# SILVER Biker

# L.B. DUNBAR

www.lbdunbar.com

2023 Graphic Cover Design: Blue Moon Creative Studio
Editor: Melissa Shank
Editor: Jenny Sims/Editing4Indies

# Other Books by L.B. Dunbar

<u>Sterling Falls</u>
*Sterling Heat*
*Sterling Brick*
*Sterling Streak*

*Parentmoon*

<u>Holiday Hotties (Christmas novellas)</u>
*Scrooge-ish*
*Naughty-ish*

<u>Road Trips & Romance</u>
*Hauling Ashe*
*Merging Wright*
*Rhode Trip*

<u>Lakeside Cottage</u>
*Living at 40*
*Loving at 40*
*Learning at 40*
*Letting Go at 40*

<u>The Silver Foxes of Blue Ridge</u>
*Silver Brewer*
*Silver Player*
*Silver Mayor*
*Silver Biker*

<u>Sexy Silver Fox Collection</u>
*After Care*
*Midlife Crisis*
*Restored Dreams*
*Second Chance*
*Wine&Dine*

<u>Collision novellas</u>
*Collide*
*Caught*

L.B. DUNBAR

*The Sex Education of M.E.*

The Heart Collection
*Speak from the Heart*
*Read with your Heart*
*Look with your Heart*
*Fight from the Heart*
*View with your Heart*

A Heart Collection Spin-off
*The Heart Remembers*


## BOOKS IN OTHER AUTHOR WORLDS
Smartypants Romance (an imprint of Penny Reid)
*Love in Due Time*
*Love in Deed*
*Love in a Pickle*

The World of True North (an imprint of Sarina Bowen)
*Cowboy*
*Studfinder*


## THE EARLY YEARS
The Legendary Rock Star Series

Paradise Stories

The Island Duet

Modern Descendants – writing as elda lore

# Dedication

For the real James

# Reader Warning:

This is a story of second chance and forgiveness.

If you've been reading *The Silver Foxes of Blue Ridge* from the beginning, you've gathered the hints of what has happened in the past to James Harrington. As a parent, he's suffered the worst of nightmares—the unimaginable. While I'm fortunate and grateful this has not been my experience, I know several parents who have lived through this heart-wrenching loss. Some have carried on. Some have not. Any errors in the emotional experience represented in this work are mine alone. However, I've made every attempt to be sensitive to a realistic situation in a fictional setting.

L.B. DUNBAR

# Prologue

## *Nineteen years ago . . .*

### [Evie]

"Yes. God, yes." My palm slaps the side of my camper as the sexy search and rescue officer slams into me.

I've never done anything as crazy as this.

"You're so fucking wet," he hisses in my ear. His voice is that of someone who's smoked a pack of cigarettes, although smoking the cancer sticks would never attract me. It's more that his raspy sound is smoky like the cloud filtering around a crackling fire. He's a flame, and I'm hot for him.

My only response to his words is a heavy grunt as my pelvic bone hits the fiberglass of my small travel trailer. The camper rocks a little from the eager thrusting of this god-like man entering me over and over again from behind. My cheek presses against the cool metal as he surges into me, filling me deliciously on repeat. It's incredible and insane.

I've just met him.

*Yesterday, I was hiking in the Smoky Mountains near Blue Ridge, Georgia. With tunes in my ear and nature as my view, I was in the zone. I never heard him coming.*

*The cracking of underbrush. The shout from his mouth.*

*He plowed into me, and we collapsed in a heap of packs and gear.*

*The cool walking stick I'd found tumbled from my hand. He landed on his back, and somehow, I was straddling him.*

*"Oh, my God . . ." I nervously giggled.*

*"Are you alright?" he questioned, coughing and sputtering.*

*"Where did you come from?" I asked, still trying to catch my breath.*

*The bluest eyes peered up at me. "I slipped and fell." The man beneath me was gorgeous. He was rugged in an outdoor manner, and his cheeks were etched like the boulders of these mountains. His abs beneath my core were rock solid while his eyes danced like a riverbed trickling to larger water. He embodied the peaks of nature around us, and I wanted to camp on him.*

"I could ask you the same question, but I see you've fallen from heaven." *His sunshine smile turned up the wattage but also warned me where there was heat, there was fire. This man could scorch a girl, and I wanted to let him.*

"Does that line actually work on women?" *I questioned as I slowly sat up on him. My palms remained on his chest. My thighs clenched around his waist, and I prayed the involuntary movement didn't register with him. When those curvy lips crooked higher on one side, I realized he hadn't missed the not-so-subtle squeeze.*

*Then I noticed his hands on my hips, holding me in place.*

"Would it work on you?"

*Ah, he's a charmer, this one, I thought.*

"What works on me is a hot bath, a no-sex massage, and copious amounts of wine." *It'd been a while since any of the above happened, and beggars would not be choosers. It wasn't really the truth. I would dip in a stream, skip the massage, and take one sip of him and be drunk.*

"No-sex massage? Well, I'm out then." *He chuckled lightly and even that was smoky and rough.* "Would you mind, maybe, getting off on me?" *he asked.*

"You want me to get off on you?" *Aghast at his boldness, his laughter turned louder. Richer. Deeper.*

"Ah, you're a firecracker," *he teased.* "And as much as I welcome the offer of you to getting off on me, I asked if you'd mind getting off of me. I'm having trouble breathing with this pack pressing into my back."

"Shit. I'm so sorry." *I scrambled free of his firm body and scampered away from him like a hermit crab.*

"No worries," *he stated, slowly lifting himself to a seated position. If I thought sitting over him was a treat, witnessing him in a casual lean on one arm with his knee propped up continued the rush of my libido. I wanted to park on his lap.*

*Instead, I shook my head to rid the sexual thoughts.*

*"I'm Evie," I offered, extending a hand, and he stared at my fingers.*

*"I'm on duty, so if you're sure you're okay, I should probably get going." He stood slowly, held out his hand, which I passed on taking since he wouldn't shake mine, and pressed myself upward to stand.*

*"Well, thanks for that." I pointed at the ground. "That was fun. We should do it again." I would hate myself for these lines after he walked away, when I'd second-guess every awkward minute between us. I'd never been so forward.*

*"I slipped." He pointed toward a ridge rising to my right, and I saw the fresh line of loosened soil in the slight incline where his hiking boot ground a path. "Be careful around here. You take care, Evie." He winked at me, a chuckle mixing with the sentiment. Then he walked away just as I figured he would.*

"Peach," he grunts in my ear, his mouth at the shell as his thickness pummels into me. The depth of his voice brings me back to the present. We should have gone inside my sleeper, but we didn't make it that far.

"Ranger?" I squeak as his body shifts, and he taps my insides in a way I've never been tapped.

"You're like a Georgia peach, juicing all over me." His teeth nip at my ear. I am slipping and sliding over him, and I'd be embarrassed if the strain in his voice didn't tell me he was thoroughly enjoying it.

At least I hope he's enjoying it.

*How could he not be enjoying this?*

This was incredible.

"Where you going, Peach? Stay with me," he stresses at my ear as his hand slips forward and his thick fingertip touches my clit. Rubbing this sensitive spot in circles like he's flint against a rock, I'm going to spark any second.

"I'm going to come," I warn him as if he doesn't already know, as if that hadn't been the end goal when he spun me for the exterior of my camper, nibbled at my neck, and asked me if he could fuck me.

He's direct.

I said yes.

I wasn't easy, though my actions appear I might be easier than I thought. My entire reaction to this rugged mountain man surprises me.

He slows his thrusts and increases the stroking on my pleasure point.

"Give it to me," he groans as he concentrates on me, and I smile to myself.

"I'm giving it to you, pal," I mutter. "Just don't ask for my heart." It's a heavy thought for the moment—for the rash decision to fuck a man against a camper in the middle of the woods when I only met him a day ago.

*Only twenty-four hours, Evelyn Sue.* What were you thinking?

At twenty-six years old, I was thinking that I'd never been so instantly attracted to someone…or so reckless.

"No hearts, honey. Just this."

I close my eyes. No hearts. Just feel him inside me. The friction. The tension. I focus on the tickle in my belly and the tingles on my skin.

"Ranger Rick," I warn with another slap of my hand on the fiberglass shell. "I'm…" The words escape me as I flatten against the metal before me. My body stills as the orgasmic rush washes over me. I'm dripping as I clench him inside me, afraid he'll slip free, afraid I'll lose the connection before I'm ready. I don't want this moment to end. My hand reaches behind me, and I grip his hip, holding him to me.

"Ready, Peach," he warns before pulling back, teasing me with escape and then surging forward. A fierce pulse goes off inside me. *Thump. Thump. Thump.* The sensation matches my heartbeat. I moan, tipping my head for his shoulder. His fingers glide back to my center and circle the nub once again.

"I can't," I hiss, my legs already shaking from the effort of standing and taking him into me.

"You will," he demands, working at me when I thought we were finished. But the jet stream in his response to my orgasm and the frantic friction against me once more rips a second geyser from me before I can catch up to what's happening with my body.

"Rick!" I scream falling into the abyss, drowning in this man's touch. I collapse, wedged between the cool camper and the heat of his body.

Then I hear his laugh.

As my breathing struggles to regain normalcy, his chuckling ripples up my back pressed against his chest.

"What's so funny?"

"Never thought I'd be okay with a woman hollering out another man's name when I'm buried inside her."

"What?"

"It's James."

"What's James?" I'm having trouble keeping up with this conversation. It's also killing the post-orgasmic euphoria.

"My name. It's not Rick."

As he'd been calling me Peach, even though I told him my name was Evie, I'd taken to calling him Ranger Rick, and completely spaced on the fact I didn't even know his name.

*Oh my God, you are such a hussy, Evelyn Sue Fitzpatrick.*

"James," I whisper.

"My name on your lips is the only name from now on," he says against my neck. He's still inside me, still pressing me to the fiberglass of my rig.

"Does that line work on all the women?" I tease, reality slowly creeping in. I've just had sex with a virtual stranger in the middle of the dark woods, miles from town. This has local news headline, ax-murder scenario, written all over it.

"Only works on one woman, Evie. Only one."

# Chapter 1
# A Reintroduction

[James]

"Why the scowl, honey?"

My vision glazes over at the question, and I'm numb to the woman on my lap. I've had a few too many tonight. Fall is always a difficult time of year for me. September specifically is the worst. This day the most awful of all. I'm in my home away from home—Ridged Edge—a biker bar just outside my hometown of Blue Ridge, Georgia, because I don't trust myself to be anyplace else. It's a place where—*despite* everyone knowing my name—I can forget who I am.

James Harrington.

That's my name, my birthright, and my curse. I didn't always hate being a Harrington. At one time, I took it as a privilege. I used it to my advantage. But a name doesn't stop you from losing everything.

The biker babe on my thigh cups my chin and forces me to look at her. I'm not about to tell her my woes. Few people know the truth, and that's the way I like it.

Trixie? Trudy? Tabby? I can't remember her name, but I squeeze her hip. She's wearing the shortest of short skirts in black leather and a white top cut so low her red bra hangs out. Her thick ass presses into my thigh. She's unfamiliar in so many ways. She isn't the woman I thought would be sitting on my legs at my age. By forty-eight, I believed my life would be many things, but none of them hold true. What a fucker I was back in my twenties. My thoughts want to wander to the past, but I reel them back in. There's no point in rehashing history. The past is the past, as the cliché goes.

"Thinking about how'd I get so lucky," I sarcastically slur of her being on my lap. She's a brunette with brown eyes, and it's all wrong. Maybe I can get lost in her, but I know I won't. I don't want to spend the night with her. Still, I don't push her off me yet. I'm not happy being with other women, but I am a man, and I have needs. I try to give what I take. The tongue works wonders. Fingers too. But there's a part of me that doesn't belong to anyone else but one woman.

*And she's gone, fucker.*

It's all my fault.

"We should get out of here," the babe whispers in my ear. Her voice is off. Smoky and rough, she sounds as tough as she probably is. It's a hard life being a bitch to a bunch of bikers. Rebels Edge—we aren't the worst out there. The club is no longer one-percenters. That history happened before me joining up with the group. The original club whittled down to more of a group of rogue bikers and lost souls who found one another. We ride. We drink. We fornicate.

Such is my life now. The life I didn't think I'd ever be living.

"Not yet, honey," I tell her as she outlines the shell of my ear with her tongue. Hosed down by the saliva, she laps at me like the kisses my pooch Silver gives me. A lick from my Siberian Husky might actually feel better.

"Ranger." The call of my biker name forces me to look up. "I think this one's for you."

Justice is the president of our non-official club, and he's also become a true friend. His silver-topped head tips toward the front of the bar, and I squint. The brightness of blond hair from yards away beckons like a beacon across a lake, but I can't make out the rest of her. She hesitantly stands before the front door, as though she isn't certain she should be here. Perhaps she's wondering how she got here.

*Join the club, sister.*

Then again, don't. Whoever she is, from this distance, I can tell she doesn't have a stitch of biker babe in her. Something just doesn't feel right about her and tells me I'm correct in my assessment.

"Nope. Not my type," I say to my friend, turning my gaze back to him and then offering a kiss to the jaw of the woman on my lap. Justice snorts and shakes his head slowly side to side. His arms cross over his solid body. He's been acting all kinds of weird over the past few months. I'd tease him it's old age, but I know the real source of his content. He's getting his dick dipped on the regular to one woman, in particular, and it's mellowing him. He's in love.

I shiver with the thought. I'd been there once—only once—then I lost it all.

Maybe the chick by the door is lost. It happens on occasion. Someone's driving toward Blue Ridge, up here in the Smoky Mountains of Georgia, and gets turned around because of a lack of GPS. She hasn't quite made it to town and doesn't realize she's only fifteen minutes outside of it.

*Keep going, honey*, I want to holler. *You'll get wherever you're going soon enough.*

Blue Ridge is my hometown. Born and bred here, I knew I'd spend my entire life near this place. After what happened, I'll never leave. Never.

"Wouldn't be so sure about that," Justice interjects, responding to my statement about type and pulling me back to the present with a deep chuckle. The lost woman finally walks to the edge of the bar and pauses at the structure. It spans the length of one wall. The rest of the room has tables scattered here and there. I'm sitting near the pool tables toward the back of the place. I'd just won a game, and somehow, the woman on my lap is my prize.

I'm not getting laid, but I'll be getting long overdue head.

"What do you know?" I snap at my leader although it comes out more a slur. I'm feeling good, really relaxed. I'd like to think the ease will allow me to stick my dick in someone random, but I know it won't. This bird on my lap could sing pretty, smell sweet, and tease me in all the right ways, and I still won't be going where I can't bring myself to go.

It isn't that I can't get it up. It's that I don't think I deserve to sample the pleasure.

"Ranger, you're asking for trouble." The tone of Justice's voice raises the hackles on the back of my neck. With my hair shorn short to my scalp, highlighting the hints of silver I've become speckled with, it doesn't take much for those fine locks to prickle. His voice has me on edge.

"Trouble is my middle name." I snort.

"Peach is your middle name," a sweet Georgian voice purrs, and I choke on air. Justice steps aside to offer me a better view of the woman speaking.

*What the fuck?*

"You're a peach," I retort, squinting at the figure who has moved closer to my perch without me noticing her. The comeback is intended to be flippant and flirty, but my tongue swells the second I've said it. The air around me stills. The woman on my lap feels like the weight of the mountains. I only have eyes for the woman standing two feet away from me.

*Can this day get any worse?*

With blond hair bright as lemonade, sapphire blue eyes, and a body like an hourglass, I can't believe I didn't recognize her at first. However, I am drunk. Or I was. I'm sobering up *real* fast. My leg begins to bounce, making the woman on my lap jiggle, and she lets loose a vibrating giggle, drawing awkward attention to herself. She sounds like a child on a kiddie ride, only I'm not offering free trips on the James Express.

"Peach," I whisper, not certain the nickname leaves my lips. Continuing to stare at the woman watching me, I can't believe she's standing before me. Is she real? *She's still so fucking beautiful.* The glare in her eyes assures me she's very real, and she's staring daggers at the woman sitting on my thighs.

In a show of possessiveness and bitchiness to the max, the biker babe kisses my jaw, licking along the hard edge and scraping her tongue against the silvery stubble. Her eyes remain on the peach before me.

*Fuck.*

"James." The blond bombshell speaks. I'd recognize her voice anywhere. I hear it nightly in my dreams, reaching out for it to drown out the other noises that haunt me.

The screams. The scraping. The silence afterward.

"Evelyn." Her name is sharper on my tongue than I intend. I'm pissed she didn't call this year. She owes me every May. She promised.

"You gonna join us tonight, honey?" The biddy on my lap teases the female before me who looks ready to stake me on a skewer and roast me over a fire.

*Good, let her be angry.* Let her be anything other than emotionless.

It was all your fault, my conscience reminds me.

I sit taller in my seat, shifting the woman on my thighs who has a firm grip on my neck at this point.

"No, I don't think I'll be joining you this evening." Evelyn's sharp tone displays how unimpressed she is with this situation. Once upon a time, she was impressed with me, though. She thought I was the shit, and she was my sweet peach.

*James and his Giant Peach.* My mother loved the irony of it.

"Evie," I hiss. Her nickname falls on deaf ears as the beauty gives me her back and walks away. My eyes follow the retreat of her firm ass—still tight—in skinny jeans. My mouth waters and my insides stir in a way they haven't for years. Justice steps back with a broad step at her retreat. He stood beside her, ever the protector of the underdog, although I'm not certain who's the underdog in this scenario—her or me.

As she walks away, the soles of her shoes clack on the tile like the ticking of a stopwatch, and I release the air in my lungs in relief. Or is it frustration? Maybe it's fear.

"Who was that?" Trixie-Trudy-Tabby asks, her voice incredulous at the sway of hips walking away from me once again.

I answer on an exhale.

"My wife."

# Chapter 2
## Second Impressions

[Evie]

*I knew this was a terrible idea.*

I hadn't been in Blue Ridge in years—almost six to be exact. I left on a cold rainy day when life felt hopeless, and I tried not to look back. I was in a bad place then. I'm so much better now, but somehow seeing James with that woman on his lap does something to my insides.

*No, I absolutely would not be joining them.*

My heart is crushed again.

"I see I've made a mistake." I'm talking to myself at this point as I've given James my back. Tearing my eyes from the hussy licking *my husband's* ear like a lap dog, I gaze up at the giant of a man at my side as I speak. He has a scruffy salt-n-pepper jaw and longish hair to match. With his arms crossed over his broad chest, he gives me a pitying glance.

I want to kick myself for thinking this was the right way to handle things. I've worked hard to place James in the past because that's where he asked me to put him.

It's another reason I'm here now. I'm thinking about my future.

Dalton Braun wants a future with me.

It'd taken years to get to a point when I felt comfortable dating, and a few more before I considered marrying anyone else. The concept seemed daunting until I realized how truly lonely and empty I've been. I wanted to be whole again, and Dalton did that for me. He was stable, steady, and good stock. My family would approve of him whereas they never approved of James.

*"He's so backwoods,"* my mother said upon meeting my husband.

She had no idea that's why I liked him so much. Admittedly, my initial attraction was all lust. It was nice to be looked at the way he looked at me. Without commitment. Without obligation. Without wanting to change me into someone other than who I wanted to be. At that time, I was a bit lost, but James didn't care. His easygoing attitude was a big attraction, as was his large, knowledgeable dick. I didn't need loyalty from him. I needed the way his body worked with mine.

Now, I have Dalton. He's good for me. He takes care of me. He's a decent man. I owe him, and I have to free myself from one man before I can even consider marrying another.

However, I'm aghast at the position I've found my husband in. I can't accuse him of cheating. I have my own guilty sins after six years, but that's another reason I'm here. I need to atone for myself, *for him*, and move forward.

Giant Santa Biker nods at me, shifting his eyes back to James, and I walk away. Again.

+ + +

Although I'd exited the bar last night, I redouble my efforts on night two. I need to see James, reminding myself this is why I'm here. I want to talk to him before the papers arrive. I thought it was only right to do this in person, so for the second night in a row, I'm seeking him out.

Tonight, I'm at the Devil's Den, the biker headquarters, or so I'm told. It's more like a mansion on the mountain, which doesn't fit the stereotype of a motorcycle clubs. I wasn't familiar with any of these places or the people when I lived here. James and I had a normal life, by a standard definition. A nice house. A loving family. He'd moved on from the grueling work of search and rescue to be a local fireman instead. He tinkered with a motorcycle. I had no inclination he wanted to join a club.

But everything changes.

I yank open the door and enter a dimly lit entryway, holding my head as high as I can. A grand staircase leads upward, and I do not want to know what goes on up there. I continue forward into what looks like an old ballroom. These ancient mansions housed balls in a time long since passed. I don't belong here, and I'd like to think James doesn't either. However, he told me when he joined Rebel's Edge. I like to think

I understand. He needed friends. He needed to feel he belonged somewhere. I'll never be over the fact he didn't feel he belonged with me.

"Are you lost, baby girl?" The sultry voice of a rugged young man behind a bar I'm certain did not exist in the original home's design catches my attention. I've been trying to take in everything around me. The thumping bass of hard rock, 70s music. The adjustment of my eyes in the dull lighting. The couple making out like teens on a couch in the corner.

*Baby girl?* I could be this boy's mother, and he vaguely looks familiar.

"I'm looking for James Harrington," I announce while my gaze struggles to pull away from the woman giving a lap dance on a man so visibly. Her tongue is halfway down the guy's throat, and his hands are up the backside of her skirt.

*Holy shit.*

I quickly look away and focus on the bartender. He's young, roughly the age of someone in college. My heart pinches with the thought.

*Michael would have been a high school senior this year.*

"Ranger know you're coming?" he asks, tipping his head while looking me up and down. It's a sexual glance. *Since when does James go by Ranger?* That was my nickname for him.

Then another thought occurs. I worry that telling this young man James is not expecting me might be the wrong answer for my safety.

"I've got this." The rough, masculine voice of another pulls my attention from the bartender, and my sight lands on the man who led me to James last night. This character is solid, broad in shoulder, and silver in hair. His face reads don't fuck with me, but he was helpful last evening.

*If pointing me to my husband with a woman on his lap is called considerate.*

He's eyeballing me much like the bartender, assessing me, but it's not appraising like the younger man.

"Evie, right?"

Stepping forward, I offer him a hand, but he glances down at it and crosses his arms instead of extending one. I clear my throat.

"Right, and you are?"

"A friend in your corner. Maybe."

I nod, not certain what that means.

"I'm looking for James again. I was told I might find him here."

The man's eyes never leave my face. "Is that so?"

"Giant sent me."

I'd always liked Giant Harrington, the eldest of the Harrington clan. James and he were close as brothers can be at one time. I knew from James that wasn't the case anymore. He'd rejected his entire family, just like he tossed me to the side.

The brooding man before me lowers his shoulders, lowering the badass biker guard a bit.

"What do you want with him?" he asks, protective of his brother-in-arms, or is it biker brother? I don't know the lingo. I'm not versed in *Sons of Anarchy*.

"It's personal," I state, feeling I owe James the decency to speak with him and let him decide how he wants to share things with others.

"Everything always was with you." Finally, some familiarity in my strange surroundings. I spin to find James behind me. His stance mirrors that of the biker now at my back. If anyone ever told me being sandwiched between two bikers would be a turn-on, I'd tell them they were crazy, but the solid man behind me and the sexy man before me are doing strange things to my lower belly.

*What is this?*

The energy vibrating off James alone results in a pulsing beat in a place that should no longer thump for him. The presence of the other man behind me enhances the rhythm. Sexual vitality swirls around me.

*Focus, Evelyn.*

There is no point in acknowledging the attraction I've never lost for my husband. It was a dead-end street. He'd moved on as was evident by the hussy on his lap last night. So had I.

"What do you want, Evelyn?" The use of my formal name felt all wrong coming from such a smoky voice. Then again, whenever he grew frustrated with me during our life together, he'd pull out the name like a lash.

"We should talk."

James glares at me. Blue eyes that were once cool water are now frozen ice. "Little late for that," he mocks. He glances at his wrist as if he's wearing a watch instead of the leather band, silver clasp, and beaded bracelet on his arm. "I'd say, you're three months too late."

It takes me a second to process what he means. *Three months? We'd* been separated for almost six years.

"You owe me a phone call," he clarifies, and I want to snap at him. Since when do I owe him anything?

A phone call. The promise rings true with me, but I don't wish to address it. Things were happening in May, and I didn't feel right calling him.

"Listen, we don't need to talk, really, I just need you to sign something when it arrives."

James stands taller, and the man at my back mutters, "Oh, shit."

I spin to face him. "I don't think we need an audience," I snark before my eyes drift to the couple still going at it like no one else is in the room. The woman's undulating on the dude's lap, but it's his hand up the back of her skirt that really has her moving. I turn back to James.

"Is there somewhere private we can speak?"

"This is as private as I get with you," James states, holding out his arms and twisting his neck to imply the middle of the room. A few people linger here and there, and a quietening around us occurs. Despite the music's harmony and the couple's grunts, everyone's listening to the center of the room.

"Don't make me do this," I mutter, lowering my voice and linking my arms together, matching his defensive stance. "I don't want to hurt you."

"There's nothing you can do that will hurt me," he states hard as steel. The comment pisses me off. I don't know why I'm bothering to make this easy on him. This man ripped my heart out and took everything from me. I never blamed him for all of it, but he's so determined to hate himself, he cast me aside like I never meant anything to him. *He* hurt me.

"Fine," I squawk, arms flailing out to the side. "I'm here for a divorce."

# Chapter 3
# What A Woman Wants

[James]

To say I knew it was coming would be the truth.

To say it hurt any less coming from her mouth directly would be the lie.

When Evie left, I figured it was only a matter of time before we reached this point. But time kept ticking, and that pesky sucker called hope left me hanging on.

*Maybe it would never come to this.*

*Maybe she'd come back to me.*

Of course, I didn't deserve her to return to me. I didn't warrant a second chance. All my luck went down the side of a mountain, and I'd never be worthy of nice things again.

And Evelyn Sue Fitzpatrick had been one of the best things in my life.

For all my bravado to hear Evie's mission, stated before the gathering, I suddenly feel sick with her announcement.

*I want a divorce.*

"Why?" It might be the stupidest question to ever pop out of my mouth.

Evie's beautiful blue eyes widen, and her crossed arms lower. Her hands meet before her, and she twists them to clasp her fingers together. I've seen this pose before on her. She'd slip into it when she had something to tell me that was difficult for her to say.

*"I broke the food disposal again."*

*"I hit a curb and hurt the tire."*

*"We lost another baby."*

My girl had been a princess in another life, and she was sheepish of natural errors. Thank goodness, I was handy enough to repair most things—just not us. I'd ripped us apart and tossed away the manual on fixing our marriage.

Evie still hasn't answered my question. Her eyes lower. Her fingers clench and unclench. Whatever she has to tell me is hard for her, and I'm making her sweat. My heart races because for all the reasons she could—and should—divorce me, there's one I fear most.

"I've met someone."

*Fucking fuck to the fucking hell no.*

However, I'm not shocked at the reality of what she's said. Evie is beautiful. A real Southern peach of a woman with that still-blond hair, those bright azure eyes, and her rocking body. She's three years younger than me, putting her at forty-five, and I always thought we'd grow old together. I knew she'd grow more gorgeous through the years.

"Well, lucky him," I mock. While some chump is fortunate to have her, he might never know how fortunate he is. Evie has a heart of gold, trust for miles, and a sweetness under her sassy side. I don't want some other guy having what's always been mine, but she doesn't belong to me anymore. From the moment I met Evie, I was in trouble of losing my heart for the first time ever and did—to her.

I'd been a player most of my life. I'd had no shortage of women and one woman I nearly wrecked with my carelessness, but Evie was different. When her body collided with mine that day in July, her lean weight pressing my pack at my back, I knew I'd never be the same.

+ + +

*Nineteen years ago . . .*

*I didn't typically seek out campers in the woods, but I did later that day. As a proud member of the search and rescue team in the area, I liked to hike the trails on the regular and even go off course on occasion just to remain familiar with every root and branch of the area. I would come across day-hikers, trail walkers, and the occasional tent campers, but I'd never purposely been looking for someone who wasn't a rescue mission.*

*I'd been searching for her all evening, though. It was strange that I couldn't get her out of my head. The way those wide blue eyes looked down at me as she straddled my middle just did something to my insides. My heart raced. My dick jolted. My stomach felt a little off.*

*I was joking—but I wasn't—when I asked if she fell from heaven. It's like I hadn't seen her, did a double take, and then she was there. I lost my footing looking at her from the ridge above and slid down the slight incline. I'd called out to her, but she hadn't heard me, and we tumbled, ending with her on top of me.*

*I'd like to have her over me again, minus a few layers of clothing.*

*Instead, I gave up my quest and made my way to a recognizable space near Bolton Lake. My family had a small sliver of property here that no one ever lived on. It was just a slice of land passed down from generation to generation like our granddad's cabin on the ridge or the brewery my family ran. We proudly owned Giant Brewing Company, officially named after my eldest brother, George the second, nicknamed Giant to distinguish between the many Georges in our family.*

*I was pressing through the trees surrounding the place when I saw an illegally parked camper on the property. The 1961 Airstream Bambi was in mint condition, and I didn't know how someone could comfortably fit in such tight quarters, let alone camp in one, but that wasn't my concern. I needed to find the owner of this small rig and tell them to get off the private property they were trespassing on.*

*Rounding the sparkling aluminum rig, I stopped short when I saw a topless woman in the lake.*

*She stood without abandon, not looking in the direction of the camper, but enjoying the peace and quiet of the dying summer day. Her hair was slicked back against her head while her face tipped up to the setting sun. Her breasts were on full display, though slightly shadowed by the waning light. Gracefully, she tossed herself backward, diving into the water in such a way it expanded her lean body, peaking her breasts and then giving me a hint of the valley at the top of her legs. Water sloshed over her legs before her pointed toes broke the surface and then disappeared. She emerged a few feet away, standing once again, only this time with her back to me. Her hair lay smooth and flat to the middle of her spine, and her hourglass shape was backlit by the dripping sunrays. She looked like a water nymph, if I believed in such mythical creatures. She was more like a siren, and her body called to mine.*

*"You're trespassing," I call out to her, finally breaking through the lust-filled thoughts in my head. She quickly spins, rustling the water around her. Whether she forgot she was naked as the day she was born or just boldly putting on a display, I'd never know, but she stared me down from the distance.*

*"Who's there?" she cried out, arching a hand over her brow to see me. I was actually leaning against the side of her camper equally taking my fill of her before breaking the news.*

*"I'm with the Smoky Mountains Search and Rescue team, and I'd gotten a call that an alligator escaped into these waters."*

*"What?!" she shrieked, twisting her body side to side and staring down at the liquid surrounding her. Her hands splash at the surface, and she slowly walks forward, still uninhibited by her nakedness.*

*Sweet Jesus.*

*Her body was stunning with the dipping sun outlining her form. Water cascaded down her skin, giving her an otherworldly appearance.*

*"Stop," I hollered, knowing I was going to lose it if she came all the way to the edge of this lake in all her glory. I could exemplify control. I'd never take advantage of a woman, but seeing her like this, was too much. My body hummed. My dick stood at full attention. I pressed off the camper and lowered my crossed arms to clenched fists at my side. The desire to rush her, tackle her in the lake, and lick every drop of water off her body consumed me.*

*She halted, exposing more than three-quarters of her body. "What about the alligator?" she questioned, searching the water again for the impossible.*

*"Do you have any idea where you are?"*

*"The Smoky Mountains," she said, tipping her head like I'm the silly one.*

*"How many alligator sightings do you think really happen in the mountains?"*

*Even with the space between us, the heat of her blue eyes hit me. I took a few steps forward, drawing closer to the lake's edge and slipping my hands into the pockets of my shorts. Her fists came to her hips, accentuating the curve of them.*

*"I know who you are." Her voice rises like she finally recognizes me. "Do you make it a habit to stalk all the girls you knock to the ground, Ranger?"*

*"Only the pretty peaches that have fallen from a tree," I teased. Her hair was glistening in the dipping sun, giving it a fuzzy peach color, and I wanted to pick her.*

*"You playing me for a fool?"*

*"Never," I teased. "But I'd like to play you."*

*She shook her head, laughing at me. "Does that line actually work on anyone?"*

*"Most girls," I snarked back at her.*

*"Well, as I'm not most girls, good luck with that one." She turned her back on me and cautiously strolled deeper in the water.*

*"You're still trespassing. This is private property. You aren't allowed to camp here." She spun back in my direction, her firm breasts hardly moving but standing erect with sharp peaks for nips, accentuated by the cold water and the cool night air.*

*"You lying to me again?"*

*"Nope. Honest truth, alligators and all. This is my family's land, and you aren't allowed to be here."*

*"Crap," she muttered, lowering her head. Her hands slip together before her like a repentant child.*

*It's at this moment she realized her lack of dress. "Shit," she added to the first explicative and slapped her hands over each breast as if the tiny cupping could disguise such ample globes.*

*"Um. Naked here," she hollered.*

*"I've noticed," I told her, not turning away even though that would be the respectful thing to do.*

*"You could . . . maybe give me a second," she stammered before adding, "Turn around."*

*"Why? Is there an alligator behind me?" I lowered for my boots and quickly sliced my fingers through the laces to loosen them. Tapping the toe to the back of one, I used it as leverage to remove the hiking footgear. At the same time, I tugged my T-shirt over my head. I dropped it to the ground and toed off the other boot.*

*"What are you doing?"*

*"I'm a search and rescue ranger like I told you. I need a better search of these waters for lost alligators, and you look like you need some rescuing." I leaned forward to pull off my socks. Standing, I unsnapped the thick fabric of my shorts.*

*"I don't need your assistance, Ranger, but thanks."*

*"Are you sure, Peach, because you look like you're struggling?" Her eyes were no longer focused on my face but somewhere near my waistline. I lowered the zipper and shrugged out of the material.*

*"What are you doing?" she choked, taking in my physique and the appendage that could not be missed straining to salute her.*

*"Leveling the playing field."*

*"I already told you I don't want to be played."*

*"Well, I want to swim . . . on my property."*

*"How do I know this is even your land?"*

*I slowly stepped forward, letting the cool water cover my feet. Damn, it's cold. Maybe the refreshing blast would lessen the aching throb of my dick.*

*"Why would I lie?"*

*"Um, alligators?" she mocked, and I chuckled. I've reached the depth of my ankles, and she stood a few feet away from me.*

*"I'm not going to touch you," I warned her, trying to keep my eyes on her face instead of letting them rove her body now that I was closing in on her. Her head tilted to the side.*

*"Oh, now you want to be chivalrous?"*

*"Chival-what? I don't know the word," I teased.*

*"Why do I feel like that's the first truth you've told me?"*

*I laughed harder, and she leaned forward, letting those firm beauties dangle. My thoughts raced to what it'd be like to have her over me, teasing me with those babies before I cup them each with a hand or, better yet, suck one into my mouth.*

*I hissed as my dick leaped. It had a mind of its own, like a puppy on a leash, eager to get closer to this woman. I couldn't get any firmer. But I meant what I said, I won't touch her without her permission.*

*"I'm never a liar," I offered. "I'm a lot of things but not that. I'm always up front and honest."*

*I watched her lips clamp together and then twist a bit as if she was considering something. She was still bent forward, hands drifting in the water as if rinsing them off.*

*"What's the most honest thing you could say?"*

*"I want to fuck you." If I thought I'd shock her, it didn't instantly show. Her lips remained together but rolled inward. Her hands stilled in the water. Her breasts hung forward, tempting me.*

*Then a splash of water hit me in the face.*

*"What the hell?" I sputtered, laughing at the same time. I swipe one hand down my face to clear the droplets and noticed she'd spun. With her back to me, she struggled to run in the knee-deep liquid.*

*"Alligator," she tossed into the night air before diving into the disturbed lake, and I followed her, wanting to rescue her over and over again.*

# Chapter 4
# Conditions

[Evie]

May. I owed him a phone call in the beginning of summer. It was the one promise we'd made to each other. I'd call him on the anniversary, and he'd answer. Every year, I was a wreck the days leading up to the call. It took me weeks to shake our conversation once it was over.

The longing for something we can't have back.

The unspoken apology deep within his tone.

The disappointment between us—in him, in me, in what happened to us.

This year, I didn't call. I just couldn't do it.

"Evie?" My name hooks my attention, and I glance up at Billy Harrington. I'm sitting in the Blue Ridge Microbrewery & Pub, owned and operated by one of James's younger brothers. Billy always was handsome in a rugged, playful sort of way. He wears a beanie cap on his head, giving him a youthful air despite his mid-forties age. With the typical light brown Harrington eyes and a mischievous smile, this man has player written all over him. *He learned from the master*, he used to tease his older brother. I wasn't jealous of my husband's sexual history. He'd already told me how he'd been around a bit. The only person I ever felt guilty over was Dolores Chance, a once upon a time friends with benefits of James's.

"Evie, is it really you?" Billy's still addressing me as he rounds the bar and nears the stool where I've been sitting, staring into a glass of whiskey I haven't started to drink. Billy's arms open, and before I can tell him not to hug me, he pulls me into an embrace, pressing me to his firm body. It isn't that I don't like hugs. I just don't want a Harrington hug because I know it could break me. My resolve to be firm against this family would crumble. My determination not to think about things I can't get back would weaken.

When I left, I lost not only James but his entire family, *my family.*

And I've missed them with every part of my being.

Billy continues to hold me a little longer than necessary, and I hate to admit how good it feels to be held. The Harringtons know how to hug. Not a lean in and pat on the back. Not an air kiss to the cheek and pull away. They hold on and hold on tight.

"William." A stern feminine voice comes from somewhere at our sides, and I press at Billy. I've witnessed a few catfights over him through the years, and I don't want any trouble. Billy pulls back but keeps his arm over my shoulder, shifting both our bodies to face a woman. She has beautiful silver hair with accents of white and hints of charcoal. Her eyes are silver steel and glaring at me.

"Roxie, honey, this is Evie," Billy introduces me. Then he clarifies, "James's Evie."

I open my mouth to correct the label. I'm nothing to James and haven't been for years, but before I can speak, I'm enveloped in another hug, and it's almost as strong as the one given by Billy.

Whispered words near my ear. "I'm so happy to meet you." The woman—Roxie—leans away but doesn't release my shoulders. Her eyes soften as she stares at my face.

"I'm . . . sorry," I question, emphasizing my disadvantage here. I glance over at Billy who's still smiling with that playful grin of his. His eyes spark as he takes in the woman holding onto me.

"Evie Harrington, this is Roxie McAllister, my forever girl."

Roxie's hands finally slip from me, and she turns to face Billy. "William, that is a horrible name."

"Well, I can think of a better one, but you haven't said yes yet," he teases.

"I don't recall the question." She arches a brow at him, and I instantly like her. I can't be certain of their status, but I'm reading this situation as Roxie has put Billy in his place a time or two. And forever girl sounds strangely similar to *girlfriend.*

"Roxanne," she states, holding out a hand for mine. We shake although it seems a little late since she just hugged me without knowing me. Then again, I imagine anyone close to the Harringtons knows of me, the infamous wife who walked away from James when he was at his lowest point.

*"He told me to go,"* I once explained to Giant.

*"I know,"* he replied, but disappointment rang in my ears. Giant wanted me to be stronger for James, but I just couldn't be.

"Are you here for the wedding?" Billy asks.

"Are you here for the dedication?" Roxie questions, and Billy cranes his neck, turning his focus to his forever girl.

"Roxie," he whispers like something is a secret.

"Who's getting married?" I ask.

"Giant," Roxie interjects, and I glance at Billy, who closes his eyes for a split second.

"Giant?" I choke. George Harrington II was as loyal as they come to his first wife. Sweet, innocent, quiet Clara didn't seem to match the brooding, solid, militant stature of her husband. She died almost eleven years back from breast cancer, and Giant was wrecked. They'd been high school sweethearts and had two beautiful daughters. I couldn't imagine him with anyone else. I also wonder why he hadn't told me himself.

James and Giant were close once upon a time, and both wanted Clara and me to be friends. On a surface level, we were friends because we were family. However, we were very different from one another. Nonetheless, I loved her as a sister-in-law. Hearing Giant is marrying someone when I didn't even know he'd fallen in love is shocking.

I'd been in touch with Giant lately as I relied on him to help me track down James. My husband was rather vague about what he did or who he did or where he went.

"Who's the lucky lady?" I ask, fighting the lump in my throat. Giant deserves every bit of goodness in his life. He deserves a second chance at love. We all deserve second chances for things.

"Her name's Letty Pierson. She's from Chicago." Billy lowers his voice, making it sound ominous as though a Southern mountain man can't marry a damn Yankee. Fortunately, the Harringtons do not discriminate that way. Billy's explanation tells me nothing about the woman, but I respond as pleasantly as I can.

"That's wonderful. I'm happy for him. When's the wedding?"

"Friday next," Roxanne gleefully states, and something in my expression causes Billy to bite his lip.

"That's soon." I smile as best I can, but suddenly feel shaky. My hand covers my lower abdomen.

"So, are you coming to the wedding?" Roxanne asks, hope ringing in her question. "It's up on the ridge."

This additional information causes my shakes to turn to tremors. I fight to still my body, but a cold sweat trickles under my armpits.

"The ridge?" I croak. The parcel of land inherited by Giant three miles up the mountain behind Pap's old cabin. Grandpa Harrington was an interesting fella, as he referred to himself, and he loved this mountain more than anything. Well, maybe it tied in affection with his love of beer and his wife, Charlotte.

"Yeah, that's where they met, sort of, so they're getting married there," Roxanne explains while I watch Billy lower his eyes to the floor. A hand comes to Roxanne's back, and I don't miss the tenderness in his touch. Billy methodically strokes up and down his forever girl's spine, and Roxie steps closer to him, like it's instinct, like he's magnetic.

"That's a lovely location for a wedding," I offer although my voice strains with forced enthusiasm. "What's the dedication?"

An awkward silence falls around us for a second, and it's clear I'm missing something heavy.

Billy's hand stills on Roxie's back. Her mouth opens, but Billy speaks instead. "Have you seen James?"

"I have." I hold my head higher, hoping to restore the shield I knew I'd need to return to this area.

"He didn't tell you about the dedication?" Billy asks.

"No." My answer hesitates, lingering as I wait for them to tell me about this secretive ceremony.

"I think James is the best person to explain it," Billy states, and the tremors begin again, rippling up my spine in unease. "Ask him about it."

"William," Roxie hisses beside him, both a warning and a reprimand. Billy leans into his woman and kisses her temple. She turns to face him, and he goes for her lips. It's quick but tender, and I blush like I'm witnessing something I shouldn't see. The action seems so innocent but intimate, and I'm the one a little flushed from watching them.

"Whatcha drinkin'?" Billy tips his head to the bar where my glass remains untouched. I thought I wanted something strong to dull my thoughts and ease the ache of seeing James again, but I haven't found the stomach to drink the whiskey.

"I should go," I say, unhooking my bag from the back of the barstool. The need for air causes my lungs to ache. I hate the secrecy I sense around me.

"Don't leave," Billy begs, stepping toward me. "How long have you been in town? Where are you staying?"

"I'm at the Conrad Lodge." Corabelle Conrad was the nemesis of the neighborhood, according to the Harrington clan. Growing up, she was the youngest girl on their secluded Mountain Spring Lane. The elusive fire road had three large antebellum homes evenly spaced along the gravel drive with a river running behind the properties. The Harringtons own one. Next door lived the Chances. Kip Chance was once the mayor of Blue Ridge and had his house deemed the official mayor's home. The current mayor is another Harrington named Charlie. On the dead end of the drive, the last home belongs to the Conrads who own the Lodge. Currently, their daughter runs the place. The Conrads were an older couple when they had their miracle baby who they spoiled even in adulthood. When I'd left the area, Cora was in the middle of major renovations to the place her parents had let run down. Now, the lodge was a beautiful resort experience.

"Hang out a bit," Billy encourages. "It's been a long time since we've seen you." He doesn't have to remind me. The six-year separation feels like my time with James was in another life. Clearly, we've all moved on, and my heart hurts with the thought.

*Nothing stays the same.*

"I'm not certain how long I'll be in town, but I'll come back. Another night," I weakly suggest.

"Mama will want to see you," Billy says, dropping his voice. His bark-brown eyes hit me hard. It's the Harrington trademark. James is the only one who doesn't have them. His eyes are bright blue, making him stand out from the pack. He considered himself an outlier to them.

"I'd love to see Elaina and George." James's parents remind me of my own socialite parents in some ways. Proper. Cultured. Opinionated. Yet in the same respect, they are nothing like my parents. For one, Elaina and George enthusiastically welcomed me into the family while my own parents never accepted James.

"Tomorrow then," Billy says.

"I—"

"I'll let Mama know you'll be stopping by," Billy adds.

"William," Roxie scolds, her eyes on me, sensing my discomfort. Her hand comes to my arm and strokes up and down. "You can call the pub and let us know what works best for you."

Billy chuckles and shakes his head beside this woman. He leans in to kiss her temple again, and she slowly grins at me. I recognize the look on her face. I remember the feeling. Such undevoted attention from a Harrington is heady stuff.

+ + +

When I return to the Lodge, a long bath seems in order to calm my nerves and settle my thoughts. I've tried to call Dalton, but he's out, and I don't leave a message. He knows I've come to this area of Georgia. He thinks I'm here for a little respite. I'm a jewelry designer, and I told him I came to check out the local fare. It feels a bit subterfuge, but I didn't have the heart to tell him the truth.

*I'm always honest and up front*, James once said to me. He never was a liar. In fact, he might have been too blunt at times.

*I can't look at you anymore.*

The words were more painful than anything he'd ever said. If he told me he didn't love me, I'd have called him out for being a liar. But not being able to look at me? That was a truth that hurt.

I've just tugged my sweater over my head, exposing the T-shirt I'm wearing underneath when there's a knock on my door. I didn't order room service or request anything from the front desk, so I peek through the peephole. Then I yank open the door.

"Jam—" I haven't gotten his entire name out when his hand lands on my belly, gently forcing me back into the room until I fall against the wall near the door, and it slams shut with the kick of James's boot. His lower half pins me in place, and I hate how a thrilling rush ripples up my middle. His hand has moved from my belly to land on the wall over my head with his other palm, and I hate how I miss the touch. I'm entirely caged in by his body, and the scent of him overwhelms me. Spicy. Smoky. Sinful.

"He been in your mouth?" James asks, his growly tone straining. His breath fans my face, but I don't catch a hint of alcohol. Mint accosts me instead. His directness hovers over me.

"What?" I choke, wondering who, what, where, why until my thoughts catch up. "I'm not doing this with you," I reply. I am not here to discuss Dalton. I'm here for a divorce.

"I asked you a question, Evelyn," he says, one hand coming to my throat. His thumb strokes along the column of my neck for a second. Then his hand shifts, the thumb and forefinger expanding as he slips his palm upward, forcing my jaw and chin to lift. He cradles my face in the crook of his fingers. He knows I like his hold on me in this position. I used to cave when he did this, but not anymore.

I hold his eyes with mine.

James tilts his hips, his pelvis pressing into me harder. His eyes drop to my lips while his nostrils flare a bit. Then his mouth crashes against mine, his tongue thrusting forward, forcing me to open for him. He sweeps the inside of my mouth, over my teeth, and along my inner cheeks before he sucks at my tongue. He isn't just dusting me off, but owning me, possessing me.

*Good God, what's happened to him?*

And what's happening to me as I groan deep from the back of my throat at the pleasing intrusion.

He releases me as quickly as he invades me, and my heart races. My chest is heaving like I've run a marathon instead of standing still against a narrow wall.

"Don't matter," he says. His blue eyes spark as they stare into mine, seeking answers, undressing my brain. "I'm the last thing to be in that pretty mouth of yours, and you'll remember it belongs to me."

His mouth comes back to mine. His tongue meeting mine instantly. This is more like a kiss than a cleansing but still a claiming. It's *almost* the James I remember, yet it's something more, and I find I ache for him. He sucks and swirls before he draws back, taking my lower lip between his and releasing me too soon.

I slip down the wall a little at the sudden release and a weakening in my knees.

"James," I whisper, stunned by his behavior.

"Your lips. One name. Mine."

He kisses me one more time, more forceful than the second yet less intrusive than the first. I melt into him, my body familiar with his, recognizing and remembering what he can do to me. The way we once blended into one another. His hard strengthened my soft. My tenderness loosened his stiffness.

He abruptly pulls back again. The effect is a popping sound from the sudden release.

"I'll give you the divorce you're craving, Peach, on one condition."

There are more than butterflies in my belly. A flock of birds has taken off in my midsection, and I'm ready to give him almost anything.

"Sleep with me."

# Chapter 5
# Memories

[James]

I'll give her her fucking divorce if she gives me this one concession.

"I am *not* sleeping with you," she stammers, pushing at my chest. She's not strong enough to physically force me away from her. It's the slight pressure of her palms that moves me. I don't want her touching me. I don't deserve her hands on me. And I don't need her hands, especially if they've been on some other douchebag and his junk.

"Suit yourself then, baby. Better call your guy and tell him no divorce."

I watch her visibly swallow and turn her head away from me. Something unsettling hits me in the gut.

"He doesn't know, does he?" I glare at her, gripping her jaw in my hand once more. "He doesn't know you're already fucking married . . . to me."

+ + +

*Nineteen years ago . . .*

*"I'm here to see James Harrington, please." A sweet voice floats into the cabin through the open door. Slowly, I rise from the desk chair as my SAR co-worker, Nova Greer, stands at the door addressing the visitor.*

*"And you are?" Nova questions a bit defensively. I never mix business with pleasure. Well, except maybe once, but that wasn't recently, and it hasn't happened in this office. Tons of sexual tension swirls around my partner and me, but I suppress it because this job matters more to me than dipping my dick in my partner.*

*Nova's question is a good one despite the fact I recognize the feminine voice asking for me. Who is the woman I skinny-dipped with in*

*Bolton Lake? Who is the woman I took against the side of a camper, both of us too eager to wait until we were inside? I had her one more time that night before I had to take the early shift for work. When I went back to the lakefront property that evening, the camper was gone. Her full name unknown. Her whereabouts a mystery.*

*That was three months ago in July.*

*Placing a hand on Nova's lower back, I nudge her to the side so our inquirer can see me.*

*"James." My name is a breathy relief, and she slowly smiles until she sees something in my expression. Her eyes lower for my hand on Nova's hip. The grin quickly disappears as I stare down at her from three stairs up.*

*"Peach," I address her, fighting my own relief that she'd returned. There was something about the wild spirit of this woman. The trust she had in me as we swam naked together as virtual strangers. We weren't strangers for long, at least not with our bodies. I'd memorized every curve and dip of her luscious frame, and dammit, I'd missed the fact I hadn't had a second evening with her.*

*I step around my partner and remove my hand from her waist. "I got this." Evie's eyes watch my touch drag against the other woman. Her blue eyes narrow. Her lips purse. I want to make a statement.*

I wait for no woman.

*I clear the three steps in one and walk down the path a bit, giving us space from the open office door because Nova's listening.*

*"What can I do for you? Are you lost again?" I crisply state, crossing my arms when I spin to face her. I'd love to ask how she found me as we hadn't shared anything personal other than first names and horny bodies. I also want to know where the fuck she's been.*

*"I have something to tell you, and there's no easy way to say it." Her hands clasp together before her. I noticed this on our second official meeting. She crosses her arms at her wrists, flattens her palms together, and then entwines her fingers, clenching and unclenching them. This must be a habit when she has something difficult to say. Her eyes lower briefly, and she takes a deep breath. Then she lifts her head high,*

*struggling like its weight is too heavy, but she must look at me for whatever needs to be said.*

*My arms remain crossed as a protective stance. The temptation to reach for her has me fighting myself. The position is also meant to intimidate, but something in the air tells me I'm the one who should be afraid.*

*"I'm pregnant."*

*Birds stop chirping. Trees stop rustling. I shake my head. I couldn't have heard her correctly.*

*"Excuse me?"*

*"I'm pregnant," she repeats. I stare at her, still not certain what that means or why she's telling me. However, my heart races inside my chest.*

*"Congratulations," I spit while smirking, concluding she fucked some other guy in the past three months while I've been on some strange celibacy path since she disappeared. Great. I find a girl I can't stop thinking about, and she forgets me so quickly she sleeps with someone else.*

*"I'm having a baby," she restates. She leans toward me as though it'll help emphasize what she's already said. Her eyes widen, those blue lakes staring up at me beneath dark lashes. Her fingers have slipped apart and fall against her dress near her thighs, tugging at the loose material.*

*"I get it. You're having a kid. Why you tellin' me?" Why did she come all the way up this mountain to give me this news? I don't want kids. The thought isn't entirely true. Someday. Maybe.*

*Those sapphire eyes narrow, and my crossed arms unfold, hands slipping into my pants pockets.*

*"Who's the lucky guy?" I mock, holding her gaze. Her slit eyes sparkle under the sunshine of a fall day. She tilts her head, mocking me in return, with an expression that reads: Do I need to spell this out for you?*

*"Wait a minute." My tongue grows thick, and my mouth dries. The slow curl of her lip tells me I'm finally seeing a light I don't want turned on.*

*"I'm having a baby," she says again, leaning away from me on this repetition, speaking more slowly as the words sink in.*

*"Say it," I demand. "I want to hear it. Say the words."*

*"We're having a baby. You're the father."*

*Both my hands fly to the back of my head, and I exhale a deep breath. I slowly turn my back on her before circling around to face her again. When I look at her, her forehead furrows, and her lower lip quivers.*

*"How do you know it's mine?" I have to ask, but the way her expression falls, it's like an arrow through my own heart. I've hurt her with the question.*

*"I told you, I've never done what we did before." Her voice lowers again, and her eyes drop from my face. She had told me that night that she'd never gone skinny-dipping. She'd also never been camping, hiking, or built a fire. The weekend away was meant to give her perspective. That's when I told her she didn't have to tell me her life details. We hadn't used a condom, which was so stupid on my part, but she told me she was on the pill.*

*"I thought—" I point to her lower region, not accusing her of tricking me, but I want to understand what happened here.*

*"I'm in that two percent, I guess, when it didn't work."*

*I stare at her, uncertain what she means.*

*"I'm not asking you for anything," she continues. "You don't need to be involved. I just thought . . . maybe . . . you'd want to know."*

We're having a baby.

You're the father.

I'm going to be a dad.

*"I take responsibility for my actions." I always have. Getting caught with Dolores Chance in my bed at eighteen. Fooling around with girls in the trophy room. Buying a motorcycle against my dad's wishes. Joining SAR when the family wanted me to work at the brewing company.*

*Her head tilts again. "Well, don't do me any favors. I don't need you stepping up out of some misplaced obligation. I just thought you should know. That's it." Fisted hands pop to her hips, one of which she juts to the side.*

*She's so freaking cute. I can't help myself. I reach for her face and lower to kiss her. She stills a second before melting under the attention of my lips against hers. I give her a taste of what I hope she's been missing as much as I have. While we kiss, my hand slips to her throat, curling around the delicate column, and I stroke my thumb along her jaw. She groans against my mouth, but the vibration under my hand is like a shockwave straight to my dick.*

*I pull back, keeping my palm on her skin.*

*"I'm James Harrington, by the way," I say. If she found my place of employment, I'm assuming she knows my full name by now, but I want to be clear.*

*"Evelyn Sue Fitzpatrick. Nice to meet you." She chuckles a bit before her eyes well with tears. Her lower lip trembles while I'm still touching her neck. My hand slips upward, cupping her jaw in the curl of my thumb and forefinger.*

*"It's okay, Peach. We'll figure this out, okay? If we stick together, we can make it through this. Just give me a minute to process everything. You finally standing before me. The news you just dropped."*

*She nods, but a tear leaks from the corner of her eye, rolling slowly down her cheek. With my other hand, I use my finger to brush away the salty liquid.*

*"Why're you cryin', baby?" I softly question, concerned she hates being pregnant, and by me, no less.*

*"I don't know. I'm an emotional wreck lately. I'm just relieved to finally find you and tell you, and I'm strangely happy." Her voice lowers on the last sentiment, and her eyes try to drop from mine, but I slip my hand farther upward, forcing her to lift her chin and return her gaze to me.*

*"I'm happy, too," I tell her, finding I immediately mean what I've said. I promised her I'd never lie, and I'm not. "I'm happy you found me, Peach."*

*I lean forward for another kiss, loving how her body leans toward mine, curling into me. Her hands come to my biceps to steady her, and then she slips them up to my neck, slipping her fingertips into the fine hairs at my nape. I release her lips but pull her against me, holding her tightly to my chest. It's rare I hug a woman—really embrace them like I am her—but Evie feels right in my arms.*

*"I'm scared," she whispers. I nuzzle into her pretty neck and kiss the side of it.*

*"I'll be a rock for both of us." Holding her in my arms, feeling her relax against me, I believe myself. I'll be the strength we both need.*

*It's strange, the sudden feelings I have for her. She's a part of me I hadn't known I was missing. I'd felt out of sorts since her disappearance, though, and now I felt differently, perhaps better with the rightness of her in my arms. There's a hammering in my chest. There's a rush through my body. I'm so grateful she's standing before me. She returned to me.*

*And we're having a baby.*

*And I'm going to be a father.*

*And I might be in love with a woman I hardly know.*

+ + +

"Another," I shout out to Bear Grady. It's the night after that powerful kiss in her hotel room, and I can't get the new memories out of my head.

*Divorce. Someone else. Her mouth on mine. Her mouth on* his.

I walked out of the room as soon as I realized she hadn't told *him* the truth.

She was still married to me. She was still *my* wife.

I'm at Ridged Edge again, where Bear is playing bartender. This is the lesser of the two evils the club owns. Our clubhouse bar, Devil's Den, isn't for the faint of heart. It's also private property. As Evie witnessed the other night, anything can happen in the open space—and does. Ridged Edge is more a mix of diehard locals, faithful to a classic bar, not that trendy place my brother Billy owns.

The men who frequent this place are my family now. I should have been the one to leave the area, but I've always been a sucker for this place. It's one reason I joined the search and rescue crew and put in to remain here. Six years ago, I had even more reason to stay local.

"How many have you had?" Bear mutters to me. He's a big man, looking a bit like badass Santa or a polar bear. Then again, our president Justice looks the same. Large, burly men with rough voices and rougher pasts are the norm here. The past does not discriminate by size or stature, though. I fit in with my silvering hair, slimmer build than these men, and an ugly history.

"Lost count after one," I tell him, tossing back the next shot of whiskey, which looks like I'm holding two in my hand. I'll be crashing here tonight unless some poor soul takes pity on me and drives me home.

*Home.* The house I had with my family. Evie and . . . I can't go down that path. I need to stick to only one memory at a time, and tonight is Evelyn.

She wants a divorce? She's going to give me something first because I'm a fucking selfish man.

A large hand claps my shoulder, squeezing hard once. I hate to be unsuspectingly touched, and I equally hate surprises, so I turn with fist raised, ready to punch whoever has his hand on me.

"Simmer down, little brother," Giant mutters to me under his breath. Since the brewing company joined forces with my club on a fundraiser for the upcoming community center, my eldest brother has been popping in here more often. Him and that damn fool woman who started everything—Janessa Cruz.

"Did you know Evie is back?" Giant asks, not mincing words as he helps himself to the stool next to mine.

"I did."

"Did you see her?" Giant questions, staring at my profile while I keep my eyes forward.

"I did."

Silence passes between us as he orders a beer from Bear. I don't need to face my brother to know what he looks like. His eyes match everyone else's in our family—a strange mix of gray and brown, like weathered bark. I'm the odd man out, and always have been with my blue set, but it's even more than a pair of eyes. My eldest brother has thick hair and a matching beard, bordering on charcoal gray but still plenty dark, unlike my hair, which is short to my scalp, dusted with more salt than pepper, and when I let my whiskers grow, it all matches.

"Gonna talk to her?" Giant finally asks. I shake my head, not certain if I'm answering Giant or trying to clear my thoughts of my wife with another man. Tapping the shot glass on the bar, I'm still waiting for Bear to give me another pour.

"James," Giant addresses me.

"Ranger," I snap back at him. He knows I go by Ranger in this room, in this club, in this town. I no longer want to be James Harrington, the pitiful fuck who lost everything. I'm Ranger. A lone ranger for that fact.

Giant ignores my correction. "What happened?" Giant might be quiet, the silent brooding type, but he's observant. We're close in age, back to back in school, and once tight until I fucked it all up.

"I saw her." Explanation complete.

"And . . .?"

I kissed her. God, I fucking rammed my tongue into that sweet mouth, wiping it clean of anyone else, and then kissed her again, reminding her of how we once were—hungry and needy.

She can't possibly kiss *him* like that, can she?

"She wants a divorce."

"Fuck," Giant mutters under his breath. A beer bottle appears before him, and he wraps a hand around it. Lifting it for his lips, he takes a deep swallow, drowning in his thoughts.

*I know the feeling, man.*

"What'd you say to that?" Giant asks after breaking from the long pull. My gaze follows the lowering of the bottle to the bar top before I answer him.

"I agreed. With an ultimatum."

"Jesus," Giant hisses. Then he chuckles. His hands double tap on the bar edge, and he laughs. "You are my brother." He guffaws.

*What the fuck?*

"That's how I met Letty. I threw down a challenge, and she accepted." Letty is Giant's soon-to-be second wife. His first one died. Sweetest girl ever but quiet and demure. This new girl has really opened up my brother. I bet they're having crazy good sex. That's the only thing I can think of that will put a smile on a man's face like the one he wears whenever he mentions his new woman.

I used to smile like that.

"Yeah, well, your Letty and my Evie are not the same women. Evie rejected my suggestion."

"What'd you ask for?"

"I want her to sleep with me."

Giant chokes, and another explicative hisses from his lips. "Well, she is your wife, but man . . . you've been separated for what, five years?"

"Six," I correct.

Giant chuckles. "I can see where that might be a problem."

"How difficult is it to sleep with your fucking husband? We did it all the time before—" I stop myself short, knowing exactly how difficult it was *after*. After everything went to hell. I've remained in that hell while Evie moved on.

"Dude, you haven't been together in years. You want to win her back, then you need to woo her a bit."

"Fuck this shit. I'm not trying to win back my wife. I just want her to sleep with me, and then I'll give her what she wants."

Giant stares at me. "Do you really want to divorce Evie?"

I don't answer him but feel the weight of his glare and the pressure of the next question. "Do you think she really *wants* to divorce you?"

"She met someone," I announce a little louder than necessary.

"You haven't answered your brother," a deep, rough voice speaks from behind the counter, and I glance over the bar to see my new best friend and club president leaning against the wall highlighting various alcohols.

"What do you know?" I address Justice. He's been keeping a big secret, roping the club into this damn fundraising thing, and dragging my name with it all to keep himself in pussy. I scrub a hand down my face. Justice wouldn't know how to a woo a woman. He's the one duped lately.

"Do you really want to divorce your wife?" Justice questions like Giant.

"It isn't about what I want."

"That's bullshit," Giant adds, and Justice nods his head once to agree.

"Fine, what I want is to fucking sleep with my wife and then get on with my life."

"Good to know things haven't changed." The soft feminine voice turns our heads.

*Evie?*

Shit.

"Evelyn," Giant croons with his deep voice and stands from the barstool. Big arms wrap around my woman as he pulls her into him. She practically disappears under his large form, and she returns the hug with her thinner arms. Giant kisses her temple before releasing her.

"You look beautiful, Evie."

"Thank you." She blushes, and I wonder what my brother's playing at, or why she's flushed by the compliment. Evie is the most beautiful woman alive as far as I'm concerned, and she damn well knew it when we lived together. "I hear congratulations are in order."

My forehead furrows while Giant softly smiles. There's that grin again of a sexually satisfied man. "Thank you, but who told you?" Giant turns to me, but I just stare at Evie. Her blond hair is pulled up in a ponytail. Her makeup done a bit. She looks too good.

"I saw Billy at the Pub."

A disadvantage of living in a small town. *It's small*. And us Harringtons are many.

"What were you doing there?" I snap as if it's any of my business or concern.

"I wanted a drink." She holds her head higher when she addresses me as though my speaking to her is beneath her. I am beneath her. I have no proper words for her. We don't have anything left to discuss. I just want her in my bed one more time, and then I'll let her go.

"Bet Billy was shocked to see you. Probably hit on you." My younger brother was insatiable for years. He flirted with everyone, including my wife, just to piss me off.

"Actually, I met Roxanne McAllister." Ah, the bookstore owner who has tamed the wild man under me in birth order. "And he invited me to see your mother."

*What the fuck?*

"I thought we could go together—"

"Fuck no," I bellow, my voice loud. "Not me. Not you."

Evie blinks at me.

"Why not?" Giant asks on her behalf, but Evie knows. When I broke it off with her, I broke it off with everyone.

"So he can move on with his life," she mocks my former words. "How's that working out for you, James?" she sneers at me, and I deserve her wrath. Her sass also turns me on, and I want to kiss the crap out of her again, right here in the middle of this bar. She's mine. Only I can kiss her.

"Seems to be agreeing with me, so what does it matter?" I immediately realize how unfair that sounds. She's beautiful. She's desirable. And she no longer belongs with me.

"I'm outta here," I say, rapping my knuckles on the bar and fumbling off the stool.

"Whoa," Giant says, reaching out for me.

"Easy, Ranger," Justice mutters from behind the bar.

Evie says nothing. She just stares at me, giving me that look of hard steel just as she did back then.

Like she did when I told her to get the fuck out of my life.

I shove Giant's hands off me and brush past Evie as I make a not-so-grand exit.

## Chapter 6

# Hard Pass

[Evie]

I wake from the soft brush of fingertips across my forehead. My lids flip open, and I stare at the man sitting next to my curled body on the bed. Rolling my head on the pillow, I look toward the ceiling, taking a second to acclimate myself to my surroundings.

*How did I get here?*

I recall driving James home. Giant caught his brother before he face-planted into the front door of the bar. He'd been swaying as he attempted to walk away. I told Giant I'd take care of my husband. I'm all too familiar with him in this state—when he's had too much to drink. Giant was concerned I wouldn't be able to get James into the house, but to my surprise, James was lucid enough to stagger up the front steps and open his own front door.

*Our front door.*

I should have left him then.

I shouldn't have followed him.

Once inside the familiar house, a Siberian Husky greeted us. James kicked off his shoes and tossed himself on the couch in the living room, and the dog yipped at him a few times as if chastising him for his drunken state. Then the animal made himself at home on the floor next to the couch where his master lay. The dog gave me almost a pitying look.

*I shouldn't be here*, I told myself repeatedly, but curiosity got the best of me. With James out cold, I'd decided to wander around. Same kitchen. Same dining room. Same everything, including this room.

My eyes shift to James, staring down at me, as I lay on the twin bed. I feel like I've been caught where I shouldn't be, yet I have every right to this bedroom.

My vision drifts from him again, taking in the state of the space. Bright blue walls with white trim. Sunlight filtering through mini-blinds at half-mast. A shelf with sports trophies and pictures of friends. A poster for the Atlanta Braves. A computer monitor and keyboard on a desk too small for a growing boy.

When I left, I took what I wanted from this bedroom. They were only trinkets—mementos of a life lived too short, but one filled to the brim. They were only things. They didn't replace him, and they'd never bring him back.

My eyes cloud. I'd cried last night when I entered this room. James hadn't touched a thing. It was dusty and musty, but everything was still in its original place. He wanted to close the door and lock away time. I wanted to enter and surround myself in memories.

*"Do you think it's okay to lie down on his bed?" I'd asked James's mother.*

*"I think you can do whatever you think is best to grieve."* That was Elaina Harrington. She didn't mince words. She told me what I was going through without trying to sugarcoat it.

I was grieving.

Then.

Now.

I realize something covers me, and I notice the quilt over my body. My sister-in-law Clara made it for him when he was nine. It was a true work of talent and skill with fabric. More memories flood my head.

Baby blankets.

Baseball uniforms.

Closing my eyes, I swallow hard, willing away the prickling tears. James remains seated next to me, not speaking. He didn't have much to say when it happened. He would never have been this close to me then. Afterward, his rejection was almost immediate.

"You didn't call," James finally says, his voice tight and wet. A soft tear leaks from each of my eyes despite my fight to control them. Slowly streaming down the side of my face, they collect in my hairline near my ears.

*I didn't call.*

"You made a promise," he adds.

A promise that I would call each year on May seventeenth, and James would answer.

I should scream at him that we made more than just the one promise. We took vows to love and honor one another, in sickness and in health, until death parted us. However, it hadn't been one of our deaths that separated us.

It had been the death of our son.

He was twelve when it happened.

He would have been eighteen in May—when I didn't call James.

I'm the one who should be angry. James could have called me. He has my number. It's been the same one for nearly twenty years. The first year after we fell apart, I waited and waited and waited for a call from him.

An apology.

An explanation.

Anything to hint he wanted me to come back to him.

He never called.

I broke first and contacted him when our son would have turned thirteen. He would never be a teenager. He would never fall in love, kiss a girl, or hold her hand. He would never go to high school or college or work a job. He wouldn't marry or have kids or lose his heart to both a woman and future children.

I lift myself to a seated position, toying with the yarn ties sticking out every so many squares on the quilt.

I should argue with James, but I don't have the energy. Six years is too long to harbor bitterness. It took me a year, until our boy would have been thirteen, to let go of the pain in my heart from my husband. The ache of losing our son will never disappear.

"How are you feeling today?" I ask, ignoring his statement to me. James shifts, resting his elbows on his thighs. His head hangs while his hands clasp together between his knees.

"I'm fine, Evie." For the first time ever, he's lying to me. There's nothing in his voice. No tenor. No cadence. Just dull, unfeeling words. "What are you doing here?"

"I drove you home," I remind him. He shakes his head, not looking up at me. Two hands cover his face, and he swipes downward against his cheeks. The morning's scruff scrapes against his open palms, sounding like sandpaper against his skin.

"I meant, what are you doing *in here*?"

Taking another gaze around the space, I give a weak smile. "Just remembering," I say. Remembering when our boy loved a game involving a bat and a ball. Remembering when we took the photograph of the three of us on the ridge. Remembering when we first went fishing, and he kept the lure as a souvenir because he didn't catch a fish.

When I entered this room last night, I didn't know how I'd respond. Would I break down into sobs? Would I feel hollow inside? Or would I smile at the memories? I did a bit of all three as I held the framed photo to my chest, ran a finger over a baseball, and smelled the quilt on his bed. I didn't know what to expect, but I know what I felt after being in his room. His spirit is in my heart, and his memories are in my head, but he isn't here among his things, this space, or our house. This is all a part of the past because there is no future for him.

"I don't come in here," James comments, straightening his back but keeping his hands between his thighs. He's staring toward the window where specks of dust float in the air. There's something magical whenever I see dust dancing in the sunshine. In my memories, there's my little boy staring at the tiny puffs drifting through the rays streaming between the blinds.

*"It's like heaven in my room,"* he said as he'd been newly learning about Jesus and saw images of heaven in a picture book. His small fingers reached forward as if he could tangibly hold the unseen.

*"You're my angel,"* I told him. He was the only baby God graced us with, and that was an entirely different subject I didn't wish to dwell on.

"I can tell," I finally address James. A huff of sarcasm fills my tone. The room is a shrine, and it's depressing. Michael would be ashamed that we'd let time stand still on him. He'd want us to enjoy life, not wallow amidst the dust and stagnant air.

"What's that supposed to mean?" James turns on me.

"It means, it's dirty in here." I pick at the quilt one more time and let it fall back to my lap. "I'm going to clean." I make to move, but James holds out his arm like a barricade at a toll booth.

"Don't touch anything." His voice drops. He's almost scary, but I'm not afraid of him.

"This isn't healthy," I mutter. Mentally. Physically. This isn't sane.

"Our son is dead," he bluntly announces to me as if I don't know this fact.

"Yes, he is, and he'd be so disappointed in us. His memories shouldn't be buried under cobwebs. This room needs to be cleaned up and out." I push at his arm, making it to my hands and knees in hopes to crawl off the bed, but I'm tackled and flipped to my back.

"I said no," James growls in my face as he presses over me.

"And I said yes," I snap back at him.

His chest heaves over mine. His heart hammers through his T-shirt. I'm pinned under his body, and then he crashes his mouth against mine. His tongue seeks mine, opening me wider for his invasion. He angles his head to take more of me, sucking at me before returning to my lips again. I'm almost gasping for air, but my hands find his head, holding him in place, unable to allow him to release me. This kiss is anger, frustration, and fear. It's *I-hate-you* and *I-love-you* and *you-hurt-me* all rolled into one, but I don't know who's saying which phrase.

Suddenly, I hear a buzzing noise, like a vibration. I turn my head, breaking the kiss, and James's mouth travels to my jaw, nipping at my skin. His lips suck at my neck until he tugs the collar of my sweater, exposing the juncture of my shoulder to my neck. His teeth scrape the pleasure point, and I hiss. The sting is like a live wire to a part of me eager for more.

The vibrating starts again, and I realize it's coming from my bag on the desk chair.

My phone.

Dalton.

"Shit. I need to get that." I press at James's shoulders, willing him to stop while not wanting this to end. We need to get this out of our system. I need to sleep with him.

"James," I hiss. "The phone."

"Don't answer it," he mutters into my skin, retracing his path up my neck and breathing into my ear.

"I have to. It might be Dalton." The moment I say his name, the air around us turns to ice. The flames of desire between us are doused, and James stills. I continue to breathe heavily.

"Dalton?" he questions, pulling back enough to examine my face, but I can't look at him. He grips my chin, turning my head so I face him. His eyes search mine. Hurt. Stung. Steeled.

James presses off me and jumps off the bed.

"Wouldn't want you to miss a call from Dalton," he growls before stalking out of the room.

The phone buzzes once more, but I'm too wound up to move. I don't know if it's that I'm turned on by the anger in our kiss, the prospect of sleeping with my husband, or the confusion over both items colliding.

I slowly roll to my side, press off the bed, and reach for the desk chair. Pulling it out, I dig in my bag for my phone. The call has gone to voicemail. I typically don't listen to messages when I recognize a number. Dalton just called me, so I should immediately call him back.

Instead, I press on the voicemail number.

*"Hey honey, just checking in with you this morning. It was late when I got back last night. I'm about to head into court, so I'll call you again this afternoon. I miss you."*

He's so sweet.

I look up to find James's dog sitting just outside Michael's bedroom, watching me, assessing me.

"I know, I'm a terrible person," I say to the pup who barks once in agreement before running off.

I stand from where I'd been sitting on the edge of Michael's bed and hike my tote over my shoulder. Making my way down the hall to the stairs, I take a second glance at the pictures hanging in the stairwell. The

Harrington men for three generations. The Harrington cousins at a young age. More photographs. More memories. Faded rectangles mark the wall from the pictures I took with me. Nails remain intact, empty of replacement frames.

When I enter the kitchen, James leans against the kitchen counter. His arms are spread, hands clutching the countertop. His head is hung again as he faces the window with his back to my entrance.

His body language reeks of sadness.

And guilt. So much guilt.

"I'll . . ." I pause, waiting for him to turn and acknowledge me. "I'll see myself out."

James spins. "How's Dalton?" His exaggeration of Dalton's name along with the visceral tone does not settle well with me.

"I'll speak with him later."

"And tell him you're still married?"

My head shakes. The anger that I try to suppress boils inside me. While I didn't have the energy to argue with him moments ago, perhaps the denotation of my libido did the trick because I explode.

"This isn't a marriage."

James's brow lifts.

"Marriage is a partnership. It's comfort. It's support. It's . . ."

"Don't stop now. Tell me more," he mocks, crossing his arms as his backside leans against the sink.

"It's vows, not promises. Sacred vows to uphold love and honor and faithfulness."

"Who's been unfaithful to who?" James mocks.

"Don't you dare," I hiss, pointing a finger at him as I round the kitchen island between us. "I saw that woman sitting on your lap, nibbling at your skin like you were corn on the cob dipped in butter."

James huffs, but I'm not trying to be funny. "I'd like to lay you out on this counter and eat you like corn on the cob, Peach. Remind you who nibbles you best."

"Jesus," I hiss, a clash of turned on and pissed off. "You don't have to be so crass."

James steps closer to me. "That's the thing about you, Peach. One minute, you're proper, and the next, you're dirty, and I happen to know you like it nasty. Reckless. Wild."

He clears another step and reaches for my face, but this time, willpower strengthens me. I lean away before he touches me.

"Don't pull away from me," he snaps, blue eyes firing like the start of a burner.

"Because that's your job?" I bark at him.

"Evelyn," he warns, but there's nothing left to warn me about. He broke my heart. He cast me out.

"A marriage is love, James. I loved you." I jab a finger at my chest. "No matter what happened, I loved you, but you told me to leave. *You* told me to get out. *You* said you couldn't look at me." I choke on the sob I'd been fighting since entering this house. "Do you have any idea how much that hurt? He had my eyes, and because of that, you tossed me aside. I didn't leave you. You left me, so don't preach to me about faithfulness."

*You said we'd get through anything as long as we were together.*

James stares at me. His arms slowly crossing over his firm chest. His hand lifts for his mouth while his finger swipes at the patch of hair thicker on his chin. His eyes are blue steel, hard and cold. He's so distant from me despite the twelve inches between us.

"You didn't call, Evie," he states as if that explains or answers anything.

"Forget the call. You could have called me. For years, I've been waiting on your call, Ranger." The reference to his nickname startles him, and both brows arch.

"It's been six years," he clarifies.

"That's right, and a year ago, I'd finally had enough. I had to let you go." My voice cracks, and James stares at me. I'm such a fool. It took me years to release him. It took him days to cut me out.

*I can't believe I almost considered sleeping with him.*

For half a minute, on our son's bed, I thought I could do it. I thought I could have sex with him.

"So, you can divorce me and fuck him," James says without a second of thought.

"Fuck you!" I scream at him. Then I hitch my bag higher on my shoulder and stalk out of the house—*our* house—just as I did six years ago.

# Chapter 7
# Woman Are Pillars

[Evie]

To my surprise, my car leads me right where James told me I wasn't allowed to go.

I'm paying an impromptu visit to his parents.

When I told James I was pregnant, the first thing he did after getting over the shock was asked if he could introduce me to his family.

*"They're going to love you."* The sentiment was nice enough, but I wanted *him* to love me, which seemed like the craziest notion because we'd only been together less than twenty-four hours. We'd been apart for three months, during which I found out I was having his baby.

Back then, he followed me to Conrad Lodge, which wasn't as nice then as it is now, and I rode with him to his parents' house. James was nervous when we finally pulled in front of the antebellum home, reminiscent of history long passed in this country. The house was beautiful, with a grand porch on two floors and stately columns accenting each level.

*As we sat a minute in the gravel driveway, James reached for my hand, kissed my knuckles, and I turned to him, never forgetting the look in his eyes.*

*Fear.*

*I softly chuckled at his tenderness. "Maybe I need to be the rock?" I questioned of him.*

*"There's something you need to know about me before we walk in there. I'm sort of the black sheep of the family. I don't match the rest of them. The military hero of my eldest brother. The do-good of my youngest brother. Even Billy, who can be a fuckup in his own right, hasn't done the shit I've done. You're going to be the best thing to ever happen to me in their eyes, and that's a lot of pressure." His concern for*

*me made my heart patter double time, but he had nothing to worry about. I had my own black sheep moment, which he'd learn about soon enough.*

*"We have so much to learn about each other," I told him, hoping this conveyed I understood his concern. His thumb rubbed over my knuckles while his attention concentrated on the motion.*

*"We already know we have one thing in common," he teased, and my brows creased in question. "Fantastic sex."*

*I swallowed against the anxious chuckle in my throat. "You've had a lot of that, haven't you?"*

*"Fantastic sex?" he continued to tease, and I nodded while licking my lips as I awaited his answer. "Only with you."*

*"You promised you'd never lie to me," I reminded him, releasing the nervous laugh.*

*"I'm not lying." He twisted my hand so he could scrape his teeth against the pulse point of my wrist, and it was a shot right to another pulsing place on my body. I wanted fantastic sex with him again, but first, we needed to meet his parents.*

The memory comes back to me as I park in the drive of Elaina and George's stately estate. It's just as breathtaking as it was nineteen years ago, and I'm just as nervous.

I exit the Jeep and take a deep breath of the autumn air around me. When I shut the driver's door, my heart races faster. As I walk up the drive, a woman with bright blond-white hair steps onto the lower porch and holds a hand up to her brow to shadow her eyes as she watches me approach.

"Evelyn Sue," she calls out to me as I near the steps. My smile grows, and something inside me wants to run to this woman, hoping she'll circle me in her arms. She did that once, letting me know I'd always be part of this family when my own rejected me. However, something stops me from rushing to her. My feet feel sluggish and heavy as I climb the stairs and meet her face-to-face for the first time in years.

"My, aren't you a sight?" she says, forcing a smile, and I'm not certain if her question is an insult, compliment, or merely an expression of her confusion. After a second of eyeing me, she flaps her hands and opens her arms. "Well, give me a hug, sugar."

I exhale with relief and lean into her, allowing her to pull me against her. She smells like gardenias, which have a distinct floral-spice scent. Every time I get a whiff, I think of her, and my chest aches for her compassion. She presses me back too quickly, holding my shoulders as her gaze roams my body.

"You're too thin, honey." I have lost some of my curviness over the years, taking up a healthier lifestyle after living a few years with self-doubt and deep sorrow.

"It's so great to see you," I whisper, feeling the too familiar prickle in my eyes. I don't want to keep crying at every turn in this town.

"Where've you been, child?" There's a hint of curiosity with her admonishment. When I left, I left the family, because it was what James wanted.

"I went back to Savannah."

Elaina sucks in a breath, knowing my history with my hometown. Her hands slip off my shoulders, and one arm loops through mine.

"Let's go inside, and you can tell me everything."

For the next hour, I explain to Elaina how I returned to Savannah but not my parents' home. I wasn't welcome there. I threw myself into my business, which had been more of a hobby before everything fell apart.

"Silver Dragonfly specializes in silver spoon jewelry. I mainly make bracelets and rings." Although Elaina already knows I dabble with the medium, I hold out my own arm to show her my work. "I'm even sold locally at Pearl's." Pearl's is a local artisan shop filled with Georgia favorites and kitschy touristy stuff. Presley Granger had been one of my closest friends when I lived in Blue Ridge. She was one of the few who knew what happened with James on a deeper level.

"You sell your line at Pearl's?" Elaina questions as if she doesn't understand something. "Have you been in town?"

"I arrived a few days ago." I realize Billy did not end up telling his mother about my return.

"Oh," Elaina states, affronted. Her simple interjection implies the unsaid. It's taken me so many days to pay her a visit. "How about other than this trip?"

Sheepishly, I look away. "I haven't." I couldn't bring myself to return even as my jewelry line expanded, and Presley demanded more inventory. We communicate mainly online and when she visits Savannah.

"Have you seen . . ." Elaina pauses, swallowing around her own son's name. "James?"

"I have," I state, trying to hold her eyes, but she looks away. Her fingertips press at her lips. Her head slowly nods.

"How was he?" To be surprised James doesn't speak to his family would be an injustice. He's told me himself he stepped away from them. He didn't deserve to be a Harrington, he said. I didn't understand his statement. His family loved him, past experiences and all. Pregnant woman and all. He gave his family the long-awaited grandson as Giant had two girls, and Mati had twin boys, but they were Rathburns. Billy never had a child with his wife, and Charlie was a single father with another girl.

However, I am surprised that Elaina doesn't know how her own son is. She makes it her business to know everything about everyone in town, and she must know her second son hangs with a motorcycle club outside of town.

"He's . . ." *Distant. Cold. Unforgiving.* I allow her to fill in the blank.

"He was so hurt when you left him," Elaina adds to my drifting statement.

"Pardon me?" I blurt, taking a moment to calm my tone. "Hurt?" I'm shocked by the word. *I* was hurt. James was unaffected. We both had another loss on our minds, and his rejection was like a second blow.

"I've tried to be compassionate to your leaving. It was the darkest hour for both of you, but still . . . it's been difficult on him as you left him."

Something isn't settling right with me in what Elaina *isn't* saying. "Since I left him?" I repeat for her.

"I realize you'd suffered the greatest of losses—the unimaginable—but James was hurting, too. I dare say the guilt drove him to do all he did. The decisions he made to pull away from the family and join that club, but it didn't help that you left him. It crushed his already shattered heart."

I turn my head, staring out the window facing the backyard where I once attended family dinners and barbecues. We're in the kitchen, and this is where the family gathers.

I return my gaze to her across the kitchen table. "Elaina, what do you think happened when I left?"

Elaina holds her head up and swallows hard. "You walked out on your husband."

I stare at her, dumbfounded. "And that's what you think? I *left him*-left him."

Elaine blinks once. "I'm not following you, dear."

I roll my lips, struggling with what information to give my mother-in-law. Do I expose the truth that James asked me to leave? He practically kicked me out of the house. He told me he couldn't look at me.

I stare at his mother, finding her eyes to be strangely similar to his when his weren't so cold and hardened. A soft blue like rippling water. A concerned gaze like a sun-filled day. James's eyes match his mother's. My son's matched mine.

"I don't think I'm the right person to explain this to you," I say, defending myself, snippy with Elaina for the first time ever. The implication is clear. James needs to explain it to her, and then maybe he can explain it to me.

"But let me say, I'd never *want* to leave this family," I add.

"I see I'm not understanding something." Elaina smiles with a confused grin and pinched brows but quickly dismisses her puzzlement. She shifts and reaches for my hand. "Evelyn, women like us need to be pillars for our men. Columns of strength supporting them."

She clenches a fist and raises her arm a bit. Staring at her, I'm baffled by her statement.

"Men want to be rocks, symbols of solidity and strength, but it's the woman in a relationship, in a family, who holds things together. Your pillar slipped out from under the roof, so to speak, dear." Her tone softens, but her intended lecture is clear. *I walked away.*

However, James was supposed to be my rock. If we're comparing polished granite to rugged boulders, where was his strength? Where was his support? I had to fight through my grief alone. I had to struggle with our separation. Where was he when I needed him?

I bite my tongue. Elaina held a different set of values and standards for her daughter, and thus women, than she did for her boys. She was tougher on Matilda as her only girl child and a bit disappointed in her lack of femininity. Mati never fully embraced being a Southern debutante. I'm the closest Elaina ever got to a daughter who might have fit the mold, like she was raised as a young girl. However, I hadn't conformed either. That's how I ended up with James in the first place.

I reach for my bag next to me and force the strap over my shoulder. Standing abruptly, I hold out a hand to Elaina, a gesture of goodwill I suddenly don't feel toward a woman I loved more than my own mother.

Her fingers curl into mine, and I squeeze once. "I need to be going, but it was great to see you again," I lie with the sting of her believing I'd ever volunteer to leave this family.

"But you're back now, right, honey?" Elaina presses herself off her chair, standing once more to match my height. Her eyes meet mine with compassion and hope. "You're the only one who can bring him home."

Her voice softens as our eyes hold. I hate to disappoint her, but she's wrong. I can't make James do anything. He'll have to make the decision on his own. Seeing the defeat in my eyes, she shifts gears again.

"You need to meet Letty, Giant's fiancée. Come to dinner next Sunday."

Sunday dinners were a ritual for the Harringtons. One meant to gather the family and keep them connected. We'd come and gone to them over the years. "Did you know they are getting married soon? And Janessa, Charlie's new wife—"

"Charlie has a wife?" The shock of another Harrington settling into matrimony, and one I didn't know had happened, is like a sucker punch to the gut. All these people were getting a chance at second love, and I couldn't even salvage my first.

"Yes, they were married at the end of August. And Matilda is engaged."

"Mati," I whisper, having forgotten that she'd lost her husband two years ago. I didn't attend the funeral as I didn't think it would be appropriate. Giant was the one to share the news with me. James didn't mention it during our annual call. It wasn't the sort of thing we discussed.

"Denton Chance. You don't know him, but he's Dolores's younger brother." The mention of Dolores lifts my head. Denton and Dolores Chance grew up in the house next door. Their father had been the town mayor when they were teens. James had a thing with his childhood neighbor. An on-again, off-again affair that spanned years which James did not realize involved deep love on her part and only sex on his.

"He ran off to be a rock star but returned last year when his mother fell ill and eventually passed away. God rest her spirit." I remember hearing about this man—a guitarist in the band Chrome Teardrops. Elaina's coquettish smile tells me she's honored to have someone famous enter her family.

"I'm very happy for all of them."

"You must come to dinner," she tenderly commands, reaching for my hand again although I'm not certain I can stomach a meal with the happy couples, especially if they all think I pulled away from James instead of him pushing me out.

"I'll think about it. I'm not certain how long I'll be in town. I need to return to Savannah soon."

"Oh pish. For what?" Elaina asks, wrinkling her nose like the historical seaside city can't possibly be better than this mountain ridge town. I can't tell her Dalton waits for me. I can't mention I might be getting married again myself one day, once I divorce her son.

"Business," I state, knowing it covers the truth in part. "It's great to see you," I say again, meaning it more this time as my heart hurts to walk away from her. I lean forward to give her a quick cheek kiss and inhale her gardenia scent one more time. She pulls me in for another tight hug—a Harrington hug—and I might shatter on the kitchen floor.

# Chapter 8
# Alligators On a Mountaintop

[James]

When the front door slammed this morning, it was like a trigger went off and I'd been awakened to what happened. Rubbing two hands over my face, I stared at the empty space where Evie stood yelling at me.

*I had to let you go.*

Isn't that what I'd asked of her? I'd told her to leave me. Leave me alone. *I can't look at you.*

She didn't understand how difficult it was to look into her hurt-filled eyes and see my son reflected back at me. It's bad enough when I close my eyes, I can see his in my mind.

There are all these sensations.

The fear in his gaze.

The feel of his skin.

The taste of his panic.

The sound of his plea.

*"Hold still,"* I'd said.

*"Don't let me go,"* he cried.

Evie's words echoed in my head again.

*I had to let you go.*

I could have started drinking right then at nine-something in the morning. Instead, I left the house, taking my pup for a long walk. Silver is my steady companion now, and I feel a little guilty that I've spent another night passed out on the couch.

As we walk through the woods near my house, I realize Evie didn't mention the Siberian Husky.

*What was Evie doing at the house last night?*

I whistle for Silver, so he doesn't get too far ahead of me. He barks back at me to acknowledge my call. Of course, I have faith he isn't going to disappear. He's rather protective. It's the strangeness of how I found him that tells me he'll never wander away.

It was after Michael's death, after Evie's exit. I'd wandered where I shouldn't have gone on the mountain, having uneasy thoughts. I'd never been suicidal. I lived life on my terms. But there were so many moments when I wanted life to end, where I thought I could not go on without him, without her. I could never bring myself to actually take action, but the idea haunted me day in and day out. I'd been up near the ridge, just off our family's property, thinking these anxious thoughts again when suddenly the dog appeared.

It was as if he walked up the ledge, marking the drop-off, which would never have been possible.

*"Where'd you come from boy?"* I questioned as the dog walked right up to me and sat down. His head turned side to side and then stalled over the valley ahead. As if I could read dog thoughts, his position seemed to answer my question. He yelped to confirm his answer. He came from out there, somewhere.

As I'd once been a member of the Blue Ridge Search and Rescue team, I felt obligated to return him to an owner and listed him as a lost dog found. As time went on, I was relieved no one came to claim him. He was pretty far from a normal hiking trail or adventure path when he found me. And that's the way I view it. He found me. I was the one lost.

I watch as the silver-gray and white furred body jumps a stump and then turns back for me, making certain I'm following him.

*"Don't lose me,"* he seems to say in his dog-stare.

"Never," I whisper to the woods, knowing it can be a lie. Never is something that inevitably has an end date despite the implication of infinity. Same with the word forever.

*"I'll love you forever,"* Evie once said to me, but I heard the words loud and clear this morning. She *loved* me, past tense, meaning no longer, never again.

God, I'm an asshole. There are two halves to something whole and I haven't been whole since Evie left. It was different from the loss of Michael. That understanding so difficult to grasp. His was an infinite end because he was never going to come back. Evelyn, on the other hand, was out there somewhere. I knew she existed because she called me once a year to remind me.

Although those calls were not so much about her or me, but a reminder of him.

*"Happy Birthday, baby,"* she'd whisper through the line.

*"Happy Birthday, little man,"* I'd choke out every damn year.

Another year gone. Another year he'd never have. Another year I had to go on without him.

And her.

I call out for my pup, not missing the irony in my nickname being Ranger and naming him Silver. He yips back and runs to me. The lone ranger and my trusty steed, or in his case, a Husky. I have no idea what his name once was, but he responded when I called him the metal and the label stuck.

As we walk back toward the house, Evie's voice travels through my thoughts.

*"You could have called me. I'd been waiting for five years,"* she said.

What could I have said to her? How many times could I say 'I'm sorry' before the words meant nothing? How many ways could I explain what happened when I didn't even know myself?

"I'm sorry," I say to the breeze surrounding me, having said it a million times and knowing I'd say it a million more, only each time there's no one to hear my apology.

Not her.

Not him.

+ + +

"James?"

When Evie opens the door to her Conrad Lodge room, I'm ready to chicken out again. I don't know what I'm doing here but my bike had a mind of its own this evening. While it's just after dinner time, the sun hangs low in the autumn sky.

I slip my hands into my back pockets and rock on my boots. "I was wondering if you'd take a ride with me, Peach?"

She leans against the door, crossing her arms. Her mouth falls open and then shuts, and I swallow as my throat dries. I was kissing her just this morning—kissing her with anger and regret, hostility and heartache.

"Just a ride. I promise to have you back at a respectable hour," I tease, hesitating with my humor.

"Fine," she huffs, pressing off the door and stepping back into the room for a jacket. I didn't check out this space the other night but it's a nice room. A queen-size bed fills the center of the space with a large wardrobe to the left of the bed. A nightstand with a fancy chair stands to the right. The room is white, reminding me strangely of our first night as a married couple. We'd booked a bridal suite in this lodge, but it hadn't looked like this room.

"Ready?" Evie asks, standing before me with her jacket on and her bag crossing her body.

"You won't need that, if you want to just slip your phone or whatever in a pocket instead." Evie leerily looks at me but she'll understand in a minute. I'd love to tell her to ditch the phone as well. I don't need some jackoff Dalton dude interrupting us again. *Dalton.* Sounds like a pretentious schmuck name and I hate him without knowing him.

My Peach. She always had men fawning over her.

I watch her tug the bag over her head. Reaching inside it, she removes a key card and the phone, tucking one into her back pocket and the other inside her jacket. My body hums, eager to get out of this room before I do something foolish like tackle her to the bed and take her mouth again.

I hadn't realized how much I'd missed her kisses until we were kissing again. Whether its frustration or temptation, the familiarity of her lips on mine has my brain all confused. My heart is hardwired to her, and the moment we connect, it's like a plug in an outlet, sexual energy flowing.

I step back and wave out a hand, allowing Evie to pass me. My eyes drift to her ass in her tight jeans. I've missed her body, too. The fit of those firm cheeks in my palm. The feel of her solid breasts in my hand. Her thighs around my hips. I scrub a hand down my face as I follow her out of the room and down the hall.

Once outside, Evie looks around when I stop by my motorcycle.

"We're riding on that?"

"Peach, don't be a prude. You've been on my bike a hundred times."

"So have a bunch of other women," she mutters, and the comment sparks a match. I stalk to her, cupping her jaw with one hand.

"No one rides my bike but me. And you." Her eyes widen with the depth of my voice and the weight of the words. She might have caught me with a woman on my lap, but I don't let women ride with me. That makes a statement I'm not willing to make with anyone but the woman before me.

Evie continues to watch me, trying to stare back into my eyes, but I can't look directly at her. It's too much. I'm still raw today. Still upset to find her in Michael's room. Still irritated with her words about his belongings. And still aggravated by the call that interrupted us.

I release her jaw and Evie gasps, like she was holding her breath. Not that I was hurting her. I'd never hurt her, at least not physically. I'm certain I've ripped out her heart and torn it to shreds, but that's different.

After offering Evie a helmet, I swing my leg over the bike and settle in. My dick stiffens with the anticipation of what will happen next. I hold out a hand to help her slide behind me, but she places her hand on my shoulder instead. Slinging her leg over the seat, she settles in behind me. Her thighs spread around the outside of mine. Without looking, I know her heat is at my ass. She's keeping herself stiff and as distant as she can, but she knows she can't ride like that.

"Gonna have to touch me, Peach," I call out after I start the engine. I don't hear a response from her, but her hands come to my sides, curling into the edges of my jacket above my hips. It's not going to be tight enough and I won't risk her falling off the back just because she doesn't want to press against me. I reach for her wrist and tug a hand forward.

What I don't expect is the shock to myself. Her flattened hand against my abs makes them contract.

"Sorry," she calls out, over the engine, but I catch her hand before she retreats.

"Hold on," I warn, kicking up the stand and balancing us before rolling forward. Evie's arms instantly wrap around me. I'm conscious of the placement of her hands, just above my waistband. Her palms remain flat, fingers spread until we exit the lot. Then her fingers curl into the edge of my shirt, fisting the material. Her chest rests at my back. In my head, I feel her breasts, naked against my equally naked shoulder blades. It's a position we perfected over the years, where she'd give me a back hug. She'd nibble at the base of my neck, hands coasting up my chest. Her fingertips would comb through the smattering of hair between my pecs. She'd kiss my shoulder and her fingertips would skim to a nipple, circling it, teasing it. I'd let her play a minute before I'd spin on her and take over.

I hadn't recalled those tender moments for a long time, but this familiar position triggers me.

Something else hits me.

Evie came with me without asking questions. She didn't argue. She didn't ask where we were going. She still trusts me, and something inside me wants her trust back full time.

We meander along backroads, winding through the darkening night. It's just light enough for me to find the two-tire trail I want and turn onto the short path before slowing to a halt. I cut the engine, feeling Evie stiffen at my back. She doesn't move at first. Hands still fist in my shirt. Her upper body at my back. Glancing over my shoulder at her lack of movement, her chin tips as she stares straight ahead.

"Why here?" she finally asks.

I don't have a direct answer. I'm a pawn in a board game over the past couple of days, and something greater than me is playing me.

"Heard there was an alligator sighting," I tease, but when Evie doesn't laugh, I clear my throat and add, "I thought we could talk here. Or just sit a bit."

It's become one of my favorite pastimes, making me sound old and dodgy when I'm only forty-eight. I just sit and ponder, brushing away what I don't want to remember, pulling forth what I do. This is one of those places I come to on occasion when I want to recall good memories.

I've brought her to the lake property.

Evie shifts, swinging her leg off the bike. She stumbles a second, and I reach out a hand to steady her. Unless she's been on a bike lately, I'm guessing her wobble is from the vibration in her thighs.

"Just lost my footing," she mutters, but I don't release her. Keeping my hand attached to her hip, I remove myself from the bike and stand before her.

She's so fucking beautiful. Her lips. Her chin. Her eyes.

Her eyes are my reminder of why I can't have her.

I close mine for a second, and she steps away from me. When I open them, she's crossing before my bike, and I follow her retreat.

"I have a blanket," I call out, pulling the roll from the space tucked under the seat and spreading it on the ground. It's water-resistant on one side while flannel on the other. I stare at the back of Evie as she stares out at the lake. Her hip cocks to the side. Her arms cross in a way she's wrapped them around herself. Her hair blows in the night breeze.

"Come sit," I state, breaking into whatever thoughts she has. Does she remember how we skinny-dipped? Does she recall that first night and her camper? Is she picturing how I proposed to her?

Evie and I had our night in July that summer. It was sometime near October when she returned to me. On a cool night shortly after she showed up at the ranger station, and after I introduced her to my family, I brought her to where it started and asked her to marry me.

It hadn't gone exactly as I planned.

*"Are you sure you want to do this?"* she nervously chuckled when I got down on one knee but hadn't asked her anything yet.

*"Peach, I've been waiting for you my entire life. I just didn't know it until we met."* Even then, I'd spent a few months wondering where she went before she'd returned. The memory feels strangely similar to this moment. She's been gone a long time, though, and those old feelings just don't exist as they did then. The newness of her. The prospect of our baby. A future with a family.

She accepted my proposal once I finally asked, and we made love right here in the grass, despite the cooler evening temps. My wild girl was not opposed to sex in nature.

I chuckle softly to myself, still waiting on Evie to sit.

"What's so funny?" she asks, turning toward me finally.

"Just . . . memories." I shake my head, but Evie slowly crooks the corner of her lips.

"Tell me," she prods.

"Just remembering two crazy kids, horny and newly engaged."

Evie snorts, glancing back at the lake one more time. "We were hardly kids."

Back then, I'd turned thirty in Evie's three-month absence while Evie was three years younger than me, but I'd done my time fooling around with random hookups and Dolores on the regular. My male-whoring days were getting tiresome by the time I'd met Evie, and I'd taken her pregnancy as a sign to settle down.

Folding down to the blanket, I make myself comfortable. My legs stretch forward, crossing at the ankles, while my arms lean back, supporting me in a seated position.

"Sit," I say, patting the spot next to me. Evie finally concedes and walks to the blanket, which doesn't feel large enough for both of us. She lowers next to me, mimicking my position a bit but placing her hands in her lap.

"Want to skinny dip?" I tease, wondering if she'll take the dare. "I promise to look for alligators first."

Evie chuckles quietly next to me. "Alligators on a mountaintop." On instinct, my hand lifts, rubbing up her back, and she stiffens.

*Shit.* "Sorry," I mutter, placing my palm back on the flannel behind her. She shakes her head, dismissing what I've done, but it's too late. Awkward silence surrounds us, and I notice Evie isn't wearing her wedding band or engagement ring. The nakedness of her finger makes me melancholy. I don't wear mine either, but I carry it with me all the time.

The lake is calm tonight. Not many people boating, if at all this late in the season. The water is cold year-round, which is refreshing near the Fourth of July but not so much in mid-September.

"Why'd you tell your parents I left you?"

"Who told you that?" I question.

"I went to see your mother. She's upset that I left you in your darkest hour."

*What the fuck?* "Evie, ignore them. I do." She knows I took my parents in small doses as it was, especially my mother, and I don't have any contact with them now even if we do live within twenty miles of each other.

"But why would you let them believe that?"

"What does it matter?" Does it make a difference whether I asked her to go or she went on her own? We were having a rough time, a private time. No one felt our child's loss like we did, and even then, I experienced it differently than Evie. I had to because I was present when it happened.

Evie shrugs, but she clarifies, "They were my family too."

We're quiet a second as I let that sink in. Evie didn't have great parents as far as I was concerned. They never approved of me, of us.

"So, Giant's getting married," she states, interrupting my recall of the people who nearly cast her aside because of me.

"Yep." I squint out at the lake.

"And Charlie's married, too."

"Yep."

I feel her eyes on the side of my face.

"You said you wanted to chat, but why haven't you told me these things?"

My mouth opens to remind her she hadn't called this year, but Charlie's wedding had been after Giant's engagement, and both happened after May.

"Guess I don't have much to say about them." I sit forward, drawing my knees up and wrapping my arms loosely around them. I can't sit like this for long, but I need to do something with my hands.

"Because you hate the idea of marriage."

"I never said that," I snap, turning to face her. She's right next to me, so in this position, my knee sticks above her thigh.

"Just don't want to be married to me," she mutters, looking out at the lake herself. Once upon a time, we had a huge fight where I told her I'd never wanted to get married to anyone. Of course, then I met her, proved myself a liar in that matter, and the rest is our history.

"I didn't say that either," I scoff, wanting to remind her that she's the one wanting a divorce and not wearing my ring.

Instead, I stay quiet, and the silence surrounds us another few seconds.

"Tell *me* something," I ask. "You sleeping with him?"

Her head snaps back to me. "I'm not doing this with you."

"Just tell me." I'd swear I could handle it, but that'd be a goddamn lie.

"I'm not talking about Dalton with you."

"He why you want a divorce?" I ask.

She glares at me, narrowing her eyes. "It's time to move on, James."

*Not happening.*

"And that house needs to go," she adds.

"What the fuck is wrong with our house?" I bark, releasing my legs and twisting to the side, leaning closer to her. My hand lands behind her backside. My attention is fully on her face.

"He isn't there," she whispers.

"You don't think I don't know that?" I growl. One leg bends upward, and I balance my elbow on it, scrubbing a hand down my face to calm myself.

"He's in your heart, James. He's in mine. He's inked on both our skin." Evie and I have matching tattoos with our son's twelve-year-old signature, his birthdate, and a few symbols of things he liked imprinted on us. A baseball. A dragonfly. An illustrated mountain range. "The house is just . . . depressing. It's only a house."

"It was our home," I remind her, my voice still rough.

"Not anymore." Evie's voice remains low as though she's speaking to a child or a frightened animal. It pisses me off.

"I'm not leaving the house," I tell her.

"We can make a note of that in the divorce."

*Fuck*. I'm not divorcing her unless . . . "Planning to sleep with me," I mock, leaning closer to her and whispering the words near her ear. She turns her head, her mouth only an inch from mine. Her eyes drift to my lips.

"I'm undecided."

"That's halfway between a no and a yes," I hiss the final word, realizing I'll take this as she's considering it again, after telling me this morning it was no longer an option. I thought I'd blown my chance. I just want one night with her.

"Evelyn, are you fucking him?" I keep my voice low, attempting to downplay the strain of asking such a difficult question.

"Have you really been innocent yourself?" she counters. Her gaze remains at my mouth, and I lick my lips, watching her eyes spark. It's getting darker, but my sight is adjusting. The warmth of her nearness tickles my lips. Another second of teasing tension passes. "You aren't answering my question."

Her asking is breathless, and her tits heave.

"You haven't answered mine."

Her lips twist, and she turns her face away from me, attempting to break the energy humming between us. Still leaning toward her, my hand behind her, I reach across us both and cup her jaw, bringing her attention back to me.

"I'll still be the last on your lips," I warn before bringing hers to mine. I don't rush as I've done the last two times. I keep it tender at first, sucking at her mouth and drawing back until each time I pull away, she follows. This is my hint she wants more. That's when I open. My tongue invades. My fingers slip into her hair and move to the back of her head, tugging her closer to me. She kisses me back, eager and excited. This is my Evie.

"There's my Peach," I mutter at her mouth before kissing her with everything I have. I want her on my lap, straddling me, riding me, but I'll take her mouth as a start. Her fingertips find their way to my jaw, scratching over the short stubble. Her head tilts, thus deepening the kiss, and our tongues clash.

Slowly, we shift. Evie's moving to her knees, and my arm wraps around her hips. With a hand on her ass, I press at her to climb over me. I remain upright, but she spreads her thighs and nestles into the crook near my dick, which strains for more from inside my jeans. Adjusting myself, Evie lands over my length. The heat of her seeps through the seam of her denim. She rocks her hips, sliding that warmth down my firm shaft, and I hiss.

"You dripping for me, Peach? You ready for me to spread you open? How about I taste you and see how juicy you are for me?"

"Jesus," she mutters, against my mouth as my hand at her hip rocks her over me again.

"Gonna make us both messy, you keep this up, baby," I warn her, surprised how close I am so quickly. Evie's hands rest on my shoulders but her gyrating increases. She presses her forehead to mine, grunting as she works that knot at the seam of her jeans, hitting her just right while she coasts over my zipper region. I'm so fucking hard, and it's tight in my pants. I want her to release me. I want her to fill her hands with me. I want that mouth swallowing me and . . .

"Fuck," I groan, squeezing both her hips, forcing her to rock back and forth faster. Her chin tips up. Her throat exposed to me, I lick her skin until I get to the juncture of her neck and shoulder. My teeth scrape over her at the pleasure point I know so well, and she stills, crying out my name. Her head tosses back like a wild animal, howling at the moon as her fingertips dig into my shoulders. She's clenching her thighs at my hips, and I swear I've never seen anything so beautiful as I come in my own jeans.

We pant.

We heave.

Then she's crying. A giant sob is my warning before her hand covers her mouth. Wide, frightened eyes meet mine for only a second before she squeezes them shut.

"No, Evie. Baby, no, don't cry." I don't want her to cry about this. I've seen enough of her tears. I don't want to make her sad anymore.

She shakes her head, and I sense her retreating before she physically pulls away from me. Wrapping my arms around her back, I keep her on my lap, and she lowers her forehead for my shoulder.

"Shh, baby. No tears," I whisper, my heart tearing into strips like a love letter headed for the trash. She cries harder. Her body trembles. I tug her tighter to me, and she finally gives in, wrapping her arms around my neck and holding onto me with equal strength. Wetness coats my skin.

"That's it, baby. Hold onto me." My voice cracks on the phrase, and I fight my own sob. I don't have any tears left. I only have anger and the ache.

"Let me be your rock," I say without thinking, and the promise hits me like a boulder.

I didn't keep it with her.

# Chapter 9
# Truth Not Dare

[Evie]

Eventually spent between the unexplained orgasm and the downpour of tears, we ride in silence back to the Lodge. James doesn't pull into a parking spot but rides up to the main entrance. The engine remains running as I swing myself off his motorcycle. The message is clear. He's dropping me off.

I don't know what I expected to happen. Him to hold me all night? Him to make me more unkept promises?

After tugging off the helmet, I hold it out to him. He doesn't take it but catches my wrist.

"Come to a party with me." The invitation crosses between a plea and a command.

"I don't know . . ." I begin, weighing the decision.

"Just one night."

Is that the night where I'll end up sleeping with him? Will he give me what I want once I do what he asks? Do I really want to divorce him?

For a myriad of reasons, I know the answer to the last one, but even then, I'm still questioning my decision, which shouldn't be questioned.

"I'll think about it."

"I'll call you tomorrow." With that statement, my eyes latch onto his. The promise should feel empty, but it wraps around me like a comforting blanket instead.

"What are we doing?" I whisper.

"What you asked." He revs the engine before I can ask what he means. A final weak smile meets me, and then he's pulling away from me, while I still hold his helmet in my hands.

Once I enter my room, I lean against the door, banging my head on the panel. How could I be so stupid as to have an orgasm with my husband? I pause a beat on the question and break into a giggle. My hand covers my lips, swollen and raw from kissing him like I haven't been kissed in years.

And then, my phone buzzes in my pocket.

I fumble for it like an eager teenager, thinking it might be James calling me already. Once removed from my pocket, I breathlessly answer.

"Hello."

"Hey, honey." Dalton chuckles into the phone, knowing the caller ID should have identified him. I hadn't looked, too excited to consider it was James.

"Dalton . . . how are you?" It's been two days since I spoke to him.

"Busy. What have you been up to? Hanging with your girls?" Dalton knows I once lived in Blue Ridge. He knows I had a son and lost him. I've referred to James as my ex-husband because it just seemed easier. However, the more often Dalton asked me out, the more he wore me down, and the deeper the lie became. He thinks I've returned here for business, including a visit to Pearl's, but I haven't seen Presley yet.

"Actually, I haven't seen my friends yet, but we have plans for this weekend."

"You'll be gone that long? I miss you."

"I miss you." My eyes close as I'm caught in half-truths. I do miss him. Of course, I miss him. He's amazing, and I don't deserve him. Guilt washes over me and my predicament. "I'm sorry, but I might be here longer than I expected."

"Maybe I should come up there?" he offers. His voice drops, and I recognize the seductive turn. Dalton is a bit reserved in his affection. He's sweet in private, but it's rare for him to be touchy or vocal in public.

"You know I'd love that, but I have plans." I swallow around more lies, although I plan to rectify this one. I hadn't told Presley I was coming to Blue Ridge, and I need to get us together. I also hope to hit up an estate sale or two this weekend. Dalton is used to me going off for a day to look for hidden treasures in people's old stuff.

"When do you think you'll be back?" he questions.

"I don't know," I say, biting my lip to tamper my tone and the exasperation I feel over my current situation. Also, I'm put off by his asking even though he's just making conversation. Somehow, I feel backed into a corner, though.

"Okay," he drones.

"I'm sorry. It's been . . . a long day."

"Are you sure you should be there alone?"

*I haven't been alone*, my heart cries, and guilt suffocates me. I'm not being fair to Dalton, but then again, what I'm doing is so I can be free to be with him. If I can let James go, I'll be open to another man in my life, right? I need to move on. In so many ways, I already have with the return to Savannah, the investment in my business, and the meeting of new people.

"I'm fine." The statement makes me cringe as it's been said too many times in the past six years. Those were James's words this morning when I asked how he was feeling, but it's evident he's anything but fine. He's stuck like I mentioned to him.

"Okay. Maybe have a glass of wine. Take a bath. You work too hard." Dalton's voice soothes me, and I weakly smile to myself. He really is good to me. The best part about him is he isn't pressuring me. He's spelled out what he wants from me—for us—but he isn't pushing me to make decisions. However, a man can only be patient for so long.

Strangely, my next thought includes how James would suggest he get me off as a means to relax. He'd talk dirty to me, use his tongue, and bring me to the point of forgetting even my own name. The tension would be gone. The comparison hits me hard as I don't want to compare two men so different but good in their own right, and James had been a good man once.

"Evie?" Dalton's concerned voice interrupts my thoughts.

"Yeah, I'm still here, but I should let you go. I'm thinking about that bathtub as you mentioned."

"Think of me," he says, catching me off guard.

"I am," I say, feeling like it's the first truth I've told him. I am thinking of him and how I need to be divorced before taking the next step with him. I need to be honest with him, but only once I have what I want from James.

"Okay, honey. Talk soon. I have court again tomorrow and that dinner meeting with Hartford afterward, but I'll call you when I get home."

"Okay. Bye, baby," I say, and the air stills. I don't typically call him an endearment. It slipped out as if I've forgotten to whom I'm speaking with.

"Night, honey." A smile fills his voice while guilt socks me in the gut.

"Night."

After clicking end on the call, I toss the phone on the bed and knock my head against the door one more time.

How could I have done what I did with James and then come here and talk to Dalton as if nothing happened? Speaking of James, how can I still react to him as I do after six years of separation? It's like striking a match and poof, I'm aflame, burning hotter than ever for him. There's something inside me still attracted to him, or maybe it's just an ache to fulfill something I can't explain. Perhaps it's just that I want closure. I want to seal the door on James and his rejection and open the door to a possible new life with Dalton.

Something is unsettling about that thought, and I press off the door. The bathtub sounds like a good call after all, but first, I need room service with all the wine.

+ + +

The next day, I have every intention of making it to Pearl's and seeing Presley, when I notice the new bookstore, BookEnds, and recall learning somewhere that Roxanne McAllister owns it. I open the door and instantly love the rightness of a place that sells books. It's a corner store with an angled front door, making it quirky from the start. A counter is just inside to the left with a large table and chairs in the front window to the right, surrounded by shelves of books. From where I stand, additional stacks are evenly matched down a singular aisle leading to the back of the store, but I immediately see Roxanne speaking with a dark-haired woman.

"Evie?" Roxanne questions, approaching me, and the brunette follows. "Letty, this is James's wife." From her arched eyebrow, it's clear she might have just been speaking about me. The tall woman behind Roxanne steps around her and walks right up to me. She doesn't offer a hand but goes in for a hug.

A little baffled, I don't return the embrace as well as I should.

"It's so great to meet you finally. I'm Olivet Pierson, but everyone calls me Letty. And soon, everyone will call me Mrs. Harrington." Letty gazes over her shoulder and smiles at Roxanne, before turning back to me. "Mrs. *Giant* Harrington."

"Oh. Oh my. Congratulations. I'm so excited for you. For both of you." I pull her back to me for a better embrace, hoping to emphasize my sincerity. I'm so happy for Giant.

Letty pulls back and smiles wider at me. She isn't Southern. Her accent gives it away immediately, and I recall learning from Giant his woman was from Chicago. I hadn't known they were engaged, though, until my present visit.

"When is the wedding again?" Elaina hadn't mentioned a date, but I vaguely remember Roxanne had.

"Friday of next week. We're getting married in a clearing near a stream. It's behind Giant's cabin, up the ridge three miles." Letty's still smiling at me, and I'm working hard to keep a grin plastered on my face.

*The ridge.* My heart races. The location slams into me, and I smile through gritted teeth. I can't find words to speak.

"Giant and I met there, so to speak, and we thought it'd be romantic to get married there." Letty's watching me as she tells me this information, and slowly her smile falters.

"Evie. Honey, are you okay?"

A shaky hand comes to my forehead, and I swipe a clammy skin.

"I'm familiar with the ridge." It's all I need to say before Letty glances at Roxanne and then back at me.

"I'm so sorry. I heard what happened up there." Her voice quiets, and the deep set of sympathy fills her words. Thankfully, it doesn't sound like pity. "I lost my brother when he was twelve. It's not the same thing, but we were super close, and I was there." It's all she has to say. It isn't the same thing, but somehow, Letty seems to understand the heartbreak and the difficulty of a place instantly.

"It's a beautiful location. I haven't been there in years." At least six, if not more.

"It's going to be perfect," Roxanne says, a cautious smile on her face. "Letty and I were going to get some lunch at the Pub. We'd love for you to join us."

I should decline. My first instinct is to say maybe another day as I had planned to find Presley. But the idea of seeing another face who remembers my past and then questions all the things about James suddenly doesn't sound like how I want to spend my afternoon. Surprising myself, I say, "I'd really like that."

If James and I were still together, these women would be my sisters-in-law. Perhaps sisters in crime would be more like it, as we'd have stories aplenty to share about Harrington men.

Roxanne excuses herself to tell an employee she's going to lunch. "Grace," she calls out. "I'm headed out with Letty."

"Okay," the voice floats from the back of the store.

"Grace Eton works for me. Do you know her?" I did, but her boys were younger than Michael would be.

"I wasn't friends with her, no, but I know of her, of course." Grace had a tragic story, widowed with five young boys years ago. When I look over at Letty, who leads us to the door, I'm reminded we all have a story somehow.

We cross the street as Letty explains how she has a son, but Elaina is babysitting for the day. "I really needed a day off." She winces as she says it, glancing at me as she opens the Pub door.

"I remember days like that," I say, hoping to convey it's okay for her to speak about her child. I was in that position on the day I lost

Michael forever. I'd asked James for a day off as Mom. I shake the guilt that normally eats at me and step into the dim pub.

Roxanne waves at someone—I don't see who—and then points to a table. I follow her to seat ourselves at a high-top table in the center of the room. After we order drinks, Billy finds us. He's sweet with his woman, and I wonder if Roxanne and I would have been friends if I'd been here when she opened her bookstore four years back. She's quirky and a bit eccentric-looking with those seductive silver eyes and white-streaked hair. She's beautiful in an unconventional way while Billy looks like a punk kid with a beanie cap on his head.

I wonder the same about Letty and friendship. She has an infectious laugh and a taller stature, matching her with Giant in physique but not expression. He's always been a broody man. Although Giant's first wife and I had been friendly, I wouldn't say we were close friends. Letty immediately seems more like my person, if that even makes sense, and I long to establish new friendships with women. I keep people at arm's length in Savannah, grateful that most I meet now don't remember when I was the rebellious young woman I once was. Letty's loud, easygoing, and talkative, and we settle into a round of beers in the middle of a Friday afternoon.

It's nice.

A variety of burgers are ordered, as that's still the top specialty item on the menu. The conversation flows. Letty shares about the wedding, and Roxanne talks about the bookstore. I explain my business in jewelry making. Thankfully, women can talk about anything.

Meals are served, but just as the waitress is setting down the plates, someone enters the bar. There's a shift in the air, and my gaze is pulled to the front door. Three bikers dressed in heavy boots and leather jackets, tight tees, and fitted jeans wait by the front. Immediately, I recognize James among them despite the silver in his hair. It wasn't there when I left, and it makes him look more distinguished. It also makes him edgier looking, and sexy as fuck, as the saying goes. My eyes don't leave the movement of his body as he follows the other men to a booth near a window. Once seated, he glances up, and his eyes find me in the center of the room.

Quickly, I look away, uncertain how to respond to his presence, while my heart begins to hammer. My underarms sweat. I feel him looking at me across the restaurant.

"Oh, my. If he looks at you any harder, he's going to drill through you to me," Roxanne says, leaning closer and speaking only to me. "I know that look."

My eyes shift to James, noticing him still staring in my direction. Hastily, I glance away again, wondering what Roxanne means, and then recall she's living with a Harrington.

"How are things going?" Letty softly asks, and I wonder just how much she knows about me. Surely, Giant has told her about his brother, his estranged wife, and the death of their child. I take a deep breath, uncertain about how to respond.

"Everyone thinks I left him." I don't know why I admit such a thing, but it needs to be said.

"Billy thinks James pushed you away. He said that's how his brother works." Roxanne's voice expressions caution in what she says.

"Giant thinks it was all James too. Like maybe he told you to leave him," Letty adds.

My eyes widen at the relief that his brothers don't think it was me. Not that I want to blame James, I just don't want his family thinking I walked away when James needed me most.

"You don't have to tell us anything," Roxanne says.

"We don't even have to talk about him. We can pretend he isn't eating you up with that gaze like he's a starving man."

I turn toward James once more and then just as fast turn back to the two women watching me. "He is not," I whine, slipping a hand nervously through my hair.

"I don't know your complete story, Evie, but if you ever want to talk, I'm here," Roxanne says, offering a comforting smile, and I decide Roxanne and I definitely would be friends if I still lived here. *Which I don't.* Because I'm here for a divorce.

"Same," Letty offers, giving me an encouraging smile. "I'm the new kid here. I need all the friends I can get."

I laugh at that, remembering the feeling well.

"Billy and I had a rough start. We hated one another at first, but there was just something about him," Roxanne offers as an olive branch of understanding when it comes to a Harrington.

"Giant and I didn't make the best impressions on each other either, but we quickly got impressed." Letty wiggles her brows. "We had a rough patch, too, though it was because I made a dumb decision."

"It happens." I hope to reassure her that I understand poor choices.

"I think it's standard for relationships to have rocky roads," Roxanne states, and Letty tag teams the sentiment with, "And bumps along the way."

*Try an entire mountain to get over.* However, I appreciate their attempts to show they understand.

"So, are you here for the dedication? Milton Duncan has his circus ready . . . I mean, camera crew . . . all set for filming," Letty states, redirecting our conversation, and a slow, steady trickle of quiet descends on the table.

I offer a weak smile and swallow the awkward lump in my throat. "Seems I'm the last to know, but what is this dedication everyone keeps mentioning?"

"Oh, boy," Roxanne says as she's the first person I heard it from.

"I—" Letty abruptly cuts herself off and glances across the restaurant.

"Perhaps James should explain," Roxanne says, mimicking what Billy had said when it was first mentioned to me. At that moment, my phone buzzes in my bag, but I ignore it, allowing the annoying cricket chirping ring tone to *chirp-chirp-chirp*. I stare at Roxanne.

"You know, that's the other thing that's been said. Once I'm asked if I'm here for the dedication, James is referenced. What does James know that I don't?" It's a question I probably shouldn't ask of these two women I'm newly acquainted with, but I need some answers as James has not mentioned this mysterious dedication.

"We have a new Parks and Recreation supervisor. She's Charlie's new wife. We should have called her to join us." Roxanne pauses with pleasure at Charlie's recent nuptials. "Anyway, do you remember First Church, just outside of town? The community received a donation of a parcel of land, and they wanted to move their congregation to another property and build a new worship center. Janessa convinced the members to sell their old property to the town, as it's a historical landmark, and it's being converted into a community center. Milton Duncan and his crew will deconstruct, reconstruct, and film the process."

I stare at Roxanne, still unclear in my understanding. "Film it?" I question.

"Milton has a television program called *Rehab Dad*. It's on the Home Network. He rehabs old homes and buildings, filming the process of restoring them to their natural beauty while updating them with modern amenities and décor," Letty explains.

I blink as a slow grin curls my lips. "That's amazing. Good for Milton." Milton is one of the Duncan boys, distant cousins to the Harringtons somehow, and a family who owns the local hardware store and a construction company. Last I knew, Milton worked with his brother Griffin while Kent Duncan runs Duncan Hardware in town. "Does Griffin work with him?"

"It's a complicated story," Roxanne clarifies. A heavy pause fills the table, and I sit straighter, taking a fortifying breath.

"So, the dedication?" I question, perhaps too cheerful, in hopes of gaining information. My phone begins to beep again—*chirp-chirp-chirp*—but I ignore the urgency of the sound. Instead, I pull it from my bag, check the caller ID, and turn the phone to vibrate mode before setting it on the table face down.

"The community center will have a baseball field and a playground for little ones with a train theme. There will be a walkway joining the old church to the center of town," Letty continues.

"Isn't that like a mile or more away?" I question, vaguely remembering the old church outside of downtown.

"Its intended purpose is to encourage exercise for the locals," Roxanne adds, and I nod, still unclear about what any of this has to do with James.

My brow lifts, suggesting Roxanne get on with the explanation.

"Janessa isn't from here, so let me add she had the best intentions when she made the suggestion. She wanted the community center to be dedicated to someone important to the town. There was a loosely led vote, and it was decided to name the new center for . . ." Roxanne swallows hard, anxiety in her silver eyes as she looks at me. "Michael."

His name is a whisper in the room, yet it's the only sound I hear.

"Wh-what?" I stammer as my damn phone begins vibrating against the wood table. In my numbed state of shock, I hastily flip it and notice three missed calls from James Harrington. My eyes leap across the room. James holds his phone to his ear, and mine pulses in my hand. Holding the phone high in my palm, I dramatically tap my finger on the ignore button. Then I click off the device and set my phone back on the table.

I glance up at a stunned Letty, and Roxanne looks up at me with concern.

"Just what the hell?" It's like an echo in my head. *What the hell, what the hell, what the hell.*

What does this mean?

"The community center will be a place for locals to gather, and the Harringtons are such an important part of the community, Janessa thought it might be an honor. The naming will occur when the deconstruction begins in a few weeks with a groundbreaking event and the official opening ceremony next spring," Letty defends.

My head turns to face James one more time. My heart races so fast I'm certain he can see it pounding in my chest across the room. His eyes narrow at me, but I twist away from his glare.

"When was all this decided?"

"There was a vote in August."

I'm floored. I'm stumped. I'm in disbelief.

"Did James approve this?" I choke, wondering why he didn't tell me or better yet, ask me if I wanted our son's name on a building, a place dedicated in his memory for the entire community.

"I think maybe you should speak to James about all this, Evie," Roxanne quietly states.

"You should have known about this," Letty interjects, sensing my upset. My agitation is slow to surface, but I feel it rising within me.

A community center. In Michael's name. Nobody told me.

I stand to my full height and forcefully tug my bag off the back of my chair.

"I'm not upset," I blurt as if I've been asked if I am. My teeth grit as I force a grin. "I just need some air."

From across the pub, I feel James watching me, but I don't turn around. If I did, the only sign I'd have for him is double barrel middle fingers. I stalk around the table, muttering, "Excuse me," as I dismiss myself and head toward the back of the room, hoping for an exit. Thankfully, I remember an emergency door near the restrooms, leading into the back alley, which holds a small parking lot. Immediately after pushing through the metal door, I allow it to slam behind me, and I plaster my back against the brick wall of the building. Tipping my head upward, I take a few deep breaths, coaxing myself to calm down.

*Why didn't he mention anything to me?*

*Why didn't he ask me how I'd feel about this?*

*Why couldn't he ever pick up the damn phone and call me?*

My head screams with these thoughts as I lightly tap it against the brick, cursing the likes of James Harrington.

"Hey." I hear his voice after the click of the metal exit door when it opens. The softness of his masculine tenor grates on my nerves like the brick catching my hair behind my head.

"No," I growl the second he closes the door and steps closer to me under the overhead balcony. "No!" I shout again, turning toward him and lifting a finger, pointing at him. "Get away from me, James."

"Hey." His tone turns sharper as he steps even closer, not heeding my warning. My body vibrates with the need to lash out at him, possibly strike him in my anger. In all the years, anger wasn't something I felt toward James. Sadness, despair, and confusion had been my emotions. Anger at God, but not James.

I was hurt, hopeless, and heartbroken, but I wasn't ever fully angry with him. It wasn't his fault. I said it so many times that it haunted my dreams. It filled my nightmares, but I believed it. He wasn't to blame. It was an accident, but this, and all the other things afterward, have all been James's doing. His neglect of me. His dismissal of me. His withholding from me.

"What is this, Peach?" he states, stepping close enough that I return to pressing myself into the brick. Only this time, it's to get as far from him as I can. He's invaded my space, and I need him to back away.

"Don't call me that," I snap. "And why didn't you tell me about the dedication?"

James's eyes narrow in on my face. "Who told you about that?"

"Everyone," I yell. "Everybody seems to know this thing I knew nothing about. Roxanne explained it to me."

"Damn her," James mutters without conviction.

"No, damn you," I bark, and James's head lifts. "Damn you and your secrets and your push to keep me out. He was my son, too, and I deserved to know." Tears fill my eyes and swell my throat. It's hard to be tough when you're about to sob, and I'm so tired of crying over this man. I blink rapidly, but a traitorous tear leaks, and I let it ripple down my cheeks, watching James as he watches with so much pain etched in his expression.

"I didn't know how you'd react. Hell, I didn't react well myself. I wanted to punch Charlie and his princess for this suggestion, and I disagreed with it from the start." James is somehow closer to me. His face only an inch from mine as his hand cups my jaw. His thumb rubs up and down the edge of my face in soothing strokes.

"Tell me," I demand.

"Charlie's new wife got the harebrained idea to name the new community center after Michael. I didn't think it was such a good idea. Then Justice, that damn fool, had to volunteer the club. He offered a ride in Michael's honor to raise funds for the place, and Giant stepped up to match the club's donation through the brewing company."

James's palm at my jaw lowers to my throat. He continues to stroke my skin, the attention becoming more pronounced, like rubbing the pad of his thumb on my neck is somehow calming him.

"Why didn't you tell me all of this before?"

"Because you want a divorce," he says, brows lifting.

"That's a cop-out," I snap. "This was decided in August. It's September. You know I deserved to know. I might even be able to support it once I get over the shock of being blindsided by it and finding out from someone other than my husband."

"Glad to see you remember who I am," James mumbles back.

"I'm not the one who wanted to forget," I yell, and the air around us stills. James's chest heaves. His leather jacket crackles as it drags over my sweater covered breasts. He's pressing against me, heat radiating off him as his legs straddle my thighs, forcing his lower body flush with mine.

"I remember"—James hesitates—"stepping out into this alley one night, so hungry for my wife I couldn't make it to the truck. I was so desperate to be inside *my wife* that I couldn't wait to get home where she needed sweet and tender in our bed. Instead, I pressed *my wife* against this wall and fulfilled a fantasy of hers." He mimics what he did, thrusting his hips in a way his current excitement is undeniable. "I remember when she let me fuck her in an alley against a brick wall where anyone could have seen us."

I remember that night. I'd been the one who had a little too much to drink, but not enough that I couldn't perform. And I was horny. I'd been handsy all night with him in the bar. Teasing him with a swipe of my finger up his zipper. Straddling his thigh as he sat on a barstool. Kissing him publicly on the neck and whispering in his ear what I wanted from him.

He gave it to me because he was my husband, and I knew in taking me against an alley wall, he wouldn't let anyone see us.

Michael had been two years old back then, and we wanted more children.

That night, I got pregnant.

And within months, lost a baby.

"Sleep with me, and I'll give you what you want," he blurts. My reaction is to shove at his chest, hard. His upper body leans back, and one foot catches him as he stumbles, but he bounces back, caging me in like the night he kissed me in my hotel room. Hands land on the brick wall on either side of my head. His arms keep him away as his eyes search my face, struggling for control of his expression.

"Your wife . . ." I begin. "Gave you that night because she loved you. She trusted you. She knew you would protect her and never let anything happen to her." I pause as my heart hammers, clogging my throat. "I don't trust you anymore, James."

"Because of . . ." James falters, choking on the name he doesn't speak.

"Not because of Michael," I shout, exasperated. "Jesus, James. You can't even say our son's name. Michael," I yell. "I am his mother. Michael's mother."

James turns his head as if I've slapped him.

"I lost him, too. Him. Michael." I'm really yelling now, and James closes his eyes, his face still turned away from me.

"When are you going to understand? It's not about Michael. Not everything is about Michael. You pushed me away. You pushed your *family* away." I choke as I consider the two women I just walked out on at lunch. They could have been my friends. They could have been the sisters I never had. "You don't call me. You don't open up to me. It's because of you. Only you, James."

# Chapter 10
# Be Angry. It's Healthy.

[James]

With my wife shouting in my face, I want to kiss her. It's the craziest reaction, but it's a reaction, and I haven't felt this alive in a long time. My body vibrates with desire. I want to rip her clothes off, kiss her everywhere, and bury myself inside her against this wall, like our younger selves who couldn't get enough of one another.

An advantage of marrying someone who was practically a stranger was discovering each other in our journey to know one another. What soap she uses to make her smell so good. Her favorite food that she can eat repeatedly. What tune does she sing in her head when she concentrates on her jewelry making. One thing we learned over and over again was the heat of our chemistry. Evie and I were off the charts together. The things she'd let me do, considering her proper upbringing and overall good girl vibe prior to me, bolstered me up. I felt like a king when I was with her.

But this afternoon, she is angry, an emotion she hadn't ever truly displayed with me. Even when everything had been my fault, Evie never got angry with me. She cried. She sobbed. She wailed, but she never rallied against me, letting me have it, telling me how I was the fuckup for all that happened to us.

I needed her to be angry with me.

I face her, and with my hand on her jaw, the other slips to her hip. In one swift move, I flip our position, so I'm pressing myself into the wall holding her against me.

"That's it, Peach, get mad," I hiss in her face. Her fingers fist in my jacket as she tugs the two halves together. Her eyes are wild, and her chest heaves. With the fire in her tonight, I let her lead.

"How many more things will you keep from me?"

"Take?" I correct. She must mean take from her. Her eyes narrow to slits. *There's the girl.* The one who needs to be angry with me.

"Keep," she hisses, surprising me. "You denied me everything. You. Us. Our marriage. You keep yourself so locked up, and you wouldn't let me in. You still keep me out, but this . . . this I cannot forgive you for."

"This?" I stammer. "Of all the things, you're mad over a name on a building."

"It's more than a name, and you know it. It's denial. Not telling me. Never calling me. Never opening up and letting me know how you felt, how you feel. What do you want, James? It isn't me. I get it. You told me it wasn't me, but what do you want?"

I stare at her. The list is short.

I want my son alive.

I want my wife back.

"Stop shutting everyone out," she continues. "Your brothers. Your family."

Her chest rises and falls as if she's been sprinting, and perhaps she has. She's been running and running away from me because I pushed her to leave. I told her to go and never look back. I wanted her to forget that I'd hurt her worse than anything that could ever happen to a mother, or to a father. I wanted one of us to forget because it would never be me.

"I'm not keeping anyone out. You could call me anytime," I state, holding her hips, forcing her body to press against mine as if she and I are the only two people who exist in this world.

"Bullshit," she yells at me. "We had a deal. I promised to call you, but you never promised that to me. You could have called me, James. You could have reached out to me. You could have talked to me."

Somehow, I don't think we are discussing a figure of speech related to phone calls. *Reach out and touch someone.* Evie means I could have reached out to her emotionally. Hell, even physically, I might have been able to use her to forget. We could have used our physical chemistry to mask what was happening to us. She didn't understand, though, that she was a constant reminder. One look at her eyes, and I saw everything I'd lost. I saw Michael, and it cut me to the bone.

I risk a glance at those sky-blue beauties raging like an approaching thunderstorm and quickly look away.

Evie's fingers release my jacket. Splayed fingers hold open like sparklers during a summer celebration, hover inches above the leather. Her hands shake like she singed them holding the leather, and I tug her hips tighter, hooking my fingers through her belt loops, hoping to tether her to me. In response, she pulls her body back, suggesting she wants off me.

"Don't stop fighting now," I grumble, turned on while equally appalled with myself. I should let her go.

Slowly, she shakes her head. "I'm done fighting, James. I'm done fighting you. I'm done fighting my feelings. I'm done."

"What feelings?" I question. Does she finally hate me? Is that what she fights? The feeling that she should hate me? She really should, even though she'd told me over and over again that she didn't.

*It wasn't your fault.*

But it was.

"No." Her voice remains stern like when I first walked out the exit door into this alley. I saw her dramatic phone tap across the pub. I also saw the conflict in her face moments before I tried calling her for the *fourth* time. Then I saw her hasty exit, and I had to follow her. I had to know what those women said to her because I knew it had to do with me.

"No, I will not discuss my feelings with you. There are no feelings to discuss."

Her denial would be cute if it weren't telling. She's really done with me. She's really letting me go, and I realize I'm a contradiction because I told her to leave me. I told her not to look back.

*I can't look at you.*

With a heavy sigh, Evie places her hands flat on my chest and presses away from me. I tug at her hips once more, hoping to return her against my lower half, but the continued struggle tells me to break free. I release her belt loops and allow her to take a step away from me.

"I'll sleep with you," she says, surprising me. Her eyes remain on my chest as she can't look me in the face. I hear the shame in her voice. "If that's what you want, I'll sleep with you. For the divorce."

For the divorce.

Not because she wants to sleep with me.

*Why would she?*

+ + +

*Nineteen years ago . . .*

*I quickly learned Evelyn Sue Fitzpatrick was not who I thought she was. I'd met a girl hiking in the woods, camping in a tiny rig, and illegally parked on private property. She was skinny-dipping in a lake, and I thought she was more nature lover, couldn't sit still, needed to be free, like me.*

She wasn't.

*Evelyn Sue Fitzpatrick was a Savannah socialite of the highest caliber, and although the Harringtons like to consider themselves royalty on the ridge, it was nothing compared to the wealth and prestige of her family.*

*Howard and Susan Fitzpatrick instantly disliked me. The mountain man hick, who wandered the woods as they saw my search and rescue position, did not meet the high standards they'd set for their only offspring. I knew all about Southern princesses and their parents, as my own sister certainly held her share of the market on spoiled. Matilda was the girl child my mother always wanted and the princess my father never dreamed he'd receive. Mati loved sports like the boys in the family, so while she was still precious in Mother's eyes, she was closer to Dad for her tomboy ways.*

*Evelyn was not raised in the same manner. She was raised to exude poise. She actually attended a finishing school, which I didn't even know was still a thing. She was groomed for a life she didn't want to lead, but I didn't know those things at first.*

*When I entered her parents' historic home in Savannah, I was beside myself with worry. Although I was plenty old enough and wealthy enough to provide for my future wife and child, I didn't know if I'd be enough. It was a surreal feeling as I'd never been concerned before about impressing a woman.*

*With Evelyn, I felt the opposite way, especially in her parents' home. I wanted to be everything to her.*

*"What exactly are your intentions, James?" her father asked me. "Is it money you want?" The offer stung, and Evelyn gasped as she sat beside me, clutching my hand as fiercely as I clutched hers. She hadn't told her parents about the baby. She said she wanted me to be the first to know. She told me she'd need my strength to tell her folks.*

*I didn't know how difficult it would be.*

*"I plan to marry her," I said, turning back to the woman sitting next to me, still holding my hand as though she'd never let go, and a strange sensation came over me. I didn't want her to let go. I wanted her to hold on to me forever.*

*"After three months and only twenty-four hours together?" her father retorted. "Name a price."*

*"There's not an amount you could place on Evie, and time isn't a factor either. I'll have the rest of my life to learn about her," I said, proud of my answer.*

*"Evelyn," her mother corrected me in calling her a nickname.*

*"Peach," I retorted, growing defensive. I didn't need their approval of me, but I wanted their blessing because it seemed important to Evie. There hadn't been a resolution that night after telling them we planned to marry before the baby arrived. I wanted to leave immediately. Evie begged me to stay one night.*

*I was given a guest room, separate from my future wife, as if the damage—so to speak—hadn't already been done. I laid in that bed wondering what the hell I was doing in that antiquated home with its halls of history. Who was the girl who went camping alone up a mountain? How did she get there from this?*

*While the Harringtons considered themselves something special in this town, their claim to fame was illegally brewing beer until it became legal. Even then, some looked down their nose on the production of alcohol, although it's a legitimate business and one that pays nicely. The Fitzpatricks were in shipping and transportation, and somehow that was considered a more noble business practice. Perhaps it was because they were doing it since the dawn of this country.*

*Suddenly, the door to my room opened, and Evelyn squeezed into the room.*

*"You okay?" I instantly asked, sitting up in bed.*

*"I wanted to see how you were doing," she said, equally concerned. I scooted over in the bed, allowing her space to crawl in next to me. She laid on her back, hands on her belly, and my hand fell there as well, feeling the tiniest of swells.*

*"What are you doing with me?" I questioned, propping myself up on an elbow as my hand remained on her stomach.*

*Her head turned to face me. "I like you," she whispered in the dark of the quiet room.*

*"I like you too, Peach, but I mean, what are you really doing with me? Why were you in those woods? Why did you do with me what you did?" It was an honest question. Why me? Why camping? Why sex with a stranger? She clearly didn't grow up traipsing in the woods. She was more a resort vacation in the Maldives type.*

*"I was trying to find myself," she whispered. "Things were . . . difficult here, and I just needed to get away. I wanted something different, something I'd never done before, and I wanted to do it on my own."*

*"Well, you certainly did something," I teased, squeezing a little at the slight curve to her belly. Her lips twisted side to side, not appreciating my joke. "I'm sorry. Explain more to me."*

*"Have you ever had expectations placed on you, you just knew you couldn't fulfill?"*

*I stared at her, feeling as if she'd read my mind. My oldest brother went off to war. He was a hero just for signing up. By default, that meant*

*I was next in line for the brewery, but I just couldn't be confined to an office. I didn't have the business sense for running a company, and I'd never been a conformist. I'd always been the rebel child without much reason. I did what I wanted when I wanted, and I faced the consequences without flinching.*

*Drunk at fourteen.* Didn't care.

*Dolores Chance in my bed at eighteen.* Oops.

*Got a wild girl pregnant in the woods.* Okay then.

*I manned up because I had fun doing what I'd done.*

*"Yeah, I know what you mean," I said to her, rubbing the palm of my hand over her belly and then pulling up the short tee to feel her skin against mine. My child was inside this woman. We created something together, and I had confidence we'd create more. We'd be more.*

*"I just wanted to get lost," she said.*

*"In order to find yourself." It made perfect sense to me.*

*"Weird, right? It was the wrong thing to do." Her voice dropped, and I cupped her jaw, forcing her eyes to look up at me. God, I'd give this woman anything she asked as long as she kept looking at me.*

*"Did it feel right when you were doing it?" I questioned.*

*"So right," she whispered, and somehow, I don't think she meant only the hiking, camping, and skinny-dipping.*

*"Then it can't be wrong, can it?"*

*She shifted on the bed, rolling to face me, and I dropped my arm, laying my head on the pillow to look at her.*

*"You're so beautiful," I said, lifting fingers to trace the edge of her face and brush back her hair.*

*"I know we've just reunited, so to speak, and we'll be marrying soon enough, but would it be too much to ask if I could sleep with you, here, tonight? I don't like being in this house, and I especially don't like thinking of you being so far away from me."*

*"I'd love to sleep with you, Peach," I said, letting my fingers drift down her face and along her neck. "In fact, would it be too bold to ask if I could make love to you? We can be quiet and go slow and—"*

*I didn't have time to finish my speech as she crushed her mouth to mine. Before I knew it, she was rolling me to my back, straddling me.*

*"Yes, please," she begged, grinding herself against me, the thin fabric of her pajamas not enough to disguise the heat and need in her. My hands cupped her face while her mouth took mine wild. She bit me, and I grunted. "Sorry, pregnancy hormones. I'm so horny."*

*She pulled back as if afraid to admit such a thing, but I held her head, keeping her face only inches from me.*

*"You can use me for whatever you need, but I'm warning you, Peach. I might fall in love with you." It was meant to be a joke, to calm her fears, but as soon as I said the words, I found I meant them. I'd fall in love with her. I already had.*

*Her smile grew until her face beamed in the dark room.*

*"Yeah?" she whispered. Leaning forward, she brought her lips so close to mine I could feel her breath.*

*"Yeah," I teased, then lifted my head to quickly take those lips. No more talking, I decided, especially with her moving over me. We didn't take it slow as we should have. We struggled to be quiet that evening. But I gave her what she wanted and knew I always would as long as she looked at me like all of me was good enough for her.*

# Chapter 11
# True Confessions

[Evie]

I step away from James in the alley, out of breath and out of patience. Tugging my bag up on my shoulder again, I turn my back to him and close my eyes. He wouldn't chase me. He'd told me he wouldn't follow. He told me to leave him alone.

And fool that I am, I hold my breath for half a second, waiting to hear if he'll call my name, hoping he'll stop my retreat.

*I won't be standing here waiting*, he'd once said.

I was the idiot who had been holding out.

Stepping forward, I walk to the end of the alley and turn for the main street where I've parked my car. I cannot re-enter the Pub after my grand exit, but I don't have either woman's phone number, and I need to apologize for my abrupt departure. I send a text to Giant asking him for Letty's number, hoping I don't need to explain myself. I'm sure she'll fill him in.

When I return to Conrad Lodge, I debate heading to the lounge for a drink. I'd hardly eaten my lunch. Instead, I decide the privacy of my room is what I need. Although I'd been alone a long time, and desperately in need of people, I don't think I'd be good company to anyone in my current state.

To my surprise, I see a newly-familiar man stepping out of a room, and I stop in the hallway.

"Justice?" He doesn't seem like the type to rent a swanky resort room for a one-hour tryst. There are places off the highway for such a thing, not to mention I'd been to the clubhouse slash mansion deep in the woods thanks to Giant's directions. It didn't make sense to me that Justice would be here, but what did I know? It wasn't my business anyway.

"Evie?" The expression on his face shows his matching surprise. "Thought you were at the Pub with James."

I stare at him, uncertain of how to respond. "I was supposed to be there for drinks with some girlfriends. James happened to be there."

Justice nods and then tilts his head. "You doing okay?"

My lips quiver at the concern in his tone and bite them hard, preventing the embarrassment of tears before a man I don't know. "It's been a rough night, but I've been through worse."

"Yeah," Justice drones as he must know a thing or two about my worse. "Wanna get a drink?" He tips his head, signaling the lounge behind me.

"I was thinking of heading to bed. It's been a long couple of days."

"One drink," he says, stepping forward and placing a large hand on my arm. I spin without thinking, leading him toward the front of the Lodge. As we walk, I sense him look over his shoulder just once, but no one else enters the hallway. For a second, I wonder if James does this kind of thing often—takes women to a nice hotel to have sex with them for an hour or so. Then I dismiss the thought.

Justice guides me to a high-top table in the corner of the Lounge. With two fingers in the air, he signals the bartender, who gives a chin dip in our direction. The biker Santa before me looks a little out of place in the dimly lit, jazz-infused lounge. Tiny candles in miniature glassware decorate the tables while the low lights give the space an intimate atmosphere. It feels clandestine to be here with him, but I'm not doing anything wrong. It's only a drink.

Two whiskeys suddenly appear before us, and Justice takes his glass in hand. Tapping on the edge of mine, he lifts his higher in salute and throws back the drink without a word.

"What are you doing here, Evie?" he asks me, and I softly chuckle.

"I could be asking you the same thing. You live in this town. Why would you need a room at a local hotel?" I tip a brow, hoping he senses I'm teasing him to avoid his question. His business really isn't my concern.

"For privacy," he states, answering me. "Now answer me."

"I'm here for a divorce," I state, sitting straighter on the barstool.

"That what you really want?" he questions, although he doesn't know me.

"Yes." The word isn't as convincing as it should be, but it is the truth. I'm here for a divorce. Justice nods as though he understands.

"That's too bad," he mutters, looking down at his empty glass, rolling it side to side on its base.

"Why's that?"

Justice's eyes shoot up to mine. "Because your husband is in love with you."

I snort, loud and deep. "Um, no, he's not."

"He is. Why else do you think he hasn't asked you for one?"

"Because he's waiting for me to make a move." I exhale loud and frustrated. "He *told me* to leave."

"Self-preservation," Justice says as if I'm to understand, but I don't. "And sacrifice. He did it to save you."

"Save me?" I huff. He shattered me, but I'm not telling this stranger my water-logged emotions. How the pain was so deep it cut out my heart. How numb I felt inside at the loss of not one but two boys in my life.

"He knew he was going down a rabbit hole he could not get himself out of, and he didn't want to bring you down with him. He'd already lost one of his family members."

"So he threw away the other?" I glare at this stranger, who has obviously become a friend to my husband. "What do you know about what happened?"

"Enough to know a man took responsibility for what no man can predict might have happened, and he's never going to forgive himself. He's come a long way, but it's not been for fighting, that's for damn certain. Never seen a man with more of a death wish. Saved his ass more than once from himself. Something in him keeps him alive, and I believe that something is you. He hasn't completely lost hope in you. He's just lost faith in himself."

I stare at Justice, not knowing anything about what he's sharing. "What do you mean, 'death wish'?"

"Base jumping, wingsuits, rock climbing, sky diving. He's been doing it all in hopes something will naturally happen to him, but it hasn't." Justice levels me with a stare, and my hand comes to my mouth.

"Why?" I whisper, although I know the reason. I don't like the reason, but I understand it.

*I should have gone with him. I should have followed him.*

"He blames himself," I state the obvious, answering my own question, and Justice nods. "How do you know all this?"

"A drunk man confesses everything, including his love for his wife."

"He stepped out on me," I say even though I haven't exactly been faithful either. Dalton's the only man in six years I've let get close to me, and even then, I'm not certain how comfortable I really am with the idea. It's only been once, and that's when I knew I had to let James go, or I'd never be able to move forward.

"Felt just as guilty about that," Justice admits.

"Why doesn't James tell me any of this?" I question, my earlier anger slowly returning. Why hasn't he told me about the community center and Michael's name for the dedication? Why hasn't he opened up about these risk-taking adventures? Why isn't he telling me he still loves me, if he does? Why? *Why?*

"Private man, I guess."

"Does his privacy include renting rooms at this resort, too?" The question hits below the belt, but I'm aggravated.

"Not my business to share."

"You just shared plenty with me," I remind him, lifting a brow.

"I like you, Evie." Justice softly chuckles. "You'd be good for him."

"I *was* good to him," I clarify, emphasizing the past tense. "Now, he doesn't need me to be good."

"Oh, he needs you, alright. He's just still clouded under that guilt, a guilt only you can help him release."

"I don't think he'll ever forgive himself. It's like an addiction. I can't help him. He needs to want to help himself."

"You're not wrong, but he needs a push to get there, Evelyn. He needs the love of a good woman to set him straight."

"I'm not that person anymore," I say, finally lifting my tumbler and letting the short pour of whiskey burn down my throat. I choke on the intake of such sharp alcohol.

"Maybe not," Justice says, eyeing me with disappointment, especially as it's obvious I can't handle the liquor I just tried to swallow in one gulp. "Too bad 'bout that."

"Yeah, too bad," I mutter, feeling my own sense of guilt mixing in with the loss I'd felt years ago and thought I'd finally be able to let go of with my husband.

"Coming to the house tomorrow for a party?" he questions.

"I've been invited, but I don't think it's my scene."

"Maybe you should come and see before you judge."

"How did you and James become friends?" I ask, suddenly wondering about this new friendship that didn't exist when I was here.

"I think I'll leave the particulars to James to tell."

"Funny, he's not much of an explainer," I mock.

"For the right woman, I'm sure he'll open up." Justice slowly smiles.

"Too bad, that woman ain't me," I retort, lowering my vocabulary.

"We'll see," Justice says before rapping his knuckles on the table and slipping off the stool. "Don't behave, Evelyn. If there's something you want, go after it."

I stare at his retreating back, covered in leather, wondering what exactly he means.

+ + +

To my surprise, James called me again.

*"Wanted to make sure you made it back to the Lodge okay."* His voice is quiet in the message he leaves. The four previous missed calls don't contain a message.

I send him a responding text with a thumbs-up emoji as I don't want to talk anymore today.

However, the next morning, I receive another call, and this one I answer with a groggy sleep-filled voice.

"Hello?"

"I'm picking you up at eight," he says before I've even finished my hello.

"For what?" I croak.

"The party."

I hadn't decided on the party, but I guess I'm going.

"I don't know how to dress," I admit. I'm not certain what a party with a bunch of bikers entails.

"Just be your beautiful self." I hate how his voice softens, and I imagine a smile I can't see. It's dangerous to assume things.

"Okay," I whisper, hoarse in tone.

"Damn, I forgot how sexy your voice is in the morning." The softening of his holds a hint of rough and tumbled itself, and a ripple rushes down the center of me. I try not to think about what happened the other night, as I sat on his lap, grinding on him like a teen, but the sensation of him between my legs returns.

"Yeah," I whisper, breathless and hot.

"Fuck," he mutters as if he can hear my thoughts. I want to touch myself. I want him to touch me. I was having this dream, and he was the star. And I shouldn't have been having the dream, but my thoughts are not my own lately.

"Eight, Peach," he says and then hangs up before I can decline his invitation.

At a few minutes before eight that evening, I'm outside the front entrance of the resort, considering James might stand me up.

"Waiting on someone?" The rich Georgian sound of Corabelle Conrad hits my ears as I pace back and forth. Corabelle owns the Lodge outright with the passing of both her parents some time back. I also know she's been divorced in the time I was gone.

"I am. How are you, Cora?" We weren't exactly friends during my life in Blue Ridge. Cora was considered the pesky neighbor of the Lane—a tattletale as a child, a know-it-all as an adult—but there was something different about her.

"I've never been better," she says, giving me a warm smile. Cora's one of those Southern belles like I would have been had I married Emmett Shaw from Savannah before James. She was prim and proper, judgmental and fierce. I never wanted to be on her bad side, but I also wasn't eager to be her friend. I haven't seen much of Cora although she runs the resort.

"That's a glowing statement," I tease. How often do people speak such a line?

Cora looks around the entrance. "There have been many changes since you left here, Evelyn. For one, I'm divorced, and it's the greatest thing to happen to me." *Ah, maybe that's it*. Divorce becomes her. Her hair isn't quite so coiffed but loosely tucked up at the nape of her neck. She's wearing jeans, and perhaps that's what's thrown me off as well because I've never seen her in pants of any type before.

"Congratulations. Is that the correct sentiment?" Will people say the same to me when I tell them I'm newly divorced? Then again, most people I know now think I already am divorced. "Looks like the Lodge is thriving," I add.

"It is. Business is good, and I've become more involved in community affairs." She coyly smiles as if there's more to her participation in Blue Ridge business than seeking gossip and spreading rumors. "I had a tough spell for a bit, but us mountain girls know how to climb out of a pit."

My brows rise at her words. I don't think Cora's had to climb anything in her life except a staircase. However, I am sorry she's divorced. There were rumors before I left that her husband, the athletic director at the high school, was having an affair with someone.

"How are Jane and Silas?" Cora's daughter and son are only a few years older than Michael would have been.

"Jane's doing wonderful. She runs the bakery near town, and business has never been better for Apple Jane." Cora winks at me. She pushed her daughter to be a beauty queen and then be the spokesmodel for her own apple baked products. "Silas, on the other hand, he's joined the Rebel's Edge."

"The bikers?" I question, choking on the club name James is a member of. I'm only familiar with *Sons of Anarchy*, having never seen an episode. Either way, I fear that both men might be involved in illegal dealings, risky business, and a multitude of debauchery. However, James told me the club isn't involved in anything that could set him in jail. All businesses are legitimate, and some members have jobs not affiliated directly with the club, which is how James maintains his firefighter position. However, I don't think this makes him innocent.

"Yes." Cora looks away from me a second. She takes a breath and lifts her head. "I'm not proud that my son had to seek others for the family he wanted. I'm working to rectify that relationship." Guilt riddles her expression as if she knows she's fortunate her son is still alive, and she's squandered their mother-son connection. This is one reason I didn't want to come back to Blue Ridge. I don't want people giving me this look. I don't want people to be afraid to admit their blessings or their mistakes. I wasn't a perfect parent. Neither was James. We just did what we could and loved our child no matter what.

"James is part of that club," I admit, uncertain if my statement helps her feel better as Cora has known James her entire life or makes it worse. In some ways, James has done the same thing—sought the club for the family he no longer believed he deserved.

"I have a . . . friend . . . who looks out for Silas for me." She weakly smiles.

"That's good," I say, hoping she finds small comfort in someone watching over her boy. I always liked to think Michael had guardian angels whenever James and I couldn't be present. Perhaps it was an angel who took him back to heaven. These are the things I'd tell myself when I couldn't sleep at night, and I prayed to understand why his death happened to us.

A motorcycle rolls into the parking lot, turning both our heads. The engine rips into the quiet, mountain night air, and Cora steps forward. A smile breaks out on her face, and she runs a hand over her hair. I still, questioning her motions. As the bike nears, Cora halts. Her expression of pleasant surprise shifts to brow-pinching disappointment. She turns her attention to me.

"I see your ride is here." She falsely grins and steps back, drifting to the front entrance doors. "Have fun tonight."

It's a strange sentiment, but I don't have time to consider it as Cora re-enters the Lodge, and James pulls up before the entrance.

Only the corner of his lip curls upward at seeing me. His blue eyes sparkle under the low lights of the entryway. He tips his head for me to come to him, and I realize as I watch his fine body straddle the powerful bike under him that I'm in over my head.

# Chapter 12
# Mystery Mansion

[James]

When I see Evie standing under the dim lights, waiting on me, I can't breathe for a second. I take in the glow of her blond hair down in loose waves around her shoulders. Her clothes are fitted once again, outlining her perfect body. When I near her, I stop my bike and see her eyes. Her lashes look longer tonight. Her makeup is a bit darker. Those sapphires gems gleam at me, and my heart skips a beat.

*Damn.*

I'm ready to skip the party and beg her to take me up to her hotel room. I'll give into that divorce if she gives in to me. My dick is already hard. Knowing her thighs are about to press against the outside of mine adds to the pent-up pressure. I should have jerked off before I picked her up, but it'd been a long day. I worried I'd whack off and need a nap, and I wouldn't miss this night.

For some reason, I was excited to bring Evie to a club party. I wanted her to see we weren't all a bunch of hooligans, fucking everything with two legs and breaking the law with every opportunity. There were plenty of clubs with order and hierarchy, and in our case, a bit of philanthropy.

"Hi," Evie says, stepping up to the bike as I sit back and hold out a hand to help her hitch over the seat. My dick pulses anticipating her nearness, but it's my heart that's thumping double time. My abs flinch again when her hands cover them. I've always worked out, keeping my body in shape, first because of search and rescue and then for the fire department. At times, I'd pushed myself even harder to be strong. I never wanted to feel weak again. Never.

Still, Evie's hands on my firm belly burn through my cotton tee. I wonder what it'd be like to have her palms on my skin again. Seeing as I can hardly handle her touch as we sit on my bike, I'm certain I'd implode if our skin met. Then again, I haven't been able to stop thinking about Evie giving into our crazy lakeside orgasm the other night, forcing me to come in my jeans, which I haven't done since I was a teen.

"All set," I say, once she's settled in behind me. Thighs on the outside of mine. Hands at my waist. Breasts against my back. I imagine the sharp peaks through layers of clothing, missing her naked back hugs once again. "Hang on."

I kick up my feet, and Evie squeals in my ear as I take off a bit faster than necessary. I'd like to hit the road and keep riding with her in this position, but I'm also just as eager to get her to the party. There isn't a man at the club who doesn't have a secret or made a bad decision, and reasons for doing either. It's why I fit with them and consider them family more than the good one I once had.

Evie and I enjoy the ride in silence, weaving deeper into the woods to the clubhouse. It's more of a deserted mansion in the forest, but it has a legitimate owner. The other night, I don't know how she found me here. She'd been talking to Justice when I entered the main room, but he swore he hadn't told her our location. As we pull through the open gate and sidle up to the side of the house, I kill the engine and take a deep breath. Evie slips off the seat behind me and hands me the helmet.

"You forgot this the other night."

"I hadn't forgotten," I say. I'd driven off, purposely leaving it behind, as it would be an excuse to see her again if she didn't attend the party with me. Taking the helmet from her, I don't look up, but when I do, her eyes have softened to a blue sky on a sun-filled day. I used to get lost in those eyes. The looks she'd give me when I was over her, thrusting into her. The tenderness when she told me she loved me. The spark of desire before we touched. Now, I struggle to look directly into those eyes. Quickly, I turn away, and Evie clears her throat, stepping back as I swing my long leg over the bike.

"This place has kind of a Playboy mansion vibe," she states, taking in the size of the building. From the outside, it looks like a haunted house, perhaps. The brick is a bit run down. A chimney slants. It was once a stately place. "Either that or a bad frat party."

"Yeah, it doesn't get to Playboy status," I joke. I won't be sharing how it's come close, but I've never been part of those shenanigans. "The club's original clubhouse was burned down before my time with them. The club dismantled a bit and regrouped under Justice about fifteen years or so back. This place is his, but he keeps it open to anyone who needs space."

"What should I expect in there?" she asks hesitantly, eyeing the two-story Georgian-style house.

"Seen *Sons of Anarchy*?"

"No, but I know of it." Her voice squeaks.

"We aren't like that, and I hate that every riding club is compared to that show."

I reach for her hand, and she takes my offer. Entwining our fingers, I take in her appearance again of skinny jeans, heeled boots, and a shirt that's sheer enough I can see a black bra underneath.

"I told you to dress your beautiful self, and now I'm regretting that suggestion because I'm gonna spend the whole night fighting off every brother inside."

"Was there a compliment in that declaration?" she teases.

"Definitely a compliment, Peach. Stick with me, okay?" Suddenly, I'm second-guessing bringing her here. I didn't think we were ready for another one-on-one session, but I still wanted to see her again. The party seemed like a happy medium until I see my beautiful wife and realize she's so fucking gorgeous I'm going to seriously come to blows with guys this evening.

My fingers seek her wedding band and engagement ring but find them still missing from her finger. Instead, I twist my fingers around hers, finding the heat of her a skin second best in their absence.

We enter through the main door, and I ignore the stares. The guys closest to me—Justice, Bear Grady, and Rocket—know who Evie is. I don't need to explain myself to the others and holding her hand should say it all. She's with me.

The club is full tonight. We never have much of an excuse to party other than it being a Saturday night. This antiquated, giant room houses a bar along a wall with a broken mirror behind it. The reflective glass is still intact in some parts against the plaster. Couches and chairs sit haphazardly in the middle of the space, while two pool tables are near the wall opposite the bar. It's an overgrown man cave of sorts with large windows blacked out by the night sky outside.

I lead her to the bar, pulling out a barstool for her to take a seat, and order her a gin and tonic. We pour our drinks heavy here, and I should have made her favorite for her. She always said I was the only one to get her G and T just right. While we're waiting on our drinks, I rub a hand up her back.

"Want to play pool?" I ask, needing something to do with her, other than stare at how beautiful she is because I'm growing hornier by the minute.

"It's been a long time," she says, shyly looking at me over her shoulder. "But sure, why not?"

"I'll be right back," I say to her, crossing the packed room for a table and setting down quarters to mark that I'm up next.

When I turn back for the bar, it's just what I figured might happen. Some jackoff hasn't gotten the message about Evie and me. Rusty Miller has taken a seat next to her, and I see red. Crusty Rusty, as he's been called in the past for his dirty ginger hair, is not one of my friends despite the brotherhood of the club. About ten years back, he set his eyes on Dolores Chance, a longtime family friend and once friends with benefits of mine. Rusty used her in ways that made me sick and hardened her heart.

Their relationship had been an eye-opener for me as I realized how poorly I'd treated my relations with Dolores. How I'd misunderstood her feelings for me and her understanding of where we were at with one another. When I tried to discuss Rusty with Dolores, she told me in no uncertain terms to mind my own business. In her words, she could make up her own mind who to fuck, how and when. She knew he fucked others. She couldn't have been happy with him, but I'd taken her warning and stepped back. I joined the club a few years after she started messing around with him, and quickly had the power to stipulate Dolores never be his old lady. Not that he'd commit to one woman anyway, but I didn't want her mixed up with club business or him.

I realize the hypocrisy as I've now brought my wife here, but there's a difference. Evie is already my old lady in biker terms.

"Move," I demand of Rusty as I return to the bar.

"Seat don't have your name on it," he says, winking at Evie. She isn't smiling, and I notice how tightly she's gripping her glass.

"What's he said to you?" I ask, drawing her attention to me.

"Just introducing myself," Rusty says, sneering at me and reaching out to place his hand on Evie's back. I shove it away, catching his wrist and pinning it behind his back. His face almost hits the bar top as I have him bent over it in less than a second.

"James," Evie screeches.

"Get off, Ranger," Rusty hisses.

"Don't talk to her," I warn him. "Don't look at her. Don't think about her." I stare at the side of his face exposed to me while I use my other hand to hold his head down.

"Fuck you," he snarls.

"No, thanks. You haven't had all your shots." Rusty is a walking STD, and I cringe when I see girls saunter off with him, but it's not my place to tell a brother how to care for women.

"James!" Evie shrieks, and I meet her eyes for only a second. With a final shove to Rusty's head, I release him. Rusty is a sneaky bastard, so I'm prepared for the swing he attempts, thinking he can slip in the punch because I backed down. I sway left as his fist glides past my head. My arm wraps around Rusty's neck, bending him backward on the countertop, pinning him to the bar again.

"You always were a damn fool," I mutter, holding him at the throat.

"You always think you can get what you want," he says, gurgling under my hold. I'm not squeezing him hard. It's the position he's in that causes his strain.

"Break it up," Bear Grady hollers from behind the bar. "Rusty, get your ass out of here."

"He started it," Rusty grunts as I shove at him once more before fisting his shirt and dragging him upward. He shoves me off.

"You were hitting on his woman," Bear explains.

"Every woman's his," Rusty states, and a sharp hitch of breath comes from Evie.

"Peach—" I warn. It isn't true.

"You're always fucking everything that walks in here," Rusty states, and I'm seeing red again. He's a goddamn liar, but I don't need to justify myself to him. Evelyn's the one with horror on her face before she can school her expression. She turns toward the bar and takes a healthy drink of her too-strong gin and tonic.

"No one's in the mood for you tonight, Rust. Get out of here. Find a woman of your own," Bear demands.

"Had one, until he got his hooks in her again." The implication is Dolores Chance, although Rusty didn't really have her, and again, his words are absolutely false.

"You fucked that up on your own, asshole. She finally wised up to you."

"It's always something with you, Ranger," Rusty mutters, straightening his shirt and purposely knocking my shoulder as he passes me.

"Ignore him," Bear chuffs, shaking his head as he addresses Evie. "We all think he's an asshole." I turn my head enough to watch Rusty disappear before twisting back to Evie.

"Who are you?" she whispers, staring up at me with wide eyes. Slowly, they narrow to slits. "What's happened to you?"

"You already know the answer," I snap even though it isn't her fault she's so damn good looking, and Rusty can push my buttons.

Evie shakes her head. "You need to stop using Michael as your excuse for everything."

"That wasn't what I meant," I hiss, swiping a hand over my head.

"Fire's going out back. Maybe you two could use some air," Bear states, and I take his meaning as he stretches his thick arms along the bar. Evie and I need some privacy.

I hold out a hand for her, but she doesn't take my offer. Instead, she takes another deep drink of her gin and tonic, and winces after it, puckering her lips. She stands from the stool and crosses before me, heading to an open French door leading to the back.

"It's this way, baby," I say, lowering my voice and catching her arm, tugging her in the proper direction. We exit to an old patio and then down the stone steps to the large lawn behind it. There's a mix of cars and trucks parked around a large pit a few yards from the house. Some people have camp chairs. It looks like a tailgating party crashed a country club.

"Pick a car, any car," I tease, but Evie remains quiet.

When we near the flames, I lead her to an old Mustang and help her sit on the hood. I stand, leaning my side against it as my eyes watch the fire dance over the stacked wood.

"That was intense," she mutters, and I swing my attention to her.

"I'm sorry about that. Think I lost my head a little with Rusty so close to you."

She slowly nods, curling her fingers around the hood's edge. "Is there any truth to what he said?" Her eyes face the pyre, and her question burns. My lips twist side to side, buying me time on how to answer her.

"I haven't been innocent, as I suppose you haven't either, Peach. But I don't claim any other women as mine. I haven't fucked anyone. That's Rusty just shooting off shit to upset you, which he's done."

"When he mentioned how you ruined his relationship with someone, who did he mean?"

"Dolores," I admit. Dolores has always been a tough topic for Evie. I can't say I'd been involved with Dolores when Evelyn and I met because we had an on-again, off-again friends with benefits kind of relationship. Unfortunately, we were definitely on when I had my night with Evie, and the guilt rests on me. Evie took it hard. She felt bad as though she was somehow the other woman when there wasn't any first woman in my life. Still, she had trouble facing Dolores and even tried to apologize to her once because that's just how sweet my Peach can be. Dolores wanted nothing to do with Evie's guilt, though, and it ate at Evie whenever we went to the diner, which was never her first choice of dining out options.

"I see," Evie mutters, but she didn't.

"Dolores and I have never, ever been together after you and me, Peach. You know these things. And now, she has a good man in her life. Someone who treats her like a queen. She's happy."

Evie swings her head to me, searching my face for the truth. While she says she doesn't trust me, she must see something in my expression because she nods once and looks back at the fire.

"Peach," I say, pressing off my side on the hood and stepping before her. I force her knees to spread, bringing myself between them so I can get closer to her. "Tell me about him."

"What?" She looks up at me, and I only take a second to meet her eyes before looking over her shoulder. I take the fortifying breath I need and ask again.

"Tell me about this new man."

"I am not discussing Dalton with you," she snaps, gritting his name through her teeth. I want to pick apart his name, but I can't. I'm too stunned by the reality of him having a name, which of course, he does, but it's much too real for me.

"Never mind. I don't want to hear about him anyway."

I lean forward, placing my hands on either side of her hips. "I just want to know if he kisses you like this." My mouth meets hers, taking her by surprise. I keep it soft, sucking at her lower lip before opening wider. I don't even force my tongue forward. I just stick to the warmth of her lips pressing against mine at first.

God, I've missed kissing her, and before I know it, my palm is at her throat, cupping under her jaw to hold her steady. I feel her swallow against my hand, wanting her thirsty for only me. We kiss with long pulls and short pecks, and I scoot her closer to me by curling a hand on her ass and tugging her forward.

"James," she mutters to my mouth. We continue for a few more seconds, the kissing heating up like the flames at my back. "James. Stop."

I still and pull back, afraid of what I'll see in those eyes. Relief washes over me when I see her dazed and dreamy like she used to be.

"I've just learned you've messed around with others. We should not be doing this," she says, lowering her gaze and reaching out to toy with the edge of my shirt. Her voice holds no conviction, but it does contain concern.

"Peach, I just told you I haven't fucked any other women."

Her head pops up, and she stares at me. I can't take that questioning look, so I gaze at her shoulder.

"I didn't think it'd be right when I was still married." My voice drops. Her hand comes to the side of my face, forcing me to look at her, but I can't hold her eyes.

"I saw that woman on your lap," she states, cupping her hand to hold my jaw steady. I risk a quick look at her eyes.

"I didn't say I was innocent, just couldn't have sex with someone else." Admittedly, the truth might make me sound like a wuss, but I just didn't feel right sticking my dick in someone who wasn't mine when I had someone out there who was my forever.

Evie's quiet for too long as I drop her gaze again.

"Your turn, Peach," I state, feeling my heart hammer, knowing the answer before she even tells me. Still there's hope, that tricky bastard, holding out that it won't be true. That she hasn't slept with him.

"Ranger," she whispers, and I hear it in her voice. My eyes close, and I accept I did this. To her. To me. I forced her into someone else's bed. I want a number. I want to know how many, and how many times, but then again, I don't.

Instead, I wrap my hand around the back of her head and crush my lips to her mouth, kissing her hard, hoping to make her forget the others, hoping she'll remember only us.

# Chapter 13
# Kissing With Fire

[Evie]

James is my husband. He's kissed me soft. He's kissed me hard. He's been slow, fast, long, and brief, but he has never kissed me the way he is kissing me with my ass dangling on the edge of this car hood. I am drunk on this kiss. Light-headed, blurry vision, heart-racing drunk. It was tongue and teeth, messy and wet, and I wanted more. My heels fell from the bumper, and my legs slid forward until I was standing, straddling James between my open thighs. My arms wrapped around his neck at one point, holding him to me as we make out like teens at a field party. I am oblivious to who was around us, who might see or comment.

It is only James and me. And this kiss.

"He touch you sweet?" James grumbles against my mouth, bucking his hips so his unmistakably long, hard erection taps against my center.

"James," I hiss, not even letting myself think of another man, let alone wanting to explain the particulars of my limited sexual history. My mouth longs to distract him, so I open to kissing him, forcing my tongue to seek his. He groans into me, the sound vibrating to the back of my throat, and I instantly consider putting another part of him in my mouth, dragging him deep and making him groan again. Instead, he distracts me by his fingers wandering my waist and dipping lower. The heat of his palm cups me between my thighs, removing that strong dick out of the way for only a second.

"I bet you're wet, aren't you, Peach? You're going to forget everyone else but me." He nips at my jaw, his hand squeezing me. "Only me."

I hum as his mouth moves along my jaw and travels to my throat, sipping at my skin while his hand holds between my legs. I grind against his palm, hungry for friction only this man can give me. God, I hate how instantly he can turn me on. I hate how quickly the switch can flip, and he knows he has this power over me. I've never been able to resist him, and it's my biggest weakness. I don't hate him. I love him. Always have. Always will. No matter how he feels about me.

Like a wanton hussy, I move my hips, forcing my center to skim over that open palm while whimpering that the friction is not enough.

"Need more, baby?" James mutters below my ear, knowing my body like no one else ever will. "How wet are you, Peach? Let me see."

Before my brain can catch up to the overdrive of my body, my jeans are unbuttoned, zipper released, and a large hand slips into my panties.

"James," I whine, fighting the struggle between saying stop and begging him to never stop. His fingers dip lower, and we both purr when they reach the trigger point.

"My girl is so fucking juicy and only for me," he groans as his fingers search just past the sensitive nub, and two thick digits surge into me. I yelp at the rushed intrusion. My head falls back, and I glance to the right, recalling where we are, where we stand.

"James. Others will see us," I whisper, stilling my movements and lowering my hands to his chest. His fingers remain in me, and slowly, he drags them back and forth, unrelenting despite my fear.

"Do you think I'd ever let someone else watch what only I can do to you?" His stance shows I'm covered as best I can be. His legs shifted at some point to straddle mine, protecting his hand in my jeans. One hand is propped at my side, arm extended to hold him upright as an additional shield to my body. I'm angled toward him in a way others might think they know what he's doing to me, but they can't be certain. My hips flinch of their own accord, sliding those fingers deliciously back and forth and drawing out the wetness only he produces.

"My Peach," he mutters, tipping his head to see where his fingers have disappeared. Even he can't fully see between the darkness of the night and the cover of my jeans, but he knows. Just from the sensation of touch, this man knows what he's doing to me. I'm melting. "So juicy for me. Want to taste that sweetness, baby."

*Jesus.* His mouth has gotten so dirty, and I hate how much I love it.

"Not here," I whisper, warning him. He cannot tug down my pants and taste me here.

"Not going there, baby. Just gonna make you come on my fingers, make you remember only these fingers can touch you like this. Only my fingers know where to press, how to please. Only these fingers know the spot." He moves so he's rubbing my clit with the pad of his thumb while he delves forward, filling me and tapping a place difficult to reach, but causing another rush of excitement. "This belongs to me."

*Ohmygawwwd.* I break against him, fingernails digging into his shoulders while my mouth comes to his neck, open but holding back a scream. Pinpricks of silver dance between my closed eyes, and I sway to the right a bit, but James catches me, holding my body pinned between the hood at my backside and the firm length of him straining in his jeans. If we were alone, I don't trust what I'd do, but I know it'd involve dropping to my knees and taking this man to the back of my throat. I want him helpless and wanton like me.

"Fuck, baby. You are a sight."

My eyes slowly open, and I pull back to watch him toying with me, rubbing softer circles on the nub that is still sensitive.

"You should stop," I whisper, loose-limbed from the first orgasm.

"But you don't want me to," he says, looking down where his hand disappears in my jeans, his fingers still moving against me. "Got one more."

"I don't want to be selfish." He gave me an orgasm the other night, coming in his own jeans. He gave me one now when I can't reciprocate. And he's working on a second one.

"My girl has never been selfish," he says, surprising me. Then his mouth drops to my neck, and his hand works me slower, but determined, I give in to another release.

When I come down from the second wave, I almost collapse back on the hood, and I would have if I didn't recall our obvious position again. James slowly removes his fingers from my jeans, and my hand instantly comes to the button of my pants, brushing my knuckles along the firm length of him. He hisses as he lifts his hand and places his fingers in his own mouth, sucking at them a second before dragging them forward.

"Not as good as having my mouth on you, but good enough," he says, closing his eyes like he's savoring a favorite treat. A giggle clogs my throat. It's not appropriate to squeal like a schoolgirl, but I want to toss myself on my back, like a teen hitting a bed, making angels in the sheets.

I'm ridiculous, and my brain is slow to catch up to what's happening.

Then reality slams into me.

*I'm so foolish.*

Hastily, I button my jeans and right my zipper, shifting my eyes from side to side, worried people will know what we've done. I've never been so public, not even when James had me against the exterior wall of the Pub. I consider the first time we had sex, against the side of a camper, and I accept that James just pushes all my limits. He might be the risk-taker when it comes to extreme sports, but he's my greatest risk.

And I need to get ahold of myself again.

"What's this?" he demands, watching my fingers fumble and my body shift.

"I can't believe I did that with you," I mutter.

"Do not erase this," he warns, and I look at him, watching his face harden. I don't want to erase it, but I still can't believe we've done this again. I've given in to his kisses, and he's brought me to orgasm faster than you can spell Harrington. I don't understand myself, but then again, I do. My attraction to James from the start was undeniable, and it's why it hurt so much when he forced me away from him.

"I need a minute," he adds, shifting his leg. I should offer to take care of him, but he quickly steps back.

"You can't leave me out here," I state, looking around the circle of trucks and cars, finding some people in positions similar to our own while others sit in small gatherings, chatting it up like it's no big deal people are making out near them.

"I'll be right back," he mutters, slipping a hand in his pocket.

"James," I warn. I am not staying out here in the dark yard, where I don't know anyone, especially after Rusty Miller just approached me and James reacted to that approach.

James grabs my hand and tugs me behind him, walking us quickly back to the house. He leads me up the stairs to a bedroom, and I stumble into the room with a double bed, covered in rumpled sheets, and a comforter pushed to the edge of the mattress.

"I'll be just a minute."

Before I can answer him, he's gone, and I'm sensing he's at the edge of his control with me. James would never ever hurt me physically, but he's a sexual being, and he needs relief from the strain in his pants. Waiting him out, I walk around the room, noticing there are no pictures anywhere. Other than the large motorcycle boots near the bed, there isn't a hint as to who's room this is. I'm stepping up to the window when I hear laughter outside the bedroom door, and it bursts open. A large body is guiding a woman within, blocking my view of her, and then they are against the wall, kissing.

*Oh, my God.* I need to get out of here, but I don't know how, other than clearing my throat as a means to draw attention to myself. When that doesn't work, I decide to slowly make my way toward the door and then call out, "Excuse me."

A silver head of hair pops up, and his body turns. He covers the woman at his back.

"What are you doing here?" Justice barks.

"James put me in here, but he'll be back in a second. I can just . . ." I point toward the hallway. "If I can just . . ." I wiggle my finger, implying I need to get by them.

"Get out," Justice snaps, and he doesn't have to tell me twice. I scramble for the door, struggling with the handle at first as it's locked. Once I have it open, I turn to face the menacing man to apologize and catch the eye of a woman hiding behind his back.

I pretend I don't notice her, and I'm assuming she wouldn't want me to know she's with him.

"I'm sorry," I mutter, taking myself into the hall and closing the door behind me. It immediately locks, and I hear giggling on the other side of the barrier before I hear a thud and then silence.

I shake my head, wondering what I've gotten myself into being in this house, being with James. He's so different than he used to be. We both are.

Deciding not to wait on James, I head back down the stairs and out the front door.

# Chapter 14
# Adrenaline Rush

[James]

When I exit the bathroom off the hall, I find the door to Justice's bedroom locked.

"Evelyn, let me in." Flat palmed, I pound on the barrier. I pushed her too far, but she's just . . . her, and when she told me about her man without telling me about him, I lost control. I need her to know she'll never feel the way I make her feel. *I'll* never feel again the way I feel with her.

"Jesus," Justice mutters, yanking open his door. He stands before me in a state of disarray, missing his shirt, jeans open at the waist. His body blocks the entrance. For half a second, I have the worst thought. "You and your woman are driving me nuts. She isn't in here, so get that look off your damn face."

The door slams in said face, and I turn about, wondering where she could have gone. The bonus is, she can't leave as she rode here on my bike, and we are too far from town for her to walk. Still, I race down the stairs, two at a time, and scan the old ballroom, now party central. When I don't find her blond hair among the others, I spin for the front door, finding it open, and step outside. I scan the yard covered with bikes and beer cans and find who I'm looking for standing off in the distance.

Stalking toward her, I slow my pace as I near. Her back is to me. Her arms wrapped around herself, holding the sides of her shirt. It's cool in the mountains during a mid-September night, and she isn't wearing a jacket. I shrug out of mine and close the distance between us. Slipping the leather over her shoulders, she flinches at the touch, craning her neck to glance at me over her shoulder.

"Hey," I say.

"Hey."

"Don't run off like that." My heart still hammers with thoughts she might have found a way to leave the party after all, and I didn't want her to go. There's so much unresolved between us, and I'm not talking about what happened years ago, but the present day, too. We keep coming together like a thunderstorm marked by lightning, and then the rain. So much rain. Thankfully, Evie isn't crying. She's just standing there, staring off in the dark distance.

"Someone wanted to occupy the room," she says with a soft laugh.

"Yeah, I heard." I reach for the back of my neck, scratching nervously at it. I shouldn't have walked away from her, but I needed a minute. There's no way I could get my dick to rest, and I knew it wouldn't take long. Just imagining her, recalling the feeling of her under my fingers, the taste of those fingers on my tongue, and I lost it.

"I saw Justice last night," she blurts, which was not what I expected her to say next.

"You what?"

"He told me about your adrenaline addiction." She glances at me again over her shoulder as I stand at her side.

"Back up. Where did you see Justice?"

"He was coming out of a room at the Lodge."

*Huh.* So that's where he meets up with her? Justice and Corabelle Conrad have a thing happening. They're trying to be discreet, but after what she pulled, roping the Rebels into riding for funds, it's become more and more evident to the public that something's happening between those two.

"And?"

"He asked me to have a drink with him."

*What?* "What the fuck?"

"When did your language turn so crass?" Evie asks.

"When did you become a prude?" I tease. She's never minded how I speak. Although I had the highest of education offered here in Blue Ridge, I hang out with a lot of mountain people. The search and rescue team had rough language, and the fire department isn't much better. "Answer the question."

"I'm not a prude," she says, a hint of the socialite she could have been peeks out in her statement.

"Not that question, the other one. What did he want?"

"He told me about your adrenaline addiction," she repeats.

*Dammit.*

"Actually, he called it a death wish."

I scratch nervously at my nape again. "It's not a death wish," I mutter, looking off in the distance. When Michael died, I didn't know how I'd go on without him. I wasn't one for pulling my own trigger, and I'd never been afraid of risk, so I purposely put myself in danger. I would have rejoined search and rescue if they didn't think I was a head case. It took all I had to prove to the fire department I was okay to continue working, but I always volunteered for the toughest situations.

As the local fire department often assisted search and rescue, I'd go down steep cliffs and deep ravines. I'd jump with wingman suits, flying into places for an aerial view or hike through rough terrain, risking everything.

"James," she softly drones.

"I just . . ." I don't know why I did it. I can't seem to live without my son, and I can't live with my wife. Death on my own does not seem like an option, but I won't deny it coming for me if it wants to take me.

"You just what?" Evie snaps, turning to face me in the dark yard. "Do you want to die?" Her voice cracks. "Do you want to leave me in this world without both of you? Do you want me to carry on every day wondering what foolish thing you'll do in hopes to what? Join him?" Her voice strains higher. Pain fills her face.

"Peach," I groan, unable to answer her.

"Then stop it," she states, arms still crossed over her middle with my jacket over her shoulders, dwarfing her frame. "Do not leave me alone without you in this world."

"Evie."

"I mean it, James. You've always been a risk-taker, and I understand that about you. It's in your blood to push limits, and it was worrisome enough being your wife, wondering every time you went out if you were coming back. But this . . . with the distance between us . . . I cannot be worrying about what stupid thing you'll do to put yourself in harm's way in hopes of something happening." Her voice rises again, octaves escalating.

"I don't want you worrying about me, Peach. I can take care of myself."

"Clearly, you can't," she states, huffing as she does.

"I'm doing just fine on my own."

"Really? You're happy with all this?" She waves out at the decrepit house.

"Hey. There's nothing wrong with these people. They're good men, and they've been good to me."

"Because no one else was good to you?" she shouts.

"Because they understand me." My arms flail out to my sides before my hands come to the top of my head.

"And I don't." Evie's eyes sparkle in the dark, and it seems easier to look at them without light emphasizing their shape and color.

"I didn't say that."

"You don't have to. Six years of separation says it clear enough."

We glare at one another in silence.

"I killed our son, Evelyn," I state, recalling the most painful words I ever had to say to her.

"It was an accident." Her calm unnerves me. It always has. She doesn't understand.

"I'm lost without him."

"You think I'm whole?" Her voice cracks once again as she points at her own chest. "How can these men understand you better than me? I am Michael's mother. I was there, standing beside you when we buried him. They were not." Tears fill her eyes, but I find anger in her again. Her lids keep those tears within, blurring the aquamarine to liquid.

"They were there at the lowest point," I admit, looking down at her feet between us.

"I should have been," she states, and she isn't wrong, but I didn't want her to see me like that. The rock I was supposed to be for her had crumbled to gravel and sand. "Who was there for me?"

Her quiet question lifts my head, and I stare at her as she swipes at an errant tear crossing her cheek. I reach for her face, but she flinches away from me, stepping back to put space between us.

"Who was there for me?" she repeats, lowering her voice.

"You went home," I remind her. She ran back to Savannah to her parents' house. I'm certain they celebrated my failure although they mourned their only grandchild.

"My home was with you." Her words hit me like a sucker punch to the gut. Evie suffered, and I tossed her out. Instead of allowing her to cling to me, the rock I promised to be, I cast her aside.

"I couldn't help you, Evie." I just couldn't support her grief as I was buried under my own. It made me selfish and weak, which buried me deeper in self-hate and shame.

"And these men did?" Sarcasm drips from her tone. "How? How did you meet Justice?"

I turn away from her, uncertain I should share this story.

"I was drunk."

Evie huffs.

"I'd been at the Ridged Edge, no longer able to face the cheer of the Pub." I reference my brother's establishment in town. "I wanted to disappear."

Evie continues to stare at me, and the weight of her glare pins me in place. I'd had the same sensation *that* day. I couldn't move my feet.

"I wandered to the tracks in town, waiting on the three a.m. train."

"James," she hisses.

"I was just standing there, hearing the sound in the distance. The light was coming for me." I close my eyes and see it as I always see it in my dreams. The roar of the engine. The blinding luminescence. The vibration of the track.

"Then I woke up in a bed in this house." I tilt my head toward Justice's place behind me.

Evelyn doesn't blink. Her wide eyes remain focused on me.

"Justice says he tackled me to the ground where I hit my head and passed out. He called Giant, but I refused to see him. I stayed here and just sort of fell into things."

Evie's face has gone white in the blackness around us. Her mouth hangs open while her body trembles. Then she launches herself at me, knocking my jacket off her shoulders. Her arms wrap around my neck, and her knees come up to my hips. I catch her under her thighs, stepping back with one foot to catch my balance from the sudden advance of her.

Her body quakes against mine as she tightens her hold and squeezes her legs around my waist.

"Don't you ever, ever, EVER! Do that again," she mutters near my ear. "James Peach Harrington, you will not die on me. I cannot live in this world without knowing you are in it. Even if you don't love me, I cannot bear the thought of you not existing."

My hands move from her thighs to her back as she's mostly holding herself against me. One palm skims up her spine and into her hair at the nape of her neck while the other smooths down to her ass, hitching her upward to adjust her weight. She shifts with me but doesn't loosen her hold and her words sink into me.

*Even if you don't love me, I cannot bear the thought of you not existing.*

*Even if you don't love me.*

My God, it's not that I don't love her. I pushed her away because I love her. I didn't want to take her down with me, and I was going down. I was slipping under my own guilt and grief with no light above me, not even her.

*I cannot bear the thought of you not existing.*

*Not existing.*

For years, all I've done is exist. I don't live life to the fullest like I once did. I keep to myself, hang with the club, and drink.

I wanted Evelyn to live. I wanted her to have a life, and I knew it could no longer be with me. I couldn't look at her, but I also couldn't allow her to look at me. *What must she see in me?*

I killed our son.

I didn't mean for it to happen.

Everyone says it was an accident.

It was an accident, but I was trained to save people.

I should have been able to do something.

With these thoughts in mind, I cling to Evie as much as she's clinging to me. My arms circle her body, pressing her into me while she's wrapped around me just as tight. My eyes close, and I just breathe her in.

"Don't let me go." The plea in her voice mixes with another tone. The cry of our twelve-year-old son blends with her words, and I freeze. My hands drop to Evie's sides as I'm instantly suffocating under the weight of her against me. Her body is too heavy. Her embrace too tight.

I don't deserve her.

My hands gently push at her hips, pressing her away from me in hopes she'll take the hint.

She does. Her legs drop, and her arms release. She slides down my body and steps back, putting space between us again. For a moment, I felt as if I couldn't breathe, couldn't get the air I needed. In her absence, I feel the same. My chest heaves as Evie takes another step away from me, and I realize the struggle to breathe comes from the loss of her. I'm ready to reach for her, tug her back to me when she speaks.

"I see," she says, her voice quiet. Her wrists cross before her, fingers entwining as they do when her palms meet. "I think you should take me back to the Lodge."

"Evie, you don't understand," I state, reaching out for her after all, but she takes another step away.

"I understand, James. Nothing has changed in six years, except me. I'm the one still holding on. My friends have moved on with their lives. People have moved into the community. Your brothers have fallen in love. You have a new group to call family. I'm the one stuck in time." She takes a deep breath. "But that's why I'm here," she says before exhaling. "It's time to move forward."

With that, she steps around me, stalking off toward my Harley, and for the first time in years, I'm nervous. She's going to move on without me.

And I can't exist in this world without her.

# Chapter 15
# Caught In Between

[Evie]

I've never been in an accident. Never broken a bone except for the tip of a finger once while working on making jewelry. But if I could imagine being shattered in a million places, it's how my body felt riding behind James back to the Lodge. Every bump hurt. Every brush against him caused an ache. I didn't know how to be with him, no more than I knew how to be without him.

I'd moved on in my own right, or at least I'd been attempting to. I'd finally said yes to dates with Dalton, which moved to hesitant kisses and cautious fumblings. One night, I almost gave in, just needing to feel the weight of someone else above me. I'd felt so guilty for almost sleeping with him but was determined to make it right, so I decided to seek out James and end us. Dalton had marriage material written all over him, and I deserved someone who wanted to be good to me.

For some reason, *Outlander* comes to mind. A historical romance about a woman falling through time and falling in love with a Scottish rebel while still married to a man in her current time period. I was always torn about her return to Frank, the man she married, although I never considered Frank a decent man, and the undeniable destiny of loving Jamie. Perhaps I was in some kind of time warp myself.

Dalton, however, was too good for me.

James and I don't speak as we ride to the Lodge. Once he pulls up before it, he doesn't kill the engine, just like the other night, and I slide off the back of the bike as quickly as I can. I hold out the helmet to him.

"Keep it for next time," he states.

"There won't be a next time, James." As he doesn't take the helmet from me, I set it on the seat behind him, and James catches my wrist.

"Do we have a deal?" Glancing up at his roughened voice, I'm prepared to snap at him and tell him how I keep my promises. Then I see his eyes. Blue so clear, it's like looking up at a perfect summer sky.

"Name a time and place. I'll be there." The words are flat. My insides feel hollow, and I'm bone-tired. I have nothing left to give him but this one night, which won't be a hardship. Sex with James was always off the charts.

+ + +

A memory haunts me as I lay in bed that night.

*"Yes, yes, yes," I growled, curling a fist into the sheets. We'd taken to doing it in this position as my belly was growing larger, and James was afraid he'd squish me. My knees were pressed into the bed. My cheek plastered to the sheet. James's fingers clutched at my hips, bruising me as he slammed into me. I'd never been so full, and my release spilled over him.*

I don't know why it's my go-to memory. Maybe it was the force of my orgasm. I cried that night. My toes curled. I dripped onto the sheet.

*Continuing to slide together, James was out of control as he pummeled into me. My hormones had increased my appetite for sex like the overly hungry pregnant woman I was.*

*"Fuck," James groaned, stilling as he pumped into me, releasing a wealth of seed. "I love being inside you."*

At that instant, I knew I never wanted to separate from the man buried within me. He completed me, as the cheesy statement goes. I wanted to always feel as I felt at that moment.

*"I love that you're already pregnant," James would tease, as it allowed him to be bare within me.* Of course, that's what got us in trouble in the first place, which wasn't responsible, but neither was skinny-dipping with a stranger.

*"I'm never going back," he'd whisper, implying how he'd never cover himself again with me. We were going to have plenty more babies if we continued at the rate we had sex. Or so I thought then.*

At the time, my only concern was James loving me. He loved being bare. He loved being in me. He loved sex with me. But he didn't love me.

*James collapsed next to me on our bed, which I struggled to call ours even though he said it over and over again. We'd been married in a small church service. I wore a white shift dress to disguise the small bump in my belly. James wore a navy-blue suit that accentuated his eyes. We had a Christmas wedding, which wasn't how or when I ever predicted being wed. My parents did not attend. I walked myself down the aisle.*

James had wanted to do right by me. He would have gone to a courthouse on that first day, he later told me. He would have married me on the mountain where we met, he said. It was all romantic sounding, if only he loved me.

And then one night, he told me he did.

*With his hand on my belly, freed from the sheet and my nightie so he could place his warm palm on my stretched skin, James said he loved me.*

*"I'm going to be your rock," he said to me. "A boulder to build your life on. I can be strong enough for both of us, and it's time you know I love you."*

*He swallowed with nerves, his hand rubbing my swell while his eyes watched the movement of his caress.*

*"I love both of you," he whispered to my belly, and I captured his face in my hands.*

*"Look at me," I whispered to him then. His eyes met mine in our dark bedroom. "I can't imagine life without you. I love you, too."*

For all our nights of wild, out of control sex, that was the first night James took me slow and deep. He wanted me to feel that love he professed, and I felt it from the top of my head to the toes on my feet. I believed him—in him—in our future.

And then the boulder crumbled, and we were nothing but dust.

+ + +

I'd fallen asleep to the memory and woken with dry, crusty eyes. I'd been crying again, and my lids were heavy and swollen. I roll in the bed, picking up my phone to find a missed call from Dalton, and guilt blankets me. In many ways, he was right. I shouldn't have returned to Blue Ridge. I could have handled everything with a simple phone call and attorneys, but something inside me told me I needed to see James.

*One last time.*

I owed it to him when he clearly didn't think he owed me anything.

With that thought, I call Dalton. I owed him as well.

"Hey, honey," he breathes into the phone.

"Hey." My voice cracks, rough from tears and a restless night.

"You okay? I tried to call you last night."

I swallow back the shame I feel at being out with James, allowing him to give me two more orgasms against a car at a bonfire. I'm turning into a hussy.

"I'm good." I almost choke on the reply. "It's been more difficult than I expected to be here."

"Come home," he whines, and I sense a smile in his voice. He's such a good man with a good heart. He's been patient and understanding with me, and we're on the verge of something real and serious. I want that with him. It's why I'm here.

He isn't Southern-born or bred but ended up here after law school, pursuing his career in legalese. He claims to love the coastline of our fair city because he grew up on his own coastline along Lake Michigan in Michigan. I haven't ever been there, but he assures me the weather down here is a million times better than sub-zero temperatures and unexpected snowstorms. I'll take his word on it.

"I can't yet," I admit, without giving away the full reason. "I have an estate sale today." Estate sales are where I do my best shopping; there and fairs or flea markets. It's a Sunday, and I'm planning to lose myself in other people's tossed treasure in hopes of my next inspiration.

"I could come there," Dalton suggests, sounding hopeful as he presents the idea. I swallow back my immediate no and fight to keep my voice steady.

"I don't want to interrupt your schedule, and you know how bored you get at these sales." Dalton once went with me to a large estate auction, intending to show his support of my craft and small business. Within fifteen minutes, he was bored while attempting to give it his best effort.

He chuckles softly into the phone. "I'd still be there for you." He would. I know he means it, with all his best intentions and his generous heart. He's been a busy man, working hard his entire life, and he's ready to settle down. He assures me he doesn't need kids, he doesn't want them, but a man like him should have them. He'd be a great dad despite what he says.

"I know, honey," I say, lowering my voice as I swipe fingers through my hair, holding back the long tresses from my forehead. *I'm such a terrible person.*

"So how much longer will you be there?" he questions.

"I shouldn't be more than a week. My girls' night out got cut short."

"Oh yeah. What happened?" The pleasant tone in his innocent question drives the shovel deeper into the hole I'm digging.

"Oh, I just saw another old friend, who wasn't so great to see." I cover my eyes, closing them, as if he can see me, which he can't because we are speaking on the phone.

"Need me to kick someone's ass?" The words surprise me as Dalton is relatively calm, and while he's solid in stature, I can't picture him ever getting in a fight. My thoughts race back to James pinning Rusty Miller to the bar top last night. The display of masculinity should have totally been a turn-off, but instead, the possessive growl and hissed warning did nothing but spike my libido. Which does not need to continue spiking around my soon-to-be ex-husband.

"It's nothing I can't handle," I tease.

"You know you don't have to go it alone, Evelyn. I'm here for you."

"I know," I whisper, guilt continuing to fill my cup and spill over, pour to the table, drip on the floor, and puddle on the rug. I'm going to hell. *I'm already in it*, and I just need to get through one thing before I'm free and clear.

I pull back the phone and check the time.

"Dalton, I should probably let you go. I need to shower and get a move on."

"Okay, honey. Call me if you need me." The message is clear. He'd be here at a moment's notice if I asked.

"Thank you. Have a good day."

"You too. I miss you."

"I miss you," I say, realizing it's not a lie, but it's just not the entire truth.

I miss someone else more.

# Chapter 16
# Morning News

[James]

The weekend passes without additional contact with Evie. I had to work, and I knew she had an estate sale to visit. Her business started as a hobby. My girl likes jewelry, and at one point, I thought she started the work because I didn't have the means to buy her everything. We were not poor but keeping up with the socialite lifestyle Evie had prior to agreeing to marry me was not something I could do, nor did I want to. I had money coming from Giant Brewing Company by default of being a family owner. Shockingly, I hadn't been cut out or written out of future wills despite my behavior toward them. I hadn't worked at the brewery since I was a teenager because I wanted to make my life on my own terms. I denied my wealth and decided to save every penny of the dividends for Michael and his college fund.

I'd just gotten off an overnight shift and was passing through town when I saw Evie's Jeep outside Dolores's Diner. It had a new name, but it was always going to be Dolores's Diner in my head, and Dolores Chance would always be important to me. She and Evelyn did not get along, but on occasion, Evie would allow us to go to the diner for breakfast or lunch. You just could not pass up on Dolores's skillet scramblers or her chicken salad sandwich.

I take a U-turn on Main Street and find a parking spot a few spaces down from Evie's vehicle. I don't typically frequent Dolores's on my own, but occasionally with the firehouse guys and every so often with my biker brothers. Entering the diner, I feel like all the air swishes out of the place. A strange vibe draws conversations to silence as I scan the room looking for my wife. Once I see her, I understand everyone's disquiet, but I don't give a fuck about what others think of me.

I stalk to her table.

"Giant?" I huff, greeting my eldest brother, who looks cozy sitting with my woman on a Monday morning.

"James," he says, lifting his coffee mug for his smug lips while Evie shifts in the booth seat to face me. At one time, Giant was my best friend. We're twenty-two months apart but back to back in schooling. It killed me when he went off to the military, but I understood why he did it—Pap was his inspiration, and Giant had a mission to prove himself. I had the same desire to be someone, but I wanted to do it locally, traipsing through the mountains I already loved, hoping to protect the forest and the people who entered it.

"Peach," I direct to my wife, whose mouth hangs open a second before snapping shut when I help myself to the bench seat next to her. My arm stretches behind her on the back of the booth.

"Good morning," she mutters.

"This certainly looks cozy," I snap, referencing their breakfast plates spread across the table.

"I wanted coffee," Giant states.

"How's Letty?" I dig, mentioning his woman and recall mine had lunch with her the other day.

Giant shakes his head with a smirk at the mention of his future wife.

"She's at home with Finn preparing for our wedding." His deep brows draw together, scowling at me. An envelope arrived in the mail, and I knew what it contained—an invitation—but I didn't open it. I don't do family.

"Giant was just telling me all about the wedding plans." Evie faces Giant while she speaks. "I'm so sorry again. I wish I'd known sooner."

Her attention snaps back to me, eyes narrowing.

"You should come," Giant states, and Evie and I swivel our heads in his direction. "The both of you."

"No," I say forcefully while Evie sweetly replies, "I'd love to attend."

An awkward silence falls over the table a second until Evie speaks, "Giant's getting married at the ridge." Her voice is quiet as she explains this to me, knowing the significance of the location.

I glare at my brother across the table. Last fall, he took his girl to Pap's old camping spot near the ancient ranger outpost, and I'd interrupted them on an impromptu visit to the place. It's a three-mile hike up the mountain behind Giant's cabin, which he inherited from our pap once he returned from the military. No one begrudged him the gift. Pap and Giant were exceptionally close, and Giant needed something to do with himself while his wife lay dying of cancer, and he struggled to re-acclimate to civilian life after years of service.

*But the ridge?* There is no way I'm going there for a fucking wedding.

I sense Evie's hand fist on the bench seat more than I see it. I clench my own hand, fighting the sensation to reach for her hand to comfort her.

"It's a great location," Evie states, her voice holding steady and low. "It's predicted to be a beautiful day Friday."

"I can't attend," I reiterate, softer than the harsh rejection moments ago.

"Why not?" Evie questions, turning her attention to me.

"I just can't," I repeat, not meeting her eyes but glaring back at my brother.

"That's not an explanation. Your brother asked you to his wedding. Did you know Billy was going to officiate?" Evie huffs with humor. "Billy? He's going to play the role of minister." Evie snorts.

I don't even want to know how Billy obtained a minister's license.

"I said I'm not going," I say, turning to her, and Giant chuckles across the table.

"You two haven't changed." He smiles as I look back at him.

"What do you mean?" Evie asks.

"You'd bicker until one of you gives in, usually James, because you'd give him this look." Giant points a finger at Evie, circling in the air as if tracing over her face, and I glance back at her, wondering what Giant is playing at. "James would melt under that look."

"I have no idea what you're talking about," I state, turning to my brother.

"Too bad," Giant mutters. "It was always fun to watch her put you in your place."

Sensing Evie's glee at wrapping me around her finger, she beams a smile in Giant's direction.

"But you weren't oblivious," Giant directs at her. "James could look at you, and it was like watching a sunny day crank up the heat." Giant fans his face like an overheated old lady, and I scowl at him and his sexual innuendo. Evie rolls her lips, lowering her gaze for the table. Neither of us knows what to say to him.

"There wasn't a couple more in love than you two," my brother continues.

"Giant," I warn, watching Evie's shoulders shrink.

My brother loved his wife, but I didn't miss the looks he'd give me when I took Evie in my arms at family functions or kissed her in public. Clara was sweet, quiet, and innocent. Theirs was a private relationship while Evie and I were very physical and open, and something makes me wonder if Giant wanted more than he had with Clara.

"It's still there," Giant states, lowering his voice like a marriage counselor, and I want to tell him he's out of line, but I realize he isn't entirely off base. I love Evelyn. I always have, always will. It's just our circumstances that have changed. Our lives fell apart because of me, and despite that love, we aren't the same people we once were.

"That's enough," I growl at my brother as something covers my thigh. Glancing down, I'm surprised to see Evie's hand there, fingers splayed over my denim-clad leg, giving it a squeeze. It's a warning not to argue, and suddenly, I know what Giant means. I'd do anything this woman asked of me, other than one. I can't get us back to who we were.

"Can you text me the information?" Evie asks, speaking for herself instead of both of us like she once did. There was always a collective "we" in everything.

I turn my head away from her, feeling the press of Giant's eyes on the side of my face. My arm slips over Evie, coming to my own lap, where I cover her fingers with a brush of mine, and she removes her hand from my thigh.

"Letty said she enjoyed lunch the other day, and she appreciates your apology, but it wasn't necessary." Giant glares at me over the table, obviously aware of Evie's exit from the Pub and my following her. He's so in love with this new woman on a level different than this first wife. It's surprising while encouraging. I want him to be happy despite my permanent bad mood and separation from him.

As if this little breakfast meal isn't shitty enough, Dolores comes around the counter and heads for the table.

"Giant," she addresses him first, then does a double take at me and almost strains her neck, taking in Evie sitting next to me.

"James." Dolores and I patched things up years and years ago, and I still feel protective of her in some ways. I feel responsible for breaking her heart, but Evie feels even more guilty when I've told her she shouldn't have ever felt that way.

"Evelyn." My wife's name is a bit sharp on Dolores's tongue, but the expression on her face is more of concern, especially as her gaze comes back to me. She isn't surprised to find me in the diner, but it's Evie's presence that's causing her unease.

"Hello, Dolores." Evie's voice cracks as she speaks to my once lover. I want to turn on Evie and tell her for the millionth time to let it go, but then again, I'm one who can harbor guilt like a champion. Evie never had anything to feel guilty about regarding Dolores. I wasn't in love with her, as cold as that sounds. Evie's been the only one for me. *Still is*.

"What brings you to town?" When Dolores asks the question, Evie flinches. It's innocent enough although I'm hopeful Evie isn't about to blurt out how she wants to divorce me. Not that Dolores would care. She has a new man in her life—some rich dude from California who was turning her grandmother's place into a vineyard.

"I'm here on business," Evie states, and I release a sigh of relief she isn't airing her true intentions. My peripheral vision notes Evie running a hand over her wrist, covered in a collection of silver trinkets from her jewelry line. It's a nervous habit, and I want to reach for her hand. Then my sight leaps to Giant, who is the only person I told outside the club that my wife wants to divorce me.

"Evie's also coming to the wedding," Giant announces, and Dolores turns her attention from Evie to Giant.

"That's right. Congratulations. Will Mati be in town?" My sister hasn't been in the area this fall with her new job. However, she's dating Dolores's wayward brother, the famous Denton Chance, who ran off at eighteen to follow his rock n' roll dreams and became quite a hometown hero although he hadn't been home in twenty-five years. He returned last summer and conveniently reconnected with my sister, who was widowed a year prior. I have no doubt Dolores knows if Mati is attending Giant's wedding or not. The diner is a hotbed of gossip.

"She will be. It's mainly family," Giant emphasizes, glancing back at me.

At one time, Dolores wanted to be part of our family, and maybe it might have happened eventually, but deep down, I always knew it wouldn't. I cared about Dolores, but I'd been waiting my whole life for Evelyn. I just didn't know it until we ran into each other on the mountain.

"Can I get you guys anything else?" Dolores asks, scanning the plates and empty coffee mugs.

"Just the check," Evie states. "I need to get going." Evie fumbles in her bag while Giant pulls out his wallet and hands Dolores a fifty.

"That cover it?" Giant asks.

"Giant, no. I got it. I'm the one who asked you to breakfast," Evie says.

"You asked Giant to breakfast?" I question, turning my head from her to my brother.

"Well . . ." she begins, but Giant interjects.

"I came in for coffee and saw her sitting here. Alone. She asked me to join her, but I would have sat down even without an invitation." Giant winks at my wife, and I want to reach across the table and throttle him like we were kids. Roughhousing—as our mother used to call it—was a sport in the Harrington household.

Dolores is still standing at the edge of the table, now holding the fifty in her fist.

"I think that's all," I state to her when it isn't her fault I'm upset. "I'm outta here."

I roll from the booth, brush past Dolores, and head out to the street for my bike. To my surprise, Giant is on my heels and lays his hands on my handlebars, straddling my front tire as I hitch over my seat.

"Get your hands off my bike," I snarl at him.

"Get your head out of your ass," he bites back.

"Fuck off." My brother and I have had words over the years—casual, brotherly—and in true male form, quickly forgiven each other until my son's death. Then I pushed and pushed and pushed until my older brother relented.

"You need to give up the shitty attitude," Giant demands, glaring at me, still clutching at my bars.

"Not gonna happen," I remark, starting my engine to drown out whatever else he has to say to me.

"Your wife is here for you," Giant states, over the roar of my Harley.

"She's here for a divorce," I practically yell back at him, announcing it to the entire block. My wife wants to divorce me. *Shocker*.

Giant shakes his head back and forth, disappointed and bewildered. "You're a risk-taker, not a runner," he states as if reminding me who I am. "And I never took you for such a fool, and a fucking blind one at that."

"You don't know what you're talking about."

"Evie still loves you," Giant says, narrowing his eyes at me.

"No," I reply, denying the thought and attributing Giant's assessment to his future nuptials. He's all in *luuuve*. Evie's in love, too, with another man. "Get off." I rev the throttle warning him to let go of my handlebars.

"Quit acting like you're the only one who has suffered heartache."

"I lost our son," I growl back at him as if he doesn't understand.

"I lost my wife," Giant counters.

"It's not the same, and you know it. Besides, you have Letty now," I argue back.

Giant shakes his head, further irritated with me. "I love Letty with everything I have, but if you don't think I'd give one more day to be with Clara, you're wrong. She can never come back to me." Giant punctuates his words by pressing off my bike. "Your wife can. And she did." He points a large finger toward the diner, which Evie has just exited and scampers down the street without a look back in our direction.

"We don't need to compare sad stories," I state, hitting below the belt at my brother.

Giant crosses his arms, moving his head side to side one more time, and says, "Now it's you who can fuck off." With that, he steps away from my bike and saunters after my wife.

+ + +

After the shitshow of the morning, I finally make it home for a long-overdue nap. I worked in a hangover haze, which I'm too old to do. On Saturday, I dropped Evie off at the Lodge and went home hours earlier than I expected. Unable to handle my own company, I got drunk. My thoughts wrestled themselves, fighting between the sweetness of Evie orgasming on my fingers and the tension of us separating afterward.

*"I never took you for a fool, and a blind one at that."* Disappointment rang in Giant's words.

My family should be used to the letdown of me by now, but somehow his words hit me hard. What did he know? It wasn't a fair statement as Giant had lost his wife, his childhood sweetheart and best friend. He knew about loss, as did others in my family. Mati lost her husband in a car accident. Billy's and Charlie's wives both left them for various reasons. We were a family of losers in a sense. But then again, Giant was getting married in a few days. Mati was engaged. Charlie already married someone else, and Billy had a girlfriend if you can believe that one. Everyone was getting a second chance to get things right or recover from the absence in their life.

"I'm the loser-est loser," I mutter to myself, hearing a rattle at my front door that won't seem to quit. Giving up on my nap, I roll from the top of my bed. I rarely crawl under the covers, missing the other half that should be filling the space opposite me. I almost trip over Silver, who lies on the floor beside the bed.

"Dude," I mutter, although I love his nearness. Trudging down the steps, I continue mumbling as someone hammers on the screen door again. "I'm coming."

Yanking open the front door, I find a man I don't know on the front step. In his hand is an official-looking envelope.

*You've got to be fucking shitting me.*

"Mr. James Harrington," he questions, although he can't have any doubts as to who I am. I must nod in acknowledgment because he continues, "You've been served."

I press at the screen door, stepping out on the steps, and the man's expression shifts. Silver rushes past me into the yard, and the man takes a giant step backward, clearing the stairs in one fumbling skip. I follow him until we are both on the grass. He holds the envelope between us like the sword I need to throw myself upon.

"I'm just the messenger," he states, standing firm with the thin package presented to me.

"Yeah," I snap, ripping it out of his hands and crumpling the edge of it. Immediately, he turns his back and marches toward a sedan parked in my driveway. He opens the driver's door and climbs inside, but I don't watch him reverse. I open the envelope, pull out the papers so only the top portion can be read, and then shove them back inside.

My fingers seek the leather strap around my neck, pulling forward the rough strip and circle the ring that dangles from it. I wear this every day inside my clothing, keeping the symbol of our commitment and love near my heart. Tugging at the strap, I yank hard, and the strap breaks against my neck. I toss the entire thing at the house, listening to it ricochet off the wood siding.

Silver barks in response to my actions.

"Goddammit," I yell, tipping back my head and closing my eyes aimed at the sky.

*She really did it.*

As I stand there clutching the divorce summons in my hand and consider my wedding band just thrown at the house, the rumble of a motorcycle approaches and pulls into the gravel drive. I look to my left to see Justice coming to a halt on his bike.

"Now what?" I grouse, stepping over to him as he cuts the engine and hikes off his bike.

"Ranger," he addresses me, his face stern until I get closer to him. "You look like shit."

Scrubbing a hand down my face before I answer him, I say, "Yeah, I've had better days." I've also had worse, way worse, and this man knows it.

"Whatcha got?" he asks, nodding his head toward my hand, and I lift the envelope as if I'd already forgotten what treachery lies within.

"Apparently, I've been served," I state, shaking the papers while crunching them harder in my fist.

Justice slowly nods, crossing his arms and casually settling his large body against his bike. He's quiet for a moment while I look back at the house, wondering where my ring fell and if I should bother finding it.

"Gonna sign 'em?" he asks, and I glance back at the manila parchment in my hand as if it's stuck to my palm, and I can't shake it off.

"Maybe," I whisper, my voice rough. But I do know. I'll give her anything she asks for, but I don't want to give her this.

"Ready for her to be out of your life?" he questions, but I don't answer, looking back at the house, squinting in the afternoon sun. I loved this house. We picked it out together, thinking it was perfect for a growing family. We never had more babies, but it wasn't for lack of trying.

Gazing at the house, I notice how sad it looks. Even as an inanimate object, the windows look like lowered lids, eyes ready to cry any second. With overgrown bushes and a dirty front screen, the overall impression is one of remorse. The roof sags a bit. This place once contained my entire world, but now it looks like it wants to curl in on itself and sleep for a hundred years.

"I guess I'll have to be," I finally answer without looking at my friend.

"You good with that?"

"What the fuck?" I bite. Of course, I'm not good at this.

"Heard you bent Rusty over a knee and spanked him the other night for looking at your woman."

"That is not how it went down," I retort, and eyeing Justice, I sense he knows this. He holds the unofficial title of president of a club that doesn't exist in the same capacity it once did. However, his authority is still felt and honored by those who were lifers before things fell apart, and new recruits rode in, like myself. There wasn't any initial hazing—no illegal dealings to prove my worth. I just gave him my word I'd keep any secrets I learned.

"Don't tell me you wouldn't have reacted the same way if it was Cora? Did he say something else?" I fucking hate that guy, and we don't make much of a secret of our dislike of one another, even if we've pledged brothers before others.

I pause, glaring at my friend, who has lived a rough life. I don't doubt the evil in his past, but I haven't seen it in the six years I've been with the Rebels. Life is chaos but not malicious with this gang of hooligans. Justice's name fits him as his philosophy with the new version of the club is fairness.

"You had breakfast with your brother this mornin'." I know how the club works. We have eyes everywhere, and I hate that those eyes are looking at me lately.

"Not a crime," I bite. We have no rule that states ex-communication from blood. Most members pick the club as a family by choice. "What's your point?"

"Just checking in. With Evie back, I thought you might be pulling back from us."

"Are you saying I can't have my family back? My wife back?"

Justice narrows his eyes at me with the rough tone I use on him but screw him. "You want your wife back?" he mutters, nodding at the papers in my hand, but I ignore him by staying on topic.

"I thought you and my brother liked each other." Giant's been coming into Ridged Edge more and more with this damn ride to raise funds and community center dedication bullshit, and the two get along like old chums.

"It ain't a matter of liking him or not, and don't make it sound like I fucking want to date him. We have an agreement between us."

"Oh yeah, what's that?"

"Looking out for your ass," he snaps, and I startle at the fact my blood brother and my biker one have a pact concerning me.

"Well, I don't need either of you looking out for me. I'm a big boy now," I groan at him.

"Then fucking act like it," Justice states, uncrossing his arms and shifting his body so he can sling a leg over his bike. "Man up."

*What the fuck?* I don't get to question him as he starts his engine, then reverses, leaving me standing in my yard, clutching my future in my fist.

# Chapter 17
# Wedding Blues

[Evie]

"I got your message." James's terse voice makes me bristle, and as I hadn't called him, I have no idea what he means.

"I don't know what you mean."

"I've been served," he mocks, mimicking someone else's voice.

A heavy pause of silence falls between us for a minute.

"Friday," he states. "Give me what I want, and my signature is yours." The menace in his voice does nothing to comfort me in making the decision to sleep with him, nor does his tone put me at ease that he'll actually sign off on our divorce once we do have sex.

"I can't on Friday. I'm going to your brother's wedding."

James snorts through the phone. "Cancel."

"Not going to happen," I state. "I love your brother, and I'm happy for him." While Giant was James's older brother, over the years, he'd also become the big brother I never had. I worshipped him for his service to our country, his honor toward his wife, and his overall generosity of heart toward me. He allowed me to check in with him once in a while after I first left, making certain James wasn't hurting any worse than I was. It was always worse in some ways, but I'd never known how bad, and apparently, neither had Giant. He had no idea of James's extreme risk measures.

"Fine. Friday after the wedding." With those words, like a warning, James hangs up, and I collapse onto my bed in the Lodge. I can't keep staying here. It's wonderfully decadent but adding up for a two-week stay, and I've decided I'm heading home on Saturday. Home to Savannah.

I'd sleep with my husband and get out of town.

If only it were that easy.

Being with James has always been fire, and my body heats just thinking about him entering me again. The length of his dick returns to my mind. The feel of his pelvis rocking against mine. The things he'd do to me to tease me, to please me. I shiver at the memories.

My phone rings a second time, still held in my palm, and I lift it for my ear without checking the caller identification.

"What?" I snap, sexually worked up while emotionally frustrated.

"Evie?"

*Shit.* "Dalton." His name is a breathless whine of relief and embarrassment.

"Honey, you okay?"

*I'm fine*, I want to state but bite back the words, chewing my lip to keep them from escaping. "It's been an interesting day."

After leaving the diner, I went to a private estate sale, one open to serious buyers before the deceased person's possessions were set up for auction. It was always a little bittersweet to consider my work involved the end of someone's life. Their once-treasures would be separated and sold. In some cases, trashed. I'd like to think repurposing an item gave it new life, a new journey, a new story, despite it being an inanimate object. Someone's silverware was now worn as decoration. Someone's silver service was now used as décor. It was wishful thinking, almost hopeful. My business had the name Silver Dragonfly, an equally inspiring name. The title came from my son. He loved dragonflies.

Recycling someone's trash into new treasure felt like a tribute to him, over and over again.

"What happened?" Dalton asks, settling in. He's a good listener. It is part of his job as an attorney. Listen. Decipher fact. Collect evidence. He took his time to learn about me and accept my quirks. Being an artisan, dating an attorney didn't always mix, but my former debutante training returned, like something filed away in a drawer, occasionally opened and dusted off to be used again. I fell into line where I needed to, and Dalton let me be who I wanted to be otherwise. My opposition to societal roles appealed to him. I didn't begrudge him. It was a happy medium between who I was once destined to be and who I became.

I don't tell Dalton about James. Of course, I can't, and the lie weighs me down, burying me further and further in my misery. Instead, I explain my day of silver collecting, and he listens despite a lack of interest in the details. He's a good sport.

When I finish, he chuckles at the shenanigans of someone wanting only one fork while I wanted the entire collection.

"So when are you coming home?" he questions, as he's been asking each time we speak.

"I'm going to a wedding on Friday," I tell him, instead of answering with the decision to return to Savannah on Saturday.

"A wedding?" Dalton chuckles, and another layer of guilt covers me. Dalton has hinted repeatedly at where he'd like our relationship to go. He's mentioned *our* future more than I can count. He accepts me, and I have accepted a future with him. I want that. I do.

*But . . .*

He didn't press me into a wall and kiss me senseless.

He didn't kiss me, so my toes curled, and I orgasmed on his lap.

He didn't finger me on a car hood until I released twice.

He is tender and gentle and takes his time, allowing me to lead us where I am ready to go.

It is actually a little boring, truth be told, but it's safe.

"Who's getting married?" he asks, and I close my eyes, fighting with the truth.

"My ex-husband's older brother. I was close to him and his first wife, and she died of breast cancer eleven years ago." Giant deserves every bit of happiness. His expression when he spoke of his future wife gave off that happiness tenfold.

"Need a date?" Dalton asks with a soft laugh.

"It's kind of a private affair. Family and closest friends." It doesn't really explain my invitation as I've been estranged from the family for six years, but then again, Giant assured me the other morning I'd always be family, no matter what I decided with James. And I had decided. Of course, I'd decided. James had been served, as he said.

"Oh." Dalton's deep voice rang with hurt, but I promised myself I'd make it up to him. I'd be a better person once I did what I needed to do. I'd be good to him, too.

"I miss you," I say, meaning every word. I did miss him. I couldn't say it enough. He was a good person. Too good.

"I miss you, too, honey. Come home soon," he adds, and I hear something in his voice I haven't heard before. *Longing*. It was a sensation I was overly familiar with. Only, I'd felt it for someone else, and it made me the bad person I was.

+ + +

I hadn't heard from James again the remainder of the week, and his silence made me nervous. Too many times, I longed to give in and call him, wondering what he meant by *Friday after the wedding*. In the end, I valiantly fought the urge, purchased a wedding present from Pearl's, and drove to Giant's cabin.

A distinct path of two tires rolled through a thick overbrush of trees before spitting me out into a grassed area with an ancient cabin, restored to its original glory. The grayed slat siding and new tin roof balanced the house with a covered front porch. A window on either side of the open front door said, come in. It was small but felt larger on the inside, and I'd been inside on many occasions, both before and after Giant's rehab of the place.

Before, when it was an empty shell and Giant was still in the military, James and I would steal up here and spend the night, rutting like reckless animals. There was something about nature that sexually unhinged me, and when James took control, I never refused him. We had an active, energetic sex life before everything fell apart. Part of that energy was my desire for more babies. Another part of our enthusiasm was James's eagerness to give me many children.

We only ever had one.

Michael was the start and end of our parenthood journey, but it wasn't for lack of trying, and it wasn't for lack of other babies. We had several more who were souls in our hearts and angels in heaven. Five of them.

I shake the bittersweet thought of all my missed babies, as I exit my Jeep parked near several other vehicles across Giant's yard. Behind the cabin is a picturesque view of the rising mountain in a burst of fall colors of orange, red, and yellow. It almost doesn't look real against the backdrop of a solid blue autumn sky.

*It's a gorgeous day for a wedding*, I tell myself as I shut the driver's door and head toward the porch. I take another fortifying breath as it's going to be difficult spending time in the clearing with the ridge so nearby. I'll be trying to remember good times to help me get through the day.

A man sits on the low steps jiggling a baby roughly a year old on his lap, cooing at him in a sickly, sweet voice.

"Who's a big boy? Is Finn a big boy? Who's your favorite uncle? Uncle Marcus is your favorite uncle."

*Marcus?* He must be related to Letty, Giant's soon-to-be wife, as I don't know of a Marcus in the Harrington family.

"Hello," I call out as I approach, and dark eyes meet mine in a pretty face. Too pretty. His hair is perfect, not a strand out of place, and his smile white and bright as he greets me.

"Hi yourself. Here for the wedding?"

"I am. Evelyn Harrington," I state, holding out a hand to shake his, and he shifts the baby to his hip, reaching out awkwardly for my right hand with his right. He squeezes mine as though we are old friends instead of new acquaintances.

"Marcus Shelton. I'm an outlaw here." He winks as though we share a secret. "I worked with Letty when she lived in Chicago. She was my boss, but we all know who really ran the show. We're like family. Isn't that right, Finn? I'm Uncle Marcus. Say Marcus."

The baby stares over his little shoulder at me, large dark eyes taking me in, as Uncle Marcus jiggles him. Marcus's head pops up, and he smiles at me even though the baby has not answered him. "So who do you belong to, or are you another Harrington on your own?"

"I guess you could say I'm an outlaw as well. I'm married to James." *For only a little longer*, I think. The thought makes my tummy flip and not in a good way.

"James. The black sheep, right? Sheep," Marcus states to the baby on his lap. "Say baa. *Baaaa*." The front door opens and out steps Giant in dark slacks and a white dress shirt rolled to his elbows. He's also wearing a vest. Mixed in with his trimmed beard and cool charcoal hair, and he's a vision of sexy silver fox.

"Quit talking to my kid like a puppy," Giant snarks, and Marcus chuckles as he stands.

"Your kid?" I choke, fighting the bile rising in my throat although I'm happy, I'm really happy for him. Marcus hands Finn off to Giant, who kisses the fuzzy head of the baby once on his hip.

"Soon-to-be," Giant says, pressing another kiss to Finn's sweet temple as Finn can't take his eyes off me. Giant gazes at the baby while he addresses him. "Finnikin Pierson Harrington, did you meet Aunt Evie?"

Tears instantly fill my eyes. I haven't been called aunt anything in a long time, and all those nieces and nephews are growing up. Giant's daughter, Ellie, even had children of her own in my absence, making me a great aunt.

"We hadn't officially met," I say, fighting the clogging of my throat while giving a finger wave to the baby who's still staring at me. Giant steps closer to me, shifting Finn.

"Want to hold him?" he softly asks. "He's a squirmer, wanting to use those legs to run, but . . ." Giant's voice drifts, hinting I can take him for the hug I suddenly feel I desperately need. It's going to be a long afternoon on the ridge where Giant will wed Letty, and I lost my everything. Without thinking, I hold out my arms, and Giant offers Finn to me. I'd forgotten the feel of a baby. The weight in my arms. The shift in balance of my own body. As if it's automatic, I sway while Finn looks at me, his wide black eyes scanning my face.

"He's beautiful," I whisper to him while speaking to Giant. Finn has fuzzy black hair and cappuccino skin with wrinkles at his wrists and the chubbiest cheeks. He's a little chunkster, and I instantly adore him.

"When do I get to see Letty?" I ask, glancing up at Giant. His soft smile says everything. He loves that woman and this child.

"Soon. She's already up the mountain. Someone wouldn't let me see her after midnight." Giant turns and glares at Marcus.

"Despite her desire to climb you like a tree, we must have a modicum of etiquette at this wedding," Marcus states, and Giant rolls his eyes at me.

"I don't know who put him in charge," Giant mutters.

"I heard that," Marcus calls out, and I laugh while I bounce Finn on my hip.

"If you don't mind, I'm going to have you leave your car here. You can ride with one of us instead." By us, Giant means one of the limited vehicles heading up the mountain. Typically, he'd hike the three miles to the ridge, which isn't possible in his current attire, and I imagine his future wife would prefer not to be sweaty and stinky in her wedding dress. Giant decided only a few trucks would tackle the path leading around the ridge and up to an old ranger's post where they could easily park. From there, it's about a hundred-yard walk through the trees to a clearing near a stream. It's going to be a beautiful setting for an outdoor wedding.

+ + +

As the wedding takes place, I keep my head in the moment as much as I can. Giant and Letty are surrounded by his family and the man called Uncle Marcus, along with his partner. It's difficult not to feel like an outsider among people I considered family more than my own, and they make a decent effort of offering me hugs and not-so-surprised greetings.

James's father, George Jr., and Elaina seem happy to see me, but they are still standoffish. Then again, it could be the busyness of the day. I meet Charlie's new family, and thankfully bypass discussions about the dedication and who decided the name of the future community building. I also try to stifle my inability to take Billy Harrington seriously as the minister presiding over this ceremony. He actually does a decent job of keeping a solemn tone while reading off the promises Giant and Letty wrote for one another.

To love one another.

To communicate our needs.

To spend time outdoors.

To never go to bed angry.

To be open to adventure.

To treat each other as equals.

Swiping at a lone tear, I smile to myself as I reflect on each vow until something pulls my attention to the woods at my side. My eyes narrow at the form I see just inside the tree line.

*James?*

My smile grows, but he isn't looking at me. His head is bowed as if in prayer as he listens to his younger brother speak. I turn back to the ceremony at hand. In my heart, I'm happy James couldn't stay away from his brother's special occasion after all. Sad pleasure swells my chest. He still loves his family. I know he does. He just doesn't think he deserves them. If only he knew how they'd all missed him. If only he knew one word from him, and they'd be welcoming him home with a fattened calf.

After Giant and Letty complete their vows and exchange rings, I turn for the shadows once more to find his outline gone. With a sweeping glance around those gathered, I slip toward the forest entrance, leading to the ranger outpost.

"James?" I whisper, stepping into the darkness of the fall foliage. I don't want to risk drawing attention to myself inside the woods, but I call out his name a little louder the second time, walking a little further under the trees. Spinning in a slow circle, I don't find a trace of him, and for half a second, I wonder if I imagined his presence.

But I didn't.

He was here, and I take a small comfort in the fact he came to witness this happy occasion for his brother, his once best friend, and his family, despite his rejection of them. Taking a fortifying breath, I reverse my direction and re-enter the clearing to find the passing of champagne. There's no formal dinner here but a collection of wedding cupcakes. Giant said they were doing everything out of order. Dinner will be back down the mountain with Giant and Letty returning later to the outpost for their first official night as husband and wife together. Apparently, the place has significance to them.

Pictures are being taken, and Giant Brewing Company beer is shared next, poured right into the champagne flutes by Billy. The family mills about, and some wander down to the stream while I stick to the periphery of things. I have new friends in Uncle Marcus and his husband, Peter, and I hang with them until Letty approaches us.

She walks right up to me and embraces me like she did when we first met. She's a beautiful bride with her dark hair pulled up in a loose roll draping low on the back of her head and a simple straight dress in white, cut with a deep V for a bodice with a loose flowing skirt to her feet where she wears flat sandals instead of heels. Giant warned me to dress casually, and I'm wearing cowboy boots and a lightweight dress with a jean jacket. It's the best I could pull together in the collection of things I'd brought with me to Blue Ridge.

"What did you think?" she asks of the wedding.

"It was so lovely." It really was with the fall foliage and the self-written vows. It's rustic but elegant.

"I know," she says softly, slipping her arm through mine and leading me away from Marcus and Peter. "I'm stealing her boys," she cries over her shoulder, guiding me toward the edge of the forest. Giant intercedes us before we get too far.

"This looks like mischief. What are you two up to, Cricket?"

Letty smiles at her new husband, but I'm the one who blushes. *Giant has a nickname for his wife?* I was endlessly teased by the family for James calling me Peach, as the fruity reference has many sexual connotations, and most of them were exactly what the dirty minds of the Harrington boys suspected.

"There's been a little change of plans for this evening," Letty states, keeping her eyes on Giant whose heavy brows crease. "We're going to camp here tonight as there will be guests in the ranger station."

"What?" Giant bellows, and those closest to us shift to look in our direction. Letty still holds my arm locked with hers.

"We can pitch a tent right here where it all started," she states.

"But I had a plan for you and that outpost," Giant growls.

"We can use it on night two." Her grin grows as she attempts to hold Giant's gaze.

"Cricket, I—" Giant cuts himself off as his sight travels over our heads. His eyes narrow. "What the . . ."

With that, Letty reaches a hand to Giant's thick forearm, the hand with her large engagement ring, and now a wedding band. "The second night," she repeats as if reminding him of something, and his eyes lower for where she's touching him. His expression immediately softens as he removes her hand, bringing it up to his lips, and presses a kiss over the ring. James used to do the same thing to me, and I absentmindedly rub at my fourth finger where my rings would rest.

*"I love seeing my ring on your finger,"* James would say, caressing the same spot on my finger.

"Accept the challenge, Mr. Harrington. I know how to be creative in a tent," Letty teases.

"But it's our wedding night," Giant practically whines.

"And we'll pitch a tent, share a sleeping bag, and—"

"I'm not certain I need to be part of this conversation, right?" I ask, cutting off my new sister-in-law before I hear more details than necessary about their wedding night plans.

Letty turns back to me as if the two newlyweds forgot my presence. Her face warms as she smiles at me again.

"He's waiting for you," she whispers, and Giant twists his attention from his wife to the woods again.

"What's going on here?"

Letty leans her head against Giant's chest, tucking her arm through his as she releases mine. "I've handled everything."

"That's what I'm afraid of, Cricket," he grumbles before pressing a kiss to the top of her head.

"Go," she mouths to me, and I smile back, almost giddy with anticipation of what I'll find in the trees.

# Chapter 18
# Campfires and Cocktails

[Evie]

To say I had to psych myself up to sleep with my husband was an understatement and a lie. James handled my body in a way that brought out my fantasies and dispelled any inhibitions. He was a sexual being, and sometimes we used sex to communicate our feelings. Grunts and groans were our conversation, and occasionally, our argument, but we always felt better after we connected on that physical level.

A divorced friend once told me, "If you can still have sex with him, well, at least it's something." It's when the thought of kissing him is unbearable that it's time to leave. It's one reason I did go. James was no longer attracted to me. He couldn't look me in the eyes. He didn't want to touch me. And while I didn't need us to stare at one another while we had sex, it came to a point he couldn't muster the will to have sex.

It's one reason his request to sleep with me was so puzzling. *Why sex? Why now?*

I chalked it all up to closure. He wanted this one final act to finalize things. James was not vindictive—at least not toward me—so he would not make this request out of spite or jealousy. He simply had his reason, which he wasn't going to share with me. We weren't talking. We were having sex. Period. End of us.

With this thought in mind, I step back into the darkening woods. My heart races. My core pulses. I am a live wire of nerves, ready to detonate at any second.

"James." His name is a breathless leak from my lips when I find him propped against a tree. His long legs in dark jeans are crossed at the ankle with freshly polished motorcycle boots on his feet. His linked arms shield his chest covered in a black dress shirt, rolled at the sleeves, but containing a tie, also in black. He personifies motorcycle menace dressed up, and with his casual lean against a trunk, he is badass meets nature, and I wanted to scale his body like this mountain. His blue eyes shine crystal clear despite the filtered light coming through the overhanging leaves.

He doesn't greet me, only stares at me. His eyes wander the length of my dress, which hits me mid-calf, meeting the tops of my scuffed cowboy boots. My jean jacket hangs open, exposing the low cut of the dress, where a hint of cleavage pops over the edge. My hair lays around my shoulders, and I nervously brush back a section, tucking it behind my ear. My lids lower, and I'm self-conscious that I still don't meet his approval.

Maybe he's changed his mind.

Taking a deep breath, I realize I can't do it. I can't pretend he wants me when he doesn't. I can't sleep with him, knowing it's a means to an end—the end of us. I spin back for the clearing and take only two steps before his arm circles my waist, halting my retreat.

His nose nuzzles into the crook of my neck, and the warmth of his breath tickles down my spine. My eyes close as I accept his chest at my back. Dipping under my jacket with his hand, he spreads his fingers, covering my belly.

"Dance with me," he whispers below my ear.

"What?" I choke, considering where we stand and how close his family is.

"Just one dance," he mutters, squeezing at my midsection, holding me in place until a memory returns.

+ + +

*Eighteen years ago . . .*

*James and I had had a huge fight around the time Michael was due to be born. A fight that sent me running away. I didn't know where to go, so I just left, driving aimlessly out of town until I remembered his pap's cabin and wondered if I could find it.*

*I was pregnant, tired, and emotionally spent. My new husband had told me he had never wanted to get married. He had never wanted children. And I lost it. He was implying I trapped him, or at least that was how I interpreted it.*

*"Well, don't do me any favors," I remember shouting at him after I threw a lemon across the kitchen at him. James ducked from the first one. He caught the second one like a professional baseball player.*

*"What the fuck?" he hollered back at me.*

*"I know you gave up Dolores and all your other fuck buddies, and for what? This?" I jabbed at my belly, feeling fat and disgusting, instead of beautiful like he said I was every day. James had been attentive and seductive on most days. He craved sex, and my libido had not waned with the pregnancy, but I was coming close to the end of my term. My hormones were kicking back up again, bouncing my emotions all over the place, and large tears skated down my face as I yelled at him.*

*"Leave Dolores out of this. And other fuck buddies?" he choked. "You have no idea what I gave up for you."*

*My mouth fell open. It was the last straw.*

*"I hate you," I yelled. He knew what I'd given up to be with him.*

*Finally, I'd ended up at his grandfather's cabin. His elderly grandfather still used it on occasion although the family was worried about him being alone in the woods.*

*"Hello, Sunshine," his pap greeted me. Pap always called me sunshine because of my bright blond hair, but I didn't feel like the sunny star. More like the darkness of the surrounding universe.*

*"To what do I owe this honor?" He had a lopsided grin, and I could see where the Harrington men got their charm.*

*"I'm running away from home," I teased even though it wasn't far from the truth.*

*Pap let out a loud laugh. The fierce body of an aging man jiggled like a jolly Santa, and he looked a bit like St. Nick wearing his suspenders over a full belly. "What'd he do?"*

*I shook my head although the tears blurred my vision.*

*Pap looked toward the ceiling of the covered porch. "Did you see this, Charlotte? I told you she'd come to her senses about that one." He was addressing the heavens where his dear wife had been to rest for a while.*

*"Let me grab us a beer . . . er, ah, in your case a lemonade." He shuffled back through the screen door while I took a seat in one of two rocking chairs on the porch. When he returned, he handed me a glass filled with ice and light yellow liquid, and held a beer bottle in his other hand, making his way to the second rocker.*

*"Tell me everything," he said once situated. At first, I wasn't comfortable telling his grandfather about the fight. As a twenty-seven-year-old woman on the verge of motherhood, I shouldn't be whining about my new husband, especially to his grandfather. However, James and I were still new to each other. Even though it'd been five months, we still didn't know much about the other, and we were about to embark on a lifetime commitment together.*

*Quickly, I got over my unease as I was lonely in Blue Ridge. I'd ostracized all my friends by doing what I'd done back in Savannah, and my parents were hardly talking to me. I spent the next half hour speaking about my relationship with his grandson and another hour listening to him tell me stories about the first year of his marriage.*

*He always made Charlotte sound sweet and too good for him.*

*"She settled on the town rascal for some reason, and I thanked my stars every day for it. Kind of like you settled in with our James. He's thankful he has the brightest star in the sky as his girl, Sunshine. I know he didn't mean what he said."*

*Sometime during my afternoon on his porch, sipping lemonade and feeling guilty at throwing lemons at my husband, James showed up.*

*"Got a call that Pap had sunshine at his cabin," James teased, but his eyes narrowed. He was still angry with me as I was with him.*

*"Take a ride with me," he suggested, tipping his head for his truck, and I climbed in. He drove us to the ranger's post and explained the history of the place in relation to their property. Their land bordered public land, and they utilized the rarely used access up the mountain to*

*make beer illegally, not unlike making moonshine, once upon a time. Eventually, they took their beer making to a factory setting and sold it legally once the law allowed.*

*James explained all this history to me for some reason, walking me to the clearing and then stopping there.*

*"Dance with me," he said, startling me after the fight we'd had and the things we said. I stepped into his open arms, and he turned me in slow circles in the clearing.*

*"I didn't mean I'd given up people like Dolores and fuck buddies." He snorted, tugging me to him when I immediately strained to be removed from his hold at the mention of others. "I meant, I'd given up my heart. You own me, Evie. Heart and soul. Body and mind. I can't live without you. Or our baby. Maybe giving up were the wrong words. I've given you my heart. It's yours for whatever you need."*

*His words melted me into his arms, relaxing against his chest as he held me. We danced in circles a few more minutes, letting the rustle in the trees around us be our song until he asked me one more question.*

*"Do you really hate me, Peach?" The question was raw and sincere. Even though we'd said I love you, he still didn't always believe me, telling me he was surprised that a woman like me could love a man like him.*

*"I'm sorry I said that." I peered up at him as I shook my head. "I didn't mean it."*

*"I love you, Evie. No matter what happens between us. I love you. You were meant to be mine, and I meant what I've said. I've been waiting for you to take my heart. Keep it."*

*James always told me he was never a liar, and this was one of those moments where the truth was all he had to give me.*

*And I held onto that truth, thinking his heart would always be mine.*

+ + +

The memory surprises me as I hadn't thought of it in years. I also hadn't been to the clearing or the outpost in even longer. I sadly smile to myself, recalling the rest of that night. We made love right there in the clearing, but it was hardly that simple as my round belly was in the way and being on my knees in the dirt actually stung. I went into labor the next day. The doctor had warned me orgasms could move things along.

Voices in the distance interrupt the memory. Those gathered must be ready to move back down the mountain.

"Let's take a walk," James suggests, slipping his hands down my arms to capture my fingers and lead me out the opposite end of the path. Still holding my hand, he guides me around the back of the outpost and onto a trail that's distinctly trampled but not as obvious as the one between the ranger station and the clearing.

My heart begins to race, and my palms sweat. I think I know where he's leading me, and I don't know if I can make this journey. Sensing my unease, James stills once we're deep enough in the woods we can't be seen by the wedding guests returning to various trucks to head down the mountain for a proper supper and continued celebration.

"I don't think I can do it," I whisper, my eyes looking over James's shoulder.

"I won't let anything happen to you, and if it gets to be too much, we can turn back." James swallows as he holds tighter to my hand. "I come here a few times a year."

I nod, trusting James. I'm certain he said the same thing to our son. Or not. Why would he need to assure our child that he'd always look out for him? Michael had to have instinctively known his father would love him and protect him above all else. James would never let him falter. He'd never let him go.

James remains quiet as he leads me forward. Our destination is a mile from here, and neither of us has footwear to traipse through the forest. I focus on that thought. We can't actually climb to *that* point. *That* spot where it all happened.

I'd worked myself into accepting that not every memory in the area is a bad one. Letty and Giant's wedding had been a beautiful reminder that good times still happened here. James and I had several camping trips as a family in the clearing and romantic nights in the outpost ourselves once upon a time. I focused on those thoughts in order to bring myself up here but going to the actual ridge—the place it all happened—I just could not do it.

Despite my faith in James, I'm too anxious. My palms sweat to the point my hand slips from his grasp on occasion, and a slow trickle of cold perspiration rolls under each arm. I'm shivering regardless of my body's heat from expelling energy. My chest begins to constrict like a coil is wrapping around me. I can't seem to catch my breath as each inhale becomes painful. The vise grip sensation causes my upper back to ache and my ribs to pinch.

"James," I whispered, attempting to squeeze his fingers, but they slip from his grip again. He instantly stops.

"Peach?" My head shakes slowly side to side. *I can't do it*. I can't go there. I can't look at that cliff.

"I . . ." The singular word is a wheeze of air, and James quickly wraps his arms around me, hugging me tightly to his chest.

"Okay, baby. It's too far to walk there anyway. I just wanted to give Giant and Letty time to get everyone away from the outpost before we went back."

I nod into his neck as my forehead presses into the crook near his shoulder. My fingers loosely hold the edges of his shirt, but I don't have the strength to return his embrace.

"Shh," he whispers, soothing me like a frightened pup, stroking down my hair. "I've got you."

I've always been afraid of heights, and I'd tease James he married the wrong woman. I wasn't a risk-taker, but then again, that's how we met. I didn't typically scale mountains, rush into fires, or climb steep heights. My feet needed to remain firmly on flat soil and preferably leveled ground without a large drop-off nearby. Still, I'd take an occasional hike with him, admiring the dense beauty of the woods surrounding where we lived and even congratulating myself on not falling off a cliff.

In hindsight, it was not a good joke.

James continues to hold me to him, forcing my face into the freshness of his soft shirt while his fingers comb down the length of my hair.

"Let's head back. They'll be gone by now."

Keeping an arm around me, James marches us forward, and I seem to blindly follow until we can't walk side by side anymore. He takes my hand once again. His fingers curl into mine, locking firm his grip as we take our time to return to the outpost area. Once there, the only vehicle remaining is James's motorcycle. We round the small hut-like cabin, which I know is a singular room inside, and James asks me to give him a few minutes. He enters the wooden structure and returns with both a small rug and a large blanket.

Snapping the rug out, he lays it next to a thick fallen trunk cut to fit like back support by a natural fire ring made of rocks.

"You come here often, don't you?" It sounds like a pickup line; however, it's anything but. He must visit often because he's too calm being here.

"As I told you, I go to the ridge a few times a year. Birthdays and . . . anniversaries." James pauses as he kneels next to the fire ring, ready filled with fresh logs and kindling. Pulling a lighter from his pocket, he lights the shreds of paper at the bottom of the stack and blows on the low flame to ignite the pyre. I watch him work, recalling a hundred backyard fires and campfires over the years. James loved to be outside, and while he fought fires as a profession, he worshipped them as well.

I don't question how James can face the ridge. During one annual phone call, he told me how he finds solace there. As long as he isn't looking for Michael to return, I understand his need for a place to connect, a place to question, a place to reflect, although I can't bring myself to go there. In the same breath, I don't know that going to that particular spot is helpful to James's mentality. It's like visiting the scene of a crime over and over again, looking for a clue that just won't be found. Not that a crime was committed. It was an accident.

Horsing around.

Loose gravel.

I close my eyes and then quickly open them, unable to face my own imagination.

James settles next to me, watching the dance of flames for a few seconds before sliding his arm along the large log at our back. I shiver, shifting gears from the past to the present.

*I'm going to sleep with my husband.*

Our situation hardly feels romantic, but as the flames orchestrate their music over the piled wood, I slowly relax into the silence of night seeping in around us. The setting actually *is* romantic.

"I have wine if you'd like, or more beer if you're trying not to mix and match," he offers, and I decide a drink might be nice. It might take the edge off just a little bit, but I won't have too much.

"That'd be nice," I whisper as it's suddenly difficult to find my voice.

"I'll make us some dinner soon unless you're hungry now. I have a grate for the fire and steaks ready."

I softly smile, surprised at his effort. He's turning this into a real date, and a rather thought-out one at that.

"I'm not hungry yet, but I'll take the wine."

Adding to my surprise, James kisses my temple before standing and disappearing into the small cabin. He returns quickly with a bottle of red and two glasses. As he folds down to the rug, he tucks the blanket over my legs.

"Warm enough?" he asks, and I nod again as though I can't speak. Slowly, I'm shifting from panicked memories to a startled woman, being wowed, and maybe wooed by my husband. He pours me a glass of wine, and after offering it to me, I inhale the crisp, fruity scent of the fall blend while I wait for him to fill a glass for himself. He taps my glass with his but doesn't speak.

"What are we toasting?" I ask, grinning with thoughts of cheerful things we could say.

"I guess the end." His quiet words hit me square in the chest, and my forehead deeply furrows. I'm disappointed in his lack of fight. Then again, he's the one who gave me the shove to walk away from him. He didn't call me back to him. He didn't chase me down. He let me go.

Bringing my glass to my lips, I take a hardy sip, allowing the sharp taste to sting my already swollen throat. James takes a drink as well and then bends a knee, propping his arm over it and letting his wrist dangle. He balances his glass on his other thigh, stretched forward in front of him. Glancing down at his lap, he takes a deep breath before looking me in the eyes.

"I'm sorry I let you down."

The words catch me off guard.

"I let you both down." His voice drops, and the seriousness slaps me in the face. It's taking great courage on his part to say these words.

"Please. Stop apologizing." It isn't so much that I can't hear the words as much as the fact James has said them too often. *I'm sorry* were two words eating him up.

"I just want you to know—" He's stopped by two of my fingers covering his lips.

"Please. No more." I'm not angry. I just don't need to keep hearing him try to explain what happened, how it happened, and how he can't forgive himself. I understand. I've racked my brain, and I'd have done nothing different if I was in his position. I've even told myself I'd never have been in the position James was in in the first place, but I can't predict where or when or how an accident would occur.

We simply cannot keep going backward.

To my surprise again, James spreads his lips and then sucks the tips of my fingers into the warmth of his mouth. I use my fingers between his lips to tug him to me, planting my mouth against his. The kiss is slow and sweet, as we both sip at the wine flavor of one another. James breaks first, moving his glass to the other side of his body and then taking mine to place it near his. Quickly, his hand comes to my cheek, and he returns his lips to mine, taking his time to savor me. The best way to describe the subtle tug and long drag of our mouths against each other is decadent. We don't pass the seam of our lips but just meet over and over again, and this alone turns me on.

Perhaps it's Giant's wedding, the recall of loss, or the warmth of this man next to me, but I'm ready to sprint ahead to sex with him. I need this connection, joining my body with his, so I lean into him, wrapping my arms around his neck.

James pulls back. His eyes meet mine for a second time this evening. Daylight is disappearing quickly, and the sky behind his head mixes in a kaleidoscope of pinks, purples, and oranges.

"I'm gonna make dinner," he says, unfolding himself to stand, and I'm left overheated and confused. Reaching for my wine after he walks back to the cabin, I tell myself he isn't rejecting me. This is his demand. This is his plan.

When he returns, I ask if I can help in any way.

"You just sit there and look beautiful, Peach." He winks at me as he squats, placing the grilling grate over the fire and then tossing steaks on the metal once it's heated.

James stands and steps back to me. Bending at the waist to lean over me, he braces his hands on the log at my back.

"Kiss me again like that," he whispers, and I tip up my head to meet his lips. We kiss again for too short a time before he pulls away to tend the steaks. I could say I haven't been on a date in a long time, but that isn't true. Dalton has extravagant tastes, and we've been to some fine dining establishments, but my mouth waters in anticipation of this fire-cooked meal of grilled steak and baked potatoes. James is putting in a lot of effort to make this night special.

When dinner is finally served on tin camp plates, he asks me about my business, and I accept that it's a safe place for us to land in conversation. I tell him about the estate sale earlier in the week and a new ring collection I've been inspired to make after attending Giant's wedding. I'd love to make a set of his and hers bands that complement one another while being rugged enough for a man and delicate enough for a woman. As I speak, my thumb swipes down my ring finger out of habit, feeling the nakedness without my missing rings. I took them off a year ago, and ironically, it was at that time Dalton entered my life.

"May I ask, where are your rings?" Melancholy fills James's normally rough tone as if the ending really is near, and I worry, for half a second, he'll jump into another risk-taking, life-threatening experience once we are over. Yet a strange calm blankets me. We will never be over. We will never be finished. Michael will be the forever bond between us, whether he's present or not. It would be a betrayal of his memory for James and me never to connect again, and thus I know that while our marriage may dissolve, our relationship never will. We will always be related as the parents of our child.

"I keep them in a jewelry box at home." My home in Savannah. I don't wish to explain that the box is a small container, meant only to hold those two precious rings, and the third one he gave me one Mother's Day. A mother's ring, he called it, as a gift for giving him a child. My throat clogs with another memory, and I swallow back the lump with the help of more wine.

"What about you?" I ask as if it's the most casual thing in the world to discuss the removal of wedding bands and where we keep them.

"Yeah, I keep mine someplace special as well." James looks off at the fire, and we spend a few seconds in silence.

After another sip of wine, I ask, "How is the department?" As a local fireman, James does more than rescue cats from trees although he's been called to do that too. He remained in search and rescue for years after we were first married and then on volunteer status once he took a position with the county fire department. He tells me about old colleagues. Divorces. Marriages. Babies born. Kids going off to college. Once upon a time, I thought those men and women would be his lifelong buddies, but it seems he's found a new niche with the motorcycle club.

"Tell me more about the club," I prompt, hoping to learn more about his affiliation with them. James pours me more wine, and I notice a second bottle has made it near the first, which is now empty.

"They aren't bad men," James defends. "Just a group of guys looking for . . . I don't know, friendship, I guess. Kinship, perhaps, is a better word. Justice runs a tight ship on keeping people clean of shit. He doesn't want any trouble. That's all in their past." James's silence after that lets me know the subject is closed.

"I have dessert," he states, rocking up to stand and collecting our plates. "I'll be right back."

I don't think I can handle another bite of food, but James returns with a brownie wedge nearly the size of a cake plate.

"Is that from Apple Jane's?" Jane Conrad is Corabelle's daughter, and she makes the most amazing desserts, specializing in apple anything. But she can work chocolate like no other, and her brownie is sinfully delicious.

"Your favorite," James says, folding back to the rug and holding out the plate for me.

"It was also Michael's." I pause a second, considering the thought. "Why here?" I suddenly question our location. It's obvious we're going to sleep together, but why so close to the ridge for this night?

"Were you trying to get me to go to the ridge earlier?" My voice turns edgy, and James's brows rise.

"Actually, no. I thought this would be"—*Romantic?*—"a nice spot to hang out, and if it's okay with you, I don't want to talk about Michael right now." This surprises me.

"We should talk about the community center and the dedication details." I'd learn more throughout the week with a quick search of local news and then a visit to Charlie's office, where I met briefly with the new Parks and Recreation supervisor, who happens to be Charlie's wife.

"We aren't talking about that either," James says, turning a bit edgy. "Tonight is about us."

"And what about us?"

"We're just gonna enjoy good wine, a fine fire, and a beautiful night." *And have sex.* It's unsaid, but it's there between us. Our churning chemistry is a slow swirl like stirring a cooking soup. The flame is growing hotter, and the liquid is about to boil over, but James still hasn't made a move.

He tips his head back, taking in the stars, and I follow his gaze. Dots of light pinprick the dark sky, and I'm waiting on James to point out the constellations. He often did that with Michael, fueling our son's love of mythology and symbolism. I haven't seen a sky like this in a while, and I had forgotten how beautiful it could be here.

James sits in a way his hand rests near my hip on the rug. The night has been full of soft touches, brief kisses, and subtle innuendos.

We continue chatting, sticking to safe topics, which aren't many. We avoid his family, our child, and Dalton. When we run out of things to ask, we turn quiet until James brings up memories of us.

"Remember when . . ."

"And that one time . . ."

"You could never . . ."

It was one funny antidote after another like a trip down memory lane, and it hurt my heart. How did we get so far apart? And why hadn't we found our way back to one another?

"I never meant it," he finally says, and I'm coming down from a chuckle about the time he filled the dishwasher with regular dish soap.

"Meant what?"

"That I couldn't look you in the eyes because of him."

"James. I thought you said no Michael."

"I did. But this has to do with you, and I'd forgotten that your eyes are distinctly different than his."

I shake my head, turning toward the flame which has burned down to a glowing ember. James hasn't added any logs or stoked the remaining wood, and I'm assuming he's intentionally letting it burn out, like the closing of night, the end of a book. There are no more chapters to be read.

"How are mine different?"

"I've been thinking about what Giant said. You have this look you'd given me, and it just turned my insides. There's that old saying about hanging the stars and lassoing the moon, and I'd do anything you asked when you looked at me like that. Giant was right. You had me whipped." James chuckles softly to himself, wiping his hand over his lips. "Still do."

My neck cranes, and I stare at his mouth as if I didn't hear him correctly.

"That look in your eyes. It's gone, Evelyn. I stomped it out. I'd pulled the sky down but only the dark part. The light has disappeared."

There would never be getting over our son. It wasn't a possibility, but I'd like to think the light returned, at least a little bit. The days slowly moved from dark to dawn to daylight. It took years, but I got where I could make it through a day, and then a week, and another month until the years passed. I had to do it all on my own, and that's where my anger with James rests. I can't go back. I don't want to go back. I only want to continue facing forward.

"When you said you couldn't look at me, you gutted me with those words," I admit. I'd told him then, but I don't know if anything I said back then stuck with him. We argued so much, but it was more like him yelling at me to get away from him.

"I know." James shifts, bending his knees to pull them up to his chest as best as he can and circling his arms around them. "I had to do it.'

"Why?" It comes out quickly and without thought. I'd analyzed James enough over the years to understand in some sick way why he did what he did, and Justice confirmed my thoughts—self-preservation. James was going down—a rock crushed in an avalanche—and he didn't want to take me with him. Instead, he might as well have thrown *me* over the mountain because I was free-falling without a wingsuit when he pushed me away.

"I'm a selfish man, Peach. You know this. I wanted you for myself, and I kept you. Then in order to keep you safe *from me*, I pushed you away."

My shoulders fall, knowing the truth but after all this time, still struggling to accept it.

"And who was supposed to keep you safe from yourself?" I ask. James snorts, shaking his head with a weak smile.

"I guess nobody, which wasn't fair either. You were always too good for me, Peach. And then, you weren't angry."

"Angry?" I huff. "I was very angry. I wanted to hate you, but I fought the blame. It wasn't your fault."

"That's just it. I think I needed you to get mad. I needed you to tell me you hated me. Maybe I needed you to push me to rock bottom so I didn't throw myself down there." James pauses a second, and my mouth falls open. "But then again, I don't fault you. It wasn't your responsibility to pick me up. I promised to be the rock, and I'd failed."

"Jesus, James. Is this what you've been thinking all these years? That you failed me? How? You're my husband. I love you. You didn't need to be the only one who supported us. We needed to lean on each other, and if you needed me to get mad, you should have told me. I would have definitely taken a few things out on you."

James chuckles bitterly again, turning his head to face me. "Yeah, I bet you would have." James and I could fight. It was rare, but when it happened, it could be a knock-down, drag-out. To him, when it was over, it was over, and we did more than kiss and apologize. Angry sex worked wonders as did make-up sex. It realigned us, and suddenly I understood why he wants me to sleep with him. If we have sex, it might adjust the malalignment between us.

I reach for his face, as he's still looking at me, and I cup his jaw covered in speckles of silver.

"Take me to bed," I whisper. Leaning forward, I kiss him tender and sweet like we've been doing all night. Our lips move together, dancing with each other but not breaching the seam once again. There's no tongue and no passion, just tortured pleasure.

James pulls back, dragging my lower lip with his before releasing me. "Let me get this fire out. You head in."

He quickly stands and turns for me, holding out both hands to pull me upward. I pick up the blanket and wrap it over my shoulders. As I make my way to the small cabin, I don't look back to watch him snuffing out the fire or picking up the final traces of our evening.

Looking back is no longer an option. We can only look forward.

When James enters the small space, I've made myself comfortable by removing my jean jacket and boots. The setting is luxurious in the dregs of this old structure. Blankets lay over another rug with an assortment of pillows and a heavy sleeping bag for a cover. There's a new heat source in this place—a small wood burning stove that I don't remember being here before. It's always had minimal electricity and rudimentary water for the half-bath and miniature kitchenette along one wall.

I'm still in my dress as I sit in the middle of the rug with a blanket pulled over my lap. James already lost his tie and loosened a few buttons on his shirt a while back. He kicks off his boots and settles next to me.

"You're so beautiful," he mutters, capturing my mouth with his before I can respond, and we quickly fall back into the line of sweet kisses and light caresses. All his tender loving is driving me wild, and I need us to get rough. I want him to manhandle me and really touch me. I want him to shove his hand down my dress for a breast and lower his head under my skirt for the heart of me. I want him over me and under me, and deep inside like he once could get.

Instead, James keeps it tame, and we make out like teenagers uncertain where to move our hands next. Eventually, we lie back. Our kisses turn more eager. Our tongues get involved. The roll of full steam ahead begins, but when I hitch my leg over James's hip, he clamps my thigh and pulls back.

"Roll over, Peach," he mutters, and I do as he asks, giving him my back. Maybe this is how he wants it, so he still doesn't have to look at me. His hand coasts up my thigh, shifting my dress a bit but not exposing much skin. His palm moves to my covered hip, skating over the swell to my waist. I move my arm, and he brushes the side of my breast, but then reaches forward and skims his hand down my arm. Our fingers entwine a second, and he pulls my hand back to my chest. Tender lips come to my shoulder, and he nudges my hair off my neck, exposing the nape to him.

We made love plenty of times in our marriage, but this feels different. It's as if he's memorizing my body, a hint at goodbye. I shift to twist toward him, but he stills me with a hand on my shoulder.

"Stay just like this, baby." He massages my shoulder, then moves to my neck and delivers heavenly pressure along my upper back.

"You're tense, Peach," he mutters to me, and I take a deep breath. It's not like we haven't had sex or that I can't. I'm actually turned on and anxious for us to begin.

But as time goes on and the pressure of his hand works at my neck and over my shoulder blades, I continue to relax into the good wine, a heavy meal, and the warmth of my husband at my back.

# Chapter 19
# Rude Awakenings

[James]

"What the hell is this?"

Evie stumbles out of the ranger station, tripping over the steps as she stomps up to me in the yard. I was crouching to stoke the fire and make some much-needed morning coffee, but I stand as she approaches me, waving the papers in her hand.

"Just what the hell is this?" she repeats, slapping the folded papers against my chest.

I stumble with a chuckle. "I told you I'd sign them if you slept with me."

"Slept," she yells, and I'm wondering why she's so worked up.

Last night, I did what I could to make it a romantic evening. I felt bad wrestling the outpost out from under Letty and Giant and their first night together, but Letty agreed my plan was important. I hadn't known they intended to use the place for their first night as husband and wife. They'd been living together for months, and I wanted to crash this old outpost, thinking no one would give it a thought. However, I recalled meeting Letty under Giant in this spot a year ago, and it turns out, they wanted the place for the night to relive the memory. Letty easily gave it up when I found her dressed and waiting in the cabin for the ceremony to start. I knew Giant would be pissed, but I wasn't worried about his feelings. I'd come to the damn wedding, after all.

"James," Evie groans, rustling the papers against my chest and stepping closer to me in her anger.

*Now* she's angry with me.

"This is what you wanted," I remind her.

"I thought you wanted to *sleep* with me."

"I did sleep with you."

"As in have sex," she clarifies.

"What?" I stammer, my voice nearly as loud as hers.

"Yes, all the 'you're so juicy' and 'no one gets in here but me,' and I thought you meant sex together, as in fucking each other." The crassness of her tone has me wishing we had fucked. I woke with the hardest hard-on and had to take a moment in the woods to right myself. I'm getting worked up again, and I'd love to give her what she's asking.

But I can't.

I don't want to fuck my wife.

I want to love her, and I want her to love me again.

Instead, we're getting divorced.

I signed the papers after getting what *I* wanted from her. One more night to sleep next to her warm body. One more night to curl up against her and breathe her in. One more night to feel as if she's mine. I didn't think I'd be able to sleep at first. Our slow kisses were difficult to keep slow and holding back my tongue was near impossible. She tasted so damn good, and it wasn't just the wine on her lips. She was safety, and rightness, and trust, and I wanted to savor her as long as I could. I worked hard not to cross a line I'd drawn. I only wanted to outline her body, memorize her lips, and hold her again.

Just one more time.

To my surprise, despite the hard-on and heartache, I did sleep. I relaxed into her light breathing, melted against her heated skin, and succumbed to a night of dreamless sleep for the first time in six years. No screams haunted my ears. No panicked eyes filled my vision. It was a quiet, peaceful bliss of nothingness.

"Sorry to disappoint you," I mutter. "It's becoming a habit."

She slaps my chest with the papers again, too angry to cry, and then she shoves me.

"I hate you," she hisses, and dammit, I laugh as I reach for her forearm and tug her close to me.

"Why?"

"Because I thought you wanted me, and you still don't."

Both hands come to her upper arms, and I tug her snug against me. "Make no mistake, Peach, I still want you with every breath I take. You own me like you always have, and now I've given you what you wanted." I release her, feeling the adrenaline rush through my body and my dick rise. I don't want us to do something she'll regret, and having sex would be a mistake, a *big* mistake. I wouldn't be able to let her go if we joined our bodies.

"I'll find an attorney," I state, nodding at the papers.

"Get me off this fucking mountain," she yells. "I want down from here." She's visibly shaking, and I reach for her again, but she steps back, putting as much distance as she can between us.

"Evelyn," I begin, but we hear the crunch of tires on gravel and look over my shoulder to see the approach of a truck.

Giant and Letty, I presume.

*Fuck.*

"I will not take their special time away from them," Evie says as if warning me not to argue with her. "Just get us out of here. For them."

Swiping my hands down my jeans, I step past her for the outpost, retrieving my jacket and keys inside. Evie stands barefoot on the cold forest floor, and I snag up her boots and her jean jacket, noting she must have stormed out of our little sleep-nest when she noticed the papers signed and lying next to her instead of me this morning.

When I return outside, I meet my brother's troubled eyes.

"Have a good night?" he quips, digging it in that I stole his evening.

"We were just leaving. The place is all yours." Evie's forced cheerful expression pushes her voice an octave higher than normal.

"You okay?" Giant addresses her, and she plasters that smile higher.

"Never been better," she answers Giant and then turns to Letty. "You look beautiful this morning, and yesterday was lovely. Thank you for inviting me."

Evie's voice cracks, and I recall their ceremony. My brother and his new bride must have written their own vows, making promises to each other for their future.

Evie's and my future will look quite different. Our vows have been shattered, and there's not enough glue to put them back together.

I've missed what Evie says next to Letty, but the women embrace while Giant keeps his hard glare aimed at me.

"I'd like to talk to you," he states.

"Got nothing to say," I tell him.

"This week." It's a warning I don't heed. Evie will be leaving, and I'm thinking I need a road trip. I need to get out of my head a bit, and maybe leaving this place will be good for me.

"We'll be going now," Evie steps up to me, pushing me back from my brother and his wife, and I shrug off her gentle shove. Stalking away from her, I reach my bike first and pace a few feet back and forth while she puts her boots and jacket back on. Once she's ready, I straddle the bike and start the engine. Evie climbs on without my assistance. I can't touch her right now, and the feel of her against me is torture.

How can she think I don't want her? I might have told her to leave me, but I never stopped wanting her, loving her.

We don't speak as we ride out. The rugged terrain jostles us down the gravel path. I keep us as slow as I can, but once we clear the dirt and hit the pavement, I need the speed. I need the rush of the bike beneath me to rid the thoughts racing through my head.

Did Evie want to have sex with me?

*Is that why she was so angry?*

Is it possible she wants to hold onto me, or did she just want the thrill of one more night as well?

I kick up the throttle. Evelyn screams behind me, warning me to slow down as her grip on me tightens. She's tucked her head into my back, and her arms squeeze me as though she'll never let me go.

*Don't let me go.* The words echo in my head.

From my son.

From my wife.

I have lost them both in different ways.

Evelyn and I have suffered the unimaginable with our child, but do we need to remain estranged from one another?

Giant's words come back to me. *Your wife is here, and she loves you.*

She loves you.

She still loves you.

She even said it last night, and I let it slip by as if she didn't know what she was saying.

The echoing possibility doesn't seem like it can be a reality.

And it's confirmed that it can't when we reach the Lodge.

After I park, Evelyn quickly hops off my bike, strutting away from me without a backward glance or a word in my direction. And for the first time in six years, I do what I should have done from the beginning.

I chase.

"Peach, don't walk away."

Her hips swish as she flips me the middle finger over her shoulder, and I'd laugh if I wasn't suddenly overwhelmed with the finality of us. If she gets away from me this time, she's really lost to me.

"Evie, please. Let's just talk."

The statement stops her a few feet from the front entrance of the Lodge.

"Talk?" she stammers, her voice squeaking on the word as she spins to face me, and her arms flail to her side. "*Now* you want to talk?"

"Let's just . . . shit, I've fucked this up. Let's just take a breath. We'll get some coffee, and—"

"No." The firmness of the word startles me. "No, I've waited years to talk to you, James. Years for you to come to me, open up to me. I had so much to say, and I was also willing to listen, but this . . . last night." She takes a deep breath, steadying herself when her voice begins to break. "I've learned my lesson with you, James. You say you love me, and I'll always love you, but it isn't the same as what we once had. You still don't want to touch me, and on some elemental level, I need that from you. I need to be close to you." Her voice cracks again, and she chokes back a sob as she pats her chest, clutching the divorce papers in her hand.

"I'll love you from afar. I've been doing it for years. I get it, James. Message received loud and clear. I'm sorry I held on so long. You're right. Separate is best. I can't be where I'm not wanted. We need to be finished."

"We aren't over," I growl, feeling more empowered than ever to fight for my wife as she turns and walks away from me for the second time this morning.

And for the second time, I follow.

I follow her into the lobby where she stops short, and I almost run into her. Looking over her shoulder, Evie faces a man sitting in a chair, knees spread, arms balanced on them. His hair is finger-combed, and his expression troubled. I recognize the look on this man's face, and I know I'm totally fucked when Evelyn says his name.

"Dalton?"

# Chapter 20
# Unpleasant Endings

[Evie]

*Dalton?*

"Dalton, what are you doing here?" I ask, stepping up to where he's sitting on the decorative chair in the lobby of the Lodge. Then I freeze. I can't recall a moment more awkward in my life. With James at my back and Dalton before me, I don't know what to do. Before me is such a beautiful, giving man who looks confused and a bit wrecked. Without looking back, I know James's expression matches Dalton's face.

"What the fuck?" James mutters, and I close my eyes, willing away the past few minutes. The ones where James follows me, and I come face-to-face with Dalton.

"I see I'm interrupting something," Dalton says, slowly sitting upright. He's such a gorgeous man with dark eyes and dark hair. His athletic build immediately says he did manual labor in his youth and was once a football player. He wears a suit well, but the one he's wearing now looks like he slept in it.

"Have you been here all night?" I ask, hearing a deep exhale behind me.

Dalton's eyes shift over my shoulder, taking in James's presence with a blank face. My heart races. This is not how I wanted this to happen. I wanted the divorce finalized before anyone was none the wiser that I was still married, but my chest aches. Before me is a possible future, but behind me, the past still hovers, as is James.

"Dalton Braun," Dalton states, standing to his full height and holding out a hand. Could this get any worse?

"James Harrington," James replies, not offering his hand in return. I refuse to look back at him but imagine him sizing up Dalton, taking in his taller height and broader shoulders. Dalton is more of a match to Giant in stature. Not that I want any man matching up and fighting.

"I can explain," I say quietly, holding Dalton's gaze when James refuses to shake Dalton's hand. Dalton nods, giving me this concession. He wears an expression of disbelief, and he isn't wrong in his mistrust. I actually can't explain this—what's been happening here, what's still lingering between James and me—because whatever still lingers unresolved nags at me.

"I think we should talk," Dalton says, diplomatic in his tone, ever the powerful lawyer I know him to be.

"We can go to my room." My voice drops. I don't like the suggestion, and my eyes shift to find James no longer in my periphery. Without a thought, my neck twists, and I notice that James is gone. Rolling my lips inward and letting my shoulders fall, I accept that it's for the best. I owe it to Dalton to explain myself.

"I don't think that's a good idea. Perhaps we could go to the coffee shop." He means the Lounge as it's open in the morning with light breakfast fare. I nod and lead the way like the disobedient child I feel inside me.

Dalton helps himself to a coffee from the self-serve counter, and I decline an offer of one for myself. I don't think I can choke anything down.

Once Dalton takes a seat across from me at a table, he just stares at me, willing me to speak. I swallow. The next statement feels like one of the hardest things I've ever had to say.

"I'm married," I whisper.

Dalton's head slowly lifts, tipping back once before rolling forward. He's displaying remarkable control, and I imagine it's how he keeps his cool when he's defending someone in court.

"As you know, my son died six years ago." I swallow back a lump in my throat and rapidly blink away the tears threatening to fill my eyes. "And I never got divorced."

My eyes remain on the table before me, but I sense Dalton shift. Both his arms come to the tabletop as he wraps his hands around the steaming mug of coffee.

"James felt at fault. Our son . . . he slid down the mountainside." A sob chokes me as I admit the story I hadn't told Dalton. *It was an accident*, I'd said—a fatal accident—and I didn't like to discuss it. Dalton accepted my simple explanation and let me keep the rest of the information.

"James and Michael were hiking, and from what James said, they were horsing around. Michael was too close to the edge, and he slipped. James caught his arm, but there wasn't enough footing for himself, so he lowered to the ridge, lying flat while our son dangled over the edge. James was trying to pull him upward, but Michael kept struggling. He needed to hold still." The words echo in my ears.

James said it on repeat to the sheriff's department after he called me. After he called them. He explained that Michael kept squirming, kicking out at the air while James kept yelling at him to hold still.

"They were both sweaty from the hike but growing sweatier with the effort of pulling Michael upward. There wasn't anything for James to get leverage on, and he fought Michael's counterintuitive actions. At one point, James's hand slipped until they only held hands."

Never having seen the accident, I close my eyes but imagine it over and over again with the vivid description James painted. The stench of panic. The fear of my son. The look in his eyes. The strength in James. Which wasn't enough.

"Our son slipped out of James's hand, plummeting over the ridge."

Placing my elbows on the table, I cover my face, caught in my own grief and guilt. Guilt at the loss of my son. I'd asked James to take him on the hike that day because I'd needed a day to myself. We'd had a summer of baseball games, and I was trying to work on fall designs as well as plan a holiday launch. I just needed a day alone. I'd been so selfish.

I didn't want to cry before Dalton. I didn't want to turn this around and have him feeling sorry for me. I deserved his wrath or his hatred, but I didn't want his sympathy.

"We never divorced," I repeat around a hiccup as I try to calm my quaking shoulders and my straining voice. "James couldn't get over the guilt he placed on himself. He was trained in search and rescue, and he hated that he wasn't able to save our child."

Taking a deep breath, I continue despite the tears still flooding my eyes and streaming down my face.

"He couldn't look at me anymore. Michael and I share the same eyes. Color. Shape. James said Michael had a look that mimicked mine, and he couldn't stand to see it. He kicked me out."

Dalton reaches for my forearm, but I don't feel the warmth of his touch. I'm numb, and his hand is emptiness against my skin.

"Why hadn't you divorced sometime in the past few years?" Dalton finally asks.

I shake my head, slowly lifting it to finally look up at him. "I don't know." I didn't. Something kept me attached to my husband despite the time and distance. We could afford a divorce. Hell, his brother Charlie and brother-in-law Chris were both practiced in law. We just hadn't taken that final step.

"What are you doing here?" I ask.

"The fact you have to ask concerns me." His brows pinch together. "But let's not discuss my feelings yet. Are you still in love with him?"

This is the million-dollar question. I want to say no. I want to tell Dalton that I've been over James for years, and the divorce was merely a formality. I want to say I love him—Dalton Braun. He is such a decent, patient man sitting before me, but I don't want to lie to him. I already had, and he didn't deserve that.

"You know what? Don't answer that yet." Dalton leans forward again, concentrating on his coffee mug a second. Then he scrubs a hand down his face. "I knew I shouldn't have let you come here alone. I could tell you were worked up before you left Savannah, and when you told me about the wedding, well, fool that I am, I thought I'd surprise you. Thought I could be your date after all, and maybe a wedding would give you romantic ideas. Ideas about us."

He's been such a patient man. We dated for months before we kissed, and more months passed before we touched. He felt so good standing beside me, and I lost my head a little bit, thinking I could move forward and take the next steps. The only way to be with him was to clear myself of James, but even if I sign some flimsy papers, I'll never be free from how I feel about my husband.

"I'm in love with you, Evelyn. I think I've shown that from the time and effort I've put into us. I want to be with you. I want us together, but I can't be in half a relationship. It's not fair to you or to me."

I agreed with him, and I hate how affable he's being. "You aren't angry?"

"Oh, I'm pissed, Evie. I'm fucking angry as hell, but what's the point in fighting for your affection if you can't give it to me completely? I don't want you to only half love me. I want you unequivocally, and that's something I can't make you do."

A song rushes through my head and what Dalton is saying is true. I couldn't make James love me, so I understand Dalton's position, and I feel all the worse for it because I'm the one doing to him what James has done to me. I'm pushing him aside.

"I came here to get a divorce." I hold out the rumpled mess of papers, smoothing over them, which does nothing to flatten them. "I didn't think it was fair to you, and I really wanted to give us a shot without the guilt hanging over my head."

"That's noble of you." I dismiss the sarcasm in his tone because I deserve it. If he wishes to scream at me, I deserve it, but this man won't do that. He won't raise his voice. He won't wrestle with me for my emotions, and perhaps that's the thing which has held me back from him. I want someone to fight for me. It hasn't been James, but it isn't Dalton either.

"I understand if you never want to see me again."

"Shit, Evelyn. You don't get it, do you? I'm sitting here. I've been here all night waiting for you. The staff had no idea where you were, and you weren't answering your phone."

I never thought to look at my phone. I hadn't given it a glance the entire day or night. My focus had all been consumed by one man, and once I put my signature on these papers, I wouldn't be linked to him other than the history we once had.

"I'm so sorry." My lips tremble again as the words are not enough. James said them to me over and over again, and in some small way, I understand him better. An apology will never be enough to take away the pain I'm causing the man before me. Two words do not take away a lie, take away the pain, or restore anyone's faith.

Dalton scoots his chair closer to mine and wraps an arm over me. His lips press into the side of my head.

"I'm going to ask you again if you still love him, Evelyn."

Tears fall harder. "I'm sorry," I whisper again without directly answering him, and with his forehead at my temple, he nods against me.

"Me too."

# Chapter 21
# Fight or Flight

[James]

The second I hear Evie invite that douche to her room, I'm outta there. I storm across the pavement back to my bike and roar out of the parking lot as though I'm trying to outrace a forest fire. As much as I want to ride free, I don't trust myself right now, so I head to the bar. Ridged Edge isn't open before noon, but Justice is typically there doing who knows what, and I need a drink. Or at least company who will stop me from doing something stupid.

When I hammer at the door with my fist, the wood vibrates in the jamb before Bear Grady whips it open.

"Where's the fire?" he blurts, eyeing me before I brush past him, forcing him out of my way.

"I need a drink," I holler, louder than necessary.

"Bar's closed."

To my surprise, I find Justice leaning over the bar talking to that pesky new wife of Charlie's.

"Janessa," I snap. "Out." Her head snaps up at me, but she's a tough woman, and she narrows her eyes to slits.

"Excuse me?"

"You're excused. Now get out."

"Last I checked, I own this bar," Justice states, matching Janessa's glare at me.

"Last I checked, I invested in it to keep it open."

Janessa's head swivels back and forth between this interchange, and I don't even feel remotely guilty for revealing a secret I swore I wouldn't share with others. I'm invested in the bar even though my brother owns the Pub in town. I did it because I wanted a place for us outcasts to go, and the unofficial clubhouse is the private residence of Justice.

"I'm here to discuss the fundraiser with Justice," Janessa clarifies as if I haven't told her to leave. I walk right up to the bar where a stack of papers sits next to her laptop and toss the papers across the place. The sheets scatter like falling leaves, and Janessa glances over her shoulder, stunned by my actions.

"Unless you want this laptop to be the next thing thrown across this room, you'll get out as I asked." I force a false smile, but my meaning is clear. I don't want to hear about the fucking ride, and I don't want to look at her right now.

Janessa Cruz is a beautiful woman with dark hair and deep green eyes. She's curvy and luscious, and all my brother Charlie's, but she's inserted herself into business with this club because of that other pesky wench Cora, and I'm not having it today.

My hand is shoved off the edge of her laptop, and she slams it shut. "Justice, we can reschedule. I'll talk to Cora." She slides off the barstool, and I follow her retreat to the front door. I want to make certain she leaves, but I don't miss Justice's eyes tracking the sway of her backside.

"That woman has some balls."

"Quit checking out her ass," I warn. "And let me know when you get yours back." Cora, *shit*.

"Just what the fuck is your problem?"

"Everything." I sigh, perching myself on a stool and placing the heel of my hands against my forehead. "Just . . . *ah*," I yell.

Justice presses off the bar top and reaches for a shot glass, filling it full to the brim with amber liquid. I slam back the offered drink allowing the burn to coat my throat and cut like a knife going down.

"What happened?" he repeats, glaring at me.

"Evelyn has a *boy*friend," I whine as I say the adolescent term, sounding juvenile and petulant. "That's why she's divorcing me."

Justice huffs and shakes his head.

"What?" I demand of the disappointed chuckle that follows.

"She's not divorcing your ass because of some boyfriend. She's divorcing you because you have your head up your ass."

*What the . . .?* Giant's words come back to me in the sound of Justice's voice. "I do not."

"Do so," Justice responds, and now we both sound like dickhead teenagers. "Look, since the moment I met you, you've been a risk-taker. You've tossed yourself into harm's way more times than I can count, but your wife returns, and you're running scared."

"I'm not scared."

"Then what happened?" His eyes widen, waiting out my explanation.

"I gave her an ultimatum. If she slept with me, I'd sign the papers."

"I remember this." Justice bitterly chuckles.

"Anyway—" I continue.

"She refused to fuck ya because of that bullshit," he interprets for himself.

"That is *not* what happened."

"Well, I'd refuse ya, giving her a bullshit ultimatum like that."

"She didn't have to have sex with me." My eyes lower to the bar top. "I just wanted her to sleep with me again. Sleep next to me." I turn my focus toward the pool tables, keeping my eyes from him. "Ever just want to sleep next to a woman because she's warm and feels good, and you just need to hold onto something decent in your life?"

Justice remains quiet for too long, and I finally give in to glance back at him. He's holding still, still holding the bottle of Jack in his fist, but he's staring at me like I just professed my soul to him.

"Yeah," he quietly says. "Yeah, I know that feeling."

I shake my head because I do not want images of Justice with Corabelle Conrad in my head.

"Anyway. Evie slept with me. I signed the papers, and when I returned her to the Lodge this morning, her douche boyfriend was waiting for her."

Justice stares at me. Glaring. Assessing. Then he shakes his head. "You are a fucking idiot."

"What the fuck, man?"

"I did not take you for a quitter."

"I am not a quitter."

"You are now." His voice rises as he slams the bottle of Jack on the counter.

"How?"

"You're sitting here, and your *wife* is at a hotel with some dick. Which happens not to be yours."

I glare back at Justice. "That's what I just said."

"Because you quit her." His eyes narrow as he leans toward me.

"I did not."

"You did."

"I—" I have no argument. I'd pushed Evie away before, and it led to this exact moment. The moment when she chose someone else over me. She was taking that guy to her room, and as much as I wanted to call him a dick, he looked like a respectable dude. He looked a bit like Charlie, only buffer and bulkier, and he could have kicked my ass six ways to Sunday, but I'd have put up one hell of a fight.

*What would you have been fighting for, though?*

For Evie.

The answer slams into me. I would have been fighting for my wife. I don't want her in a room with some dude in a suit who can probably talk circles around Evelyn like Charlie can, arguing his case, defending his honor, and winning her over.

"Fuck," I yell again, tossing my head back and slapping a hand on the counter. It's as if I'm thrown back nineteen years ago all over again.

+ + +

*Nineteen years ago . . .*

*"I was engaged." Evie's voice was sheepish, and she couldn't look at me. Her wrists were crossed in that habit I'd learned the two weeks we'd been together. I took her to my parents. She took me to hers. It didn't end well with her folks, and I tried to assure her I had enough family to love her three times over.*

*But her words had stunned me.*

*"Explain," I demanded through gritted teeth. She'd just gotten off the phone with her mother, and she was obviously upset about something.*

*"A week before I met you, I broke off my engagement with Emerson Shaw. He was a family friend. We'd been kind of destined for each other since birth."*

*"What does that even mean?" I scoffed, wondering if that was really even a thing.*

*"It means, since childhood, all I've heard is how one day I would marry—marry Emerson—and we eventually were engaged."*

*I stare at her, disbelieving what I'm hearing. Engaged? She'd been with another man as recent as a week before me. I didn't have a right to judge as Dolores had been around for me, but still . . . I hadn't known what to think.*

*"What happened?" Was she having second thoughts about marrying me? I hadn't officially asked, but we'd been openly talking about it. It was going to happen. We just hadn't gotten to the when, where, and how, or a ring and my official proposal.*

*"I just couldn't do it." She shrugs, her eyes avoiding mine.*

*"Did you love him?" I hate that I'm asking and hate that I'm not going to like her answer if she says yes.*

*"I thought I did, but I think it was more the conditioning. Like I was supposed to love him because he was a friend, and our relationship was convenient."*

*"Yeah, but was it satisfying?" It was another question I didn't want answered. She shook her head, and a mischievous grin curled her lips. Well, at least I have that going for me, I remember thinking.*

*"So what's got you so upset, Peach?"*

*Her eyes avoided mine again, and I knew if we were going to get anywhere in our new relationship, we needed to be honest with one another. I'd always been honest with Dolores, and I felt bad that she misunderstood where we were going because I'd told her where I stood. I hadn't wanted to get married—until Evie.*

*"Peach, you need to talk to me."*

*"My parents don't approve." She didn't have to spell it out. We already knew this about our situation and me. They didn't think the beer-producing bastard, as they'd called me, could provide for their little princess.*

*"They're suggesting I come home and speak with Emerson. Mother already has, and she says he's willing to marry me. He'll accept my indiscretion even."*

*The air around me stilled, and I couldn't breathe. I couldn't be hearing what I was hearing.*

*"Are you fucking kidding me? Your . . . indiscretion." I spit. "That's my fucking baby," I said, pointing at her belly where she wasn't showing more than a little swell and only if she was naked, which only I was going to see. No one else was getting her naked but me.*

*Evie doesn't respond to my outburst, so I let loose another one.*

*"Is that what you want? Do you want to go back to him?"*

*Evie's eyes stay lowered. "Mother says it'd be the responsible thing to do, and I've acted very irresponsibly."*

*I stared at my future wife, wondering who she was. Where was the eager woman on the mountain? Why was she acting so meek in discussing her parents, and why the fuck was she listening to them?*

*"Peach, you're twenty-six years old. You can do what you want, which includes running back to him or sticking with me."*

*Finally, she looked up at me, those blue eyes bright and frightened for some reason.*

*"They promised not to punish the child for the sins of the parent." Liquid pooled in her eyes, and I could see this was hard on her. She'd rebelled for the first time in her life, and it had been a doozy of a rebellion.*

*"Fuck that noise, Peach." I took a deep breath, placing my hands on my hips and turning my gaze away from her for a minute. After taking another breath that did nothing to calm me, I turned back to her, narrowing my eyes. "It's him or me, Evie. Your choice."*

*A tear rolled down her cheek, and I hated giving her an ultimatum. Essentially, I was telling her to pick her parents or me. I also hated that she couldn't immediately pick me, but we were still new in our situation. Two weeks wasn't enough time to declare unconditional love, but I was there. I knew it in my heart before I spoke the words. I was going to love her with everything I had.*

*If only she'd pick me.*

*"Peach," I quietly said her name. "Are you with me?" I was holding my breath. I'm not certain my heart even beat as I waited out the longest sixty seconds of my life.*

*"I'm with you, Ranger."*

+ + +

While my heart is racing, and I fear what I'd find on the other side of this hotel door, I can't let it happen. I can't let her choose another man without putting up a damn good fight. I hammer on her hotel door, my palm flat to emphasize the urgency.

"Evie, open up."

Any second, I was going to draw attention to myself, and someone was going to call security if Cora even had any at the Lodge. That would be the moment I broke in the damn door between my wife and me.

When the door slowly opens, Evelyn's body fills the sliver of space. Before me stands a solemn woman, eyes swollen from tears, face ruddy and raw. Her eyes remain lowered as her hand clutches the door like the wood is holding her up.

"Peach?"

She shakes her head and steps back into the room, leaving the door slightly ajar. While the vein in my neck pulses, I enter the room to find Evie as the only occupant. She crawls back up on the bed and curls into herself, and I shut the door behind me. Quiet tears shake her body.

"No, baby," I hiss. Climbing up behind her, I tuck her under my arms and pull her back to my chest. To my surprise, she rolls to face me. Her fingers clutch at my shirt, and I hold her tighter to me. I can't get her close enough. I want to kiss the tears off her face and bury myself inside her, and make her forget about another guy, as I did all those years ago.

That night, nineteen years ago, I made love to Evie all night long, reminding her how good we were together. The next morning, we went house hunting and eventually selected our home. Maturity told me I should not use sex to heal her aching heart now. Instead, I needed to press her to me while my own heart was ripping in half. I could do this for her. I could allow her to have her tears for another man.

"Do you need me to kick his ass?"

She shakes her head, tightening her fingers in my tee and nuzzling her nose into my collar.

"Did he touch you?" I'll kill him if he harmed her. I'd also like to kill him if he touched her, but I accept there might have been a goodbye kiss. At least, I hope there was a goodbye. *Fuck the kiss.*

I have to ask. "Is he waiting for you somewhere?"

She shakes her head again.

"Are you waiting for him?" I whisper, afraid of her answer, but still clutching her tighter to me.

"No," she says and finally looks up at me. Her eyes are full of tears, and I've never seen her so sad. Although sad is the wrong word. I have seen her sad. Today, she looks lost.

I press a kiss to her forehead, and she tips back, her expression pleading, her eyes begging. I know what she's silently asking of me, but I can't give it to her. I can't be her rebound. He was the rebound, and now he's gone.

Cupping the back of her head, I pull her back to my chest, closing my eyes against the fight to take her mouth like she wanted.

I will not fuck my wife.

I will *not* fuck her.

I will lie here and hold her.

I will love her.

For as long as I live, I will love her no matter how much I've hurt her, no matter how much she's hurting.

"I won't let go, Peach," I whisper to the top of her head, pressing her into me. I hold her as if I can pull her inside me where she already lives in my soul.

# Chapter 22
# It Was Always Him

[Evie]

Sometime during the evening, or maybe the middle of the night, James leaves me alone in the hotel room. I'd fallen asleep and slept for nine hours, a new record. I was emotionally worn out between the two men in my life and lay on the bed staring at the ceiling when I woke.

Admittedly, I'd come to the conclusion there was really only one man in my life—James.

He always would be a part of me, even if we needed to be apart. We'd been saying our I love yous muddled in with our goodbye, and while I no longer had Dalton in my life, it was time to move on. Dalton had been a spark that taught me my flame could still ignite. Maybe not a full fire, maybe not a roaring burn, maybe not a forest inferno, but a flame nonetheless, and it was time.

James did not want me.

Still, I wondered why he returned to my hotel room. *What was he doing here?* He thought my tears were for another man, but they were for everything. There was a loss with Dalton, but the greater loss was James. I'd been telling him I loved him. I'd practically begged him to kiss me. However, James drew a line, and that line was yesterday when I looked up at him, begging my husband to want me again.

He didn't.

I needed to just let him go. I couldn't seem to break through all the pain he carried, all the pain he caused me. He'd been saying things loud and clear for years with his absence, and despite pretty words professed yesterday morning, I had to accept what he was telling me. He loves me, but he doesn't want me. We'd always be in each other's soul, in the place where Michael rested, but we would not be part of each other's bodies. It was just too much for him.

And I couldn't see a way to make it work between us.

I roll off the bed and take a shower, which eventually turns cold. While I want nothing more than to crawl back into the four-poster bed before me, I had one last thing to do in this town before I returned to Savannah. I check out of the Lodge. I'd overstayed by another night, missing check-out yesterday morning, and I briefly wonder how I hadn't been kicked out yet. I'm packing my things in the back of my Jeep when Cora startles me.

"I'm sorry to see you go," Corabelle says to me in the parking lot. It's a strange comment, considering we weren't friends before, and I'm trying to pretend I didn't see her tucked under Justice's arms at the clubhouse.

"That's nice of you, Cora, but I need to get back to Savannah." However, I didn't feel a burning desire to return there.

Cora shakes her head, staring off in the distance. "Is that where you belong?" Her words are harsh and a bit contrived.

"I think it's best," I state even though I don't believe that. However, I don't know why I'm offering this woman anything.

"Best for you or for James?"

"I'm not certain that's any of your business," I snap, placing my hands on my hips as I stand at the back of my Jeep.

"It's funny whose business it is in this town, Evelyn Sue. The Harringtons *are* this town in many ways, and picking your son's name to represent our community center is a big deal."

"That wasn't my decision," I snark, as I hadn't had any part in the decision to construct a community center or who to name it after for that matter.

"No, it had been mine." Cora narrows her bright eyes at me. She's petite in stature, but her attitude makes up for it. Perhaps that's the reason she's always been a bit saucy and sassy.

"Why would you do that, Cora?" I honestly want to know. What is the benefit of naming a damn building after my child?

"For one, it's a community center, and as I said, the Harringtons are a large part of this town." She means the brewery, which employs many from the area as well as Charlie being the mayor and Billy owning a thriving business downtown. When I consider Roxanne owns a bookstore and Mati Harrington lives with Denton Chance on his grandmother's property, which will be a vineyard soon enough, it's as if the Harringtons are spreading like a vine.

"But I'd also hoped it would bring you home." Cora stares at me. "This is where you belong, Evie." It's one of the nicest and most ridiculous things she could say to me.

"You hardly know me, Cora." I mean, honestly, we've known *of* each other for years, but we aren't in the same circle of friends. Then again, Matilda Rathstone hadn't been friends with Cora, yet I've heard they are best friends now. Funny how life changes things, like maturity and perspective.

"I might know more about you than you think." She holds my gaze, but I have no idea what she means, and I'm about to ask when I hear a motorcycle off in the distance. For half a second, I hold my breath, thinking James has come back for me. Then I laugh at myself as the size of the man on the bike tells me it isn't my soon-to-be ex-husband.

"That's my ride," Cora says, tipping her head toward the approaching biker, and I smile at her.

Yep, funny where life can lead people, and how people can change where they're headed.

+ + +

I find myself outside James's front door. After knocking, I decide to just let myself in. I still have a house key, and surprisingly, it still works. Once I'm inside, I immediately head to the kitchen for some reason. Old habits die hard, I guess, but then I panic.

*What if he has someone here with him?*

Can I see him with another woman again?

After witnessing the woman on his lap two weeks ago, I'd be in my first fight ever if I saw him with someone else. It almost makes me laugh to consider his reaction to Rusty Miller at the clubhouse. Then I remember his reaction to Dalton. *Nothing*. James did nothing, said nothing. He just stood behind me, waiting out my reaction before stepping away.

I stand in the kitchen, leaning against our old island. It's a small square room with an entrance to the hall and another to the dining room. James was gone quite a bit when we first bought this house, working in search and rescue, still seeking adventure while I was home with a newborn baby. I'd given up my job when I broke the engagement to Emerson Shaw. I wanted a clean slate, and little did I know, it would happen in Blue Ridge.

In this home, I decorated and painted walls. I started my hobby, which turned to a business and eventually became my income. There were just as many memories of me and my personal journey in this house as there was the path I led as mother to Michael and wife to James. However, I was done with this house. It wasn't mine anymore and hadn't been for a long time.

After removing the folded papers from my bag, I smooth them over the counter and search for a pen in my bag next. As I'm doing this, the front door opens, and James enters with a dog at his ankles.

"Treat," James says, and the dog rushes for the kitchen where I stand frozen by the island. James looks up and notices me, stopping himself inside the kitchen entrance.

"Evie?"

I drop my gaze when the dog comes to me, jumping up at my arm and throwing me off balance a bit. My bag falls off my shoulder and lands on the floor.

"When did you get a dog?" I'd noticed the Husky the night I brought James home, but he hadn't come up in our limited conversations since that night. James scratches at the back of his head, lowering his eyes to the dog, rummaging in my bag.

"Silver. No." James steps forward, and the dog backs up, hopping off for the dining room.

"Silver?" I chuckle at the animal's bounding energy.

"Yeah, the Lone Ranger and his steed, Silver." James laughs nervously. "But it's really more because of his coloring." The Siberian

Husky has a coat of snow white and peppered silver, plus incredible blue eyes.

"When did you get him?" The dog rushes back into the kitchen, and James leans forward, capturing the sides of his dog's neck, aggressively scratching at him.

"It's kind of a strange story," he begins, focusing on the animal while I wait to hear this tale. James looks up at me and quickly looks away, still rubbing at Silver's neck. "I'd gone to the ridge. It was springtime but not quite Michael's birthday."

My hands reach out for the island, spreading my arms to hold me upright. I stare at James's hands, stroking the dog.

"I was sitting there, just mindless . . . and then this dog appears out of nowhere. Like he just walked up that damn mountainside."

"James," I whisper-hiss, shaking my head and closing my eyes.

"It's not much different than finding a dragonfly on your arm at Michael's funeral."

My eyes pop open, and I lift my head to find James watching me.

As we stood next to Michael's grave, the place he'd permanently rest next to James's grandfather, a dragonfly appeared out of nowhere and landed on my arm. I took it as a strange sign that my baby was there. He wanted me to be okay while he knew I was still a wreck. He wanted me to know he was okay even when I couldn't accept his young life was over.

I nod at James, accepting his tale of the dog while disbelieving it can be anything more than a lost animal in the woods. A beautiful creature who found my James when he needed companionship and compassion.

James stands tall, releasing the dog, and I hold out a hand for the beloved pet. He licks my hand, sniffs at my wrist, and then yips once. I flinch although I'm not frightened. He just startled me.

"So what are you doing here?" James asks as the dog saunters out of the kitchen, and I recall why I stopped here.

"I'm leaving town." My lips twist side to side, anxious with my explanation for some reason. "And I thought I'd come by and sign these for you."

I press the papers across the countertop. James's eyes drift to them, but he doesn't need to see them up close to know what they are. This reminds me that I was looking for a pen when I dropped my purse, and the contents still lay just outside it thanks to the dog. I bend for my bag, but when I stand, James has rounded the island and bats the accessory out of my hand, forcing it back to the floor.

"What the—?"

"Is this what you want?" he asks me, crowding my space as his body stands flush with mine but not touching me.

I stare up at his blue eyes, looking from one to the other for a second before answering him.

"It doesn't matter what I want," I tell him, believing those words. What I want is to turn back time on so many things. Some can be undone. Some cannot.

"Evie." James takes a deep breath, and I feel the brush of air against my face. "Tell me what you want."

My eyes pinch, taking in the drop in his rugged tone. He's nearly growling at me as he leans forward, so my breasts brush against his chest. Layers of clothing prevent contact. His quilted flannel. My jean jacket. I stare at him, uncertain what he's asking of me.

"I can't," I whisper as my gaze lowers for his lips. Those lips that kissed me good night every night and sucked at my breasts. Those lips that captured my fingers the other night and pulled at my clit once upon a time.

"Peach," he groans, the weight of his chest pressing against mine, firm, solid, knowing. "Tell me."

"Kiss me," I say, swallowing my pride as my heart hammers and blood races through my veins. *Kiss me one last time.* James crashes his mouth against mine while his hand cups my jaw in that way he does where I fit in the curve of his thumb and forefinger. His mouth takes mine like I'm his last drink, his last breath. His tongue rushes forward, and I'm leaning back against the island at the sudden intrusion. My head tilts, deepening the kiss as my arms wrap around his neck, fingertips rubbing up the back of his head.

"This all you want?" he asks against my mouth, taking it again before I can answer him. He tilts his head, coming at me from the opposite angle, dipping his tongue deep once again. He releases me and sips at my jaw, blazing a trail to my ear. "Tell me what else."

The growl in my ear sends shivers down my spine, which don't go unnoticed by James.

"Tell me." He groans again, biting at my neck and then sucking at the skin.

"More," I whisper, closing my eyes, wanting so much more yet afraid to tell him. If he suddenly pulls away, if he suddenly rejects me, it will be the final straw.

"What's more, Peach?"

"Everything."

"Gonna need to be specific, baby." His lips suck hard at my neck, and I'm certain he's leaving a mark, imprinting himself on my skin as though he has in my heart.

"I want you to fuck me." I've surprised myself with the request as well as the tone of my voice. James halts, pulling back to look me directly in the eyes. The eyes he claims he can't gaze upon. The look in them is one he no longer wants to see.

"You want that?" His smoky voice ripples over my skin, shooting straight to one desperate spot on me.

"Yes." I exhale, but before the last breath escapes me, his mouth crashes mine again. With hands at my hips, he lifts me for the island top, spreading my knees. His hands lower for my backside and tug me to the edge, pressing me against the hard ridge in his jeans. We're kissing as though we've never kissed before, and we'll never kiss again, and I can't get my mouth close enough to his. My jean jacket is roughly removed from my shoulders, and I shrug out of it without breaking from his lips. I yank at the snaps on his quilted flannel, spreading it wide to feel the softest of T-shirts underneath. James shucks the flannel.

With two hands back on my cheeks, my fingers lower for his belt, working it through the latch. James releases me and starts removing my boots, tossing them to the floor. He rushes to shove my dress up to my hips at the same time his mouth comes back to mine, drawing me into another lengthy kiss before pulling away.

"Ain't no going back again, Peach," he warns me, but I'm so worked up I can't think. Despite six years of distance, James is just as firm as ever, and I tug at his T-shirt to feel his skin. He yanks it over his head in that one-handed removal all men have perfected, and then he's tugging at my underwear. Once he has them over my hips, he yanks them down my legs, and I fall back on the island, catching my head before it hits the surface. He gazes down at my body, and his eyes smolder while his large hands rub up my thighs, spreading me wider.

"Jesus, Peach," he hisses, staring down at my center laid out on display for him on the counter. We've never done it like this, so reckless and carefree in broad daylight in our kitchen. *Our* kitchen.

His hands skim up my thighs over my pelvis to my belly. Curling over my sides, he pulls me upright and continues lifting his hands to remove my dress. Over my head it goes, leaving me in only my bra. James is done fooling with clothing, and he tugs down the edge of my bra cup and opens his mouth wide to take my breast. Sucking hard, he swirls his tongue around my nipple, and I wrap my hands around his head, holding him in place against me. He twirls around the tight nub and then presses his teeth on the sensitive skin around it.

"There's so much I want to do to you. I don't know where to start. I want to be everywhere at once," he says, tugging the other edge of my bra down, trussing up my other breast and lapping at it before sucking the same way he worked the first. Full mouth. Tender tongue. Another nip.

He pulls back too quickly, and I cry out, but his mouth comes to mine, and he leans me back while still kissing me. We continue kissing, mouths seeking while his fingers tweak my nipple and his other hand moves down my side. My arms are linked around his neck while the heat of me presses against his abs. I need some friction, and I latch a leg over his hip. He's still wearing his jeans, but I want to feel him against me. Instead, that wandering hand comes between my thighs, and his thumb strokes over my clit.

I gasp, releasing his mouth and slipping back to the countertop. James glances down where his thumb circles the nub and slowly stands, still watching where he's touching me. He fumbles with the remainder of his belt, unzipping his jeans with one hand and shoving down the sides to expose himself. My mouth waters at the coarse smattering of hair and the hard as steel erection popping free. Taking himself in hand, James rubs from base to tip and then places the end at my entrance, rubbing it up and down against my opening.

"So fucking juicy. Better than I remember." He's speaking to himself while addressing my most intimate area, and I watch in fascination as he draws himself back and forth where I weep for him to enter.

"James," I groan, and he looks at me, wonder written in his expression. "*Please.*"

He's tortured me long enough. He tugs me forward by my hips and then surges inward, and we both let out an exaggerated groan.

"Oh my God," I moan.

"So good," he counters. He slides back and forth, filling me over and over as my head rolls on the island top. My eyes close from the sensation of him inside me. It's freeing while he fills me, sliding in and out over and over again, and then he pulls free.

"No," I choke, turning back to face him. My eyes pop open as I stare at him between my spread thighs.

"Just want to do everything," he mutters as if speaking to himself, and he bends at the waist, leaning forward so his mouth covers me. I lurch upward at the sudden swipe of his tongue.

"My peach," he hums against me as he takes a second lick. He purrs louder before fixing his mouth to me and thrusting his tongue forward. Leaning back again, James devours me like he hasn't eaten in weeks, months, years. I don't want to consider him doing what he's doing to anyone else but me, and by the way he's feasting on me, I can't imagine it anyway. This is all him on me. This is us.

His tongue continues to torture and tease, and I feel myself dripping down my seam to the counter. My fingers reach for James's head, but he grips my hands and holds them down at my sides, not losing a beat with his attention on me. My legs shake. My knees bounce. I can't feel my feet as a ripple rushes up my shins, and another flutters down my middle. Everything inside me races to my center and crashes together, and I scream. I've never been a screamer, but I scream at the orgasm ripping me in two and breaking me in half.

James increases his tempo until my thighs are quivering. I can't control my body, and I'm ready to cry out for him to stop when he breaks free of my clit and stands upright, grabbing his shaft before thrusting into me again.

"So wet," he hisses, hammering into me as I coat him everywhere. "God, Evie, I love you like this. Want to feel you spill all over me."

He watches himself disappear inside me, and I hold my head upright to watch as well. The power in his abs cinch and clutch as his hips rock forward, back and repeat. He's still holding my wrists at my sides, losing himself inside me, and then he tips, and his penis rubs me in a new way, dragging over the sensitive nub before getting lost inside me again. Another ripple is building. My feet start tapping, and my legs jiggle. James releases my wrists and reaches for my shins, shoving my legs upward and forcing my knees to bend to my chest. I'm in the most precarious position, open to him in every way, and he focuses on sliding into me, rushing to the brink.

"I'm gonna . . . it's going to happen again." I'm warning him because I don't want to be selfish, but I'm so close. I've experienced multiple orgasms, but it's rare, and I've cut myself off sometimes by sensing it's taking too long to reach a second peak.

"Get there," he demands. "Coat me in your juices, Peach. I want to feel you dripping all over me."

*Sweet Jesus*, that mouth. But between the trick of his shaft dragging against me and the open position of my knees plus his dirty language, I break, letting out another loud groan of defeat. My body is betraying me, or maybe it's a victory. This is what I've needed from him.

James continues to hammer into me, but he releases my shins, and my legs drop back over the edge of the counter. He takes my hands and pulls me upright, slipping free of me, and I moan, "No."

I don't want to leave him dissatisfied or incomplete. His mouth crushes mine in a hard kiss as his finger and thumb catch my jaw, and then I'm standing. Flipped to lean over the island, I'm pressed forward. James reaches around me, shoving the divorce papers to the floor, and my nipples hit the cool counter. I yelp, tugging up my bra while James grabs my hips.

"Peach. I need this." He slams into me, and I cry out as a hand comes to my lower back, holding me in place. James rocks into me, driving in deep with this new angle, and I'm struggling for something to grab on the slick top of the island. He tugs my hips back and continues pummeling into me, breaking me apart in a new way.

"Peach," he warns, before he stills, jolting inside me. He pulls back to instantly return, the pulsing continuing as he fills me with his seed. My eyes close as I rest my cheek against the countertop, knowing I'll never be the same.

## Chapter 23
# Bedside Promises and Fatherly Advice

[James]

*Holy shit.*

My breath comes in deep drags as I lay spent over the back of Evie. My arm moves as if in slow motion, swiping up her side and reaching along the length of her arm until our fingers curl together. I press a kiss to her shoulder.

"Holy shit," I say aloud this time. Evie huffs under me, and although I'm certain I'm crushing her under my weight, I can't move yet. "You can't say shit like that to me, Peach."

"What shit?" she mutters underneath me.

"You wanted me to . . ." I can't repeat the word although I'm not shy about using that vocabulary. She wanted me to fuck her, and I did just that, like a man experiencing his first time and his last all at once. Evie shudders under me, and I slowly push up and off her. My dick slips free of her heat, and I rub a hand down her spine. She's so beautiful and pliable spread out on the counter like this.

"Can't move," she says, and I softly chuckle before concern hits me.

"Did I hurt you?" My hand rubs up her back, and I pause. *Fuck.* I went a little rough on her in my desperation. I just had to be inside her, but I wanted her permission. I wanted her to want this as much as me.

"No," she replies, pressing herself upward on shaky arms. As she spins to face me, I tug up my pants, which have fallen to my thighs but no farther. I reach for her underwear, tap her ankles so she can step into them, and then I pull them up for her. Evie's hands come to the edge of the island as her knees bend, and she catches herself.

I reach for her side.

"I don't know if I can stand." She chuckles in dismissal of her still trembling body, and I scoop her up in my arms.

"James," she shrieks, but I'm not putting her down. I carry her to our bedroom—*our* bedroom—and drop her on the bed. Then I crawl over her, caging her in with my arms as columns near her shoulders and knees on either side of her hips.

"Don't leave," I say to her, trying to hold her eyes. It's still difficult for me, but this is more about the intensity of her eyes than the connection to our child. She looks afraid, and I don't blame her. "Stay right here."

"I don't think I can move anyway," she says, her voice lowering. She averts her gaze as if it's catching up to her what we did, and she's embarrassed by it.

"Look at me." I capture her jaw, holding her face, so she sees me. "Don't run away. Stay here a little longer. Stay in Blue Ridge."

"I'm not running," she whispers, and I remind myself I'm the one who told her to leave, so I need to use as much effort to ask her to stay. I fall next to her on the bed, wrapping my arm over her waist. "But I do need to go back to Savannah eventually."

"What's in Savannah that you can't do here?" I ask, still concerned she's going back to that man.

"My equipment. My studio." She's leaving out that she has an apartment there, but she doesn't need it. This is her home. Here. With me.

"We can get you new things."

She rolls her head to gaze at the ceiling and groans my name.

"Evie. Please. I know I don't have the right to ask for anything, but I'm asking. Stay here. We don't even have to sleep together." My lip crooks up because there's no way I'm not sleeping in the same bed as her.

"Live like roommates?" She wears a quizzical expression when she looks back at me, asking for clarification, and I laugh until I realize she's serious.

"Fuck no," I state too quickly, and Evie blinks. "Roommates who share a bed," I tell her, and Evie sighs, looking up at the ceiling again.

"Don't you think it's a little premature?" Her question starts my heart racing again.

"Everything we do is fast, Peach. This is us." She looks at me again. "We'll take it one step at a time. First, we nap." I collapse my arm and lower my head to the pillow looking at her. I can't believe she's in our bed again. I can't believe she's this close to me, or we did what we did on the countertop.

*Jesus, where did all that come from?*

Evie and I have always been hot and heavy for one another, but that kitchen encounter was on another level. I stare at her as I stroke her cheek, brushing back her hair over her ear.

"Stay with me for a little longer. Just a few days, maybe." Or weeks, months, years. "I know I gave up on us, but don't give up on me." It's so selfish I hate myself as soon as I say the words, but I'm not opposed to suddenly begging her not to leave me.

"A few days," she says, rolling to her side and facing me, curling under my chin and into my chest like she did last night when she was crying over some other guy. This is a new position for us, and I want to question if this is how she laid with him, but I don't ask. I don't feel I have the right to answers, and I don't think I can handle the truth. Instead, I want to hold my wife pressed against me, and eventually, we sleep.

+ + +

"Where are you going?" she says, twisting at the waist to look over her shoulder at me. I'm tucking in my shirt when I gaze over at her.

"I need to work this afternoon." Thank goodness for an internal clock that works when my shift moves to nights a few days a week. As I'm the guy who doesn't have a family, I often take the later shifts and overnight ones so the others can spend time with theirs. Staring down at Evie, I'm rethinking the idea of not having a family. She is mine.

"You're giving me a funny look," she says, rolling completely to face me, and I realize her gaze is just as disconcerting.

"So are you." I squat beside the bed, and my heart beats triple time when she reaches for my face, palm scratching as it swipes against my stubble. "You're looking at me like I might disappear."

"I'm afraid I'm dreaming," she admits, and my hammering heart stops quick.

"It's not a dream, baby." I take her hand and bring her palm to my lips, kissing her there.

"We have so much to talk about," she says, bringing us back to the reality of our circumstances, and while I know she's right, I don't want to talk. Not yet. I'm afraid *she'll* disappear again if we do. For now, I only want to think about her dozing in our bed, waiting for me to find her when I return in the early hours of the morning.

"I don't need to tell you to make yourself at home. This is your home, Peach. This is where you belong."

Her eyes search my face, and I read a thousand questions in them along with some deep concerns, but I need to get to work, and I don't want to burst our bubble. Giant's right. I'm a fool because I'm willing to pretend for a little longer that my wife might love me again and come back to me.

When I get to the fire department, I'm trying to keep cool and not worry about whether I'll find Evie in our bed or the signed papers on the counter as a big fuck you. I shouldn't have taken her like I did. We needed to make love, make up, and then figure things out. Then again, we've never been slow out of the gate. I chuckle to myself, recalling our first time together, and I'm hard just thinking about it, comparing it to earlier in the day.

I'm saluting the chief as I'm heading to the TV room when I hear him call after me.

"Ranger." The brisk voice of the chief catches me off guard. "Someone here to see you." He nods toward the TV room, and I enter to find my father sitting in a seat. I hadn't noticed his car out front as I pulled around to the back to park my bike. My dad used to do this when I first ditched my family, trying to corner me at work until I told him I might lose my job. It was the only thing still going for me, and my dad knew it.

For some reason, he let me off the hook of working for the brewing company easier than the others. He kept his own executive position until he felt Giant was ready, as if always knowing the first son would take over the business despite his military background. As the second son, I was the second string in his plan, but I always thought he wanted Billy to work for him. Young William could not handle that pressure as he was almost as fucked up as me but in a totally different way.

What surprised me most about my father's original visits is that he didn't typically pry into his adult sons' lives once we were fathers. He was of the belief a man did as a man does, and his family is his family. He didn't offer advice or tell me how to raise my kid. He let me do my thing, so I didn't understand why he was coming after me when I walked away from them.

I don't address him as he looks up at me, staring at me a long minute before he speaks.

"It was good to see Evelyn at Giant's wedding," he states. "Your mother said she stopped by the house, but I was hoping you might bring her by again." My dad knows that isn't happening.

"You need to tell your wife to back down a bit." I can't even bring myself to call her my mother. It's not that I hate my parents. It's that I feel I don't deserve them. I disappointed them on a completely new level with the loss of my son, the true Harrington grandson. Michael was a new beginning for the Harrington name after my father had four boys and all of them but me had daughters. Now, it's the end of the line. It was better for them that I finally walked away.

"She tore into Evie," I tell him, although I can't imagine Mother being that harsh, not to Evie.

George Harrington Jr. sits up straighter and narrows his eyes at me. "That is not what I heard. However, your mother and I think we've misunderstood a few things."

"I heard you talking about her at Giant's wedding." They weren't saying anything bad, just curious about her attendance and my absence.

My father blinks. "Were you at the wedding?"

*Nice of him to notice*, but then again, I was purposely hiding out in the trees. I didn't need my appearance turning the attention away from Giant or causing a scene on his big day.

"Is Evelyn back?" he questions, not letting it go that it's none of his damn business, but I don't miss the hint of hope in his voice. However, it's our marriage and our fight. We don't need my parents meddling, especially my mother, who is always trying to fix things. I remember her trying to hook up Giant and Charlie with various blind dates.

"I don't know," I state, lowering my voice and keeping my answer vague while telling the truth at the same time. I have no idea if my wife will stay or if she'll leave me.

"What are you doing to keep her?" The question surprises me. It isn't accusatory, just curious.

"Aren't you the ones thinking Evie's shit, for leaving me?" It's an unfair statement.

"You know, son," he begins, and I bristle at the label while he completely ignores my accusation of them judging Evie. "We also lost people that day. We lost our grandson. We lost our daughter-in-law, and we lost *our* child, too."

Instantly, I'm vibrating with anger. "It isn't the same thing." His child did not die.

"It might as well be. We lost three members of our family."

I stare at him aghast. *How dare he compare our situations.* "I'm still standing before you."

"But you aren't really. You're a ghost to us, and so is your wife. We miss you. All of you."

Evie's told me over the years that she didn't know how to reach out to my parents, and I told her not to bother. I didn't wish to discuss them on our short, once a year phone calls, so Evie would drop the topic, giving into my surly attitude. I looked forward to her call all year, and I didn't want to waste it talking about my folks.

I don't respond to his missing us. I'm still humming with irritation.

My father lowers his head, slowly shaking it side to side. "You know, I always thought I taught you better than this. Thought you understood that a man's position is the rock of his family."

I stare at him, remembering all those times I'd told Evie I'd be her rock. She could lean on me. I don't recall hearing such advice from my father, but him saying it to me now makes me wonder if subconsciously somewhere, sometime, he did mention it.

"That's a little sexist," I state instead, throwing in his face his age and beliefs.

"No, it's not actually. Your wife is the sweet spot. You're the solid one. It's how your mother and I ran our family."

I don't recall that being the case. Mother was the tough one while Dad was the softy, telling us not to get caught when he found us drinking in the trophy room of their house or when he caught me on a few occasions over a girl in that room. There was only the one time where it was my mother walking in on Dolores Chance and me in my bed when we were eighteen.

"A rock doesn't roll over his wife. He doesn't push her aside, and that's what you did, didn't you?"

I don't answer him, turning my head, giving him my cheek.

My father slowly stands. "We want our son back," he states. "We want his family."

"So do I," I snap, quaking so bad I need to fist my hands to keep myself from screaming at him, embarrassing myself at my place of employment. *Does he not understand I'd give anything to have my son back?* I narrow my eyes at him before I speak. "I need to work."

I'm hoping the statement reminds him where we are and prompts him to leave.

"Bring Evelyn home to us, son. Come home, too."

I stare at him, ready to admit I'm trying, that I'm hoping, but I need to bring Evie to me first, and that's a long climb up a steep mountain. My palms sweat with the thought. We've already gone over the cliff, and I just don't know if I can save us.

My dad steps up to me, patting my shoulder in what I take as patronizing.

"Be the rock I know you can be."

With that, he exits, leaving me feeling more like a volcano ready to erupt and break apart everything under my siege.

# Chapter 24
# Aftereffects

[Evie]

After hearing James leave the house, I slip from bed both sore and confused.

*What had we done?*

However, I can't fight the smile on my face or the giggle tickling my throat.

Deciding I need a shower before I can function, I roll from the bed and find Silver on the floor next to my side of the bed.

"Hey, baby," I whisper to him, and his head perks up. A noise comes from his throat as if he's answered me, and I stand, walking around the room to discover my dress and boots along with my bag have been brought to the bedroom. I enter our old bathroom finding it absent of everything feminine. It isn't so much that James erased me, but the empty shelf where my personal items once sat in the medicine cabinet is a reminder I haven't been here in years.

When I enter the shower, I'm engulfed in the scent of James. His bodywash. His shampoo. I'm no longer part of this space, and I wonder if anyone else has been here. Has he brought someone to our house? Had he taken someone to our bed? Had he had a shower with another woman? These are thoughts I shouldn't think, but it's difficult to dismiss them, and in light of my recent break from Dalton, it's also unfair.

I have no more tears left for the emotional roller coaster I've been on. I could sleep for a hundred years, but a warm bed is not where I need to be. Depression is a lingering possibility, but I fought it with therapy and exercise. Years ago, a routine helped me level out my life and move forward as best I could.

On that note, I need to work. My few days in Blue Ridge has turned into two weeks, and with James's invitation to stay a little longer, I need to make some decisions. We have so much to discuss, and I'm not hopeful we can just pick up where we left off before Michael. We're both different people now because of Michael and because of a decision we've made without the other. We need time to navigate what happened earlier. If it's even something to ponder, or was it a fluke? Were we just worked up and giving in to a suppressed craving for each other? Or was that the closure we needed?

I don't want to consider such thoughts, especially with everything else racing around in my head. Instead, I finish my shower, dress in day-old clothes, and head to my Jeep for my suitcase in hopes of something fresh. When I return to the house, I take the bag to the bedroom, curious if we'll sleep together again or if James wants us to be roommates like I said. Perhaps it's better if we are in separate rooms, but I can't bring myself to take my bag to the guest room.

I take my laptop to the kitchen, noticing Silver is following me everywhere out of curiosity. Eventually, standing at the island like I often did, I open my email. Not even a half hour passes before my mind is wandering.

Then it happens.

I hear a noise, and my brows pinch. Exiting the kitchen, I cross the front entry and stand in the living room. I hadn't inspected much the night I brought James home. I walked these rooms but didn't look at anything in particular. Michael's room on the second floor had been my destination.

Amidst the old couch and James's favorite chair, my mind plays tricks on me. I hear laughter. The soft cackle of a young boy laughing in an infectious manner. I turn for the staircase, and my imagination recognizes the sound of growing feet pounding up the staircase in haste. In my mind's eye, I see him sitting in this living room with a Braves game on, hear him yelling at the television set over a bad call from the umps.

I don't believe in ghosts, and I don't feel Michael's presence here, but it's too much.

Another noise draws my attention, and I follow it, eventually coming to the laundry room to remember Silver, finding him curled up on a doggie pillow, yipping in his sleep.

"Jesus, Silver. You scared the crap out of me." I lower to pat him, hesitant as he doesn't know me, and I don't know anything about him other than the crazy story James told me. My fingers spread in his soft fur, and I scratch along his neck as James did. I'd once been told never to look a dog in the eye, but I can't help noticing the crisp blue watching me.

"Where did you come from?" I whisper to him, and he lowers his nose, nudging at my wrists. Leaning forward, I press a kiss to his head, inhaling his doggy scent and noticing a woodsy fragrance to him. He lowers to his belly, melting under my attention to his ears, but I don't know what I'm supposed to do with him. Does he need to go for a walk? How about food?

I have no instructions for him, but notice he's stocked in both water and nourishments.

*"Mom, can we get a dog?"* I hear it in my head. Michael's sweet voice mixed with a whining beg. I don't know why I never said yes. I should have said yes a little more often.

On that note, I decide I need to get out of this house. While it isn't haunted, it's haunting me, and I don't think it's healthy to stay here all day alone.

I send a quick text to James wondering if there's anything special to do with Silver, but when he doesn't answer me in ten minutes, I leave the dog where he is and get out of the house.

+ + +

Once I'm in town, I wander the streets as I did a week ago without entering anywhere. Eventually, I find myself meandering along the route intended to be the future walking path.

James and I still have yet to discuss the community center and his involvement, if any, in its development. I'd learned some information from an internet search, but I really wanted him to give me the particulars. Stepping outside of town, I walk east, sticking along the soft gravel edge of the road leading to the old First Church property. It was a beautiful old building, and I never imagined one could turn a church into something other than it was intended—a place of worship. But I understand that the place is antiquated, and if the congregation had other land to build on, it might have been cheaper than renovating this original building.

As I near the site, I'm surprised to see quite a few vans and trucks for a Sunday. A cameraman is following around a man dressed like a too-polished construction worker while another group of men lingers near the hood of a truck. Drawing closer to the vehicle, I don't recognize anyone and simply wave. I take a moment to stare at the old building, imagining it polished up and spiffy both inside and out. I picture Michael at an event inside—maybe attending a Halloween party. Perhaps he'd be outside, playing on the future ballfield, winning a championship game. Maybe he'd even hang out on a swing even though he was old for play equipment. Whatever he might have done here, he would have liked the center.

*"Cool,"* he would have said, knowing it was to bear his name. Children will come here for years, families, too, and hopefully, they'll recall the spirit of a boy who loved his town.

"Excuse me," I call out to one of the workers near the truck. "Can you tell me when the groundbreaking ceremony will be?"

The website for the park district still said date to be announced, and I didn't want to discuss the center at the wedding with Charlie.

"We're on target for the ceremony to be in two weeks," answers a pleasant man in his forties.

"Thank you."

He nods at me, and I head back to town, making some decisions as I walk. Nearing town, I decide to eat at the Pub again. Inside Blue Ridge Microbrewery & Pub, I expect the crowd to be thin for a Sunday evening, but the place is pretty full as I take a seat at the bar.

"Evie?" I turn to find Letty Harrington standing behind my stool.

"Letty? I thought you and Giant would be on your honeymoon."

Letty waves a hand. "We only had the one night," she teases, and I recall the ranger outpost James and I stole from their wedding night.

"About that. I'm so sorry. I had no idea about James and—"

Letty places a hand on my forearm, stopping me from continuing. "I think it was very romantic, and I hope you had a good night." Her eyebrow wiggles, and I chuckle at her suggestive expression. I won't be sharing any secrets with her, but I smile in response.

"It was a nice night."

"Nice?" Letty squeaks. "How is James Harrington nice?" She laughs. "That man is only nice if you mean *niii*-ice." She exaggerates, emphasizing the heat of my husband. I'd be irritated if she weren't giving him a compliment.

"He has to be good," she says, leaning in, and I laugh despite my unease at her suggestive words.

"What are you two talking about?" Giant asks, walking up behind her.

"Girl talk." Letty winks at me before turning to him. "And Harrington men."

Giant looks toward the ceiling a second. "Ignore Cricket, Sunshine. She can come on a little strong at first."

I chuckle at how well he knows his new wife, and she leans into him. "Don't mind grumpy Giant. He's more fun than he lets on."

*Oh boy.*

"Okay, I think it's time to get you home." He wraps an arm around his bride.

"We should get together." Letty reaches for my forearm again. "I need to learn all their secrets from another outlander. Or are we considered out-ridgers?"

I laugh at her reference to the historical term and the name of a popular book, *and* her new word. Giant huffs a laugh as well.

"Woman, you are always chirping about something."

"Let's do something. Is coffee tomorrow too soon? I'm trying to keep Finn out as much as I can while the weather is still nice." It'd been a mild autumn so far, and a hike through the fall foliage might not be a bad idea.

"Let me just check with James." The words tumble out of my mouth before I realize what I've said. I don't need James's permission, but it's more the implication that James and I are speaking. Or maybe it's just an old statement of habit. Giant gives me a knowing arched eyebrow while Letty smiles deeper.

"You can tell me all about what that statement means when we meet," she says, and Giant shakes his head.

"Okay, Cricket. Out we go."

I chuckle after the two newlyweds.

"They're sickening to look at, aren't they?" A man addresses me from behind the bar. He's average height with broad shoulders, a bit of a belly, and pants that don't seem to zip all the way. His hair is a little wild, and his beard rugged, but he smiles as he tips his head after Giant and Letty.

"They're sweet," I say in response.

"What can I get for you?" he asks, his voice deep and matching his stature. He's a misplaced lumberjack, in my opinion, with his flannel shirt and corduroy pants.

"I'll take the fall blend and a cheeseburger." I don't even need to glance at the menu.

"Spoken like a woman who knows her way around here, but I haven't seen you in here before."

"Clyde, don't be flirting with my sister-in-law," Billy Harrington says, coming behind the bar himself, and I shake my head. I'm surrounded by this family today. Clyde turns bright red, stammering as he tries to clarify he wasn't flirting, just taking my order. He shuffles away as Billy approaches, and Billy leans against the bar to address me.

"Hiya, love."

I roll my eyes. "Now who's the one flirting?" I tease.

"Me? Flirt? Never." Billy laughs, and I smile. I've seen him with his forever girl, as he calls her, at the wedding, and he's so in love it's a surprise he still knows how to flirt.

"You did a great job at Giant's wedding."

"Can you believe that shit? Me a minister, and those vows." He laughs at the list of conditions as he jokingly called them during the ceremony and then corrected himself to say he meant vows.

"When are you going to make your own list of conditions?" I ask, and Billy smiles, giving me a mischievous wink.

"Already have a list. Just waiting on her to say yes." This surprises me, but I'm happy for him. It seems each of the Harrington men is achieving a happily ever after lately. All but James.

"Who is that man filming around the old church?"

"*Rehab Dad*?" Billy chuckles. "That's Milton Duncan."

I laugh with him. I do not recall Milton looking like the fine man in construction gear. That man was a builder, bolder, and very silver.

"He's filming the groundbreaking?"

Billy nods once. "And handling the rehab of the church, bringing it up to code while converting what they can. Duncan Hardware donated the materials, and Milton's donating his time. It's been a real community effort."

"James mentioned the ride by Rebel's Edge and Giant's match from the brewery."

Billy smiles slowly, nodding again.

"This Oktoberfest, we're hoping to make enough to donate the play equipment outside and the field renovations."

"Oktoberfest? Oh my goodness, how could I forget?"

"Week before Halloween," Billy proudly states, reminding me of the annual event he's taken from the back alley to a massive street tent. I'd only heard about it through Giant.

"How are you holding up?" Billy asks, softening his tone.

"I'm doing okay," I answer, looking down at the bar top.

"Is he giving you a hard time? Need me to kick his ass? I can set Roxanne on him."

I laugh. "I think I can handle James."

"Can you?" Billy questions, his tone turning serious. *Can I?* It echoes back through me. Have I handled him so far or tolerated him?

Have I done what he asked or enabled his grief? These are questions not lost to me but keeping me awake some nights.

"I think so," I state, drawing confidence I don't feel. What are James and I doing? And what are we going to do next?

"You know, I always thought you were too good for him." Billy teases. "You should have run away with me." He's playing, and I know it. He says these things to irk his brother, poking at the bear, so to speak. I shake my head at him, dismissing his antics with another chuckle.

"Always the player."

"Not anymore. Roxanne made an honest man of me. That's what a good woman does, I'm learning. You did the same thing for James." His serious tone returns.

"I tried," I say.

"No one blames you for anything, Evie. We all know you were too good for him." I've been told this on repeat, along with James's desire to push me away to save me from him. It's all too much, and I'm tired.

"He still loves you," Billy says, drawing closer to me with his arms on the bar top.

"So everyone says, but James."

"What don't I say?" I turn to see James behind me, and I feel my evening coming full circle.

"What are you doing here?"

"Watching my brother flirt with my woman like always."

My brow lifts at the reference to me as his, and when I turn to Billy, I notice the same expression on his face.

James loops his arm around my neck, gently resting it there and kissing my temple while his glare remains on his brother.

"Well, would you look at this?" Billy says, slowly standing upright and keeping his gaze on his brother as well.

"Evie?" Billy questions of me, asking me with his eyes if I'm okay with the position I'm in.

"I'm good."

"Burger and the fall blend," Clyde says as he sets it before me, and James speaks over me.

"Hey Clyde, could I get the same? Evie and I are taking a booth for some privacy."

Clyde turns red in the face again and points at a booth near the front corner. James reaches for my plate and mug, and I slip off the stool.

"See ya, Billy."

"I hope to see you more often, Evie."

# Chapter 25
# Fights and Fumbles

[James]

I was on a dinner break. I didn't have much time, but since Evie hasn't returned my calls, I decided to drive to the house. Riding through town from the firehouse, I find her Jeep outside the Pub and stop. Once inside, I see that damn fool Billy deep in discussion with her, and if I hadn't seen him with his new woman, I'd think he was hitting on Evie like he always has. But my brother is finally in love again. When I overhear my name, it stops me in my tracks, and I really want to know what they are discussing. Instead, I keep my cool, carry Evie's plate and beer to a booth, and we sit. Suddenly, I'm reminded of a hundred nights just like this where she would meet me somewhere for a quick bite, so we could see each other.

"I see my brother's up to his old tricks," I scoff, and Evie gives me a shy smile across the table.

"I don't recall you being so possessive." She brushes her hair back from one side of her face and looks up at me with those beautiful eyes.

"I've always been possessive of you, Evie. You're mine."

Her lips twist at the defensive tone. "You've had a funny way of showing it."

"What's that supposed to mean?" I shoot back at her, aiming my gaze over the table at her once again.

"Nothing," she lies.

"Are you trying to start a fight with me?" I don't know why I'm egging her on, but I instantly recall pushing her to her limits earlier today, and I'd love a repeat. I'm strung tight myself, hating that I had to leave her alone so quickly after what happened, and worrying I'd return home to find an empty house.

She doesn't answer me. Instead, she picks up her beer for a sip, and I continue watching her, puzzling over the look on her face.

"What happened today?"

"What do you mean?" she asks, setting down the glass and picking up a fry on her plate.

"Did something happen?" My voice lowers as I attempt to rein in my temper mixing with concerns.

"I walked over to the church."

"And?"

"It's going to be a nice building. The groundbreaking is in two weeks."

"What the fuck?" I scowl.

"What do you have against that place?"

"I don't have anything against it. I just don't think it's a good idea."

Evie looks down at her plate. "But why? You don't think a building in his name is an honor?"

"Of course, it's an honor. I just . . ." *Fuck*, I don't know what. Maybe it's the constant reminder that my son will have a building named after him because he isn't here to be in it. Maybe it's that it feels like my family went behind my back to honor Michael without me. I just don't have a specific reason other than I don't think it's a good idea.

Evie continues to stare at me, waiting on more, so I turn it around on her. "Why do you think it's okay?"

"Because Michael loved his hometown, and he loved being outdoors. The walking path will be a place for kids to ride bikes and people to wander. They're building a baseball diamond there. He'd love that."

"He loved the woods," I remind her, and her eyes shift to the window at her right.

"I suppose if they built a community center in the woods, then you'd accept this better?" she retorts.

"I don't want to accept it at all. I don't want a building named after our son."

Evie takes a deep breath. "Well, what if I do? I'm his mother." Her words are like a wake-up slap.

"Of course you're his mother, but—"

"But what? Are we back to this where you're the only one who lost him?" Evie shakes her head and crosses her arms.

"Okay. Fall blend and a burger," Clyde announces, setting the plate before me. "Need anything else?"

"No," I snap, but Clyde isn't looking at me. He's watching Evelyn.

"Sweetheart?" Itching to jump from this booth and tackle him to the ground, I fight the urge to do either. Maybe I'm the one looking for a fight because I'm messing this up, and I feel her slipping through my fingers.

"I'm all good, Clyde," she says sweetly, and I can't take my eyes off her. In less than five minutes, Clyde is smitten with my wife, and it's a reminder she could have anyone she wants when I want her to want me.

As Clyde walks away, I scrub a hand down my face, trying to pull myself together. "What else happened today?" I ask, deflecting the community center conversation and her comments with Clyde's interruption.

"I saw Letty and Giant when I arrived here."

"Jesus," I mutter, taking a sip of my beer. "And then you saw Billy. It was a Harrington invasion."

"I only need Charlie and Mati to bring it full circle," she says, her lip crooking up in the corner. She's looking at me, wary of me, and I hate that she feels this way. I reach across the table for her hand, and she glances at my outstretched fingers for a second before stretching forward to join mine.

"People are going to talk," she whispers, leaning over the table.

"What? They're going to say I'm holding hands with my wife?" I mutter. I don't care what this town thinks of me. I just care about the woman sitting across from me. "Are you still my wife?"

*Did she sign the papers?*

She drops my hand to reach for her burger without answering me, and my mouth waters as I watch her chew. She notices me observing her, and her lips crook up again. Her eyes twinkle, and I recognize that spark.

It's an arrow to my heart and a trigger straight to my dick. I want to clear this table and take her right here, returning us to this morning.

She shakes her head at me, and I tip mine. "What?"

"Don't you what me, Ranger?" she mocks, taking another sip of her beer. She knows me so well, and I watch her throat roll, wanting to place something in that mouth to make her swallow.

"You're not answering my question," I circle back.

"What was the question?"

"Are you still my wife?"

"I'm undecided," she says, and the comment strikes hard. I nod once, deflecting again because I don't wish to get into it at the Pub. I'm reminded of when I propositioned her about sleeping with me, and her undecided didn't mean no. It also didn't mean yes.

"I've *decided* I want to find you in my bed when I get home tonight."

"Demanding much?" Her lids lower, but she looks at me underneath her lashes. I'd like to demand all kinds of things from her.

"I mean it, Peach. I want you to stay."

"For how long?" she asks, and we're returning to the start of this conversation.

*Forever*, whispers through my heart, but I don't admit that yet. I don't feel I have the right to ask.

"Let's just take it day by day," I state, and that statement doesn't feel right. *Does she want more time?* Do we need to set a limit? If it doesn't feel like it's working in a day, a week, a month, what will that mean?

"I'm struggling in the house."

"Why? What happened?" I ask before taking a bite of my burger.

"It's going to sound silly, but I thought I heard something earlier, and it freaked me out."

I stare at her. "Like what?"

"Just Silver, but the memories in my head, I don't like them." She looks down at her plate again as if guilt mixes with her admission. "I don't think it's healthy to be there."

"You don't want to remember things?" My voice cracks, choking on the burger bite in my mouth. Does she want to forget all of it? Or just me?

"I don't mind the memories, but I can't let them haunt me." Her eyes zero in on my face.

"And you think I have?" I counter, feeling the edge to fight with her building again.

"I don't know what you think. We aren't talking about anything yet."

I swallow the heavy bite in my throat, setting down my burger as though I'm throwing down a gauntlet. "I think you need to be in our bed when I get home. I think I'm going to lick you until you cry my name, and then I think I'm going to fuck you into remembering all the good things."

She blinks at me, eyes hooded again, and I want to reach under the table and press my hand at her center to feel how hot she is.

"I think you've changed," she says, her voice low, but she isn't wrong.

"And?" I prompt once more.

"And I think I need time to figure out if I like the change." She's had six years, I want to say, but I remember those years are between us because of me, and we haven't been together during that time. "It's going to take more than fucking me on the counter to bring me back here."

*Jesus.* She's the one who's changed, and I like the assertive dirty talk.

"Okay. Challenge accepted," I say, picking up my burger and taking another bite. After I chew, I say to her, "We can kiss on it in a minute."

And within fifteen, I have her pressed up against the side of her Jeep, letting the entire town see me reclaiming my wife because she's returned to town, and I'm not letting her leave this time.

+ + +

I don't find Evie in our bed when I get home around midnight. Instead, she's in the shower, just standing there, letting the water run over her. I can see her through the foggy glass doors, taking in the outline of her body. She's curvy where she needs to be, full in other places, and firm in her ass. I crack the door, and Evie slowly turns to face me as if she was expecting me.

"Whatcha doing in here?" I ask, staring at her wet form, watching water cascade in rivulets down her body.

"I couldn't sleep."

"More noises?" I question, wondering if she heard something else. I've had moments like that, memories dancing in my head when I hear Michael call out *Dad*.

"Just memories." Her voice is sad, and I wonder if being here is too much for her, after all. She looks up at me, her eyes cautious, and I step into the shower, clothes and all.

"James," she shrieks, but I have her pressed up to the steamy tile, and my mouth plastered to hers in seconds. That kiss on the sidewalk wasn't nearly enough to satiate me for the rest of the night.

"You're so fucking beautiful," I mutter against her mouth, feeling all my anger and all my fear rolling out of me as I press against her. My clothes are getting soaked, and her body is slippery. We need to get closer. I tug off my shirt as best I can, hearing the slap of it as it drops to the wet tile floor.

"This is insane," she says, holding my jaw and bringing her mouth to mine again. She kisses me like she can't get enough of me, and I never want her to have enough. I never want her fully satisfied, so she comes back for more and more and more. Both my hands cover her breasts, kneading the firmness of them at the same time, squeezing them together.

"What are we doing?" she asks, as I break our kiss and lower my face to those breasts.

"God, I've missed your body," I whisper, ignoring her question before I firmly cup one breast and bring it to my mouth. I suck at her hard, drawing my lips to the hard nip, peaked from the water, and now tighter from my mouth on her. I scrape my teeth over the firm nub, and her fingernails scratch the back of my head. I move to her other breast, sipping water off her body and repeating the suction until I nip her again before my tongue surges forward, mixing with hers. We kiss like this, heavy and hard, as the water pelts our skin.

"Have there been others here?" she says. Quickly, I return to her mouth, tongue surging forward, until she presses at my shoulders, wanting an answer.

"We aren't going there, Evie. We need to let that part of us go." I mean it. "I don't want to discuss that guy, and I'm not sharing stories of other women with you. I'm here. You're here. It's only us in this shower."

"And what about our bedroom?" she questions, her voice dropping as her hands still against my wet chest.

"I never brought anyone here. *Never*."

She slowly nods, and her eyes fill with liquid. I don't want any more tears. We need to start somewhere, and as much as I hate thinking about her fucking that guy, I need to stop. We have to let go of past transgressions.

"I never slept with him," she clarifies, finally admitting something I never wanted to ask.

*Thank fuck.*

"We move forward, Peach," I say to her, cupping her jaw and taking her mouth again. Kissing seems like the only way to assure her. She nods against me as my hands slip down her throat, over her breasts, and slip to her hips. I wedge one hand between us. My fingers curl between her thighs, over her clit, and dip easily into her.

"Fuck, you're always so ready for me." She always is. Her hips rock, dragging my thick finger deeper, and I add a second one. She cries out.

"Sore?" This morning, we were out of control, and I don't know what came over me other than the sheer desire to connect with her. She shakes her head, reaching for my belt, struggling with it under the spray of the shower. Once she has it undone, she unzips my work pants, slips her hands into the edge of my boxer briefs, and shoves everything to my hips, springing my dick free from the soaked confines. Both her hands wrap around me, and my head rolls back. Her thumb coasts over the tip, seeping a bit in eagerness, while her other hand squeezes me at the root, tugging me gently toward her.

"Peach," I hiss. "That feels so good." She continues stroking me as I continue fingering her until I feel her quivering against me.

"Getting close, baby?"

I pull back a bit to watch my fingers dipping into her while her hands jerk me. Fuck, we are a sight, and I lift my head to take her mouth again to find her watching me. Her mouth curls in that new way, a sly grin on her face as she knows what she's doing to me.

"So wet," I tell her, looking her in the eyes.

"Only for you," she says, and I'm a man unleashed. My fingers work harder, deeper, faster as my thumb strokes over her clit.

"Give it to me, Peach," I demand, needing her to get there so I can get into her. Her hips dance, undulating faster over my fingers, and I watch her move in the palm of my hand. She's squeezing me harder, tugging me tighter, and I can see us both building to a crest. She moans as she comes, sliding down the wall a bit as her knees give, but I have her in my hand, and I'm not stopping until she's on the brink of a second one.

"James," she whimpers. I push away her hands, grabbing myself and bending my knees. I thrust upward, easily slipping into her. I grab the back of one thigh and lift her leg high, opening to me, and she screams. Instantly, I feel her coming apart again around me.

*Jesus.* Has it always been like this? How could I let this go? How will I make her stay?

"That's it," I grunt as I plunge into her over and over again. "Only my name on those lips. Only me."

Her fingers are clutching at my shoulders, sliding to my shoulder blades, holding me against her while my hips move, filling her as deep as I can get, wanting to give her all of me.

"Peach," I groan, stilling as my lower back pinches, and my balls tighten. My dick surges, jetting off inside her with all that I have in me.

I feel like a new man. Like I'm baptized and born again. My entire body tingles with the release, and I'm spent, falling against her a second while pinpricks of silver dots dance before my eyes.

Aftershocks rumble inside her, and she clenches around me. "Woman," I moan, fighting the urge to profess my love and beg her to return to me. Her hands smooth down my back, and she shivers. I remember we're still under the shower spray and the water has gone cold. Slipping out of her, I catch her at the waist and lean back. I stare at my wife, hair plastered to the side of her face, eyes bright from two orgasms.

"Bed, Evie." And I'm thankful she doesn't want to fight my demand.

+ + +

I hardly sleep that night, rolling into Evie every chance I can get. Just when I think one or the other of us is dozing off, a fingertip traces down an arm or a leg shifts, and I'm stiff again, climbing over her. I'm a man nearing fifty, but I feel like a fifteen-year-old. I can't get enough of her, and we discover each other over and over again.

By noon, I need to get out of bed and get ready for work, but I'd really like to stay in this sweet cocoon of ignorance and bliss Evie and I have going on. We didn't share any words other than *fuck me,* and *harder,* and *you're so juicy,* and *I want you again.*

We have big things to discuss at some point, like what's next for us. For now, I've bought myself more days as Evie tells me she'd like to stay until the groundbreaking ceremony. She doesn't ask me to join her again. She makes a decision for herself only. I'd be foolish to believe we can just move forward and pick up where we left off as if the past six years aren't between us. But it isn't that easy, even if I lived the past twelve hours pretending it could be that simple.

After my shift, I'm again relieved to find Evie in the house and in our bed. Standing beside it, I take a long minute to look at her sleeping peacefully on her side. Her hair spills behind her on the pillow, and her lips are parted as she breathes in shallow breaths. Her eyelids flutter, and

I wonder what she's dreaming of behind them. I'm thankful every day she doesn't have the nightmares I do. The sounds in my head. The unforgiving eyes staring back at me. The feel of my son's sweaty hand.

Taking a deep breath to push away the thoughts, I stare at the mother of my child.

*How do I keep you this time?*

Once again, I find myself unworthy of this woman, and my conversation with Giant from weeks ago returns.

*"You want to win her back, then you need to woo her a bit."* I'd been so flippant that wanting to keep her hadn't been my intention. I didn't need to win her. I just wanted to sleep next to her. But I should have known one night would never be enough. I'm a selfish man. I'd want more.

It nearly crushed me to find another man waiting on her in the Lodge lobby the other morning, but when I knew he was gone, it was an eye-opener for me as well as an open door. I'd planned to chase her to Savannah, beg her to come home with me, and promise her I'd do everything she needed.

I hadn't expected her to turn up at the house with those fucking papers. And I never expected to take her on the counter. Or the shower. Or numerous times last night in our bed.

Evie and I were always crash and crash again, but we needed to slow down. We needed to step back before we burned out.

I needed to *earn* her back.

As I'm watching her, she shifts, and her lids pop open. She takes a deep breath as though she's confused where she is for a second, and I lower to sit on the edge of the bed next to her.

"I didn't mean to wake you." My voice is rough but quiet, and I reach out to tuck hair behind her ear.

"When did you get home?" she asks. Her sleepy voice is sexy, and my heart hammers in my chest. *Home.* Can she see this house as her home again? Will she stay in Blue Ridge for longer than another two weeks?

"Only been a few minutes."

"What time is it?"

"Just after midnight." It'd been an uneventful night. "I'm going to shower." I need a minute for some reason. Although I've been waiting my entire shift to get back home and fall into this bed with her, I need a second to collect my thoughts before I ravish her again. Before I can move, she sits up, wrapping her arm around my neck and holding me in place. She looks at me for an intense second and then leans forward, pressing her lips to mine. As she slowly draws me into her, thoughts of a shower are forgotten.

Within minutes, we heat, and I'm climbing over her, tugging down the sheet and cupping her breast over my T-shirt she's wearing. Fuck, I just love her tits and the way they've always fit my hand. Her nipple is a sharp point pitching the soft fabric, and I want to touch her skin.

But I stop.

*Slow down, buddy.*

Pulling back, I look down at her under me.

"I'd like to date you."

"What?" She chuckles, raking her fingertips over the top of my head through my short hair. I shiver under the sensation, liking the feel of those nails against my scalp. My eyes flutter closed a second.

"I want to date you. I think we should get to know each other again. The new us. The changed us. I know how I feel about you. That will never change, but I want to get us both back to that old feeling."

Because I'm not certain my wife loves the new me and I don't think I can go back to the old James. I have changed, but so has she. We are both irrevocably different because we loved and lost Michael, and we need to navigate who we are now.

"What are you proposing?"

"I don't think we should live together yet."

Her hand slips from my hair along my cheek and drops from touching me. *Fuck.* I take a deep breath, continuing on with my plan, hoping she'll follow me.

"I want you back, but I feel like I need to earn you. I need to make things right between us. We need time."

Evie shifts, her body language suggesting I get off her, but I don't move, caging her body in with my legs between hers and my elbows supporting me on either side of her arms. "Time is all we've had . . . and wasted."

I want to disagree with her, but in retrospect, I never wanted her to see me as I was—daring and destructive for a few years. I needed some of that time we spent apart to sort myself out. I had to get my shit together. It's still not all the way there, but I'm a little better. Day by day, I feel myself being better with her. I need her, more than I considered I didn't, and I don't want to lose her again. I don't want to push her away. I need to do right by her this time.

"Evie—" I start, reaching out for her jaw, but she pushes my hand away and presses at me to get off her. I still don't move, pinning her under me with my chest over hers and my legs shifting to straddle her thighs.

"Are you suggesting roommates or separate houses? Are you asking me to give up my life in Savannah to *date* you?" Bitterness rings in her voice, and I stare down at her. "I can't live in this house again."

"You've spent two nights here," I remind her.

"It's too much." She's already shared her opinion about Michael's room being a shrine to him.

"Don't be like this." My voice cracks.

"*You* don't be like this," she counters. "I've given up six years waiting on you. I'm finally here, and you still don't want me one-hundred percent." She shoves at me, and I give in, rolling off her. She quickly sits up, covered in my tee, and swings her legs over the edge of the mattress, giving me her back.

"I do want you." I reach out for her, rubbing along her spine, but she stiffens. I press upward to lean behind her, but she stands and spins to face me.

"We can date. Talk. We can start over," I say, hating how weak I sound by asking her for this.

"You signed the papers," she reminds me as if it's my admission to something.

"Didn't you?"

"I can't keep waiting on you, James."

"Because there are better men out there," I snap, noting she hasn't answered my question, and the glare she gives me is like a stab to my heart.

"What happened to not mentioning others?" Her voice drops, and her head lowers, her hair tumbling around her face. "Some things we aren't ever going to get over, James, and we needed to work through them together, not separately. We needed to support one another. We've already been separated. You pushed me away because you needed space and time to heal, but I needed *you* during that time. I needed you to pull me closer and keep me grounded like the rock you promised to be. Over time, I realized that was a lot of pressure on you, and I needed to figure out me for me. When we should have leaned on each other, we didn't. What does that say about us?"

"It says we had a rough time."

"For better or worse, James. That was the vow." Evie huffs, knowing it was more than a rough patch. It was a devasting blow to our foundation, and it was my fault. Now, she's standing before me again, and I'm asking for a second chance.

"Fuck," I groan. "What do you want from me?" I'm suddenly bone-tired. "I just don't know what to do for you or how to be what you need. I don't know that I'm that rock anymore."

"You never had to be the only thing we stood on, James. I just wanted you to need me," she says and walks to the bathroom, closing the door behind her.

## Chapter 26
# Home. Sweet. New Home

[Evie]

I just did not know what I wanted from him. I wanted him to love me, and I was certain he did on some elemental level, but I wanted something bigger than that. I wanted James to need me, and he hadn't. He'd pushed me away. Then there was the fact I had needed him, and I couldn't trust that he wouldn't shove me aside again.

His proposal to date me was sweet once I took a few minutes to wrap my head around it. However, a night at the movies or watching a ball game on the couch wasn't going to cure anything. Even with sex as our communicator, it wasn't enough. We needed big conversations and grand gestures. Physical attraction had brought us together nineteen years ago, but we needed an emotional connection to keep us in place.

In some ways, I might have been overreacting. Maybe it was the fog brain of incredible sex over the last forty-eight hours and the reality of bad decisions. I'd given in to James so easily *before* we talked, and we needed to discuss things. We needed to come to an understanding about our guilt and blame, both of which we suffered. We needed to accept transgressions, which wasn't easy, and then there was the real fear. What if we didn't like the new person we'd become?

I go to the guest room for the remainder of the night, and James is gone the next morning when I wake. The light of a new day doesn't bring much new perspective other than I know living in the house, but separately, is worse than living hundreds of miles apart from each other.

In need of coffee, I find myself at the diner. It should have been the last place I went, but I need out of the house . . . and coffee. I also need someone to talk to, so I called Letty on my way here. I sit at the newly renovated counter, swiveling on a vinyl stool, and place an order for coffee while I wait with a blonde in her late twenties.

"Evelyn Sue, right?" she says to me, surprising me after she takes my order, and my brows arch.

"I'm Hollilyn Abernathy. I'm engaged to your nephew Jaxson Rathstone, Mati's son," she informs as if I don't recall Mati or one of her twin boys. "We met at the wedding, but it was kind of a crazy event." Her smile is warm and encouraging of conversation, but I don't know what to say to her. I didn't get to speak with Mati much at the ceremony, but I'm certain everyone was curious about my attendance.

Thankfully, Letty walks in carrying Finn.

"Hi, Evie. Hey, Hollilyn. How're you feeling, honey?" Letty asks her as she waves at me.

"Are you sick?" I ask.

"I'm pregnant again." I stare, and she explains. "That Jaxson just can't keep it in his pants, and even though I had CJ last November, I'm pregnant again."

Letty beams at Hollilyn. "I think it's very exciting. As Finn's adopted, I never had the experience. I'm going to be all over you, wanting all the details."

I'm a little worried Letty means it.

"Let's grab a booth," Letty says and walks to one near the back.

"I can't thank you enough for meeting me," I say. "I don't have many friends here." I sound like a pathetic teenager, but I never got around to making plans with Presley or Hetty. There'd just been too much going on.

"Of course. Look, my best friend in Chicago was a gay man, and my sister and I did not get along. I'm taking applications for new friends *and sisters.*"

I love this woman already.

"Plus, it's nice to get out of the cabin for a bit." Letty turns to offer Finn a container with dried cereal, and we place orders for breakfast with Hollilyn.

"He's so cute," I say, watching his chubby little fingers lift the perfect O-shaped treats.

"I love him, but some days, I need a break. A little not so much mommy time." She stops talking and looks up at me. "Was that insensitive? I'm sorry. I'm going to be awkward. I'm just so excited to get out of the house for a few hours without it being a necessity like a grocery store run."

"Please, don't make it awkward. I understand and remember. When children are little, you love all the new experiences, but sometimes, it's difficult to remember to be an adult."

"Exactly," Letty stresses. "I have a million questions about motherhood, but if you don't mind, I'm going to give it a rest for a little bit. I want to know about you. I'm new here. What do I need to know about these Harringtons?"

I laugh. "I've been gone for six years. I think you might know more than I do."

"So, tell me about James. He's the mysterious one. When I first learned about the Harringtons, I had to keep them straight by assigning their profession to them. We had bar owning brother, mayor brother, volleyball coach sister, and then the black sheep." It appears Letty isn't going to hold anything back in her inquiry.

"I guess you could say he's always been the rabble-rouser of the family. He wasn't so much a player like Billy turned into, although James had plenty of sexual encounters that got him in trouble as a teen." Dolores Chance immediately comes to mind again. "But he just didn't care what others thought. He was a risk-taker, and he pushed back on his parents' rules and discipline. When Giant went off to the military, James wanted to be doing something he considered equally valiant but closer to home. He never saw himself running the brewery, so he entered wilderness tactical training and became search and rescue certified."

"And now, he's joined the riding club. I heard that's a new development."

"I still can't make out what that means for him. Are they trouble? He tells me no. Are they honest? I'm not convinced they aren't."

"Giant tells me they used to be trouble, back in the day, whatever that means, but apparently, Justice has taken the effort to disband the old regime and regroup more as a riding club. I don't know if that means everything they do is legal, but they aren't selling women into slavery or moving drugs if that's what you're thinking."

"I don't know what to think anymore," I mutter.

"You know, I know you don't know me, but you can talk to me. I had Marcus back in Chicago. You met him at the wedding, and he was my sounding board as well as the voice of reason at times."

I appreciate this offer, and as Giant and James still aren't close, I don't feel like I'm betraying anything by talking to Letty. Still, I don't know what to say.

"I think I'm just struggling with what to think." I laugh at myself.

"Just talk. Giant says I'm good at it, but I listen, too."

"You know James and I are separated." I'm looking down at my coffee.

"But not legally," she interjects, and I pause to glance up at her.

"I came here to ask for a divorce."

Letty nods. "I did not know this. But the cabin?"

"James had given me an ultimatum. He'd sign the papers if I slept with him. Sleep-slept with him."

Letty covers her mouth. "That's so romantic."

"Is it? I was angry. I'd been psyching myself up, thinking he wanted to have sex with me."

"Did you want to have sex with him?"

I huff.

"Okay, silly question," Letty interjects. "Of course, you did. I mean, have you seen James? He's got that whole edgy, older vibe to him in his dark clothing. And let's not forget he's a bit broody like his big brother." Letty's waving her hands, exaggerating the effect of the oldest two Harrington boys. "But I also understand how confusing it would be. You aren't together for six years, and then bam. Chemistry."

"James and I have always been like that." I laugh. "A rock and flint. Sparks everywhere." James was supposed to be that rock, but as I said to him, that was a lot of pressure on him.

"I don't understand the issue then." Letty smirks good-naturedly.

I spend the next half hour explaining to Letty about how James and I met, and then how we'd lost our son and how that affected James. I tell Letty everything for some reason, including how he pushed me away, and now that I'm here, he's pulling me back.

"He wants to date me."

"How does that work if you live in Savannah?"

"It doesn't," I say. "I'd have to move back here or find a place to rent. I don't think being in the house together is a good idea."

"Why?"

"Because James is stuck in that house, and I *don't* want to be there. I've already moved on. Being kicked out has that effect," I say sarcastically, although I don't mean it bitterly. I just don't want to live there anymore.

"Ah. I had the same issue, obviously, living in Chicago. Giant and I did the long-distance thing, which I don't recommend. I also understand to move your life for someone is not a decision to make lightly. It's a big commitment."

Don't I know it. I'd already done it once for him, and while I don't resent it, it's more the fact I followed him here. For once, it'd be nice if James chased me.

"I just don't know that I can trust him to open up and not push me away again if something else happens. It's called for better or worse for a reason."

Letty chuckles. "As we didn't have traditional vows, I'd like to say I don't understand, but I do. Again, commitment. Let's start at a basic question, though. Do you still love him?"

"Of course, I do. He's Michael's father."

"But more than that . . ." Letty prompts.

"I feel alive when he touches me. He's always saying to me that no other man will make me feel the way he does, and he isn't wrong. It's only been James for me, and I didn't want to ever lose that. I thought we could make it through anything as long as we stuck together." That's the promise he'd made me.

"I wish I had answers for you. I really do. All I can say is we're fallible because we're human. We don't always make sound decisions or choices, and we don't always know what's best for ourselves. Without knowing James's thought process, I imagine he thinks he didn't deserve you after he lost the thing most precious to you in life. Finn is my everything, and I'd put him before everything else. That doesn't make Giant second best. It just puts him in a different column."

What Letty is saying makes sense. I'd already thought of these things myself about James.

"The bigger issue is, how do we go back to who we were?"

"I think that's just it. You don't. You move forward, and the only way to do that is an old-fashioned process called dating." Letty gives me a soft smile as I look over at her.

"So I'm supposed to date my husband?"

"Sounds like it."

"What if we don't like what we learn?" I ask.

"What if you don't? You move forward alone. You've already done that. You've already proven you can do that. But what if . . . you learn you like the new yous? What if you learn you like it better than it was before?"

I consider the sex alone, which has been very different from our previous sex life. We were already good together, but things like countertops and shower stalls hadn't been our thing. It's as if we were revamping our old selves into something new already.

"I guess I might be finding a long-term rental," I say as Hollilyn comes up to bring us our breakfast.

"I can help you with that," she interjects as if she'd been a part of the conversation.

"Okay," I exaggerate.

"Denton, Dolores's brother, has been buying up homes. It's a long story, but he's rehabbed a few smaller places just outside of town and rents them out. I can check with him to find you one."

"Okay. Thanks," I say. "Now all I need are my supplies and equipment. I need to get back to work."

"Silver jewelry, right? You know, when we renovated the place last winter, we got all new silverware, but Dolores still has the old stuff. I could ask her if she wants to sell it to you."

"Well, aren't you just the little businesswoman," Letty teases, but Hollilyn beams with pride.

"I'll make a few calls and be right back."

As she walks away, Letty chuckles. "This diner knows everything, I swear."

"Yeah." I laugh. "So you think this is a good idea? Living separately and dating again. We've never really dated."

"Definitely. You still need space to step away from him and give yourself perspective as you date. It sounds like your relationship might have been instant Harrington fog, and it's never given you the time you need for yourself. You don't need to rush back together unless I'm missing something."

We don't need to rush. I don't need to live with him to work at us. We have all the time in the world.

+ + +

When I get back to James's place, his motorcycle is in the drive. I don't want to fight with him, but I'm mad that he might be right, and I'm doing what he asked. I'm here to get my things and move into town for the next two weeks, so we can date each other.

As I enter the house, I see James sitting on the couch. The television isn't on. In fact, there's no sound in the house.

"Where have you been?" he growls, and I'm taken aback by his tone.

"Excuse me?" I blink, placing my hands on my hips. James shifts his head, craning his neck to look up at me with a powerful glare.

"I said, where have you been?"

"I went out." I don't know why I don't expound, but I don't like his attitude. "What's going on here?"

James has returned to staring at the blank television while I spoke, but he looks up again.

"I thought you left." His growly tone contradicts the fact he wants me to leave again. He wants us to live separately, and that's what I intend to do.

"I only went to the diner," I acquiesce. "And it's not like I knew where you were."

"I left you a note." His gruff voice groans as he speaks to me. His fingers fist on his thighs. I don't understand why he's so worked up.

"I didn't see it."

"I thought you left," he repeats, and it slowly seeps in. He thought I'd walked and ran away again. *Is it running away if someone tells you to leave?* I step toward the couch at the same time James stands, filling my space so quickly I step back with one foot to catch myself. His hands catch my upper arms to steady me.

"Where was the note?"

"On the bedside table." I hadn't even noticed it. I just rolled from the bed and went to take a shower. Taking a deep breath, I try to hold his eyes.

"I'm sorry I didn't see it. And I'm sorry if I made you worry." His hold on my biceps loosens a little, and he strokes up and down my arms. He closes his eyes for a second, and I take another breath for what comes next. "I'm doing what you asked." *Again.* "And I've found a house in town to rent for a few weeks."

"Evie, I—"

"You were right," I say, covering his lips to stop him from speaking as I interrupt him. "We should date. We should get to know one another as we are now, and see if . . . if we even like each other. I'm willing to stay in town for a few weeks to see how we do. I agree with you. Let's date."

"Peach." James shakes his head, lowering his forehead for mine. "I don't want you to go."

"This will be good for us. We've never really dated, right? We've just been wham-bam-thank-you-ma'am, so this time, we can take it slow."

James's head releases from mine. "You've never been wham-bam-thank-you-ma'am to me." I chuckle because he knows what I mean. We were hot and heavy from the moment we met. If we want a second chance, this time, we might need to take it slow.

"I know," I whisper, sliding a hand down his chest. "But we'll try it this way, this time."

James exhales heavily. "Okay." He doesn't sound confident, but this really will be a good thing.

"Where are you staying?"

When I tell him the address, he glares at me before repeating it back to me.

"What's the problem?" I ask, and James bitterly chuckles.

"That's Dolores Chance's old place."

My heart drops. This cannot be happening, and how does he know exactly which home was hers?

"Don't go there," James says, returning his grip to my arms.

"I've already agreed to meet Denton there at ten."

"Fuck Denton," James hisses.

"Nope. This is what you wanted." James steps back from me, giving me space as he narrows his eyes.

"I can't believe this shit." He swipes a hand down his face, and I find the strength to say what I say next.

"And I think this is a good time for us to part. I'm getting my things, and you need to cool off. Take your dog for a walk or something."

James doesn't even spare me a response. He stalks off for the laundry room where no doubt his pup has been hiding, and I move back out of the house. Again.

And find myself moving into Dolores's old place.

+ + +

Once I meet Denton, and I'm settled with keys and information about utilities, he is the one to tell me Dolores is willing to sell the old silverware to me. I just need to return to the diner for it. A new concept has hit me, and I'm thinking of making an entire line from the old dinnerware, calling it the Magnolia Spread maybe. I miss my studio, and I need to make plans to drive to Savannah and back with materials and a few belongings. I can't believe I'm staying a few more weeks in this town, and I'm caught between giddy and disgruntled.

I'm excited that my creativity is returning, and the familiar buzz of wanting to start a project hums within me. Some of that energy I'm even attributing to the town. I feel strange right here, even if this is Dolores's old house. I feel like I'm home when I've been aloof for the last six years. Even though I have an apartment and a little studio space I rent, I've been discombobulated in Savannah. Being back in Blue Ridge feels right.

I spend the afternoon in Duncan Hardware looking for supplies. To my surprise, I find a soldering kit, complete with a torch and soldering paste. I stop back at the diner for the silverware pieces, and I have an early dinner as I'd skipped lunch. Then I settle into my new home, looking up materials to order and forming a plan to move my things from Savannah. It isn't late, but it's dark outside when I hear the roar of a motorcycle ripping down the street and coming to a growling halt before the house.

Still filled with the fever of new projects and a fresh start, I assume it's James. I don't even glance out the small front window of the one-bedroom house. I just open the door and find *not* James on the step.

"Rusty?" I choke out his name, immediately leery of his presence. From my understanding, Dolores hasn't lived here since January or something like that, and she has a new man in her life, though I have yet to meet him. Still, this was her house for years, so I'm wondering what Rusty's doing here.

"Heard a new bird moved into this nest." Rusty makes no attempt to be subtle. His red-rimmed eyes take their time to scan down my body, and I shiver. Holding the edge of the door for support, I try to think fast. I don't want him on my step, and he won't be getting in this house.

"What are you doing here, Rusty?"

His eyes are focused lower on my body, and he licks his lips in an eerie way before his gaze leaps up to my face.

"Heard you're living here alone, beautiful. Thought you might like company." I could tease him and ask him if those lines work on any woman, but Rusty does not seem like the type to tease, nor do I want to appear as if I'm flirting with him.

"I'm good, but thanks for stopping by." I step back, pressing the door toward him, but his foot comes forward, and a hand slaps at the wood. Rusty takes a deep breath, holding his position, which appears like he's coming inside. He's not.

"I don't think James would like you being here."

"Seeing as James ain't here himself . . . fuck James." Rusty's voice drops with a sinister edge to it.

"I understand you two don't get along but—"

"Don't get along? We aren't fucking twelve. He hates me, and I hate him. Thinking he can just join the club and do as he pleases. Taking all the women and turning some against me." Rusty's chest heaves, his breathing growing more exaggerated.

"James didn't do that," I defend even though I have no idea. I could be missing something. Maybe Rusty had a girl, and James did something with her. The thought makes me sick, but I hold my ground, hand still on the door while Rusty's foot props it open.

"You don't know nothin' about your man now," he sneers. I'm not about to admit Rusty is right.

"I know he wouldn't take a woman from another man." I don't know this, and when I consider I took him from Dolores, I just feel all kinds of wrong even though it's been almost two decades.

"Just because he's a fucking Harrington, he thinks his shit don't stink."

What a terrible saying, and I don't have any response.

"Rubbing his nose all up in Justice's ass, earning him second in command." Rusty swipes at his own nose as he speaks, and I worry once again. Is he high? Is he on something? And how am I suddenly connected to the likes of him? Secondly, I had no idea James was considered second in command. Does that make him vice president *of a motorcycle club*? I'm in over my head, and I want Rusty off the step.

"Rusty, I think you need to leave. Whatever your issue is with James, it's with James. Not me."

For a second, I think I hear the roar of another cycle coming down the street, but I can't be certain, and as my falter in attention on Rusty prompts him to tap the door with the strength of his steel-tipped boots, I'm walking backward before I know it with Rusty pressing at my belly.

My heart races. I can honestly say I've never been so frightened in my life. My ass hits the backside of the couch in the position where it sits, and I'm leaning as far from Rusty as I can get, when suddenly, he isn't before me, but being dragged out the door.

Profanity like I've never heard meets my ears as I follow Rusty into the dark yard where James is punching him, and Rusty bends at the waist. Justice stands nearby.

"You fucking piece of shit," James yells, landing a second hit to Rusty's nose. Blood immediately spurts out, and Rusty cries out with another round of words I've never heard strung together in such a way. Too stunned to scream, I watch in horror for another minute before Justice intervenes.

"Enough. Go to your woman now." James gets another punch in before Justice repeats, "Now."

Rusty is dropped from James's grasp and folds to his knees in the yard. James takes a step back, taking several deep breaths. His chest heaves and nostrils flare. He shakes out his blood-covered hand and then looks up at me.

"I'm okay," I say for some reason, and the next thing I know, I'm in the toughest embrace. Two strong, vibrating arms surround me, holding so tight I can't breathe. "I'm okay," I say on repeat, wrapping my hands around the back of his head and stroking over his hair, petting him as I try to soothe him. I've never seen him in a fight. I've never seen him so angry, and I realize he's in this position because of me.

"I'm sorry," I mutter to the side of his head. "I'm so sorry."

"No," James snaps. "No, you have nothing to be sorry about." He leans back, placing hands on my shoulders and scanning my body. "Did he touch you? Did he hurt you?"

"He didn't. He . . . scared me. That was all."

James shifts his upper body, but I clutch at the sleeves of his leather jacket. "No, please. Stay with me."

His head swings back, and his arms circle me again. With my elbows over his shoulders, I lift myself, and James catches me under my thighs, walking me backward into the house. He kicks the door shut before placing me on my feet.

"What about Rusty?" I whisper, finding the past few minutes catching up to me. My voice quivers. My body trembles uncontrollably.

"I should kill him." I know James doesn't mean it, and I cup his face, trying to soothe him as his hands continue to stroke from my shoulders to my elbows and back up. "Justice is on it."

When I look up at him, he's still wound tight. Nostrils still flaring a bit as he grapples for air. Our eyes meet and hold. I refuse to let him look away from me. One hand of his slides higher until he's cupping my jaw, and then his mouth is on mine. We kiss through all my fear and his anger—biting and sucking, and taking all we need before we can calm down enough to separate.

"I don't want to fight with you," James mutters, pulling away from my mouth and pressing his forehead to mine.

"I don't want to fight with you, either." I pause for another calming breath. "And I'm so thankful you're here."

"Let me take you home," he says. "You aren't safe here."

For half a second, I consider it, and James is pulling away from me. One hand still on my upper arm and one reaching for the front door.

"Wait," I call out. "No, stop." James freezes, turning back to me. "I don't want to go. I want to stay here."

James's brows come together so tight a crease forms between them.

"We still need this. Don't let Rusty ruin it for us."

"I can't let you stay here, Peach. I'll go out of my mind worrying about you."

"You said Justice is handling Rusty."

James sighs heavily. "He is, but I still don't like the idea of you here alone."

Placing a hand on his chest, I peer up at him. "Then don't leave me alone here tonight."

"Evie, we said slow," James replies, but I see his struggle. He'd like to rip my clothes off and bury inside me, and I want that too, but we need to *try* to go slow.

"Maybe-maybe tonight, you could just hold me." My voice isn't more than a whisper, and I gaze down at my fingers spread over his tight tee, feeling his heart still racing under my palm.

"I can do that, Peach." He sighs once more. "I'll do anything for you."

## Chapter 27
# Ice Cream. I Scream.

[James]

I never wanted to hurt someone as much as I did that fucker Rusty Miller. He was going to get his own for scaring Evie. Hell, he was going to get it twice for touching her. I'm afraid to consider what could have happened had I not gotten word from our eyes everywhere that Rusty had pulled up to Evie's new house. Dolores's old one.

I still can't believe that shit, but I'd have to process that another time. For now, I need to hold my wife and keep her as close to me as I can, because I'm paranoid I'll lose her again.

We don't make love that night. We just lay pressed together, as tight as two bodies can fit, without being naked and attached. I'd never been in this house when Dolores owned it other than one time, and that time also involved Rusty. It felt like a bit of karma, or bad luck, or just something awful, and I didn't want Evie here. However, she was insistent she stay, and I wanted to honor her wishes. I was done fighting with her.

I overreacted this morning with the missed note, especially since her things were still in the house. Tonight, I would have returned there alone, and her absence would have been felt all over again in a new way. It wouldn't be the deserted sensation of when I kicked her out. It would be the hollow emptiness of knowing she'd left because we were going to date.

It was so backward I almost laughed out loud. Instead, I tightened my hold on Evie, who wasn't sleeping yet in my arms.

"You still scared, baby?" I ask, and she speaks into my chest where her head rests.

"Every time I close my eyes, I see his eyes looking at me. He's on something, isn't he?" Yeah, Rusty Miller had an addiction to shit he put up his nose, but I didn't want to address Rusty's issue. It's the other thing she said, about his eyes, that got me. While our situations were one-thousand percent different, still, the look in someone else's eyes can haunt you. I know. I didn't want that for her. I didn't want her to close her eyes and see Rusty's every night.

"I know what you mean about his eyes," I say, my voice hoarse as I speak in the quiet darkness of this bedroom. I'm still wearing my T-shirt and jeans while Evie wears the same. I couldn't release her long enough to let her change.

Her head shifts on my chest.

"It's horrible to close your eyes and see the panic, or fear, or hate in someone else's eyes." My voice croaks, and I swipe at my eyes, squeezing at them as they burn.

Evie shifts in my arms, and I squeeze at her to stay in place. She only shifts a little bit, perching up on an elbow in the crook of my arm around her.

"I remember when Michael was only one. He needed shots, and he was so chubby. His fat little thighs had so much meat on them. The nurses were going to double team as he needed two, one for each leg. He was looking at me, wondering what these ladies were doing on either side of him, and then they counted to three. As they pinched his skin and poked him, he had no response. Just a blank face. It was only when they pulled back, praising him for being such a brave boy that it hit him something happened, maybe even stung on those little legs, and he burst into tears. That look on his face as he was looking at me." Evie chuckles. "It broke my heart."

I laugh a little, thinking of my own story about a look Michael had given me. The one where he hit a ball at the house, and it broke a window. Our eyes met, like oh shit, and then he burst into tears thinking Evie would be so mad at him. It was only glass. Nothing we couldn't replace.

I share my story with Evie, and for the next few hours, we go back and forth, recalling tales of our son and his shenanigans. Remembering facial expressions and words, and those moments when parents must be stern but whatever happened was really too damn funny. And there were even memories we shared that pulled up Michael's little temper as well as his sensitivity. We laugh at things that probably aren't that funny, and Evie sheds a tear at things she felt guilty about, like never saying yes to a dog.

Before we knew it, morning seeps through the closed blinds, and we finally drift off to sleep.

+ + +

I wake feeling strangely refreshed. It was a long night, but the memories we shared brought me much relief, and we were able to forget about Rusty for a few hours.

As I shift out from under Evie, who is draped over my sleeping arm, she opens her eyes.

"Where are you going?" That sleepy voice of hers is so sexy in the morning.

"Gotta hot date tonight, and I need to go home, get a few things done before it."

"Oh yeah." She chuckles. "Ditching me in the morning, for some hot piece at night."

"The hottest piece," I tease, leaning over her. "Morning, baby."

Her expression softens. "Morning, handsome." Her hand cups my jaw, and then fingernails scrape over my scruff. I want to kiss her, but I'm trying to be good.

"Is there a no sex rule on our dates?" she asks, her voice still sleep-rough and smoky.

"Let's not go crazy," I tease, but I'll do what she wants. If the sexy times we've had have been too much, we can step back. I just want us to spend time together.

She smiles up at me, still scratching her fingernails through my facial hair. "You've gone so gray."

"Yeah, it sucks."

"You look distinguished." She smiles larger. "I think you look hot." Her face turns bright red although I don't know why giving me a compliment has this effect on her.

"Well, look at us. Two hot pieces, fitting together."

"Together," Evie whispers, and I kiss her. I keep it short and sweet, and that almost gives me blue balls because the moment our mouths meet, I want her in every way. Under me, over me, on her knees as I come at her from behind. I want to fill this woman, so she doesn't forget me, so she doesn't want to walk away.

$$+++$$

"Bowling?" Evie says to me as I pull up outside Bing-Bowl. The place is owned by Bear Grady about twenty minutes outside of town.

"Bowling," I announce before opening the driver's side door of my truck. The nights are getting cooler in October, and while I'd love to spend every second on my bike, I'm trying not to freeze Evie out.

I walk around the front of the truck while she helps herself out on the passenger side.

"My mama raised me right, so next time, wait for me." I nod toward the door, and Evie smiles large. Damn, I want to see that smile more often, and I make it my mission to do just that.

We bowl that night and make out in my truck in the driveway of her rental.

We go to Ridged Edge, and Evie holds her own with some of the guys like Bear, Rocket, and of course, Justice. We play pool, and we laugh, and her perfect ass teases me every time she bends over the table. Outside the bar, against the exterior wall, I finger fuck her as she jacks me off.

We even take a day trip to Savannah to gather more of her clothes and all her jewelry-making equipment, plus some of her stock and business stuff, essentially emptying out her studio. For me, it's a silent victory. A hint that she'll be permanently staying in Blue Ridge. We park on the way back to town at a scenic roadside stop, and I eat her out before she gives me a spectacular blow job.

I want to have sex with her again, but these little bits and pieces are enough for now. The building anticipation is off the charts. It's almost as if not having sex with her is winding me up more than actually doing the deed. Don't get me wrong, I want to fuck her six ways to Sunday, but I can be patient. When we finally come together again, I know it's going to be special. Not that every time hasn't been special in the past, but this will be different than the harried meeting on a kitchen counter or in the shower.

We go to the Pub for dinner one night, this time more officially together than before, and I ignore all the stares. I never dated when Evie was gone, so it isn't prying eyes on me for that so much as people are staring at me with her. It makes a statement to the community to sit with my wife, huddled in a booth, holding hands, kissing her temple, and nuzzling her neck. We aren't obscene about it, but I don't stop touching her, making it clear to anyone who wants to question it.

My wife and I are back together.

We aren't perfect. We won't ever be. But we're trying hard to learn about each other as we are now.

And we talk.

We talk about Michael, and we talk about us.

We talk about her business and my work at the firehouse.

We don't talk about my family.

This only needs to be about Evie and me.

"Let's get ice cream," I say one night after I pull into her drive, and she meets me before I've gotten off my bike. It's an unseasonably warm night, and we won't have many more, if any, of these this fall.

"Ice cream," Evie teases. We didn't have an official date planned for tonight although we've seen each other every night or afternoon if I've had to work. We had ice cream a million times with Michael and his baseball teams, but I can't remember just Evie and I getting ice cream together.

"There's a new place called Lick It, just outside of town."

"That is not seriously the name." She laughs.

"It is. I swear. They even have an ice cream called Blue Balls. It's really blue." I'm certain it's only vanilla ice cream with food coloring, but it's a fun name, and you get two scoops in a cup.

"Let me grab a jacket."

When Evie returns, we head out for ice cream. The seasonal shop is a drive-up slash walk-up kind of place. It will be closing soon, signaling the end of their season. It's a little bittersweet for some reason, and I don't even like ice cream that much.

"How did you know about this place?" Its location on the opposite side of town may be something only locals might know about.

"I've been here before," I say after we place our orders. It turns out Blue Balls is blueberry-flavored ice cream, so I pass. I wouldn't be licking any balls anyway. I go for the soft-serve swirl threatening to melt down my hands if I don't eat it fast enough.

"With who?" Evie pries, and I try not to falter. So I didn't date, but I might have been here once when a momentary lapse in judgment was present, and I might have offered to buy her a cone. And then she might have offered to do something to me, and I won't be sharing any of this with Evie. It was years and years ago.

As I've taken too long to answer, Evie narrows her eyes to slits and glares at me. "I see."

"No, you don't see," I say around a lick of ice cream, and I watch her as she licks at the mint chocolate chip on a sugar cone.

"You've brought someone here before," she says as if spelling it out for me. She swirls her tongue around the scoop on her cone once more.

"I didn't," I defend, taking another long swipe of my own. Evie opens her mouth and sucks at the top of her scoop, leaving behind a sharp point.

"Did you kiss her?" It's said in a juvenile tone as though we're girlfriends instead of husband and wife.

"No," I choke out. I didn't and again, not sharing details. I lay my tongue flat on the cool ice cream and spin the cone in my hand to cover my tongue. Evie watches me as I watch her lips suck at her scoop once more.

*Dammit, how am I getting turned on by this?*

"Did you touch her?"

"Evelyn," I warn.

"Did she touch you?" She opens her mouth once more and bites that the hunk of ice cream, pulling it into her mouth, and I imagine the heat of her tongue melting that creamy substance down her throat.

"Evie," I warn once more. I follow her lead and suck nearly half my swirl into my mouth at once. Evie's eyes widen before they narrow once more.

"She suck you?" She asks this slow and drawn out, slurring the words together to sound seductive and sinister rolled into one. Keeping her eyes on me, she lowers for her cone and sucks up another bite, jiggling the cone up and down a few times, emphasizing her words more.

"That turn you on?" I blurt. I don't know what she's playing at, but her eyes are hooded while her expression is hard. "Thinking about another woman taking me deep, shoving me to the back of her throat? Want to see that happen? Want to watch me get off in someone else's mouth?"

"I'd cut a bitch," she says, surprising us both, and then we laugh. Evie laughing harder than me. She's never spoken like that, and she's definitely never been in a fight before, but something about Evie wanting to do such a thing has my chest puffing, my dick hard, and ice cream teasing time is over. I toss the remainder of my cone and then take hers from her hand.

"Hey, I wasn't finished," she cries, her voice still ringing with laughter.

"Oh yes, you are. And now, you're gonna finish me."

+ + +

As we ride off to the lake, and I pull onto the secluded property, I don't really intend to make Evie suck me. I just want to be alone with her and definitely put that mouth to some use, like kissing me.

"What are we doing here?" she says, her voice still a little snippy after the ice cream incident.

"Cooling you off," I mutter when she slips off the seat, and I follow, standing next to my bike. I take the camp blanket out of the seat and spread it on the ground. Holding out a hand for her, I help Evie lower to the ground, but I've no sooner sat than she's straddling me, and I'm falling to my back.

"Whoa." I chuckle. Evie reaches for my hands and brings them over my head, holding my wrists beside my ears. She isn't tall enough to pull off the capture me move, but I let her have her fun for a minute. Her hair dangles around her face as she looks down at me.

"Would you like that?" she murmurs. "Would you like me to watch someone else take you?"

"Peach." I laugh, struggling with the sincerity of her question. "No. I don't need you to watch someone else do that to me, and I don't want someone else doing it to me."

"Are you sure?" She drags out the final word and scoots down my body. "You wouldn't like it if she pinned you down and undid your belt?" As she speaks, she does just that—my belt is unbuckled—and the button on my jeans pops next.

"Evie, what are you doing?"

"Maybe you'd like her to be hungry for you? Release you from the confines and take you deep."

"Jesus." *What the—?* "Gah." Evie has me in her hand before I know it. With one hand awkwardly holding me, she works at pushing my jeans and boxer briefs down enough to fully expose me.

"What are you doing, you little vixen?" I mean, I know what she's doing, but I'm wondering what she's playing at.

"You'd like that, wouldn't you? A vixen to match your fox. She'd take you in hand, but it wouldn't be enough."

I want to tell her to stop playing around and stop speaking as if it's someone else who would do what she's doing. But she's doing what she describes would happen to me, and I'm growing stiffer by the second.

"She'd squeeze this thick dick and wet the tip." Evie leans forward and licks across the slit at the end of me like I'm that ice cream cone. My head pops up to watch her and then falls back when her tongue laps at my crown.

"Fuck, Peach."

"She'd stroke you. *You're so hard*," she growls. "And she'd take you to the back of her throat."

Oh *God*. Evie opens and swallows deep. I hit her throat, and her tongue swirls around me. Her cheeks cave, and she sucks hard, sliding up my length and popping off the end. Her hand takes over a second, working on my slippery, slick skin.

"She'd beg to have you. *I want to ride you*."

"Evie," I hiss, warning her to stop teasing me. Both with her tender touch and dirty words, I'm under her spell. I reach for her hips and jackknife upward, but a hand comes to my chest.

"Lie back. This is my show," she whispers.

Jesus. *Fuck*. Jesus. I fall to my back again, staring up at the heavens. This woman will be the end of me.

"Better yet," she says, dipping her face to my dick again. "Maybe *she's* watching me. *Her* mouth watering because she wants a turn, and she isn't going to get one." Evie's mouth takes me again, and I'm so freaking turned on at the idea of someone watching her suck me, I come in seconds. My hips thrust upward, and I tap the back of her throat. She gags, but I can't stop myself, and she doesn't stop me. My dick pulses, and I come undone in long waves of relief.

When I can't take it anymore, I tug at her underarm, and she releases me. She wipes at her lips, exaggerating the cleanup, and flips her hair over one side of her head.

"You're a proud kitty, aren't you?" I tease, and she chuckles.

She looks down at me and pouts. "Too bad, you can't do more." I'm forty-eight, and she's busting my balls because I'm not eighteen and ready in five minutes to slam into her.

"You get those pants off and let me worry about you." I nod at her, unable to move my body, let alone rouse myself for something else with her. But I'll make it good. Remaining on my back, I watch as she stands, gives me a little strip tease of wiggling her jeans and underwear off, and then she straddles me again.

"Straddle my face, baby."

"James," she hisses. It's not like we haven't done this before, but it's been a while since we've been this wild.

"She's watching you. She wants to see what she can't have. Or do you want her to have a turn?" I tease, and Evie crawls over me, growling once more. I guide her by her hips to where I need her to go, and my mouth meets her center with all the eagerness she took me. She's on all fours, keening and mewing like a little kitten, and I'm loving it.

"Ranger," she cries out, and I smile against her, playing along with her dirty little fantasy. I'm growing hard just thinking about someone watching her get off on me. Again, not that I want someone to watch her when she's all pleasured and crying out with *yes, yes, yes*, but the fantasy is titillating, and I'm ready to take her again. She comes on a loud whine. Her head back like the night she howled at the moon on my lap. Her hips forward, forcing dripping heat against my face. I love her like this. It's reckless and uncensored, and she is just everything to me.

When she settles, I take her hips again and move her down my body until I position her at the tip of my dick and slide into home. Evie sits upright, riding me fast, taking what she needs. Her hands dig into her hair, lifting it higher over her head.

"She still watching you?" I strain as Evie sucks me in a new way, clenching at me as she bounces up and down. My thumb finds her clit, working it in rapid circles while she works me.

"There's a him now. He's watching. He wants a turn."

"Fuck that," I hiss, bucking upward and driving into her faster. "No one's gonna know how wet you are. How you slick my dick and slide all juicy on me."

"He wants it too," she whispers.

"He can just keep watching, bastard. Because he's never getting what's mine," I bellow. Evie's hands come to my chest, and she rocks herself up and down my shaft, lost in the fantasy until she slams down on me, and I grunt. She arches her back, her head dropping forward and her mouth hanging open as she groans.

"Oh my *gawwwd*." I come undone myself, clutching at her hips, holding her in place, and letting her milk me dry a second time.  Then collapsing against the ground—arms splayed at my sides, legs loose and liquid—I'm spent. Evie folds down to my chest with me still inside her.

I blink up at the dark sky seeing my own set of stars after what we just did.

"That was fun." She giggles, and I press a kiss into her head on my chest. My heart races within, but it's more than that. I feel alive, really alive despite the sexual exhaustion, with this woman over me.

"Fun, but it ain't ever gonna happen," I moan. "I will never let someone watch you or watch me take you."

"I know," she says softly, and I search for disappointment in her tone but don't find it. "I was only playing."

"You play all you want, baby. Just only with me."

# Chapter 28
# False Negatives

[Evie]

When James takes me back to the rental, I slip from the motorcycle as I do after each date and stand next to him. He looks at the house like he longs to come inside, and I'd like to invite him in, but I don't. I don't know if it's the house itself, the fact it belonged to Dolores, or if it's just that we're trying not to cross a line, but he doesn't come in, and I don't ask.

However, after what we just did, I'm not sure there are any lines left we haven't crossed.

I don't know where that came from. One minute, we're having ice cream, and the next, I'm getting all worked up while pissed off that he obviously bought some other woman an ice cream cone, and then she gave him head in return. I should be skeeved out, and in some ways, I am. Then I just lost myself to the fantasy, and he played along.

As I stand next to him, I cup his jaw like he cups mine. I'm not half as forceful as he is, but I still work the edge of my hand to tip up his face. He smells like me, and I still taste him.

"Just want you to remember who's the last one on those lips," I say all gruff and grumbly like him before I lean forward and lick at the seam of his mouth.

"Jesus, woman." He laughs hard and tugs me to him, wrapping his arm around the back of my neck. He holds me like this and kisses the top of my head. "You're so fun, Evie."

I laugh myself at that and then pull back. Every night when we separate, a little sadness fills me despite the good time. I don't want to keep sleeping alone at night. I don't want to separate from him, but I understand what we're doing and why.

"Maybe you should pick a date," James says, his voice still playful. In the last two weeks, he's loosened up, smiled more, and laughed a lot.

It's such a nice change in him. It's nice for us. We aren't skipping the heavy stuff. We just aren't bringing it up every five minutes.

"Actually, there is something I want to do," I state sheepishly, looking down at his belly and curling my fingers into his shirt. He's still straddling his bike.

"Anything," he says.

"I think we should go to the groundbreaking event together."

"That is not a date," James immediately retorts.

Not every date is a pretty one, but I want to attend in Michael's name, and I think James should be there *with me.*

"I think it could give you some closure." I keep my tone low, and my voice soft. I don't want to tell James what to do or how to feel or when he should work through his grief, but his grief, anger, and guilt have lingered a long time, and he needs to work through it. Perhaps the groundbreaking ceremony will help. Something positive will be built in Michael's name.

"Not going to happen. Pick something else," he states, and I sense him working to keep calm, but an edge still fills his voice.

"You said anything," I tease, trying to restore us to the playfulness by the lake.

"No." The word is firm and definite.

"Why aren't you even considering it?" I really want to understand his opposition to the event.

"I . . . I just can't do it, Evelyn. Why can't you understand that?"

Honestly, because I just couldn't. I don't know how he can be in that house, surrounded by all the haunting memories of Michael and the shrine he's kept in his room, yet he can't go to a little dirt digging and a presentation in Michael's name.

"I guess, I'll just go alone," I say, hoping a little guilt from me might prod him into agreeing to go, but I can see his rejection is firm. He starts his bike to emphasize this conversation is over. I stare at him, waiting for him to say something. Kiss me good night. Tell me he'll call me. But he doesn't do any of those things. Looking over his shoulder, he walks the bike backward until he U-turns, and then he's out of my drive. I stand there staring after him, wondering what just happened.

Later, I lie in bed, thinking about things.

When Michael's body disappeared over the ridge, a search and rescue team was activated. James was not allowed on the search. His mental breakdown prevented it, and no one thought it'd be a good idea for him to find our son. The local sheriff's department, along with members of the fire staff, used their best search and rescue members before June Barne came to our home to deliver the news. It wasn't a relief, although it should have been. No one wanted to stare at an empty casket. At the time, we'd been on autopilot. Our son was coming home, though not how we had planned, and days later, he was laid to rest near his great granddad. Pap would look after him, we said, though the words were rote and uncertain.

Then James and I began to fight, and it wasn't long before he'd kicked me out of the house. We were nearing our thirteen-year wedding anniversary at the time, but we wouldn't make it to the date. I was gone within weeks of the funeral, and I had to fight my way out of my grief on my own. I'd come to terms with not being in Blue Ridge. It hadn't seemed real that our child was in the ground at the cemetery outside of town. Michael was everywhere else—the breezy wind, a sunny day, someone else's child's laughter. I took the little things and lumped them together to give myself closure by the end of one year. Part of that process had been calling James on Michael's birthday and asking him to celebrate with me, even from a distance. I lit the candle on a cupcake and blew it out with one wish.

*Peace in my heart.*

Forgive James.

Miss my child.

Move forward.

I wasn't convinced James had gotten there. He held onto the house, Michael's room, and his things. He was everywhere but not in the way Michael would have wanted us to celebrate his life. The community center was going to be a celebration of his town and of the people who lived here and loved him. It would be a place to gather for events and baseball. It was a perfect testament to him.

+ + +

I didn't hear from James the day after our ice cream date, and then I received a texted image. I didn't respond, didn't know how to address it. I'd already been feeling like being with James was too good to be true, and the picture proved it.

Instead, I turn off my phone and spend a solemn day at the cemetery. Then I take a long drive around Blue Ridge with no real destination. Just a drive to lose my thoughts in the twists and turns of mountain roads and beautiful scenery.

My phone stays off. James doesn't come to the house.

At the groundbreaking ceremony the following day, I don't feel right about being here. I'm present in the name of my son, but my smile is false, and my nerves are shot.

"You doing okay?" Letty asks me as she stands next to me, and I shake my head. She must feel the vibration coming off my body. I'm on the edge of shattering. It's Michael's loss and James's rejection all over again.

"Just a little while, and then we'll get you out of here," she says, rubbing a hand up my back. I don't even feel her touch, but the collective 'we' in her words settles over me. The entire Harrington clan is present, surrounding me, supporting me.

George Jr and Elaina each hug me, and Junior lingers.

"Evie, Elaina and I wish to apologize." I startle at their words and sense Letty stepping back from us. "We think we greatly misunderstood what happened between you and James because James is James, and you were silent. And we feel just sick that we let you slip away like he did."

Junior holds my shoulders as he speaks, keeping his tone strong but words soft.

"We've missed you, Evelyn. Missed all of you. We want our son back, and we want you home, here with us, where you belong."

Tears I didn't know were leaking roll down my cheeks.

I should tell them about the texted image. I should let them know I'm at the end of my rope with their son. I've had enough from James, but I hold my tongue and let Junior pull me into him.

"Bring him home to us. You're the only one who can," Junior whispers, without realizing the extent of his words. The impossibility of it because James has made a choice again.

And it's not me.

Elaina gives me a hesitant smile as Junior presses me back, and then she steps up to hug me again. "Pillars sometimes crumble," she says as she holds me. "And then we just build them up again."

She has no idea, and I'm out of gravel and mortar to rebuild myself, to rebuild us.

The picture haunts me like a ghost on my phone.

Junior and Elaina step away from me, and Letty is back at my side. Her eyes scan my face reading the frailty of me. This wasn't a good idea. I shouldn't be here. This is one more thing James might have been right about.

It's almost eleven, and the club is due to arrive soon. There's a presentation of their funds, the matching contribution from the brewery, and then the shovel dig. It's all for photo ops and the news, and then I'm out of here. My presence is like a head nod of approval for this venture, and while I think it's a good thing, and truly an honor in Michael's name, I don't need to be involved in the rest of the project. A ribbon-cutting ceremony will take place in the late spring, possibly near Michael's birthday in May, and I'll have to cross that bridge when I get to it.

When I hear the rumble of motorcycle engines approaching, my stomach is in knots while my heart skips a beat. I'm so angry with James, distraught over the image and his absence, that I don't want to look up at the paraded arrival of his friends. However, it's so loud as they arrive with the sheriff in their lead, all heads turn to them, mine included.

I watch as they park, but my eye is instantly drawn to only one biker. The man riding beside another who looks like Sam Shepard stepping off a movie set in the 1980s.

James.

He came.

I want to be excited and relieved. If there's only one thing I know about motorcycle clubs, it's the position of a woman on that back seat. It makes a statement, and thankfully, his is empty despite what I'd seen in the picture shared with me. The picture he sent me off his phone.

When James left me the other night, I had a sense of where he'd go, but I would never have dreamed what he'd do. After we played out our little ice cream scene, I had a strange sense of accomplishment. Like we were going to make it as long as we were together.

From the image sent to me, I see we are not.

I don't want to run anymore, and if this is a means of James trying to push me away again, he's accomplished the feat.

*Message received.*

The bikers park, and I turn my attention to the podium. Charlie lingers, preparing to speak before allowing his beautiful new wife to do the honors of accepting large checks both in amount and paper size.

I remain by Letty, still surrounded by the Harrington family, the ones who miss me, and I've missed them. I can't walk away from them again. I'll mend my fences with them differently, separately.

Letty wraps an arm around me, and I look up at her with a weak smile. I can do this. Just a little while longer, and then I'm done.

James stands with this biker family, instead of walking to me, and it's a statement as to where he's stood for the last six years. He's with them.

Charlie opens the ceremony. Janessa speaks. Justice steps up for a photo op with the club's contribution. Giant is next with his matching funds from the brewery.

Letty gently nudges me, and I see Charlie waiting on me, holding out a hand for me to approach him. I slip out from under Letty's hold and walk to Charlie. I feel like it's the passing of the guard. When I near him, he guides me to where I need to stand. I'm quivering, and my hands tremble as I reach for the shovel. My body feels like it could break into a million pieces. I don't think I have the strength to lift the garden utensil.

The pomp and circumstance of this ceremony is lost on me. It's only dirt and stone beneath my feet.

"Just drive the shovel in as best you can and then scoop a little dirt out, flip it over maybe," Charlie explains, his voice low as he speaks to me.

I nod without looking up at him, and images rush my head.

A large pit. Shovels waiting to fill it.

My eyes blur, and I close them against the past.

An arm circles my body and covers my hand on the shovel handle.

"I've got you, Peach," he says, and I stiffen under his touch.

He's ruined me. Again and again and again, and I've had enough.

We lift the shovel together, awkwardly, and then drive it into soil already loosened for our ease. James leans around me, and together, we lift a small collection of dirt, flipping it over as Charlie had suggested.

"Stay right there for a photo. Just one more second." As director of parks and recreation, Charlie's wife pleads, but I'm done. I shake my head, and James must sense I'm finished.

"That's enough," he growls, keeping his arm around me and guiding me away from the small mound. Pictures flash. Hands clap. There are voices, but I don't hear anyone.

I keep my head down and let James lead me away from the spotlight.

As we step onto the black pavement of the parking lot, it's only then that I hear someone speak.

"Ranger, I need to talk to you," she calls out to him, and I stop short. James stumbles next to me.

"Nope," he barks out at her, and my head lifts. I look over at her and then at him.

"Evie, I know what you saw, and I can explain everything. I've been trying to call you for two days."

I ignore what he says, speaking my own mind instead. "Is she the reason you couldn't come to this event with me?"

"Evie, I—"

"Ranger, this is important," she interjects over his voice, coming closer to us.

James shifts us, putting his body between her and me. His hands cover my shoulders, and he dips his knees, trying to get me to look only at him, but I only see her. Her and him. Her mouth on him. Her eye looking out at the camera, looking out at me.

"Is she the one to suck you off?" The words are bitter and filled with upset. I'm just spitting vitriol, and I shrug his hands off of me.

"What?" James chokes. "No. Ignore her. Listen to me." He reaches for me again, but I step back. We're making a scene, but I don't care. We can make the biggest scene in the world, and I wouldn't care about anything. I'm so over everything.

"James, I'm pregnant." The words freeze my heart, and I stare at my husband, whose mouth falls open while his eyes shut.

I can't believe what I'm hearing. It doesn't seem true. It doesn't seem possible. But I know what I'd seen, sent to me, by him.

"Evie, you know that's not true," he says, his voice not registering with me. His eyes have opened. His mouth moves, but I don't hear him.

"What I know is I have a picture of the two of you from the other night. The same night that we . . . and I can't believe . . ." I falter in my words. I've been in a cloudy bliss for two weeks, and before that, two weeks of emotional turmoil. I don't know what to believe anymore. I wanted to think we were working toward repairing us. I wanted to think the easy chats and casual dates were bringing us closer in a new way. I wanted to think we were going to start over and be together again.

But I was wrong.

My head turns in slow motion. James is still saying something to me, but I don't hear him. I'm only focused on getting out of here. Off this pavement. Out of this town. My eyes land on Justice, casually leaning on his bike. I step away from James.

"Evie," his voice strains, but I don't turn back for him. My legs move faster, my feet work harder, and before I know it, I'm power walking to Justice, calling out to him.

"Justice," I cry out to get his attention. His forehead furrows as I near him. "Get me out of here."

I've hardly finished the words when his bike roars to life, and my leg hitches over the seat. Captured by cameras and a stunned community, I grab the edges of Justice's vest as he guns us out of the parking lot, and I don't look back.

+ + +

I don't know where we're headed, and I'm briefly worried we'll end up at the mansion where James can easily find me. However, Justice takes his time to travel through the mountains, riding easy around curves, and slowing over hills, and eventually, I settle into the warmth of his back. It's a little awkward to hold a strange man, but I can't let go, and I need the mindless ride to wrap my head around what I heard.

*James, I'm pregnant.*

It's on repeat, mixing with all the times I said it to him, and all the times I had to tell him I'd lost another one.

And then we lost the only one we had.

I lift a finger and tap Justice on the shoulder. "I need to stop," I holler over the roar of the bike under us.

"Hold on," he calls back, but this is urgent.

"No. Now. I'm going to be sick." I need off this bike, and the second we pull to a halt, I'm struggling to get over the seat in my dress.

"Whoa, girl," Justice says, catching my arm and trying to help me. I'm barely clear of the bike when my stomach heaves, and I bend at the waist, losing what little food I've eaten lately.

"Shit." Justice groans, and the engine is cut. He's at my back in seconds, smoothing a hand up my back as I continue to retch without anything coming up.

This can't be happening to me.

*James, I'm pregnant.*

"Okay, baby girl. Settle down." Justice's command is intended to soothe, but I'm shaking as I try to lift my head, which throbs. "What the hell happened?"

"She's pregnant," I sputter, not concerned I'm sharing something private and personal between James and that woman.

The one thing I can't give him. Six attempts. Five failed. One lived and then died. This is the one thing I can't do for him, and he's done it with someone else.

"Who's pregnant?"

"The girl. The woman on James's lap. The one he was in the picture with the other night."

"Dammit," Justice hisses. He pauses for a second, taking a deep exhale. "She's not pregnant by him."

I slowly look up at him, assuming he's trying to protect his brother biker, but I don't need to be coddled. I heard what I heard. And I saw what I saw.

"You're covering for him."

"I'd have no reason to lie, so you're gonna listen to me. I've known Ranger for some time now, and while I've seen him struggle with his shit, there's one thing I'm certain of, he has *not* dipped his wick in another woman. It's one reason I think he's so ornery. It'd be impossible to get a woman pregnant without having sex, but I'm thinking I don't need to explain the birds and the bees to you, Evie."

"How can you know?" I ask him, swallowing back the disgusting taste in my mouth. "How do you know he didn't sleep with someone in six years? Or two nights ago?"

"He told me he didn't."

"Yeah, well, he told me, too, but she just announced it in the parking lot."

"She's a goddamn liar and a good one. Tabitha's a hanger-on. She's been trying to get her claws in Rusty for years, and my guess is this has something to do with him."

I straighten, staring up at Justice. I'm not certain I can trust his word, but something tells me I shouldn't doubt him either. He knows the men under him—the good, the bad, and the evil ones.

"I've got no reason to lie to you or cover for him. If I thought it was true, I'd be telling you to either accept it or cut him loose. Shit happens."

I stare up at Justice, his deep eyes holding a wealth of stories, and I imagine not many of them decent. But he's a good man. Somehow, I just know this about him.

"At some point, you've got to trust each other again, or you'll have nothing left," Justice warns me, and I know he's correct. I just don't know if it's that simple for me.

## Chapter 29
# The Chase Begins

[James]

This is just not happening to me. I'm staring at Tabby in disbelief that she's just said what she said in front of my wife, knowing it's a damn lie. On top of that, my wife just ran off and hitched herself over another man's bike.

"I don't have time for this," I say, turning for my own bike and making haste to get on it. Tabby is following me, the click of her heels on the pavement behind me. I toss over my shoulder, "You know this shit is not mine."

"It is who I say it is," Tabby retorts, and I stop short, turning on her and pointing a finger at her. She halts with a jolt.

"You can't do that, and you know it. I'll even have a paternity test, but you damn well know I was never in you." I sneer at her, disgust rolling over my skin. While she might have touched me, sitting on my lap and kissing my neck the night Evie entered Ridged Edge, I wouldn't trust Tabby one bit near my dick, and this proves why. She's a player, and she's trying to play me, but it's not going to work.

However, I was the fool who went to the clubhouse the other night after Evie asked me to attend the groundbreaking with her. I might have been drinking, wallowing in my inability to give in on this one concession with my wife, and ended up playing pool with Tabby. Justice warned me I was making a bad decision, but did I listen? I'd misplaced my phone. When I found it, I went to text Evie and noticed the image as the last text sent to her.

I knew she'd be pissed and maybe misunderstand, and I should have gone to her immediately, but it was three in the morning. She didn't answer any of my texts or calls the next day, and I knew it was bad. I had hoped showing up at the groundbreaking would show her how I felt. I was here for her. I would do what she asked. We could do this together.

I've ruined things again.

I hitch my leg over my bike and bring the engine to life. Tabby stands next to me. In some ways, she reminds me of Dolores from decades past, clinging to a man who didn't really want her. That was Rusty then and now.

"You send that picture to my wife of us?" I ask. I don't even know when it was taken but not the other night, not any time I can remember, but it is me, and it is her, and I hate myself for the last six years. "Never mind."

It doesn't matter if she sent it or not. I need to find Evie and explain. I need to tell Evie it isn't what she thinks, and then I need to stop trying to prove myself and just tell the woman I love how I feel about her.

+ + +

After I've checked all the places I think she might be—her rental, the pub, the clubhouse—I circle back and start again. Growing desperate, I pass our house, my parents, and eventually the cemetery, although I can't bring myself to enter. Michael was never there for me. He's somewhere off the ridge.

As I continue to ride, searching out my wife, I think about how this must have sounded to Evie. I can't imagine any betrayal greater than thinking I'm fathering another child, with another woman, after I lost us ours.

My God, she'll hate me before she knows the truth.

I consider once again what Evie's said to me when we discuss Michael. He's in our hearts and in our heads, but he isn't in our home. I don't believe in ghosts any more than Evie does, but I can't dismiss Silver finding me. I also can't explain the noises Evie said she heard, only to discover it's the pup. Her mind was playing tricks on her just as mine has done. I'm not saying our son has been re-incarnated or anything of the sort, but I believe in some kind of higher power and the spirit of the universe. It's trying to speak to me, and I haven't been listening.

The thought slows my ride, and I decide to check the clubhouse once more as Evie left with Justice. Maybe he brought her there and set her up in a room to settle her down. It wouldn't be ideal, but I just need to find her.

When I arrive, the mansion is hopping with the energy of a ride and the scene Evie and I created both during the groundbreaking and after.

"Not often a man watches his wife run away with another man," some fucker says to me, and I'm on him before I can blink. I'm looking for a fight. When I was a kid, I'd seek them out, wanting to scrap and for no reason. I had a good life, a good family, a best friend in my brother, but I still was out of sorts. Then I met Evie, and with the baby quickly on the way, I felt like I'd settled into myself. It only took me until I was thirty to do so. At forty-eight, I'm coming apart at the seams again.

I've gotten in a few good punches before I'm dragged off the dude and hauled to the staircase.

"Get up there," Justice yells behind me, pushing me forward. I catch myself on the steps and press off them, standing to my full height and spin to face him.

"Is she upstairs?"

"I'm not telling you a damn thing until you settle down."

"Is she up there?" I repeat, leaning toward him although he's larger than me. Justice and Giant would be strong competition in a who's larger contest, but I'd be taking some licks if I went off against him.

"No. Now, chill."

"Chill? What am I, five?"

"You're fucking acting like it."

"I need to find my wife."

"What you need is to give her some space."

I huff. He's got to be kidding me. We've had six years of space between us, and it hits me. I've said the same thing to her. We needed time, but we've already had so much time between us. We need time *together*. We need to stop dating and start living with one another.

"I don't know how to make it work," I admit, falling to my ass on the steps and placing my hands over my face.

"Look, man. I am no advice expert on relationships, but you and Evie, you've got something. I see it lingering and scraping to happen. Either grab on tight or cut it loose. Something's got to give. You can't run here when she's pissed you off, and she can't feel like you're pushing her out. Compromise. I don't even know what that means, but that's what people tell me makes it work."

I'm hearing him, but it's not sinking in yet.

"Where is she?" I ask, and Justice shakes his head.

"Not yet, brother. You need to sort your shit before you see her."

"You know Tabby's kid is not mine," I tell him, willing him to understand it isn't humanly possible to be mine.

"I know. Just . . . take a breath, yeah? Give Evie the night to wrap her head around this day and that scene."

The groundbreaking. She was coming apart, and I could see it across the lot. My family was hovering over her, but it wasn't enough. I should have been next to her. I should have sucked up my pride and my stubbornness and just been there. She hadn't asked anything of me in six years, but a yearly phone call and a divorce.

Is she finally done with me? Is it really over for us? I don't even know where those papers are.

"Why are you protecting her?" I ask, staring up at my friend. I trust him with my life because he saved mine, but I don't understand his dedication to my wife.

"I might know a thing or two about being pushed away, and it's hard to come back, especially if you're kicked over and over again." Justice tips his chin at me as if dismissing me and stalks back to the main room. I stare at the front door for a minute and then make a decision.

+ + +

Arriving home, I find an empty house, and it hits me hard. I'm alone. These walls have been a barrier to keep me in, and I need to be let out. It's too quiet in here. The silence is deafening, but I sit still on the couch and absorb the dull sensation around me.

Michael isn't here.

Evie's words cycle through my thoughts. He hasn't been here for a long time, and I've known it. I thought if I left his room alone, I'd feel his presence when all I've felt is loneliness. I thought if I left this house, I'd be leaving him behind, but I'm not. I've left myself behind. Six years gone, and I've missed my wife as much as I've missed my child.

She's been standing before me, telling me over and over again how she's been waiting on me to bring her back, and as much as we've said *I love you*, I'm not showing her enough.

Our dates have been fun and easy, but when it comes to the hard stuff, I've backed up. Again.

I lean forward, placing my head in my hands, elbows on my knees, and I listen to the silence around me. I don't want to be alone anymore. I want Evie's soft smile, and sweet kisses, and us fucking on the kitchen counter, but not this countertop. Not this house. We need to start fresh, and I sit here most of the night thinking of how to start.

Silver slips his head onto my lap, tucking it under my arm, and I absentmindedly reach down and scratch behind his ears.

"What am I gonna do, boy?" I ask, and his eyes shift.

"I just want her back," I mutter, and his head lifts. He looks off toward the staircase and yelps. I stare in the direction of his gaze and take a deep breath.

In the early hours of the morning, I head to Michael's room.

# Chapter 30
# Borrowed Time

[Evie]

"I'm so embarrassed," I say to Letty, who hands me a glass of wine. "And I'm so sorry about this."

"Do not apologize. We're happy to have you," Letty tells me. After Justice took me for a ride, and I not so eloquently got sick on the side of the road, he brought me to Giant's cabin. How he knew how to get here, I don't know.

*"Thought it best if she's someplace where he can't find her yet. Take some time to cool off and get his head straight,"* Justice told Giant, who met us in his yard.

Giant seemed to agree, and Letty came right for me. *"I was so worried about you. That was quite a scene."*

It was. And like I've said, I'm so embarrassed.

After Letty shuffled me into their house, she made me take a long shower. I cried my final tears for James Harrington, and then took a long-needed nap. Eventually, I told them everything.

Now, it's just Letty and me.

"What are you thinking?" she asks.

"I want to believe it isn't true, but the shock was like . . . wham! . . . straight to my heart." I flatten my palm over my chest. "I couldn't give him more than one baby and thinking he was going to have one with someone else, that just hurts."

Letty smiles. "I know the feeling. I wanted a child so badly, but my fiancé didn't. Then he fucked my sister, and he wasn't my fiancé anymore."

"Oh my God, that's awful."

"I know. I decided to adopt." Letty shrugs. "It isn't the same as carrying a child, but it's still wonderful. What're nine months when I have his whole life ahead of me now?" She isn't wrong, but I think of Michael. You never know how short life can be.

"I feel like there's something more here. Something deeper happening," Letty says, and I look up at her from the bed where they're letting me sleep for the night. Their cabin has plans to be expanded as they want to live here instead of Giant's house, but the renovation hasn't started yet. I'm in the loft, an area above the one bedroom and kitchen below. I have two queen-size beds on the floor, and that's it. No walls. No other furniture fits up here. I sit with my legs crossed and hold the wine glass in my hand.

"I don't know if I can trust him. Trust him not to walk away or push me away. He was upset the other night, not angry, just upset that I wanted to go to the groundbreaking, and he rode off without . . ." *Kissing me.*

"Why was he upset?"

"He doesn't want the building in Michael's name. I think he thinks it will be too much of a reminder. Like our son has a building in his name because he isn't here."

"That's understandable."

"But the decision to name the community center wasn't up to us. Sure, we might have stopped it if we'd known sooner, or perhaps if we had more time to grapple with the idea, we could have accepted it. It's just been a lot, and he's just so . . . stubborn. And I'm tired, Letty. I'm just tired of being on the outside of him and his life." I shrug. "But he won't let me in."

"I understand that completely," Letty says. "James is scared. He's scared if he lets you get too close, he'll hurt you again. He'll lose you, and this time, it will be out of his control. Before, he told you to leave him, but if something else gets in the way to take you away, well, that's different."

"He should want to hold tighter, not give up."

"I agree," Letty says. "But the same goes for you. He pushed you away, and you walked, and I totally understand why you did it. Love takes a fight, Evie. You have to fight for him if you want him back."

"But when do I accept that I'm down for the count."

Letty puts a hand on my knee. "I don't know. Maybe when you accept you can live without him, more than you can't live with him." She's teasing but maybe not. "I'm convinced he loves you. He gave such a compelling explanation for wanting that outpost. It was so romantic that he wanted a night there with you."

"What was James's argument?" I laugh without humor.

"He wanted his wife back."

I stare at her. "That's it."

"That's it," she says. "Isn't that enough?"

In many ways, it was.

+ + +

The next morning, I wake early to the sound of a dog emphatically barking and raised voices somewhere outside. I scramble from the bed in a large T-shirt of Giant's that Letty let me wear and climb down the ladder leading to the loft. Yanking open the front door, I stumble onto the low porch and find Giant and James arguing with one another.

"I just want to see my wife," James grunts, lifting his hand for his head and pacing in a small circle before facing his brother again. His eyes lift over his brother's shoulder, and he sees me standing on the porch.

"Evie." His voice cracks as he steps forward, but Giant stops him with a large paw on James's chest. James glances from the hand on him to his brother's face.

"Please, man. Let me go to her." His tone begs, and I take a long look at his edgy face. He's so broken at this moment, almost as much as when we lost our son, but not quite the same. This is a man on the edge of losing everything. His eyes are wide while his cheeks are shallow. He's biting the inside, causing his jaw to clench. His hands form fists at his side. He's holding it all in when he wants to push at his brother.

"James," I call out, and he shifts his gaze from his brother to me. I've crossed my arms and hitched my hip, staring at him. "Come here."

287

It's said like a disappointed mother to her petulant child, but still, it's a command. Giant mutters something, and James nods without an answer. Slowly, I watch James approach the low porch. It's only two steps up, but I stand near the edge, and I point to where I want James to walk. Right in front of me. His eyes don't leave my face, and I'm grateful he doesn't start talking, yammering with apologies and explanations. I just need one minute. When he's standing directly before me, a head lower than me because of the porch height, I open my arms.

For a second, his brows lift, and then he falls forward, his forehead resting on my sternum as I wrap my arms around his head. I hold him to me, and his fingers come to my sides, curling into the soft material of Giant's tee. He's tugging at it, pulling me forward as he presses his head near my breasts. Slowly, his fingers unfurl, and he wraps his arms around my waist, holding me tight against him. I stroke my hand over his hair, lowering to kiss the top of him. He shudders under me, and I just drink in this minute.

"It's not mine," he mutters without mentioning woman or child.

"I know."

His head shoots up, and he looks at me. I expect him to be angry that we've fought for nothing, but instead, his expression remains broken.

"I'm so sorry. I don't even know when or where the picture was taken, but it's old, and it's over. I'll leave the club if it brings you back to me."

It's quite a statement, but I don't want him to give up his new friends. I think Justice has been good for him, moving into the role of big brother and protector, like Giant once was.

"I don't need you to give up things for me. I need you."

It's that simple, like Letty said. I've needed him for years, and I feel like he's just within my grasp again. We just need to reach out for each other.

"Peach, let me take you somewhere. I swear, it's the last thing I'll ask for. Just . . . I need to go there, and I want you to go with me."

I swallow. It's a hard proposition. He wasn't there for me at the groundbreaking, but then again, he was. He showed, and he held me. We did it together even though it was hard leading up to it and difficult afterward. When it came to being there because of Michael, we were there for each other.

"I don't have anything with me for a hike." I'd worn a dress to the ceremony and wore the same thing here yesterday.

"I brought some old things from the house and picked up a few things from the rental." I didn't even want to know how he got in the rental. "Please, Evie. I swear it's the last thing I'll ask."

"You haven't asked for much," I remind him. He asked me to leave, and then he never asked for anything more.

"Do you want me to ask you to come back to me? I'm asking. Do you want me to ask you to love me? I'm not above begging. I want us, Evie. I want us." His voice cracks, and his lids lower. His head falls to my chest again, and he grips the edges of the shirt.

"Okay," I whisper, my heart breaking all over again for this man, but this time it's different. It's breaking *for* him, not because of him.

"Quiet that dog," I say as I realize that Silver has been running around the house and yipping each time he passes James and me. "Letty and Finn are still sleeping."

"Silver," James snaps, leaning back from me. "Stop." The dog acquiesces, and James heads to the truck for my things. Giant walks up to the porch where I wait.

"You sure about him, Evie?"

"I want to be," I say, offering him a sad smile. Giant nods, and James returns to the porch.

+ + +

We drove to the old ranger station, and from there, we walk. I notice James's attire for the first time. He's wearing old jeans, ripped at one knee, and a Henley shirt with a quilted flannel shirt over it. His old hiking boots are on his feet, and he looks like the James I remember. Nothing wrong with all black T-shirts, tight dark jeans, and motorcycle boots, but this is him. He's in his element walking through the woods, looking up and around him.

He brought me my old boots as well and found me a pair of jeans at the rental house along with a sweater and a lightweight jacket. We walk in silence for a large part of our trip. James holds my hand, ignoring my sweaty palms. His pace is always faster than mine, but he stays slow, taking our time. Silver bounds around us, running ahead and then coming back. He yips and barks on occasion, but he's equally in his element as well.

"Before we reach the ridge, I have a few things I think I should say."

I don't respond. I suppose I have things to say as well.

"I'm sorry for all the drama. I meant what I said. I can pull out of the club."

"I don't want you to do that." James needs friends, and he's found them in men like Justice and Bear.

"I don't want to talk about Tabby. Justice is handling it. He thinks everything is linked to Rusty. Can we just be done with that?"

I nod to agree. It doesn't make sense why she'd say it's James's baby, but it's not, and it's over. I have to believe what he tells me. He's not a liar, and he's always held fast and true to that about himself.

"And I've decided to sell the house."

"What?" I stop walking a second, and James stops to face me, but his eyes don't look up. "Why?"

"You were right. It's too much for me. I've let it keep me prisoner, not only to Michael but also to you. Being there made me feel like you weren't completely gone, but it was never right. You should have been there physically, not just memories among the furniture."

I squeeze his hand, and his head lifts but turns to look off in the distance.

"I also cleaned out Michael's room." His jaw clenches. I know it was difficult for him to do such a thing.

"I could have helped you," I offer, torn between the fact he did something without me again and knowing he needed to do this on his own.

"I know, but I had to do this for me." I understood. I'd already taken with me what I had wanted when I left.

"What did you do with his things?"

"Boxed up some stuff. Made a pile to donate. I'll rehang pictures and such in a new house." He looks back at me. "I'm hoping it will be our new house."

I stare up at him.

"Evie, I want you to move back in with me, or me with you. I just want us together. Dating's fun, and I promise we'll do more of it. Creative things." His mouth slowly tips up as he recalls our ice cream outing, but his smile doesn't reach his eyes. "But I need you day to day. The good and the bad ones. And nights too."

"Nights too," I whisper, and I nod to agree. "I've missed you."

His lids lower a second, and he swallows hard. "You have no idea how much I've missed you."

"I want to kiss you, but not yet." His smile grows a little bit more, and he turns away, continuing to lead me forward.

"Just so we're clear, it would be okay to kiss me," I tease.

"Oh, I'm gonna kiss you, Peach. Just want to do it somewhere special." His hand squeezes mine as we walk forward.

It's about a mile up from the outpost, straight up to the ridge. I feel my heart racing the closer we get. I've never been back here once Michael had the accident, but James came here often. I remind myself I'm doing this for him. He wants to bring me here for some reason.

We break free of the trees to find an array of flat boulders, jutting out from the mountain and over the valley below. My palms sweat. My heart hammers.

"Not too close," I whisper, and James stops. Silver beat us here, but he's circling the rocks, coming close to the edge and then hopping back to us.

"Right here is good." We still, and James drops my sweaty hand. He swipes a hand down his face and looks off in the distance. I want to see what he sees, but I don't. My imagination has the best of me, and I'm envisioning things I didn't see. I close my eyes, hoping not to go there, but then I have to open them because it's too much.

"I brought Mom, buddy," he whispers, and then Silver barks. I flinch, too overwhelmed by James's words and the echo of the dog's bark. My body trembles, and I can't breathe. It's a beautiful setting. A glorious day with mild temps and a soft breeze, but I cannot catch my breath. My ribs feel like they are caving in, clawing at my insides. My back aches, pressure squeezing like a vise wraps around me.

Silver is frantically pacing around us, brushing at our shins and calves, and I don't know why but it's bothering me. I feel like he's pushing me.

"Silver, stop," I snap, spinning in a circle as if chasing my own tail. James has stepped forward, drawing closer to the edge. My fear of heights is catching up to me, and my entire body trembles.

"James," I choke, my voice too quiet for him to hear at his back. The dog walks to him and sits at his side a second.

In the whisper of the breeze, I hear the soft sound. *Mom.*

It's clear as the day in my ears although it can't be real. *Mom.*

The sound becomes the rhythm of my heartbeat. *Mom. Mom. Mom.*

And in my head, I'm yelling, *What? What, Michael?* in response to the incessant calling that only kids can do on repeat.

*Michael.*

I shake my head, and the world swivels with me. The trees move sideways and the sky tips, and I'm going over until the world turns black.

# Chapter 31
# Broken Hearts

[James]

The repetitive beeping of the heart machine fills my head. I'm afraid to close my eyes and recall what I'd seen. Nothing. I hadn't been focused on Evie but concentrating on Michael. Reliving the moments. Restoring my memories. But also have my silent talks where I apologize again to my son for not being strong enough, and I apologize to him for not being a man to his mother. I was in this cathartic stance, ignoring the warning yelps of Silver when I heard the thud and turned to find Evie.

She'd fallen over, and I didn't know why or how.

All I could see was her body dangling precariously close to the edge of a rock, blood trickling from her head. Her feet hung off the side of a boulder, like any second she could be sucked downward, and I panicked. Frozen in time for half a second, I didn't move, while Silver had her arm, dragging her to the center as best he could.

I fell to my knees and crawled to her. Not even graceful or careful, I tugged her away from the rock's edge and back toward the forest. I probably did her more damage than good. Collapsing to the forest floor, I tug her between my legs, holding her to my chest and checking her pulse. She was still breathing, still alive, and I might have cried instantly in relief. Cell reception was shit up here, and I should have brought a two-way radio for better contact. There was a lot of blood, and I had to remind myself over and over that head wounds bleed more heavily.

Still, she wasn't responding to my calls of her name.

Lifting her in my arms, I struggled but carried her the mile back to the outpost. I fell a few times with Silver at my feet, yipping at me like he wanted me to hurry. Like I was running out of time if I didn't move faster. I wasn't strong enough to carry her as far as I did, but I was determined to do such a thing. Once I had her in the truck, I had cell reception and called for an ambulance to meet me at Giant's.

Chaos ensued, and I blindly followed the EMT to the hospital.

Evie had a mild heart attack. The doctor believed it was stress-induced.

*"She's only forty-five,"* I told as though I was the medical practitioner.

*"Number one killer of women in their forties is heart disease."* The statistic shocked me, and I wanted to google it to see if he knew what he was talking about.

*"You just said stress, not disease,"* I argued with him.

*"What do you think can bring on heart disease?"* I didn't care for his answer, and suddenly, I felt sick. Had all we been through caused this in her? Had all I'd done to her led to a broken heart—literally? I'd rip out my own and give it to her if I thought it would make her better.

They were going to run some additional tests once she woke. In addition, they believed she had a concussion. The doctor explained her mind needed to rest after I told him where we were and the significance of it.

*"And you carried her a mile through the forest?"* a female intern questioned as I explained.

*"I'd do anything for her."*

*"That's so romantic,"* she muttered, turning pink in the face.

Romance had nothing to do with it. I was in love with my wife and damn stubborn to keep her this time.

I lower my head for Evie's arm, one of my hands wrapped around it while the other holds her hand. I don't know how long I'm in this position, but the touch of her fingers over my hair startles me.

"Hey," I croak, feeling like I might have dozed and hoping I didn't miss anything.

"Hey, baby," she whispers, her throat sounding dry. I release her and stand.

"Need water?"

"What happened?" She stares up at the ceiling, and I reach for the Styrofoam cup with a straw.

"Here," I offer her a sip, and she pushes it away when she's done.

"Tell me," she softly demands, and I explain as best I can her fall, my finding her, and then her stay here in the county hospital.

"I had a heart attack?" Her hand slips over her chest to her heart. "I'm too young for that."

I chuckle. "I told the doctor the same thing. He thinks it was panic-induced like you just couldn't take anymore and collapsed." I reach for her hand. "I'm so sorry I pushed you. All I've done is push and push and push."

Evie's head rolls on the pillow, and she stares up at the ceiling. "Did you hear him?" Her voice is so quiet, and I know what she means. She looks back at me, stunned by the admission, and hesitant as though I'll think she's crazy.

"I hear him all the time," I tell her. Sometimes it's at the ridge, but sometimes it's in the house or on my bike, or just anywhere. It's all phantom sounds in my head, and I know this, but it always startles me.

A tear seeps from the corner of her eye, and I bite my lip. I don't want her to cry anymore. We'd had such a great few weeks, laughing and talking, sharing stories and kissing in between. We hadn't done heavy and then bam! So much heaviness, and it was all surrounding me.

"I'm not good for your health, Evie," I tease, but there's something serious in my tone.

"You're the only thing healthy for me," she whispers, and the tears burn my own eyes. I lower to the seat again and pull her hand to my lips. There's something burning a hole in my pocket, but it needs to wait. I'd planned to do it on the ridge, but I'd given her a fucking heart attack instead.

"What's next for me?" she asks.

"Rest. Recuperation. You'll stay here for a few days and then need a few weeks at home."

But which home? Mine or hers? I already told her I wanted to be with her night and day, and she agreed. There's no way I'm separating from her now.

"We can stay in the rental while the house is on the market," I tell her, answering all questions before they're asked. I've already made plans to collect the rest of her things in Savannah and store them until we have a new place to live.

"I thought I lost you," I admit, and my voice cracks. I close my eyes, holding her knuckles to my lips, and feel the wetness of my own tears seep down my cheek. I could not lose her too. Not like this. I'd give her up a million times, but I could not lose her to something higher powered than either of us.

"James," she says, her voice quiet as she speaks to me. "Come here." The fingers on her other hand wiggle, and she works to move over in the bed.

"Too many tubes and gadgets. I'm not risking anything with you," I warn, but she smiles at me, something I want to see more than those tears.

"Come up behind me. Hold me, please."

Dammit. I'll do anything she asks of me. Anything, from this day forward.

+ + +

Evie rests in the hospital for a few days and then spends more time in bed at the rental house. I ended up extending the rental agreement until spring. It's a tight fit, but we need the togetherness, and our new house won't be ready until then. I can't wait to tell Evie my plans, and I'm excited about things, but I don't want to freak her into another attack. The doctors say she's strong and young, which I kept telling them, and she should make a full recovery with diet, exercise, and stress-free living.

The first way I'm helping her is by going to a grief therapist. I hate talking about my feelings, and I'd balked at this idea a thousand times in the last three years, but almost losing my wife as well put things in perspective for me. I need to help myself in order to help her.

I knew there'd come a day when she'd ask me for the "anything" I promised I'd do for her. The tough *anything*, and it came not even a week after her return to the house.

"I want to attend Sunday dinner." The ritual we'd attended off and on over the years at my parents' home until I took a six-year hiatus.

"Your mother came to see me every day and sometimes your father, too. I love them, James. They've been good to me despite our little hiccup of misunderstanding." She levels me with a teasing stare as that was my fault, but Evie admits she could have reached out to them, and they admitted the same. With everyone broken at the same time, it was hard to know which pieces to pick up and which ones to leave alone.

"I don't know," I say to her as we lie in bed facing each other. Evie rests often and then pushes herself. She's bored, she says, and she's tired of feeling confined. I admit I'm hovering, and she hates that, but worse, she hates that I'm refusing to have sex until the doctors approve it.

"James. It's time." She reaches out for my cheek and tenderly cups my jaw. "For me."

She's learning how to use those words and get her way, and I chuckle.

"You might need to hold my hand through the entire thing," I warn her.

"Baby, I'm never letting go again."

# Chapter 32
# Homecoming

[James]

As we park in the driveway, I stroke Evie's fourth finger. The one still absent of my rings.

"There's something you should know before we go in there."

Evie chuckles. "Do you know that's the same thing you said to me when you brought me here nineteen years ago?"

I shift in the driver's seat to face her.

"Jesus, do you realize it was roughly this same time of year?"

"Almost," she teases. "So what did you want to tell me?"

"I'm scared." It's hard to admit, but I'm fucking scared out of my mind to enter that house. Evie has played interventionist and assures me my parents want me to join them for the Sunday ritual.

"You have no idea how happy this will make them."

Yes, they'll be happy, but I'm still dying on the inside. I've been so mean to them. I know their disappointment. I lost them the male line. I lost them their grandson. I've turned away from them and took Evie away from them.

"It's not going to be perfect. We all need time, but this is a start." She squeezes my hand. "Kiss me."

The request is easy enough, and I do feel better once we do.

"Don't let go of me," I whisper, meaning more than my hand.

"Never," she says, and for the first time in a long time, I believe in that word again. We'll never be apart again. Even in our deaths, I'll find her. We'll find each other as we did on that mountain. As we did again, even after all we've been through.

I glance out the front window to find my three brothers standing on the lawn.

"Oh shit," I mutter, and Evie laughs.

"The welcoming party?"

"More like the mafia."

Evie laughs harder. "I'm trying to imagine it. Mafia mountain men. Nope, doesn't work for me. It's the flannel that throws me off." She nods at my brother, and I notice two out of three are wearing one. "That reminds me. You look amazing."

She glances back at me. I'm wearing dark jeans, a blue button-down with rolled sleeves, and a gray pinstriped vest. When Evie saw me walk out of the bedroom, she dropped her purse and her jaw.

*"What? What's the matter?"*

*"Besides wanting to strip you back out of that clothing and ride you like you're a bike? Nothing."*

*"Jesus," I muttered, rushing up to her and taking her mouth, forgetting to keep things slow.*

*When I pulled back, she moaned. "Quit babying me."*

*"I'm going to pamper you for the rest of your days," I teased.*

*"Can it include you wearing that vest and nothing else?"*

Good Lord, she was going to be the end of me in the most pleasant way.

"You're beautiful," I remind her. I've been telling her every day but showing her as well with little things like shared baths and massages. It's hard to keep my hands off her, but she takes care of me as well.

"Let's do this," I mutter, and we step out of the truck. The second I can, I take Evie's hand again, and she wraps her other hand over both of ours.

"James," Giant says, keeping his eyes on me.

"Giant." I pause, nodding at him. "Billy. Charlie."

It's quiet for a second, and Evie moves, but I squeeze her hand. I can't release her, and I don't want her to leave me alone with them.

"You look beautiful, Sunshine," Billy says to Evie, and she blushes.

"Up to your old tricks, I see, William," I reply instantly.

"Wouldn't have it any other way," Billy says, holding my eyes before slowing smile. "Can't help it, your wife should have run away with me instead." He winks at Evie, and she chuckles.

"William, play nice, or I'll set Roxanne on you." My wife has become good friends with her new sisters-in-law.

"We all know how much he loves Roxanne on him, so I don't think that will be a punishment," Charlie says, patting Billy's shoulder and surprising us all with such an obvious sexual comment.

"Yeah, you just keep out of the upstairs bathroom. Some of us actually need to use it for its purpose," Billy retorts.

"You had sex in the bathroom upstairs?" Giant lifts a brow.

I bite my tongue. *Didn't all of us at one time or another with someone?* I glance back at Charlie and realize no, not him.

"Janessa liked the view," Charlie admits, and Evie's mouth falls open.

"I don't think I should be here for this."

Charlie chuckles, and I notice *Goody Two-shoes Charlie* seems to have loosened up a bit.

"I am not using that bathroom," Giant mutters.

"Better stay out of the trophy room, too, then," Billy smirks. "That old couch is like a science experiment."

"Mama replaced it," Giant says, straight-faced before his eyes meet mine, knowing that old couch had significant specimens of the unmentionable kind on it. Letty and Giant came to visit Evie in the hospital, and then Letty's been at the house to distract Evie.

"Jesus, what is this?" Mati calls out from the front porch. "A pissing match or a welcome home party." She stomps down the steps and right up to me. "You coming in or what?"

"I'm coming in," I say quietly.

"Good to see you, big brother," she says, and loops her arms around me, surprising the shit out of me. Evie still holds my hand, so I awkwardly pat my sister with one arm.

"I'm used to this kind of brotherly bullshit," she says, tipping her head at the boys behind her. I used to be one of them, torturing our sister while protecting her.

"Mama's waiting," she whispers, and I nod. As I step forward, Charlie steps up to me. We both still, and he holds out a hand, all formal and politician-y.

"Welcome home," he says, still stiff, but once our hands meet, he pulls me to him and slaps my back.

"Oh fuck, I'd rather hug your wife than you," Billy mutters when Charlie steps back. But to my surprise, he comes at me with open arms. We got along the least despite being middle brothers to Giant and Charlie. Perhaps it was the competition to see who could be worse. I won. I clearly won.

Billy smacks my back hard with both hands, and I sense him making faces at Evie over my shoulder.

"Call me," he mock whispers. "There's still time for me to save you."

I playfully push him back. "Gonna trade me for Roxanne." The teasing stops all motion.

"No fucking way," Billy says, and his face hardens. Then it falls as if he gets it. It isn't great to have someone always looking at his forever girl.

"Fuck you," Billy mutters, but he's joking.

"No thanks," I turn my head to Evie, and when I look back at Billy, he's biting his lip, fighting the comeback. He wants to say something so bad, he's ready to burst, and I slowly laugh.

"I think he bested ya, Bill," Evie says, and Giant chuckles. He comes up to me next, and it's a struggle with us. We haven't lost touch completely as he'd been inserting himself here and there over the years, checking on me—as Justice said—when I didn't even realize that's what he was doing. He still knows more about me than the rest of my family, knowing Evie's promise to call and my visits to the ridge.

"Stop being a stranger, brother," he whispers to me, and I nod, feeling my eyes burn. I blink a few times, realizing along with my parents, I hurt him too. My big brother. My best friend. I pinch my eyes together and look up at him.

"You too," I mutter and release Evie's hand when Giant cups my neck. He's going to pull me in hard, and I expect it before I've even wrapped my arms around him, holding on a second longer than the rest.

"Good to have you home, kid," he mutters to me, and I remember all those times he went off to fight in the military, and we didn't know if he'd return alive or not. I was always grateful to have him back, and I'd say the same thing to him.

"Good to be home," I whisper, still feeling strange but also good about this.

As we break, my parents stand on the porch, my mother under my father's arms, and she breaks from him, approaching me first.

"Mama," I say when she stops before me. I lick my lips and look at Evie, who smiles and nods her head. "If it's okay with you, I'd like to join you for supper today."

My mother's eyes instantly fill, and her hands clasped before her chest. "Your seat has been waiting for you," she says and looks at Evie. "For both of you." Her arms open, and I step into them. I'm never going to have the relationship the rest have with her, but she's still my mother, which means I have my own relationship with her. She holds me longer than I'd like, and I look at Evie over my mother's shoulder.

Her brows pinch. "I'm starving," she says, hoping to pull Mama off me. "What's for dinner?" It does the trick, and my mother pulls away.

"Dinner, yes. It's a heart-healthy diet," Mama begins, and three grown men groan as my mother reaches for Evie's hand. "It's going to be good for all of us," she adds, leading Evie away from me. My wife looks at me over her shoulder, wondering if I'll be okay, and I realize I need a minute before I enter the house.

My siblings all follow my mother inside, but my father remains on the front porch. I walk to the edge of the steps leading upward.

"Sir," I say in greeting. My dad remains quiet. He isn't angry or sad, not disappointed or even upset. He's just watching me, knowing that I need to do this. He might not have rushed me like Mama or Mati. He might not have joked with me like my brothers, but from man to man, I need to do what I do next.

"Dad, I'd like to come home." My voice cracks, and I feel like a child but also an adult. Very adult. I've done him wrong for no reason other than my own issues of weakness and failure.

"Our door is always open to you, James." When I was a kid, my dad was my hero in some ways. I knew his story from Pap. George Jr. had been a bit of a rabble-rouser, and Pap would always look at me when he said those words. Then Junior married Elaina, a debutante from Atlanta, and he was a changed man. He filled her with kids, gave her a beautiful home, and ran a successful company. But at the end of the day, he was still a man and still a father.

"I'm sorry, Dad," I whisper, and he softly smiles at me, walking down the steps to meet me where I stand.

"I know you are," he says, not accusing me, just understanding. I'm only a man as well. I'm a father and a husband, and it doesn't make me perfect. It makes me human and a rock. Solid, strong, and powerful, yet able to grumble either by slowing chipping away at me or dropping me on my ass. I've had it all happen. But as rocks tumble, collecting dirt and soil and compacting themselves with other things, they rebuild, and one day, a tiny rock becomes a mountain. It just takes time.

## Chapter 33
# The Trophy Room

[Evie]

"Hey," I say, opening the door to the infamous trophy room in the elder Harrington's home. It's late, and I took a nap after dinner. I didn't want James to leave as he was slowly melting back in with his brothers.

*"Just a little rest,"* I told him and Elaina, who was equally worried I'd overdone it.

*"We can go,"* James said to which I replied, "No," and Elaina begged, "Not yet." I knew her fear. If he disappeared, he might not come back. But I had faith at James's reception that we'd be back for more Sunday dinners.

I laid down in Giant and James's old room and instantly fell asleep with the relief of dinner going well. There were hiccups. It wasn't perfect, but we would get there. James would get there.

"I slept so long," I tell him, entering the room and closing the door. It's dark outside, as it's November, but it's also later than I expected us to be here.

"That's okay. You alright?" he asks.

"Yeah. How about you?"

"I think I'll leave you two alone." Charlie's voice surprises me. I hadn't noticed him in the overstuffed chair facing the television. He stands and comes to me, pressing a kiss to my forehead. "It's good to have you home."

He turns to his brother. "Both of you."

Charlie dismisses himself. He doesn't have far to go as he's the house next door.

"Did everyone else leave?"

James chuckles as he holds out an arm. "Hours ago, baby."

"I'm sorry," I say, coming up to him and climbing over his lap instead of tucking into his arm on the couch. "New couch, huh?"

This room holds a few tales I never want to hear about four teenage boys drinking underage and diddling with girls. The brother with the most stories is under my thighs. It's called the trophy room because it once housed all the sports and activity trophies of this family, but the shelves of the full wall entertainment center now hold frame after frame of the expanding family. Somewhere on those shelves are baby pictures of Michael and a wedding photograph of James and me, but I'm not interested in looking behind me. I focus on the man before me.

"Whatcha doing, Peach?" he asks as his head tips back on the couch, and I lower myself, getting comfortable in the crook I want on him. His hands lazily come to my hips.

"Where are your parents?" I whisper to him. I have no idea how late it is.

"They went to their room a while ago, and Charlie and I were just hanging out. Mama didn't want me to wake you. I think she was hoping I'd spend the night and never leave."

I chuckle over him, swiping a hand over his silvery hair and scraping my fingers back up his head. I lean forward and kiss him, slow and sweet.

"Evie," he groans. We haven't had sex since I was in the hospital. He's treating me too tenderly lately. My mouth becomes more insistent over his. "Peach, the doctor said nothing strenuous."

"Mm-hmm," I purr against my lips. "Then we'll need to go slow and quiet." My mouth returns to his, and he lifts a little, taking me harder, tongue thrusting forward.

"We shouldn't do this," he says, and I curl my lips at him as I slip from his lap. Hitching up the skirt of my dress, I tug down my underwear and return to his lap.

"I heard this is the place to get a piece of James Harrington," I tease, and James shakes his head.

"Mama's gonna kill me for messing up this new couch," he mutters, leaning for me and taking my mouth hard again. We kiss hot and heavy for a few minutes before I pull back and reach for his belt.

"Better only be messy in me then," I tease, and James's head falls backward again.

"Jesus," he hisses. "That mouth."

"I just want to remind you who you belong to." I deepen my voice as I speak, imitating his tone. Once I have the zipper down and my hand in his briefs, I squeeze him. "This belongs to me."

He crashes his mouth against mine again, and he works his pants a little lower to free him from the confines of the denim. He breaks from me and shoves my skirt upward, laying the material at my hips.

"You sure about this, Peach," he mutters, his eyes focused on me spread over his lap and my hand wrapped around his thick shaft.

"Need to remind you where you belong," I say, keeping the deep tone as best I can. When his thumb comes to my clit, I squeak.

"Quiet, Peach," he warns, and then he hisses. "You're getting messy all over me."

"Better do something about that then," I tease, and he holds himself upright while I lift on my knees. Balancing on the tip of him, I kiss him once more.

"James," I whisper his name with all the love I have for him. "Only you on my lips."

"Evie. Jesus, I love you." He guides me down over his hard length, and I pause as he fills me. My mouth falls open at the fullness, but I hold in the groan of relief. He's where he belongs. In this house. In my heart. Inside me.

"I love you, too," I tell him, holding his eyes once more as he holds mine, no longer afraid to look at me. In fact, he's looking at me with all the love I ever had from him and more.

"Go slow," he warns me.

"Nah, you and I are always fast, baby." I start rocking my hips, drawing to the tip, and then lowering to swallow him in again, but we can't keep slow, and gradually, the pace builds. I'm lifting and lowering, and his mouth captures mine, thrusting his tongue in me to match the way I'm riding over him.

"So close," I mutter, wrapping an arm around his neck and cupping his jaw like he cups mine. "I love you, I love you, I love you." The words punctuate the rhythm of my heart and the tempo of me working over him, until I still, slamming down on him and feeling the release wash over me. I clench, and he hisses.

"Shit," he mutters and tips up his hips to match me. His neck strains. His fingers squeeze my hips. When he comes down from the high, his head lifts from the back of the couch, and he looks right at me with the bluest of eyes. We stare at each other with sex-satisfied smiles.

"We're gonna make it, aren't we, Peach?"

"We're going to make it, Ranger. As long as we're together." I kiss him softly. "Take me home."

And James nods because home is wherever we are together.

## Epilogue
# Short but Sweet

### [Evie]

It has been ten days since that Sunday dinner. It took courage for James to enter their house and wordlessly ask forgiveness of everyone. Then he asked to speak to his dad privately, and they disappeared into his father's office for a long time. When James came out, he was like a new man. I didn't ask what they discussed. It was between father and son, but James seemed lighter, better, and then there was what we did in the trophy room.

As we exited the room, his father stood outside it, head lowered, hands in his pants pockets. I slipped behind James, shy about what we just did. As James held my hand, he addressed his father.

*"Dad, we're gonna head out now."*

*"I think that's best," he said, a sly smile on his face. "Glad it wasn't your mother who came to check on you."*

*James chuckled, and the two men looked at each other. It must be an old joke. "At least, she's your wife." He winked at me, and the implication was clear. He knew what we were doing, and I wanted to melt into the floor.*

"Where are we going?" I holler over the roar of the engine. It's been a brisk ride, but James wanted to enjoy a rare beautiful day in early winter. When we pull off the side of the road, I'm confused.

"Is this it?" We aren't anywhere but the side of the road, although I have a sense that the lake is somewhere to our left.

"Do you trust me?"

"Yes." I mean it with everything in me. I trust him to keep me safe and protect my heart.

"I want to blindfold you."

"What?" We've discussed some kinky things lately, and we've been pushing some boundaries as we discover one another's bodies.

"Just . . . do this." His eyes soften as he looks at me over his shoulder, and I nod. He shifts, and I slip off the bike. Pulling a bandana from his pocket, he folds it and wraps it over my eyes. "I know it's going to feel weird riding blindly, but it's only a short ways. I have a surprise for you."

The glee in his voice fills me with eager anticipation.

"How will I know to lean with you?" I ask, as I fumble onto the bike and curl into his back.

"You feel me, Peach." And I do. James and I were one in many ways, and as his body moves, so does mine.

He goes slow, and the distance isn't far as he promised. The pavement turns to gravel under his tires, and then we stop. I shift off his back, and James offers his hand on my arm to guide me off the bike.

"I've got you," he says, and I smile to myself. I've got him, too.

James's hands come to my shoulders as he's behind me, and he moves me a few steps before holding me still.

"Okay," he says as he pulls the bandana from my eyes, but I still keep them closed. "You can look."

When I open, I begin to laugh. "What is this?" I stare at the vintage silver Airstream parked on the land at Bolton Lake.

"Surprise," he says to me, and I lean back against his chest. He kisses my neck.

"Please tell me this isn't our new house," I tease.

"Why not? I checked all around for alligators." It's good to hear the tease in James's voice, the lilt of excitement and flirt. I turn in his arms, slipping mine around his neck.

"You know I'll live anywhere with you, but a camper in the winter isn't top on my list."

James leans forward, kissing me, tender and sweet, and if he has his way, we might be up against that aluminum on wheels, chilly or not.

"Where did you find this thing?" I say, pulling back and twisting to look at the camper again, but keeping myself tucked into his chest.

"I rented it. Last weekend before it gets really cold, so I thought we could use it as a little getaway." He'd been doing this. Trying to make our dates as unique and unusual as he can.

"I want to show you something, though." He releases me but takes my hand, and we circle the camper, facing out at the lake.

"What a view," I whisper, remembering the first time I pulled the rig into this spot. I'd been running away from home, trying to find myself. Instead, I found James. Or he found me. It didn't matter as long as we were together.

"I want to see this view every day with you, Evie." I nod to agree and then turn to face him. He takes both my hands with his and rubs his thumbs over my knuckles. "Remember when I spoke with my dad at dinner?"

He swallows hard. It's going to be a long road to fix what he's lost with his parents, but they've been open to his return.

"I asked for his forgiveness for disappearing and being disrespectful all those years." James pauses, keeping his eyes on his thumb over my knuckles. "And I apologized for making them worry about me and promised I'd try to do better. I'd be crushed if Michael had ever shut me out, and I realized how much I hurt my father because he's *my* father."

"Wow," I say softly. That's a lot to have shared.

"Yeah, wow."

I wait him out as I sense he has more to share.

"Then I asked him if I could have the land. This land." I look up from where I've been staring at his thumbs rubbing my hands and into his face.

"Here?" I ask, although that's exactly what he said.

"I thought this would be a good place to start over. A new beginning. We could build a house here. And we'd have that view every day."

I nod again, turning to look out across the water in the fading afternoon sun. It's getting darker so much earlier this time of year, but the lake still glistens.

"It's a nice view." I smile as I speak. "And no alligators? Sounds like a great place to live."

As I tease him, I feel him lowering before me, still holding my hands.

"James?" I choke as he reaches into his pocket.

"Then I asked my dad for permission to marry my wife again." A new ring is presented to me. One different than our first. The silver band holds a large diamond, and I recognize that it's my original stone in a new setting.

"Evelyn Sue Harrington, would you do me the honor of marrying me? Again." He pauses before adding, "Let me be your rock."

"Only if I can be yours." We look at one another, hopeful of starting over. "I would love to marry you again, James Harrington."

He slips the beautiful diamond ring on my finger and stands, reaching up for my jaw before kissing me hard. I laugh at the rush of his lips against mine, but he continues working my mouth until I give in to him. We kiss like we first did, only that time we were in the water.

"I have one more thing for you inside the camper." He smiles sheepishly.

"Oh, a big surprise in your camper," I tease. "Bet that line works on all the girls."

"Only needs to work on one, Peach." He winks and leads me by my hand inside the small rig. It's tight, and I sit on the edge of the bed. James reaches inside the compact refrigerator and pulls out a single cupcake.

My brows pinch as I watch him stick a candle in the frosting and light the wick. He kneels before me again on one knee.

"Every year, you'd call me, and every year I'd count down the days until that phone rang."

I whisper his name. We've let all this go.

He shakes his head and continues. "And I know it was always a sad call even though it was a celebration of his life." We only spoke on the happy occasion marking Michael's birth, not his unfortunate death. "I'd hear you blow out that candle and close my eyes, making my own wish. I'd wish for you, Evie. Like all those years I'd been waiting on you and hadn't known it, I'd silently wish for you to forgive me, love me, and come back to me."

I cup his jaw with the hand now holding a new ring. "I'm here for you."

"And I promise to be there for you. From this day forward. I like the idea of building where we conceived Michael. Where you agreed to marry me, now twice. Where we made love, made up, and now, where we promise to be it for each other all over again. Let's celebrate. To day one together, make a wish, baby."

A tear rolls from my eye, and I quickly swipe it. It's a happy tear finally. "They are already coming true," I whisper because being back with him is the only wish I could wish for that could come true.

We gently blow together, and the flame goes out. In the quiet, we smile at one another.

"So remember that little fantasy play after we had ice cream?"

I smile deeper, fighting the grin as I chew on my lip. It's a great memory, and a night I won't soon forget.

"How do you feel about frosting?" His blue eyes sparkle as they did years ago, crystal clear and full of hope.

"I'd say I'm willing to play along," I tease.

"Ah, my Peach is always ripe for me." He winks before giving his lips to me, and he isn't wrong.

I'm ready for him and more.

SILVER BIKER

Thank you for taking the time to read Silver Biker.
Please consider writing a review on major sales channels where ebooks
and paperbooks are sold.

Want a sip of Evie and James in the future?

SILVER BIKER BONUS

If you love small town, silver foxes, visit Sterling Falls.
Start with *Sterling Heat*.
Having a baby in a bakery gives new meaning to taking the bun out of
the oven. Having that baby delivered by a sexy, curmudgeon baker isn't
part of the birth plan.

**Flip the page for a sample.**

Did you start at the beginning of the *Silver Foxes of Blue Ridge*?
*Silver Brewer*
Opposites attract when the grumpy giant mountain man meets a chirpy
city woman who wants his land.

Read where the Harringtons were first introduced in *Second Chance*,
Mati Harrington and Denton Chance's friends-to-lovers,
second chance romance.

# A sample of *Sterling Heat*

## Chapter 1
*October*
[Enya]

Falling on my backside in front of a handsome man was the last thing I expected to happen today.

Then again, the day has been full of surprises.

After leaving the small-town bakery with only minutes to spare before it closed, a torrential downpour came out of nowhere as I stood on the shop's stoop. Balancing my tote and a paper bag containing one of the most delicious-looking baby-Bundt cakes, I snapped open the travel umbrella I'd found in the bottom of my oversized purse and risked the deluge.

However, when stepping onto the sidewalk, a gust of wind careened along the storefronts on the quaint main street and jacked my umbrella. The flimsy thing snapped backward to look like an art deco buttercup flower, offering no protection from the cold, pelting rain which rode the wind and came at me sideways. In an effort to right my worthless umbrella, I spun on my heels in hopes the gusts of the gale would snap the thing back into its proper position. The wind took me as well, forcing me backward when the umbrella momentarily expanded. As I tried to maintain my balance, the heel of my over-priced stiletto slipped into a grate in the sidewalk. Struck by the ridiculous physics of a thin spike wedging into an even slimmer slat opening, my ankle gave way and I collapsed onto my ass.

"Miss, are you alright?" The broad and slightly rebellious-looking man from the bakery I just left asked me.

*Perfect. Just perfect.*

For a moment, I sit on the rain-drenched sidewalk, allowing the chilly drops to batter me, plastering my hair to my face and further drenching my already soaked dress.

This is what I get for wanting to celebrate.

For wishing for something more in my life. For grasping at something I never thought I'd have.

I almost laugh until the concern in the dark blue eyes of the large man standing over me has me swallowing instead. His jeans are saturated at his ankles, above a pair of solid biker boots. His white T-shirt is plastered to his body, the opaque material accentuating dark hairs on his chest and the solid muscles of his upper arms. He's thick in the midsection. Firm might be a better description. A paw of a hand extends toward me and slowly I lift mine to accept his help.

My umbrella is nowhere in sight. The bag containing my miniature cake tragically sits in a shallow puddle on the sidewalk. My foot has slipped out of my shoe. My wounded pride is the only thing present. I've never been so embarrassed. And my backside uncomfortably aches.

"Let's get inside, yeah?" he yells over the torrent of rain, swiping at his face to clear the drops. His eyes are kind. His voice rough. A sprinkling of silver peppers among his temple and over his ears.

I nod and accept his assistance, as he holds my hand and gathers up the remains of a soggy paper bag. Once we enter the cool breeze of the bakery, he tosses the waterlogged sack on the counter and turns to face me. The thickness of his hand is a comfort as he pushes back my hair, effectively exposing my mortified blush. His gentle fingers glide through the wet strands, tucking an errant lock behind my ear. His thumb trails a blaze of warmth down my cheek. Heat infuses my whole body, from my frozen toes to the tips of my ears. It's a welcome sensation beneath the cool air-conditioning.

I shiver. Teeth chattering. Tailbone throbbing. I'm off-balance wearing only one shoe.

"We should probably get you out of those clothes." The depth of his voice has my body humming in a new way, but I still choke around my next word.

"What?"

"Got a change of clothes in that bag?" He nods at my tote which surprisingly remained looped over my arm; however, water drips through the seams. I'm certain everything inside is as soaked as the leather. Why do bag companies make totes without closures? And why did I own something that couldn't protect my belongings?

Oh right, it matched my now-ruined shoes.

"No." I can't hold my teeth still.

"Only speak one word at a time?" His rugged tenor matches the hitch on one corner of his lips, suggesting a smile is hard won from him. Still, the expression is doing strange things to my lower belly.

Or maybe that's something else inside me fluttering.

*Don't be ridiculous.* I only took a test this morning. Surely, I can't feel anything yet. Although I'd read home-tests are ninety-nine percent correct, I won't know anything with certainty until I see my doctor.

"I-I'm sorry. I ruined the cake." Hopefully, he can't decipher between welling tears and water on my face as I'm on the verge of crying over a silly lemon cake. Then again, maybe it's simply my emotions which have been pinging all over the place since this morning.

"No worries." He pauses, stepping back to size me up while tipping his head. His hand still holds mine or maybe mine is clinging to his. I don't want to let go. His palm is so warm. His fingers strong. "I have a T-shirt that might fit you more like a dress, but it'd be warmer than what you are wearing."

At thirty-eight, everything in me should clang like warning bells. I don't know him. I'm not from this town. No one knows I made this stop. But while his sapphire eyes could be interpreted as dangerous, the heat in them glides over me like a protective blanket.

I nod, blindly following him to the back of the bakery, limping on my one heel.

When we step inside the office, he releases my hand. Rummaging through some boxes, he pulls out a large T-shirt with Curmudgeon Bakery on the back. He scowls at the shirt before handing it over to me.

"It's going to be loose on you, but it will be dry. I'll step out while you change, but if you hand me your things, I'll toss them in the dryer."

I weakly smile. "It's dry clean only." A tumble in a dryer would ruin the material of my dress. If it isn't already destroyed.

His eyes roam my soaked outfit, like a physical caress. From the collar of my dress, trailing right down to the saturated hem plastered to my thighs, those warm eyes peruse every inch of me. He takes a deep inhale through his nose, his wide chest puffing out with the movement, before pausing a second. Then he turns his head to the side. Without a word, he slips around me and softly closes the door.

Once he leaves, I glance down at my dress, suctioned to every curve and dip of my figure. My nipples are protruding peaks giving away how cold I am. Or is it something else? My body reacting to the way he was looking at me. The heat in his gaze. Warmth fills my cheeks once again. I shiver at the possibility he might have liked what he saw.

Shaking my head, I dismiss crazy thoughts. He wasn't looking at me in any way other than he might stare at a drowned rat. With shaky fingers and chilled limbs, I work to remove my clothing. Deciding my bra and underwear will only cause discomfort under the dryness of a fresh shirt, I remove them as well. With the oversized T-shirt on, I run my hand over my backside, confirming the length covers my butt. Every attempt to bend forward forces me to catch my breath and wince at the pain in my tailbone.

Glancing around the office, it's an accountant's nightmare. Papers stacked like lopsided pancakes on the floor. A box brimming with receipts rests on a file cabinet. The desktop is covered in haphazard piles. But the thing that attracts my gaze the most is a large zipper sweatshirt draped over the back of the desk chair. Taking the liberty, I swipe up the soft cotton and wrap myself in another layer for warmth. The collar smells like vanilla and motor oil, which is a strange yet surprisingly refreshing combination. I smile to myself as I inhale what I assume is the scent of the curmudgeon baker himself.

A soft knock comes to the door, but it opens before I answer. "I figured you might want these. I don't have shoes that would fit you." That crook of his lips happens again. He's making a joke. He's also holding out a pair of socks when he glances at my feet. His feet must be four sizes bigger than mine. "Or you can keep hobbling on one foot."

When he looks up, the flame in his eyes flares. His gaze lowers from my face to the sweatshirt dangling too long on my arms and the T-shirt that hits just above my knees.

"Thank you." My voice is still unsteady but I'm not certain it's the cold making my throat rumble. I shrug and smooth my fingers down one side of the open zipper. "I hope you don't mind."

He shakes his head, and I take the socks from him, wincing as I bend forward to slip them on.

"Are you hurt?"

"Besides my pride?" I joke then reality hits me. Am I hurt? Did I do any internal damage? Is everything still good in there? "My backside is killing me."

At the mention of my ass, he chokes, and I glance up to find him swiping his thick fingers around his mouth, stroking at the bristly hairs on his chin. He looks more like a biker than a baker but he's the man who filled my cake order. He has swapped his wet clothes for a dry pair of jeans and a light gray Henley shirt. His close-cropped hair is damp. A towel hangs over his shoulder.

"Are you the Curmudgeon baker?" I ask, righting myself and wincing again as pain shoots up my spine.

"A joke from my family," he mocks.

"But are you the owner of Curmudgeon Bakery?" I tip my head. He's solid brawn, and I can't imagine his hefty fingers delicately decorating baby-Bundt cakes, but the judgement is unfair.

"Yeah." His gaze lowers to the floor and the corner of his mouth tips up again. Pride fills his voice while his cheeks pinken the slightest bit.

"What? Only answer one word at a time?" I tease.

His head pops up and those dark eyes dance with mischief. He stares at my saturated hair. "I brought you this." Dragging a towel off his shoulder, he hands it to me and arches a brow. "And that was four words."

With a cheeky smile, I mutter, "Thanks," and rub the material over my face, inhaling a stronger blend of vanilla mixed with laundry detergent. My makeup must be a frightful mess.

He tilts his head toward the storefront, "How about some coffee?"

With a nod, I finger comb my long hair as best I can. Following him into the bakery while wearing his socks, I twist my hair around itself, forming a messy bun. He points to a long wooden bench, and gingerly I sit, wincing before trying to balance on one cheek.

The sexy baker rounds the display counter, and I take the opportunity to glance at his well-sculpted backside. *Nice.*

He pours two mugs of coffee, and then comes to the table, setting down each steaming container. "I'll be right back."

Disappearing through a door marked Private, he quickly returns and holds out a bed pillow. "For your ass."

I laugh as he takes a seat across from me in a chair. "I'm Enya, by the way. Enya Calloway."

"Nice to meet you, Enya Calloway." He lifts his mug, watching me over the rim. In typical conversation this is where he should tell me his name, but he doesn't offer, and I don't ask.

There's something very unconventional about this man.

As silence grows, I glance around the bakery. Display cases line one side while the long, wooden, booth bench where I sit, and a scattering of tables line the opposite wall. The floor is giant black and white squares while subway tiles decorate the wall giving the place an old-world-bakery atmosphere. Or maybe it's New Age as the stark white, clean lines have made a resurgence. With the hum of the air conditioner no longer buzzing, music can be heard.

"Imagine" by John Lennon fills the space.

"Beatles fan?" I hitch a brow, glancing at him over the rim of my mug. He shrugs, all casual coolness across from me, watching me drink my coffee. One arm rests against the back of the chair beside him; the other hand cups his mug. Silence has never been so comfortable, but I can't keep quiet for long. I glance up at a quote on the wall.

*There is NO HOLE in Kindness.*

The capitalized Os are shaped like donuts.

"Strange quote."

"This location used to be a donut shop." He offers, as if that explains everything.

"Donuts have holes."

He shrugs. His smirk matches my smile. "Bundt cakes do as well." He tips his head to read the quote himself. "It was here when I bought the place. Figured it brought the previous owners thirty-two years of business luck. I left it on the wall."

Taking a second glance, a faint outline surrounds the quote, as if fresh paint didn't match the original color.

"Maybe it's a metaphor. Like kindness is cyclical."

He shrugs again and scoffs while lifting his mug. "Maybe it was a nicer way of saying don't be an asshole."

Glancing back at the quote, I mutter, "Maybe." Unfortunately, I've known a few assholes in my thirty-eight years. Lowering my gaze, I look at him again. "Got any other quotes for good luck?"

His lip quirks up on one side and he tips his chin. "What do you need luck for?" Those heavy blue eyes scan my face.

Do I need luck? I should already feel like the luckiest woman in the world. But my eyes instantly well. Damn my emotions.

"I'm pregnant." Saying the words aloud for the first time feels strange. A little unreal. A lot exciting.

His arm along the back of the chair slips to the seat. His hand on the handle of his mug flattens on the tabletop. His entire demeanor shifts, and that hint of danger becomes more apparent. An invisible wall goes up around him. He leans forward.

"Husband must be happy." His rugged tone, which once sounded friendly, is now jagged.

"No husband." With my gaze aimed at the table, the wood surface blurs from the threat of tears.

"Boyfriend, then?" His voice croaks on the term.

I shake my head. How do I explain my situation to a stranger?

"You're the first person I've told." A sour lump fills my throat when I'm actually ecstatic deep down.

"Shit." The gruffness filters into my ears, but all I really hear is the pulsing of my own heart.

*I'm going to have a baby.*

Suddenly, I'm hefted off the bench and wrapped in thick arms. My head is pressed to his chest where the rapid rhythm of his heart is a steady song. Thrown off guard at first, my arms are trapped between us, but slowly, I loosen them and circle his waist. Tears slip down my nose.

I don't know why I'm crying. This is what I wanted.

Still, I'm scared . . . and his simple questions remind me I'm doing this alone.

"Want me to kill the bastard? I know people." The ferocity in his question tells me he isn't joking but there's no one to harm.

I shake my head against his solid pecs, anxiously giggling despite the flow of tears. "I'm good."

His hand glides down my back, pausing just above my ass. His other hand cups my head, holding me against him. I close my eyes, inhaling the vanilla and motor oil scent of him. We stand like this for long enough the awkwardness of hugging a stranger should settle in, but I don't want to move.

And I don't know why I told him this monumental truth.

As I pull back, his hand at the base of my spine keeps me close to him. His eyes search mine and I wish I could read his thoughts. I wish I could tell this stranger all of mine.

Wishing is what got me where I am, though. Pregnant and alone at thirty-eight.

"I was here to buy a Bundt cake. A little celebration of sorts." The explanation sounds even odder than telling him I'm pregnant. While some might pop champagne, I can't. A *baby* Bundt cake felt appropriate for a future birth. In roughly eight months, I'll have a birthday to commemorate.

He huffs, swiping back at the hair coming loose from my makeshift bun. Abruptly, he releases me, and the reality of standing in borrowed socks and a stolen sweatshirt hits me. He must think I'm a nut.

As he walks away, I shamelessly check out his backside, rounded and firm in tight-fitting jeans. He circles the counter once more but quickly returns to where I stand. A baby-Bundt cake sits on a small plate and two forks are in his hand. He nudges me to return to my seat and he slides into the chair across from me again.

Placing the plate between us, he holds up a fork and nods for me to do the same.

"To babies and Bundt cakes." His tone rings slightly somber. He taps my fork like we are clinking glasses of champagne and then he pushes the plate in my direction, suggesting I take the first bite.

The moist lemon cake perfectly balanced with a rich buttercream frosting melts in my mouth. As I close my eyes, I moan, not even exaggerating the orgasm on my tongue. The texture. The flavor. Chef's kiss.

When I open my lids, his eyes smolder at me, and the strangest fantasy fills my head.

*He's the father of my baby and he's so excited by my announcement he wants to take me on this table to commemorate the good news.*

My eyes widen. Horror fills my face in a heated rush. My imagination would only complicate matters.

Softly, he chuckles, pulls the plate closer to him and fills his fork. As I watch him take a bite, he sucks at the utensil, taking his time to savor the experience within his mouth. A place on me that has no business beating, pulses like a kitchen mixer, strong and fierce. Slowly, he removes the tines, taking his time to release the fork, now clean of cake. My mouth dries, curious about the mystery of his tongue. Wondering what his lips might feel like clamping onto parts of me. How firmly does he suck? How roughly does he kiss?

My body heats but shivers return with the carnal need to ask these questions.

*I still don't even know his name.*

However, as we share this piece of cake, and the silence between us fills with another Beatles tune, I fight back my lust and come to a decision.

A simple act of kindness might be more seductive than spreading me on this table.

No holes *is* a metaphor. Kindness goes around and around in quiet gestures, like fresh socks, a warm sweatshirt, a celebratory piece of cake, and a secretive smile.

And one day, I hope to repay the curmudgeon baker for his generosity in a grand way.

Continue reading *Sterling Heat*.

# More by L.B. Dunbar

<u>Sterling Falls</u>
Small town. Big heart.
Seven siblings muddling their way through love over 40.
*Sterling Heat*
*Sterling Brick*
*Sterling Streak*

*Parentmoon*
When the mother of the groom goes head-to-head with the single father
of the bride.

<u>Holiday Hotties (Christmas novellas)</u>
Holiday novellas certain to heat the season.
*Scrooge-ish*
*Naughty-ish*

<u>Road Trips & Romance</u>
3 sisters. 3 destinations. A second chance at love over 40.
*Hauling Ashe*
*Merging Wright*
*Rhode Trip*

<u>Lakeside Cottage</u>
Four friends. Four summers. Shenanigans and love happen at the lake.
*Living at 40*
*Loving at 40*
*Learning at 40*
*Letting Go at 40*

<u>The Silver Foxes of Blue Ridge</u>
Small mountain town, silver foxes. Brothers seeking love over 40.
*Silver Brewer*
*Silver Player*
*Silver Mayor*
*Silver Biker*

<u>Sexy Silver Foxes</u>
When sexy silver foxes meet the feisty vixens of their dreams.

SILVER BIKER

*After Care*
*Midlife Crisis*
*Restored Dreams*
*Second Chance*
*Wine&Dine*


Collision novellas
A spin-off from After Care – the younger set/rock stars
*Collide*
*Caught*


Rom-com standalone for the over 40
*The Sex Education of M.E.*


The Heart Collection
Small town, big hearts - stories of family and love.
*Speak from the Heart*
*Read with your Heart*
*Look with your Heart*
*Fight from the Heart*
*View with your Heart*


A Heart Collection Spin-off
*The Heart Remembers*


**BOOKS IN OTHER AUTHOR WORLDS**
Smartypants Romance (an imprint of Penny Reid)
Tales of the Winters sisters set in Green Valley.
*Love in Due Time*
*Love in Deed*
*Love in a Pickle*


The World of True North (an imprint of Sarina Bowen)
Welcome to Vermont! And the Busy Bean Café.
*Cowboy*
*Studfinder*

L.B. DUNBAR

**THE EARLY YEARS**
The Legendary Rock Star Series
A classic tale with a modern twist of rock star romance and suspense

Paradise Stories
MMA romance. Two brothers. One fight.

The Island Duet
Intrigue and suspense. The island knows what you've done.

Modern Descendants – writing as elda lore
Magical realism. Modern myths of Greek gods.

# (L)ittle (B)lessings of Gratitude

This book was written in 2020, a year that will go down in history because of COVID-19 and cultural upheaval. It's been a difficult year to be creative, and yet James Harrington, and the entire Harrington family have been on my mind for a while. If I didn't know where their lives would lead before this year, this book might never have been written. However, James and Evie are two of the rawest characters I've ever written and a trope I desperately wanted to write – a true second chance.

My gratitude in this year goes first and foremost to Mel and Jenny. Their patience with my deadlines has been generous and unbelievable, and once again, I'm humbled by the people in my life. Thank you Shannon for another edgy, striking cover design. Believe it or not, it's difficult to find sexy silver fox photographs, and Shannon's skill gives just the hint I need. I'd like to thank Karen for her eagle eye proofreading and additionally, Jenny McCoy Alfred, for last minute detailing.

To all the readers in Loving L.B., God knows you have been my salvation this year. In laughter and tears, you stand by me, and I by you, and it just makes this journey all the sweeter every day.

And finally, to my family: Mr. Dunbar and second chances; MD, MK, JR, and A, who are the best gift and ultimate experience a mother could receive. I'm more grateful for you than you'll ever know. You're my greatest dream come true and I love you more than anything.

# About the Author

www.lbdunbar.com

L.B. Dunbar loves sexy silver foxes, second chances, and small towns. If you enjoy older characters in your romance reads, including a hero with a little silver in his scruff and a heroine rediscovering her worth, then welcome to romance for those over 40. L.B. Dunbar's signature works include women and men in their prime taking another turn at love and happily ever after. She's a *USA TODAY* Bestseller as well as #1 Bestseller on Amazon in Later in Life Romance with her Lakeside Cottage and Road Trips & Romance series. L.B. lives in Chicago with her own sexy silver fox.

To get all the scoop about the self-proclaimed queen of silver fox romance, join her on Facebook at Loving L.B. or receive her monthly newsletter, Love Notes.

+ + +

# Connect with L.B. Dunbar

www.ingramcontent.com/pod-product-compliance
Lightning Source LLC
Chambersburg PA
CBHW051204220726
48293CB00014B/1868